Fairmist

Book One of
The Whisper Prince

Todd Fahnestock

FIRST EDITION

Cover photo by Ivan Bliznetsov
ivanbliznetsov.com

Cover design by Todd Fahnestock and Sean Olson
toddfahnestock.com

Library of Congress Cataloging-in-Publication Data

Fahnestock, Todd
Fairmist / by Todd Fahnestock – 1st ed. p. cm.
ISBN-13: 978-0-9863756-1-3

Dedication

To Lara.
When the sun rises, I reach for you.
You are my magic.

Acknowledgements

It took a village to raise this child, and there are so many who made contributions. I want to thank all of my advance readers who took time to read the first makings of this story, and the second and third and...well, there were dozens of you and more than a dozen drafts. Thank you for all of your contributions; I am grateful. I would especially like to thank:

Lara Fahnestock: Of course. For being my first reader. For being my EVERY-draft reader. For being my emotional babysitter and coach. For staying up late with me. For getting up early with me. For that smile that let me know the book was done. None of this happens without you, my love.

Aaron Brown: For the creepy children and the poem. For the game-changing 6th draft reading and the diplomatically brutal 13th draft reading. Your unwavering belief in this story helped me get it to the finish line.

Giles Carwyn: For pinpointing Grei's personality issue so succinctly.

Elliott Davis: For the Debt of the Blessed instead of Ceremony of the Blessed.

Megan Foss: For being an eternal fan and a great friend. How many hours have you spent reading early drafts of my stories? You were there since those first tales of *Wildmane* in college, and you have remained ever-eager. Also for coming up with Kuruk's driving motivation. You helped make him sing.

Liana Holmberg: For being my Editor, for lovingly, ruthlessly pushing me. I treasure what I've learned from you. And also for guiding Adora's choice of paramour. Skinny ascetic or hot Highblade? No contest. And for the name Galius Ash!!!

Chris Lamson: For being a steadfast fan and an insightful reader. Your support makes a world of difference.

Marie Lu: For "a kiss and a cut". For loving Galius Ash as much as I do, and for making Grei chase the Imperial Wand.

Chris Mandeville: You were my first draft fuel supply and my last draft taskmaster. Your excitement about this book was food for me. Thank you for letting me turn your house into my own personal writer's retreat. The Ringblades were born in your basement. And lastly, for NOT doing what I asked you to do in my final draft.

Donald Maass: For loving this story and giving it its best shot of getting picked up by a big publisher.

Tami Miller: What a fan! Your extreme enthusiasm about this novel drives me to write more. I love your bitter hatred of Lyndion.

Mom: For, as always, reminding me about the basics.

Dena Morrissey: For being such a pillar of support during the middle drafts! You listened to me blather on about writing for longer than anyone should have to endure, draft after draft.

Sean Olson: You took a good idea and made it professional grade. Thank you so much for the cover!

Steve Patterson: For giving me a steady wind in my sails to get this book out into the world. Your support means a lot.

Veronique Redican: For constant faith in the story and the spiritual aspects of the book.

Emily Sherwood: For making space for my writer's retreat, and for being so wonderfully supportive of the creative process.

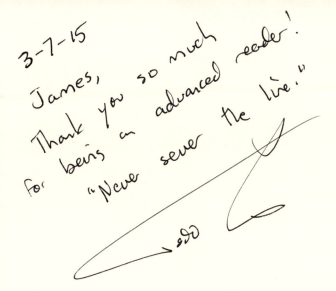

Fairmist

Book One of
The Whisper Prince

The Prophecy

A lost fair lady looked into the mist
The Whisper Prince whispered of love
The lady saw slaughter, and terror, and rifts
The prince, he whispered of love

Love came swimming along the lost road
Her heel painted with blood
The shadows came charging with wrath born of old
Their claws dripping with blood

With blood and from fire the shadows unwound
Losing souls too many to measure
The flesh and the faces of others were bound
And the shadows all took of their measure

Their measure felled hordes; their fires untamed
But the prince, before them, he stood
One hand on the rose, one hand in the flames
The prince, before them all, stood

All stood when the horns of the realm gave alarm
Too late for all and for one
But he sent them away
And never did say
Why a princess lay down for his charm

Prologue

THE SLINKS paced them at the edge of the tree line, their silhouettes and burning eyes visible. They stayed silent, distant, but they may as well have been sitting behind Darven, their teeth scraping his skin, reminding him: *stay the course*.

In the darkness below, the city of Moondow held its breath, street lamps flickering like orange jewels. It was peaceful, but Darven conjured a vision of the city in flames, slinks chewing flesh, mothers screaming. His mortality thumped in his neck. Beat. Beat. Beat.

He paused, and the five heavily armed Imperial Highblades pulled into tight formation behind him. The thick clouds pressed low, close enough to touch. Darven searched overhead for a hint of silver in the black, but there was nothing.

"It looks like Fairmist," he said softly.

"Yes sir," the captain of Darven's Highblades acknowledged without emotion. It was not his job to think about such things. It wasn't Darven's, either, but Darven's thoughts were heavy like the clouds above. It was an ill omen, Moondow looking like Fairmist. Fairmist was where the world had ended. Almost.

The other Highblades remained silent and at attention on their well-trained mounts. They would sit there all night without complaint, through rain or raging storm, whatever came, until Darven gave another command. They would cling to their duty until their hands were bones.

Never sever the line.

Darven knew what they were thinking. The Imperial Wand did not pause on ridges and stare at clouds. It was a break in routine, and every Highblade had been on edge about odd behavior since the emperor's champion, Jorun Magnus, had gone crazy and betrayed them all.

Darven nudged Snowfall with his heels and the giant cat started down. The malformed slinks stopped at the edge of the forest, as they always did. They never entered a city and only stayed long enough for Darven to see them, to remember what would happen if the empire didn't pay the Debt of the Blessed.

A fine rain began, as though the clouds had been waiting for Darven to move. He flipped his cowl up over his head and followed the packed path, which turned dark with tiny dots. Halfway down, the dirt became flagstones winding up to the wall of Moondow, which had been built to protect the city from outlaws or, if they should get this far south, Benascan raiders.

But it wasn't a raider who came to Moondow tonight. Darven would not slay their men or rape their women. He was here for one person only, chosen to pay the Debt. All others were safe as long as they did not interfere.

A local Highblade perched atop the wall and shouted down. "State your need!" A young man's voice.

Perhaps it was dark enough to make the sentry believe Snowfall was a horse, or for him to miss that there were six riders: the incomplete number, the unlucky number, seeking a seventh.

Darven reached up and flipped back his cowl. Even in the darkness and rain, the young man would see the long, snow-white hair. Darven remembered when his hair had lost its color, over those first few months after his promotion. It had something to do with the emperor's artifacts. The wand and the crystal. They marked him. All those who bore a wand had the white hair, and everyone in the empire knew it.

The young man's gaze flicked over the five Highblades and came to rest on Snowfall. The sentry's partner appeared next to him, staring down. "Open the gate!" the older man said roughly, shouldering the young sentry so hard their armor clattered. The young man scrambled to the winch, and the heavy doors groaned opened.

The second year of the Debt of the Blessed, Moondow had kept her doors shut, refusing to allow Darven inside. He and his escort had ridden back to Thiara without a word. The emperor returned two days later with a hundred Imperial Highblades and another of his artifacts. The gates of Moondow dissolved into sand and the hundred rode within. By sundown, the city's delegate and all of her local Highblades lay dead in the city square.

Tonight the gates opened and Darven's escort entered unchallenged. The two sentries stood back, watching. Darven found the emperor's crystal, tucked against his chest inside his tunic. It was warm, and he knew it would become almost too hot to touch when he neared his quarry.

The young sentry closed the gates behind them. The older sentry reluctantly approached Darven. He had a thick mustache and was fit for a local Highblade.

"Apologies for the delay, Lord Wand," the older sentry said, bowing.

"Your partner was doing his job," Darven said. When you possessed real power, there was no honor in flaunting it. Best to be quick. Best to be done. He shifted to the subject at hand. "You have lived here long, Highblade?"

"All my life," he said in a low voice.

"Salandra Gell," Darven said.

The man's head bowed further. He knew the girl.

"She's a sweet girl," the old sentry said, not making eye-contact. Captain Bayn stiffened in his saddle. Citizens of the empire did not question the Debt of the Blessed. They were not even to discuss it.

"Her sister already serves the emperor, a Ringblade," the older sentry continued making his case, as if he didn't know the consequences for standing in the way of the Debt, as if even the most convincing argument could make a difference.

"Then her family will understand," Darven replied, trying to give the sentry a chance to save himself.

Captain Bayn actually looked at Darven this time. The hard man's face was expressionless, his jaw muscles clenched. But he would do nothing until signaled.

"Of course they should," the old sentry replied in a scathing tone. "The Debt of the Blessed is our salvation." He spat.

Darven felt unbelievably weary, and he looked away, looked for the absent moon in the iron gray overcast. Rain pelted his face.

Once, his duty had been clear. Then Champion Magnus had gone berserk in the palace, killing his fellows until that bitch Selicia brought him down. His rampage had thrown everything into question. He was the emperor's champion, the Highblade after whom all other Highblades had modeled themselves. Bravery without thought. Uncanny strength. A peerless swords-man with absolute dedication to empire and emperor.

Had he known something they did not? Was the emperor wrong to enforce the Debt? Or had Magnus simply gone mad like they said?

The Debt of the Blessed was necessary; it was all that kept the slinks at bay. Magnus knew that. Everybody knew that. The Slink War had nearly consumed the empire. Hundreds had died in a matter of days. A single slink was ten times as strong as a person, ten times as fast; they were overwhelming. During the Slink War, they had swarmed, ripping heads from bodies, pulling arms out like weeds.

In the midst of that slaughter, only Champion Magnus had killed one. Just one. Thousands had fought the slinks, but all other weapons had bounced off like sticks. Magnus was the only one to bloody them back. He was what they had all aspired to be. And now he was the traitor, the Highblade who had severed the line.

Never sever the line.

Darven broke from his reverie. He had paused too long already. He turned back to Captain Bayn and reluctantly nodded.

Captain Bayn's horse leapt forward and his sword flashed out. The old sentry fell back, but Bayn cut halfway through the man's neck before he could shout. Blood splashed over the flagstones, and the sentry fell with a soft gurgle, dead before his head smacked the ground.

Captain Bayn cleaned his sword on the edge of his red cloak then sheathed it over his shoulder. His horse danced in a neat circle. Darven glanced at the younger sentry, who was pale and shaking, gaping at his dead partner. The boy was poised to flee, but he stood transfixed by the growing pool of blood mixing with the falling rain.

"Young man," Darven said. "Where might I find Salandra Gell?"

The sentry gaped, unable to take his gaze away.

"Young man."

Captain Bayn moved his horse into formation behind Darven, and that seemed to jolt the young sentry back to life.

His jaw worked. "There's a water wheel, in the river. For the mill," he stammered.

"I know it," Darven said.

"The Gells are the millers."

"Long live the empire," Darven said, laying his reins against Snowfall's neck. The great cat huffed as he turned. The young sentry slumped to his knees in the blood.

The river wheel was on the far side of Moondow, and they rode straight through the city. Lights went on one by one in the row of houses. Curtains were pulled aside. Citizens came into the street in their nightclothes, heedless of the rain, following the Imperial Wand and his procession. As the numbers grew, the tension built, but they kept their distance. Every citizen knew what would happen if they stood in the way.

They reached the mill with hundreds of Moondow's citizens behind them, whispers slithering between them, and Captain Bayn gestured. His Highblades spread out around the little mill.

Darven dismounted, went to the door and knocked loudly seven times. Imperial Wands always came at night. Daylight offered confidence, sights and sounds they knew. Night was uncertain, and people were more tractable when they were uncertain. That meant less need for the wand.

He waited for a time, then knocked again.

"Who is it?" a voice came from the other side of the door.

Darven drew the steel rod of his namesake. Even he didn't know everything the wand could do, only what he had asked it to do in the service of the emperor. He could feel it radiate power, and he kept it tight by his side. Families chosen by the Debt were unpredictable. On Darven's third Debt of the Blessed, he had received a knife in the ribs for his carelessness. That had never happened since.

"Imperial Wand," Darven said. "Open the door in the name of the emperor."

After a long moment of silence, the door opened.

A man about Darven's age stood in the doorway. He wore breeches and a long tunic. His bald head shone in the Highblades' torchlight. His wife, small and attractive, stood a few paces behind him. Her eyes were wide, and she covered her mouth with her hands. She began murmuring prayers into her fingers.

Behind them was his quarry, a slighter figure standing in the shadows, not as small as the mother nor as tall as the father.

"Salandra Gell?" Darven asked, though he did not need to ask. She was the one; the crystal burned as she stepped into the light. She wore a dun-colored nightdress and was barefoot. Her eyes, brown like her mother's, seemed inhumanly large. "You have been chosen," he continued.

"You have been blessed. Because of you, the empire will endure."

Tears welled in those large eyes and streaked silently down her cheeks. She made no sound. No sobs or shudders. Every Debt had a detail Darven never forgot, and he knew that Salandra Gell's silent tears would stay with him for the rest of his life.

"It is the will of the Faia," the mother whispered, rocking forward and backward with her eyes closed. "We must accept."

The father's face was a tortured mask. Veins bulged in his neck, and his arms were rigid at his side.

Darven waited. It was almost always best to wait for them to come to him.

Behind him, one of Moondow's citizens yelled, "Give her up!" Murmurs of approval swept through the crowd.

"She is the Blessed!"

"Bring her out!"

The father's rigid body slumped, and he fell to his knees.

Salandra moved to her father and knelt next to him, took his arm.

"It must be someone," she said. "Better it is me." He just looked at her, as though he was desperately trying to memorize everything about her. Salandra turned, went to her mother. "I love you," the girl said softly, laying a light hand on her mother's shoulder, but the mother didn't stop rocking back and forth, didn't stop her litany of mumbled prayers.

"Bring her out!" The voices rose again from the crowd. They wanted the Debt paid. They wanted the Imperial Wand and his Highblades on their way. Once Salandra was taken, they could go back to their regular lives, safe again. At least for a time.

Both father and mother stared silently at their daughter as she moved toward Darven.

He took the girl's hand and led her out of the house, away from her parents. There was no point prolonging it. It didn't get easier. He took her to Snowfall, and the sea of people parted to create a wide path out of the city, waiting for them.

"I can make you sleep," Darven said to the girl. "If you would prefer."

"No," she said. Darven helped her mount the great cat, then pulled himself up behind her. His Highblades formed ranks, and they rode out of the city together.

The girl did not utter a single word the rest of that night or the entire first day of the ride to the slink caves. She rode in Darven's arms by day and was guarded by the Highblades at night. She never complained, never tried to escape.

In the morning, they mounted up and began the final leg of the journey that would end in her death. She was calm, almost as though she had already surrendered and her spirit floated alongside her body. She looked all around with a serenity that humbled Darven.

They were less than an hour from the slink caves when Salandra finally spoke.

"Princess Mialene was the first," she said. "The emperor's own daughter?"

"Yes," Darven said. "Seven years ago almost exactly. Barely a week after the war."

She seemed about to say something more, but hesitated.

"Go ahead," he said. "I will answer any question you ask."

She turned in the saddle, just a little. The rolling gait of Snowfall caused them both to bounce.

"Did she go willingly?" Salandra asked quietly. "Did she charge ahead like they say?"

That was the story the empire knew: Princess Mialene Doragon riding to the hidden slink caves on her own to pay the Debt of the Blessed for all Thiarans, her hair flying in the wind. To show them all what must be sacrificed if they were to survive.

But Darven had gone with the emperor and Champion Magnus to Princess Mialene's room that day. He remembered her frightened face when she opened the door. She had only uttered one word: *Father?*

That plea had contained every question an eleven-year-old girl could ask a father who was giving her up to death. She wilted when he would not look at her, and she cast about for someone else. Her gaze had found Champion Magnus, and she seemed to find strength there. She quieted and allowed them to take her to her horse.

The princess kept her gaze on Magnus the entire ride. When they reached the slinks' cave, she watched him with absolute faith, knowing he would save her. That was what champions were for.

Darven remembered the light in her blue eyes dying when he lifted her from the saddle and placed her on the slope. She had changed then. Docile mouse to wildcat. She screamed, leaping on Magnus as he mounted, clinging to his leg. He removed her silently, and they had all galloped away.

Magnus had never looked back, but Darven saw his tears.

Darven suddenly realized he had paused overlong in his reminiscence, and turned his attention back to Salandra. He should lie to her. He should tell her the official story, but he had promised he would answer her questions.

"She screamed for us to save her," Darven said.

"And her father let you take her?"

"He ordered it."

She hesitated, and her voice was a whisper he could barely hear. "Why do they lie about it?"

"Because we must all have the courage to live up to the legend," he said. "Because it is the most noble sacrifice anyone can make. You are saving all of our lives."

"My sister is..." she began, and her voice caught. She cleared her throat and continued. "Ree is brave like that. There was never anything she wouldn't face down. She's a Ringblade, you know."

"I know."

"She would have ridden to the slinks' cave. I can do no less."

He nodded.

Then she whispered, "I don't want to die." It was not meant for him. It was a plea so soft it wrenched his heart. Perhaps she meant it for the Faia.

She went silent. They crested the rise, and a slope of broken shale led down to a hole in the ground. The slinks were in there. Hundreds of them. Thousands. He imagined them crawling over each other like roaches, longing to emerge and devour the world. Instead, they would only devour this one girl.

They stopped at the edge of the slope, and she turned in the saddle. He memorized the slope of her nose, her smooth cheeks. She looked down at the distant hole in the ground.

"What is your name?" she asked quietly.

"I am Darven," he said.

"Tell my sister..." She hesitated. "Just tell her I was brave."

"I will."

He dismounted and helped her off Snowfall. She began walking down the loose shale, picking her way carefully.

Darven clenched his teeth. His five Highblades stayed on their horses behind him, unmoving, and he thanked the Faia that they could not see his weakness.

Darven served the empire. He had collected his scars with pride. "Never Sever the Line" was the Highblade creed. It meant standing shoulder to shoulder with your brethren against the empire's enemies. It meant obedience to the emperor. It meant protecting those who could not protect themselves. They were all strands in a great web, and one severed line could mean the destruction of all. Highblades held that web together.

He watched until Salandra reached the cave and started down into that dark abyss. He had composed himself by then. He mounted Snowfall and yanked on the reins. The big cat let out a huff and turned.

He did not wait for the screams. He and his Highblades rode out directly.

It was another two-day ride to reach his home. He had a

small cottage in the duchy of Felesh, a wife and an eighteen-year-old son who was already a soldier in the Benascan wars. Lawdon would take his Highblade test when he returned at the end of the year.

Darven's escort left him in his yard and rode on to Thiara. He gave Snowfall his dinner and the drugs that kept him docile, and put him in the special stable that had been constructed for him.

Darven entered his house. Veenda was there, her lovely shape silhouetted against the afternoon light, her brown hair filled with more gray than he remembered. He had only been gone a week, but she seemed older every time he returned.

She always stood in the main room when he arrived, off to the side, letting him know she was there, but she never said anything. It was an agreement they had. They did not talk about the Debt of the Blessed.

They watched each other for a long, silent moment. In the early days, her eyes had been filled with love when he returned from his duty, and perhaps sorrow for him. But not anymore. Her gaze looked the same as the old sentry's from Moondow. Silent rebellion. His own wife despised him. The emperor had given his daughter to the slinks as the first Blessed, but the Imperial Wands gave nothing. They only took.

He nodded at her, feeling like he wanted to say something this time, but he found no words. He wanted to tell her about the bravery of Salandra Gell. No one else would remember her courage except him, and that was a sharp jewel that cut his heart, priceless and painful. *The slinks have won,* he thought. *We yet live, but they have destroyed us after all. Was this was what Magnus suddenly realized? Was this what drove him to madness and dishonor?*

He turned, went into his equipment room and closed the door. He took off his cloak and hung it up, removed his belt and dropped it onto the little bench. He sat down and removed the crystal from his tunic, set it carefully on the desk next to a box of scrolls for writing reports to the emperor.

The crystal was cool now. It wouldn't grow hot until he was called upon again. Again and again.

Darven bowed his head, trying to find that purpose that drove him forward, that dedication to empire and emperor, but there was only an empty hole where it had once been.

He took a scroll from the box, carefully unrolled it and dipped a quill into the inkpot. He kept his promise and wrote a short letter to Ringblade Ree: Salandra's last words, her last request.

He set two flat stones at the top and bottom of the scroll to keep it from rolling up, tossed fine sand upon it. He glanced at the belt on the bench next to him. It had two sheaths on it. One for his dagger and one for the wand.

He took the dagger from the sheath, touched the edge. He had sharpened it before he left. A Highblade always kept his weapons sharp. One of the first lessons.

Darven put the dagger expertly against his throat and slashed. It stung, and he felt his life's blood gush down his neck. A good cut. An honorable cut.

He shivered, and with the last of his strength, he put the dagger back on the bench over the wand. Blood dripped and smeared across the belt.

Brave Salandra.

Never sever the line.

Part I

The Faia and the Forest Girl

Chapter 1
GREI

GREI HAD swallowed the lie. He had closed his mind, numbed his heart, and told himself the Debt of the Blessed kept them alive. But the Debt had killed them all; they just couldn't bear to admit it. It had peeled away their sense of rightness until they weren't people anymore. They were walking husks with dead hearts.

The sacrifices had to stop, or he had to die trying.

His mind was clear and sharp now, and he saw every detail around him. It was past Deepdark, and the floating droplets of Fairmist glowed like tiny moons in front of him. The eternally wet cobblestones reflected their light back, making a painting of smeared stars.

He let his breath out slowly and looked across the deserted courtyard around the Lateral Houses. There were no Highblades to be seen.

It had been seven years since the Forest Girl had kissed him, put whispers inside his mind and made his heart fit together like puzzle pieces. Everything had made sense in that moment. Nothing made sense after. And Grei had let her whispers fade away.

He believed now that her whispers were the rightness in his heart. They were the indecipherable truth, the only sliver of sanity in this slinked empire. And he had betrayed her. He had broken her off like a branch and tried to bury the memory.

He'd only been a child when she kissed him, and the dead-hearted people of Fairmist, his father included, had told him the whispers were wrong; they'd beaten the rightness out of him. He'd tried to please them. He'd tried to make something else matter more than the Forest Girl. He'd tried so hard.

But the Debt of the Blessed had taken another child this spring. Another and another and another, endless. One every month from somewhere in the Thiaran Empire. Grei clenched his teeth. He couldn't go back in time and make his ten-year-old self braver or stronger. He couldn't save the Forest Girl, but maybe he could save someone else. Maybe he could pull down the lie and find a way to stop the Debt of the Blessed.

Tonight, outside *The Floating Stone*, Grei's rebellion ignited. The newcomer Blevins had flashed a bit of treason that reflected Grei's own, and Grei had moved toward him like the floating droplets moved downhill:

"What do the slinks do with the Blessed, anyway?" Blevins asked. "Why only one a month?"

That arrow sank into Grei's mind, quivering.

The right question was: How do we get rid of the Debt? But in seven years, the big drunk was the only person to question the Debt's purpose at all, and he had the courage to say it aloud, in the middle of the tavern. Everyone else turned their attention to their beers, but Grei drifted to the man.

"Why?" Grei asked. "Why only one a month?"

"I don't know," Blevins responded. "But somebody does."

"Yes. Where?"

Blevins gave him a squinty gaze and a dark chuckle. "You want secrets, Stormy," he painted the nickname on Grei

like they were friends, "Shake the secret-keepers. The
Ringblades are the slithering serpents of the empire. They go
everywhere, hear everything. Ask them."

And her whispers, the gibberish whispers of the long
dead Forest Girl, returned.

Those whispers tickled his mind now as he looked at the
Lateral Houses, small castles created by the Faia hundreds of
years ago, their bulk held up by magic. They looked like they
had fallen over on their left sides but hadn't made it all the
way to the ground. They were perfectly level with, but five
feet above, the cobble-stones. Only a single, twisting
walkway connected each to the ground like a tether to keep it
from flying away. He had watched Highblades enter before.
Gravity mindbendingly shifted beneath them as they stepped
forward, slowly turning sideways to match the door.

The Lateral Houses were supposedly the home of the
Highblades and Ringblades in Fairmist. Except there were no
Ringblades in Fairmist. No one had ever seen one. You
couldn't walk down the street without tripping over a
Highblade. But there were no Ringblades.

Grei ran across the courtyard of glistening cobble-stones
and slid underneath the Lateral House on the far left, sending
up a spray of water.

Two of the Houses had Highblades coming and going at
all hours, but the third stood empty, waiting for a Ringblade
to pay Fairmist a visit.

He crouched forward through the haze of floating droplets. Water trickled down his face as they touched him. Only
when they contacted something did the droplets fall, finally
acting like water did in the rest of the empire.

He glanced up at the tons of stone above him, and the
back of his neck prickled. A stray thought ran through his
head: What if the Lateral Houses fell if touched, like the
water? He hunched lower and kept moving.

He reached the far side and waited at the edge of the
shadow. No one shouted. There was no high-pitched

Highblade's whistle.

He focused on the Forest Girl's whispers in his mind, quiet and beautiful. Whisper whisper whisper. Rising and falling. Maddeningly indecipherable.

He craned his neck and looked up the side of the wall, taking care to stay within the house's shadow. He'd have to be quick.

With a grunt, he lunged into the droplet filled air, turned and leapt onto the house, clinging to the sideways window. He pulled the steel shim from his sleeve and shoved it into the "bottom" of the window to his left—

—but the unlocked window slid sideways without effort, and it stunned him. Were the Highblades and Ringblades so confident that they felt no locks were needed?

He pressed his lips into a firm line, pushed himself up and tumbled through.

Gravity shifted, and he fell sideways like someone had shoved him. He was expecting it, and flipped in mid-air. His feet hit the previously vertical floor and stuck.

The vertigo was powerful, tried to pull him off balance. He waved his arms and managed to stay upright, then glanced out the window.

All of shrouded Fairmist was on its ear. The joy filled him unexpectedly, and in that single moment he felt right. This was where he belonged, not broken down by the delegate's torturers, not moving in the walking death of Fairmist's citizens, but here where the whispers rushed through him like a breeze. Here, he wasn't a boy they could bend. He was a man. The thrill spread through him, and he laughed.

"Are you amused?" asked a woman's voice.

He spun, his joy constricting in his throat.

Backlit by the glow of the window across the room, the Ringblade stood ready. Her arm was high, a wide circle of sharpened steel in her hand.

Time stopped. Grei was caught. He hadn't expected to see a Ringblade. No one ever saw a Ringblade. He had hoped to find writings, secrets left behind, something to explain the Debt of the Blessed and how it might be stopped.

"How did you get through the window?" she asked in a calm voice.

He looked at the window, then back at her. Clearly she had seen him and how he'd entered. She meant something different, something he didn't understand.

He mastered himself. She would kill him, but maybe he could discover something before he died. Or maybe he could jump through the window and escape, run far enough to tell someone.

"I'm looking for answers," he said. "About the Debt." The words sounded too loud and too raw. It was like speaking treason straight to the delegate's face.

He couldn't see her expression, only the black silhouette of her body. He tried to see what she had been doing before he broke in. There was a rumpled bed next to her, clothes draped across the bedpost. Was she wearing anything? He squinted, trying to see her better, but the light behind her made her body dark.

"What is your name?" she asked. She lowered her weapon.

"Grei," he said.

"Don't move, Grei," she said, turning her back to him, facing the bed. She *was* naked. He shifted—

She spun, flinging the deadly ring. It whizzed by his ear, clanging twice off the corner walls behind him. He dropped to the floor, his heart in his throat. The weapon rebounded to her, and she caught it with the sound of ringing steel. Her catching hand was protected by something, a gauntlet.

"Don't move," she repeated quietly.

His heart hammered, but he let out a long breath and stood up again, with a full view of her this time. She was in her twenties, several years older than he. She had shoulder-length brown hair, an oval face, and very large brown eyes. Her breasts were full and round, with sickles of moonlight lighting their curves. The muscles in her arm stood out starkly in the window's light, the ring poised to fly again.

The whispers changed. Their sibilants morphed into voices, repeating something, a sing-song refrain. It was still all gibberish —no words—, but the change filled him with a rush of joy, and he felt invincible.

"Kill me then," he said.

She paused. "Are you slinked?" she asked.

She thought he was unhinged by the slink sickness that ravaged the minds of those who thought too much about the Slink War.

"No," he said. Grei's whispers weren't like that. He was sure they weren't like that.

The corner of her lip turned in a smile. "Then you're a brave one," she said. Her arm lowered. "Or are you stupid?"

"I'm dead already. You, too. Just like them out there." He gestured to the city of Fairmist outside the window. "What does it matter if you kill me again? I need the secrets you keep, and I mean to have them."

She paused, as though she was about to say something. Instead, she sat on the bed, crossed her legs. She made no effort to cover herself. Instead, she beckoned to him.

He cleared his throat. "I want to know about the Debt of the Blessed. It has to be stopped."

She watched him, then patted the bed next to her. "You sit here," she said.

He hesitated, then went to her and sat down. Every hair on the back of his neck stood on end. She was so lovely, but she was also a Ringblade. A silent serpent of the empire. This woman slit throats in the night, killing those the emperor told her to kill.

Her fingertips touched the back of his neck. "I'm going to ask you a question," she said softly, like a lover. "And you're going to answer me. If I think you're lying, well…" She held his gaze with hard brown eyes, and he understood the deadly meaning. "But if you tell the truth, I will give you secrets."

After a quiet moment, he nodded.

"The Faia built these houses," she said. "They decreed that only protectors of Fairmist may come here. Highblades in the first two houses, and Ringblades here. Any civilian who even touches a Lateral House runs away. You are not the first thief to try to break into the Lateral Houses. But you are the first to succeed. So my question is this: How did you get through that window?"

He reached for the unused shim in his sleeve. "I was going to—"

She caught his wrist, fished out the slender piece of steel.

"You're a thief?" she asked.

"No."

"A protector of Fairmist?"

He thought of the Highblades. "No," he said with disdain.

She paused, cocking her head to the side. "You're telling the truth."

"The truth is what I want to—"

She slid her fingers into his hair and kissed him, pressed her body against him.

His heart fluttered like a frantic bird. Her lips were full and soft, and her tongue touched his. She gently held the back of his neck, keeping him close. Threads of warmth spread through his chest, and he put his arms around her.

"My name is Ree," she whispered, breaking the kiss. Her breath was sweet. "That secret is yours to keep, brave boy."

He gasped and jerked back as hot pain bit into his ear. He touched it and his fingers came away bloody.

She brought the dagger down from behind his head. A smear of blood stained the blade, and she made it disappear behind her back.

He swallowed down a dry throat, touched the notch she had made in his ear.

"A kiss and a cut," she said. "For your collection and mine. Do not come back here or I'll keep more than a fleck next time."

She took his hand, her fingers strong and calloused, and led him to the door. She opened it to the Fairmist night. The walkway spiraled to the ground where the world was dizzyingly sideways.

"Go," she said. "The Faia will not let you fall."

He started down, holding his ear, dizzy from the kiss, from the pain, from his body turning slowly with each step. He had never felt so confused. Floating water touched his face and dripped down, and the world slowly righted itself. When he was on flat ground, she spoke.

"Grei."

He turned. She stood in the doorway, lithe and beautiful, sideways against the misty backdrop of the city.

"You are a protector. You just don't know it yet," she said. "That is the secret you seek."

She closed the door.

Chapter 2

REE

RINGBLADE REE returned to the imperial city of Thiara under the cover of darkness. Ringblades trained for the dark, and Ree's night vision was excellent. It was one of the first tests for initiates. More than half of them failed there and did not proceed.

She rode to the northern edge of the great city, tethered her horse to the a limb of the cypress tree and went to the red wall of Thiara, which was constructed by human hands out of blood granite. If Fairmist was the city of water, then Thiara was the city of sun, with her crimson walls, gold-veined marble towers shining in the daylight, and the blazing Sunset Sea behind it all.

She didn't worry about the horse. One of the Ringmaids would come along and properly stable or sell it.

She found the correct stone on the dark blocks and tapped out the sequence.

The secret door opened on silent runners, falling back and sliding to the side just enough for her to slip through, then reversed its course and began closing.

The moment she stepped through she slid downward at a

steep slant. As she had been trained, she kept her feet and her balance. The drop was far, at least three stories in the scant light. But she knew the count. One. Two. Three. Four. Five. Six. Seven.

She hit the ground and took the expected impact nimbly, stepping into the twenty-fifth Ringdance and counting again to seven. There were seventy-seven dances altogether. The last, the seventy-eighth, was death. Of course, as Ringmaids she and the others had joked about the seventy-ninth dance: paradise.

The twenty-fifth was one of the shortest dances, made for entering through this, the Poison Door. She placed her feet perfectly. One slip and she would die.

The dance ended exactly at the count of seven, just as the door far above thumped shut, plunging Ree into absolute blackness. She was on her tiptoes on a tiny shelf one inch above the floor. Her back pressed against the wall, and her fingers hooked through the steel rings set in the blocks for just this purpose.

A quiet hush filled the tight space as poison poured out of four spouts at the base of the walls. It spread smoothly and quickly across the steel grate, only half-an-inch deep, before sinking through. The poison was harmless as long as it only touched the metal of the grate. If it touched something living or once-living, like bare feet or the leather of boots, it became a gouting fume that would kill a person in seconds.

Ree waited for the count of seventy-seven, when another quiet rush reached her ears as the neutralizing oil poured over the poison.

She stepped down, beginning the first step of the twenty-sixth Ringdance, weaving through the dark and past the triggers of the thorn axe and the scorpion net. The dance came to an end, and she reached the door at the far side of the corridor. The last motion of the twenty-sixth was a leap straight up to brush the lever in the wall above the door.

No sound came from the lever, but she knew it alerted those on the other side. Ree swiveled and put her back against the wall as she regained her breath. Sometimes Selicia required a Ringblade to fight to gain entry. Training was never over. Ree must be ready.

A hatch in the top of the door slid aside, and the shaft of bright light would have blinded her if she had been looking at it. As she had been trained, she stared at the base of the door as her eyes adjusted.

"Who calls?" came a voice that Ree recognized well. She smiled.

"Your Ringsister," Ree answered.

"I cannot see you."

"A Ringblade moves, but is not seen," she repeated the Ringblade creed.

The latch clicked and the door swung open. Ringblade Liana stood on the other side, a coy smile on her face. Ree loved the way that woman smiled.

"Welcome back, Ree."

"It is good to be home."

Liana leaned down, and they kissed. Ree luxuriated in the fullness of the woman's lips. She let the kiss linger. The fate of the empire could wait for a good kiss. Finally, since Liana obviously would not be the first to stop, Ree gave her a playful nibble on her lower lip and pushed her away.

"How was Fairmist?" Liana asked, as if she hadn't just taken Ree's breath away. The tall, dark woman seemed invincible with her wide shoulders and muscled body. Her short hair and striking lavender eyes were exotic and delicious.

"Wet," Ree replied, thinking of the mysterious Grei and smirking at her private joke. Liana raised a jet-black eyebrow, and the corner of her lip quirked.

"You have an adventure to share?" she asked.

"You'd like it." Liana was the best of them at the forties, the dances that dealt with sensuality, sex, and snaring an opponent's mind by offering the body. Liana and Ree had grown close through the sharing of those tales. She and Liana had been Ringmaids together, the only two of their year's fourteen initiates who made it.

"Then you must be anxious to tell it to Selicia," she said, but her tall body blocked the way. Liana came from far over the Sunset Sea, even further west than Venisha, a small kingdom called Shalar. She was as tall as a Benascan, though the physical similarity ended there. Ree brushed her lips against the rich, black skin of Liana's shoulder.

"Duty first," she said.

Ringblades reported to the Ringmother first, all others after. And the news that Ree possessed could change the empire. Ree might have found the one they were all looking for.

After re-setting the latch on the Poison Door, Liana escorted Ree past the open arches to the dance rooms. It was unnecessary but sweet, a gesture of deference to Ree, as though she had not grown up in these halls, as though she didn't know every corner, every shadow and spark of light.

Three Ringmaids strained through dance fifty-one, Ringblade Zela watching with a stern eye. Zela looked up, saw Ree, and smiled briefly before glaring back at her charges.

Ree had missed the quiet solitude of the Sanctum, deep below the city. She missed the vaulted ceilings and the quietly flickering lanterns. The polished red walls shone. She ran her fingers along them, feeling their cool smoothness. This was safety, tucked away under the city with only her Ringsisters around her. She missed their companionship, their quiet conversations and late-night dinners. She missed the practice rooms, smelling of exertion, where the few Ringmaids trained each year. There was a mix of alertness and security in this place. This was the only place a Ringblade could let down her guard. This was where they all looked at the empire from inside the womb and contemplated where they would move events. This was home, more than her parents' mill in Moondow. This was where Ree Gell had become a woman, where she had learned what being female meant and the power it held.

She and Liana fell into stride together, enjoying the companionable silence.

They passed the row of Ringblade apartments, each blocked only by a red velvet curtain. The dusky walls were adorned with familiar art. She had grown up with those paintings and wall hangings. Some showed bloody battles, meant to shock the viewer. Some were quietly forbidding scenes, like the lone woman standing naked in the field of long grass before black skies, or the woman approaching the engulfing dark of the Jhor Forest. Each painting's unspoken story centered around a Ringblade, whether large and bloody or tiny against the world. Ree's favorite depicted a Ringblade dancing in the Sunset Sea, a wave towering behind her. The colors were stunning. Blues and greens of the fierce ocean rose in front of the rosy sunset for which the sea was named. The bronze figure of the Ringblade was a small but powerful contrast to the elements.

They passed the row of paintings and Liana stopped at Selicia's curtain. She turned and bowed low to Ree as though she was the imperial princess.

When she straightened, Ree shook her head, suppressing her smile. By the Faia, it was good to see her.

"Does Selicia know about your dramatic streak?" Ree asked.

"A late dinner, Ree? I'll wait up for you," Liana suggested.

"That would be the Seventy-Ninth. Thank you."

Liana moved silently up the low hallway, hips swinging. She gave a brief backward glance before she turned the corner and was gone. Ree grinned at the display that Liana had put on, Ree was sure, just for her.

Ree took a deep breath and turned to the velvet curtain that hung at the threshold of Selicia's room, embroidered with the empress' gold symbol.

The entrance to the Sanctum was fraught with deadly barriers, but within, there were no doors and no locks, only soft curtains. There were no secrets or theft here. The respect of her Ringsisters was the most important thing a Ringblade owned, and they were free to share the information they gathered, as long as they shared it with Selicia first. No Ringblade had ever betrayed the sisterhood as far as Ree knew, not in the three hundred years it had existed.

Ree did not knock. She did not clear her throat or clap, nothing to indicate she was there. Selicia said that if a Ringblade was not aware enough to sense someone outside her own room, she deserved to be surprised.

Ree counted to seven, then stepped through the curtains.

Selicia stood in the center of the room. A dun-colored nightdress draped from her strong shoulders to mid calf. Her long, black braid almost touched the floor. She usually had it coiled and clipped to her shoulder. She had either been sleeping, or was about to do so.

But there was no drowsiness in those depthless black eyes or anywhere on her angular features. The puckered red scar on her cheek was still bright, twisting the left side of her face from eye to jaw, just above the vein in her neck. Jorun Magnus' blade had come half-an-inch from killing her before she brought the legendary warrior down.

The Ringmother exuded strength. She was small, but her presence filled the space, made her seem taller. The Ringmother could be surrounded by a dozen Lianas and still seem like the largest Ringblade in the room.

She was in her forties, lean and muscled, and she could spin through any of the Seventy-Seven Dances with more precision and power than her youthful counterparts. Ree couldn't imagine facing her in combat. Jorun Magnus had been unbeatable; only one woman in the world could have taken him down. This woman.

"Welcome back, Ringsister," Selicia said in her soft contralto. "Would you like to sit?" She waved a graceful hand at the three red silk cushioned chairs around a small table in the corner.

"My thanks," Ree said. "I have been astride a horse for two days. I could stand."

Selicia gave a ghost of a smile, there and gone, as though she had expected the answer. Probably she had.

Ree was excited to share her news about Grei, the boy who could apparently either flaunt the magic of the Faia or was somehow chosen by them. He might be the Whisper Prince, someone for whom the emperor had been searching for quite some time. The Whisper Prince was the key to an old Faia prophecy that was of interest to his imperial majesty. So Ree had notched him and saved the blood. No matter where he went, she could find him.

Ree waited for Selicia's word to report. Ree had been sent to Fairmist several times over the last two years to see if there was any new Faia activity. Never had she returned with anything to report. Never until now.

But Selicia did not speak the ritual words. She did not ask Ree for her report, and suddenly Ree felt there was something wrong.

Selicia's lips pressed into a line, and she said, "I have news for you, Ringsister. I urge you to listen to it, then take a late dinner with your friend as she suggested, and later sleep. When you wake, I wish to talk more of it, if you would."

Ree's heart began to pound. She immediately thought of her parents, wondering if something had happened to them. Benascan raiders? But they had not come as far south as Moondow since just after the Slink War.

Selicia watched Ree with those black eyes, perhaps reading her mind, then she said, "Your sister, Salandra, was chosen."

Ree's heart lifted for an instant as she thought Selicia meant her sister would become an initiate in the next cycle, would be brought to the Sanctum to pit her wits and her body against the Seventy-Seven Dances. But Ree's heart dropped at Selicia's solemn expression.

"No," Ree said, her voice barely a whisper.

Selicia took a long, even breath. "I am so sorry."

"The Debt," Ree said, her lips numb.

Selicia held out her arms to Ree. It was the first time the

Ringmother had ever done that since Ree had been initiated. It was the first time Ree had ever heard of Selicia making such a gesture. She did not cross the room as a friend might, but only made the offer, which meant Ree could refuse.

Ree remained where she was.

"When?" she asked.

"Last night."

"Selicia, you must intervene," she said, knowing what the answer must be, knowing that it was treason to even ask. "Just this once."

Selicia watched Ree, never once breaking eye contact. She lowered her arms, answering without words.

Of course not. If the emperor would not intervene on behalf of his own daughter, no one would intervene on behalf of a Ringblade's sister. Salandra was dead.

Ree clenched her teeth. She was expected to hear the news, to grieve silently, as Ringblades did everything else, and to bury Salandra as though she had died in an accident, or from a raider's axe. She mastered her emotions, and nodded.

Selicia watched her eyes, and Ree saw caring there, but also duty. Always duty first.

After what Selicia must have decided was an appropriate amount of time for Ree to collect herself, she returned to the normal. To the routine. To duty.

"And what words do you bring to me, Ringsister? What tales of the unseen?" She spoke the ritual words.

Ree's tongue had turned to stone. Salandra was dead, never to be spoken of again, and Ree was left with routine and duty. She had served the empire faithfully, and the emperor had killed her sister. Ree's obligation dictated she trust in the wisdom of her emperor and, most importantly, to report on her mission to Selicia.

"Fairmist continues as ever, Ringmother," Ree lied smoothly, as they had trained her to do. Except lies were for the outer world. Never in the Sanctum. Never against the Ringmother. "The Faia remain absent."

Selicia nodded, and her eyes turned concerned again.

"Then let us speak more tomorrow."

"Yes." Ree bowed her head, feeling as though she had swallowed something rotten. She turned and moved through the curtains. She did not think of Liana even once. She did not think of a late dinner.

She had left a horse tied to the giant cypress tree. The Ringmaids had almost assuredly not taken it yet.

And Ree might yet reach the Imperial Wand before he reached the slink caves.

Chapter 3
KURUK

KURUK HUNCHED his thin shoulders over the table, focusing on the tome. He worked to keep his fingers cool as he handled the pages. The old paper was made for the plump sacks of water humans used for fingers. His claws would poke burning holes if he didn't concentrate, and it required more effort to maintain his concentration with every month that passed. The pressure had increased; every day was a battle. He fought them all, had held them in check for seven years, but in each moment there was a chance he might lose control. In each moment, he fought.

He reached the end of the page, slid a translucent claw between the brittle sheets, and flipped to the next. The old human histories calmed him, settled his mind.

"Kuruk," Malik said from behind him. His brother entered the cavern, flame rising from the top of his blond hair. Kuruk wanted to say something, but he restrained himself. Malik had poor control, and control was the only thing that kept them alive. Once they brought their brothers home, they could allow themselves to be careless. But not until that moment.

He and Malik had once been human, and their boyish faces resembled children unless they projected something else into their enemies' minds. They could have passed among humans unnoticed in their natural forms except for their translucent claws, and of course, their eyes. Their eyes told every nightmare they had endured.

"A crusader approaches," Malik said.

Kuruk felt the news like another sack of sand laid on his shoulders. The onslaught was constant, and he was weakening. There was no respite. That would make two this year already. Two too many. The humans must be so afraid that they did not dare approach the slink cave.

Kuruk rose reluctantly, concentrating and closing the cover of Emperor Cozelt's second history without burning it.

"You have read that before," Malik said, looking at it.

"Something caught my interest. Their history—*our* history," he corrected himself, "is vital. It calms me," Kuruk said.

Malik nodded, but Kuruk could feel his brother's doubts.

"Did you read the passage I gave you about the Whisper Prince?" Malik asked.

"I did," Kuruk said.

"A human with the powers of a Faia."

Kuruk put a hand to his head. The beating inside his skull increased suddenly, drums pounding full force. The whole of Thiara shrieked at him, all of them scratching to get out. Smoke curled up from Kuruk's eyelids.

Malik had seen these attacks before, and he waited with his breath held. If Kuruk lost the battle, their plan was over. Kuruk gritted his teeth, shoving the screeching back until it was contained. Fire leaked out of his fingertips, burning five neat holes into the cover of Emperor Cozelt's history. He snatched his hand away and Malik drew the flames into his own hand, snuffing the fire.

"I'm sorry, brother," Malik said.

Kuruk slumped, leaning on the table. "The Faia hold the

door, Malik. But we are stronger. We will bring our brothers home." He drew a shuddering breath.

Kuruk pushed himself upright and moved to the archway. They walked together down the long corridor. Their human lives had been so brief compared to their century of torture. He wanted that life back, wanted the home that had been ripped from him.

He had read the books. He had watched the humans. Tried to remember. He built his future life in his head. And when the moment came, he and Malik and all of their brothers would be human again.

Now there was a Whisper Prince somewhere in the empire, called by prophecy. A human who might challenge them. Like the damned Jorun Magnus.

Their brother Bahktish had fallen to Magnus and his Faia-cursed sword, and it had been Kuruk's fault. Kuruk had told his brothers that they were impervious to human weapons, and they should have been. Then Magnus had slain Bahktish.

"Patience and silence are our allies now," Kuruk said, as much to bolster himself as to give Malik heart. "It will be over soon."

Malik said nothing. Kuruk could feel his brother's frustration, the fury mounting, and he shared it. Seven years was too long to wait. But they had to maintain their control. Their master, still trapped in fiery Velakka, would have them succumb to their fury, revel in its power, and burn Thiara down. But Kuruk knew if he did, his humanity would vanish forever. Kuruk wanted his humanity. He wanted it back.

"Turoh is ready," Kuruk said, calming his brother, calming himself. "Not a failure after all. It will just take time. We are so close now. We will not falter."

They neared the cave's opening, which humans saw as a pit to their greatest fears. Only those who brought the Blessed knew where the slinks resided. But every now and then, an adventurer discovered them. Then they would receive a visitor, someone who would come to take revenge for the

Slink War, or for the Debt. Malik called them crusaders.

Tonight's crusader was female. Unlike Velakkans, humans were divided into two different types. One kind gave his mucous to the other, who kept it in her body and grew offspring. Later, the offspring had to be pushed out in another expulsion of fluid. Kuruk quelled his abhorrence at the thought, forced himself to remember that this was how he and his brothers had come into the world. He told himself it was not repulsive. Born in water. Human water. Squalling. Mother cooing. Love.

When Kuruk had asked his master about love, Lord Velak had laughed. It had been scornful, meant to burn the notion from Kuruk's mind, and Kuruk had laughed with him. But Kuruk remembered love. He remembered his mother's embrace, her soft lips on his forehead. Her squeezing arms, warm around his body. Her fingers tickling him until he was breathless with giggles. Love meant safety; it was the only memory Kuruk had of such a thing.

He didn't let his master's laugh strip love away from him. He wanted that back most of all.

Kuruk watched the woman crusader move across the loose rock that led down to the hole of the cavern. To him, she seemed slow and ponderous. Since he had begun watching her, her fourth and twelfth step had turned a rock, caused noise that carried easily to his ears.

To a human, though, she would seem graceful. Deadly. A Ringblade.

Thin metal squares had been fit to her forearms and forelegs, and her body was sheathed in soft black cloth because her own hide was vulnerable to the sharp edges of the world. The slightest puncture would cause her to spew her red water.

She crouched and crept forward, moving herself in a bad mimicry of a spider. Her breasts, the round mounds of fat on the front of her chest, hung against her clothing. The purpose of them was to create and pass fluid to children after they were born. Kuruk had read about them. He didn't remember his mother's breasts. Only the warmth of her arms.

"Humans are not to come here," he said to the crusader. His voice echoed off the rock walls. "Unless you wish to be the next Blessed." An empty threat. Kuruk had recently taken a Blessed; he was at his weakest. It took him almost a full month to recover.

The female's head shot up. Her steel-clad hand rose at the same time, bearing the sharpened ring that gave this group of fighters their name. She peered through the darkness, trying to see him.

He waited, searching. A breeze blew past Kuruk, and he smelled her fear.

"Show yourself!" she called.

He held his arms out to his sides, and she tracked the motion, focusing on him, seeing the nightmare form he had chosen: An eight-foot-tall creature with wide shoulders, long, thin arms that reached almost to the ground. Great jaws in a small head. Red, burning skin and cloven animal hooves. He looked like his master's minions, like the innumerable slinks that had torn through Thiara seven years ago.

With a grunt, the female flung her ring.

He held up his forearm and whispered to it. The sharpened steel clanged off, rebounding. The woman leapt to her right, caught it with her gauntleted hand.

"I've come for my sister," she said.

He watched the woman, doomed to fail here, completely overmatched. He imagined that his mother had fought this hard for him, died this bravely before the rough hands grabbed Kuruk from his bed. He wanted to save this Ringblade. He wanted to tell her he knew her pain. They were kindred. But for her to regain her sister meant he must lose his brothers.

"Salandra was brave," Kuruk said. He could give her that, at least. "She paid the Debt with honor."

Then he reached into the Ringblade with whispers she could not hear and began working on her mind. His forehead heated, and he felt the dangerous screeching again. He wished he had time for mercy. And perhaps wishing was enough. Perhaps the wish alone guarded his speck of remaining humanity.

"Give her back and I will leave," she said. In her fearful heart, she knew that her weapons could not hurt his slinks. Yet here she was, willing to sacrifice herself to free her sister.

"What is your name, Ringblade?" he asked.

"I am Ree. There has been a mistake with the Blessed. Selicia sent me to retrieve Salandra."

"No, she didn't," he said softly, and his estimation of her diminished. He hated liars. The men who had snatched him and his brothers were liars.

The Ringblade shifted, her grip tightening on her weapon.

"Give me my sister," Ringblade Ree said through clenched teeth. She flung her ring. This time, she followed it, leaping over rocks and sliding on the shale to reach him. Kuruk blocked her flying steel and moved to brace her.

She swung at him with a curved blade she pulled from a sheath across her back. He whispered again, making his arm hard enough to turn metal. He backed up a few steps, deflecting her strikes, giving her a cut to her shoulder with his claws, then one on her leg just to the side of the armor plate.

Kuruk took a breath, steeling himself, then moved at a speed that was difficult for him to achieve and almost impossible for her to see. He grabbed her arm, jerked it into his teeth and bit down several times quickly, severing it as fire raged from his throat. Her blood boiled in his mouth, and her burning flesh filled his nostrils.

Kuruk's brother Bahktish had loved the taste of blood. Of all his brothers, Bahktish had been the most like a Velakkan. It was this bloodlust that had distracted Bahktish when Magnus set upon him. Kuruk had found his brother over a half-chewed corpse in the palace, his head severed at the neck.

Kuruk hated the taste of blood. Humans did not eat each

other; it felt foul. He could barely hold it in his mouth.

The female screamed, falling backward, dropping her sword as she grappled with her smoking stump. Her arm burned with the fire his teeth had left behind, the flesh curling and turning black. She drew a shuddering breath, biting down on her next scream, which leaked out in a whimper.

Kuruk spat her own blood upon her and advanced. Her feet scraped frantically as she tried to draw back. He went to work on her now, heightening her fear, bringing it to a pointy desperation before he crushed her mind.

He dropped her severed arm, grabbed her and flung her backward. She flew silently and hit the rocks, slid to a stop.

With an anguished shout of determination, she pushed herself upright with her good arm, holding her severed stump close to her chest as though she might cradle the hand that wasn't there. She was still trying to fight, and she fumbled desperately with her belt, drawing a thin dagger. She looked at Kuruk through squinty, agony-filled eyes.

Her gaze moved past him, saw the hundreds of slinks emerge from the darkness behind him, their eyes glowing, their claws clicking on the rocks, their teeth bared in excited smiles.

Kuruk breathed fire at her, and the female backed up the slope, filled with horror.

"Take her," Kuruk said.

The horde of slinks leapt up the slope, howling. The female turned away, stumbling and running as fast as she could. She crested the ridge and disappeared, the slinks hard on her heels.

Kuruk held on until she was out of sight, then fell to his knees. He clenched his hair with his fists, breathing fire. The screams in his head were like claws, slashing his mind. They wanted out. Every moment, they longed to escape, but he couldn't let them go. Not until his brothers were safe.

He didn't know how long he lay there, fighting the pain, fighting the overwhelming wave that wanted to drown him.

But eventually, he realized that Malik was with him,

holding his head and whispering softly.

"You are strong. You are invincible. You can hold them all."

"I can't..." Kuruk whimpered. "I can't."

"You are Kuruk. You can do anything."

"Malik..."

Malik opened his mouth and flames coursed over Kuruk, engulfing him. There was only heat and red fire, like in Velakka where they had been transformed and turned invincible. Made inhuman.

After a time, Kuruk was filled with the strength of it, and he was able to beat back the scratching, the howling, the relentless pounding.

"Yes," Malik said. "You can do it."

Kuruk took a shuddering breath, but he didn't sit up. He didn't know if he had the strength. At long last, he could think. He could breathe. He could speak.

"Every moment," he gasped. "It is almost too much. I don't know..."

"You will find a way. We follow you, Kuruk."

But am I strong enough to lead you?

"Tell me about the Whisper Prince," Kuruk said quietly, closing his eyes again and resting in his brother's arms. "Tell me of our new threat."

Chapter 4
GREI

GREI QUIETLY closed the door to his house, shutting out the wet. It had been more than two weeks since Ringblade Ree, and he hadn't wasted a moment of it. His head hurt, as it always did when he thought too much on the Debt of the Blessed. The singsong voices had descended into whispers again.

He was tired, and the warmth was welcome. He hung his cloak on the pegs over the water tray by the door and let it drip. The rest of the house was quiet. Then, a mug clacked on the table in the common room. Grei let out a long, quiet breath. His night was not over. He could feel the anger from here like heat, and Grei moved inside with slow deliberation.

His father sat at the table with the mug in hand. His frown was a damning slash over his chin. Tendons stood out in his wrist where he clenched the handle.

"Good of you to come home," he said tightly.

So he had heard at last. Grei had spent every waking hour since Ringblade Ree searching for information. He had been to the caves at the base of the Highward, had paced the ground in the Wet Woods where the emperor had bargained with the slinks. Grei had spoken with families who had lost loved ones to the Debt of the Blessed. He had tracked down those who had lived through the slaughter in Thiara seven years ago. Yet with all that, only two people had chosen to talk with him. He had learned precious little about the slinks he didn't already know, and nothing about the Debt. His frustration was turning to desperation, and he feared the whispers would abandon him again. He was running out of next steps.

He stood silently in front of his father.

"Lady Suffayne," Father said. "She said you were talking to Luran."

"I've been talking to a lot of people." Luran was the son of a palace cook, and one of the few people Grei's age who would talk to him. Luran's father had been in Thiara when the slinks came.

"Lady Suffayne withdrew her order," Father continued. The mug was now shaking; pewter rattled against wood.

"Because I was talking with Luran."

"About the Slink War, Grei." Father stood up. "About the Debt!"

"Yes."

"It's treason. We are not going down this road again."

Grei glowered. "You're not."

He paused. "Do you want me to send you to the delegate's men?" he asked in a low voice.

And there it was. So quickly. *I'll give you back to the torturers.* Grei felt the numbness they had created and fostered during those days in that black room. Days that seemed like weeks. He would never allow himself to go numb again.

"You do what you have to—"

"I won't have it!" his father yelled, slamming the mug onto the table with a loud bang. No one else in the house stirred. Grei could picture his brother Julin huddled in his bed, covers to his nose. His step-mother Fern probably stood at her window, twisting her fingers together, silently agreeing with Grei, too afraid to stand with him. That hurt more than his father's shouting. "This is not a game," his father growled. "This is our life."

"This is no life," Grei said.

"The emperor—"

"This is the way we make it."

"You pig-headed boy! You want to kill yourself? Fine! Don't take this family with you!"

"Don't ruin your business, you mean?" Grei shouted.

Father stood up, livid. His whole body shook.

"I should have let you die," he said in a lethal voice.

Grei stalked back to the door and snatched his cloak.

"I should have saved your mother instead!" his father said, following.

Grei flung the door open and slammed it behind him. The floating water droplets touched his face and his chest and dripped down the front of him. He leaned his head back against the door, hearing his father breathing hard on the other side.

He clenched his fists. The gutters trickled, forever draining onto the stone streets, and there was the distant slither and hush of Fairmist's citizens going about their night activities. The Harvesthome Festival wasn't far off, and some were getting ready to stuff themselves with pastries, drown themselves in ale.

Forcing his tense arms upward, Grei pulled his long hair back into a ponytail, tied it, and adjusted his cloak to shield him from the floating droplets.

He crossed half the city in seething silence, over the deep and powerful Fairmist River. He approached the Temple of the Faia, a circle of seven marble pillars carved centuries ago by the finest artisans of an early empire, back when Baezin was emperor and goddesses walked among humans. Its stout crudeness, compared with the empire's modern structures, made it seem indestructible. The Fairmist River could escape its banks and sweep through the city, taking all the other houses with it, but the temple would still stand.

Seven short beds of roses surrounded the temple, making a wide red circle with paths in between. A giant urn stood in its center, waist high and two feet in diameter. The water within rose like a stalagmite, pointing at the curved ceiling. Several inches beyond that unnatural peak, a sphere of water as big as Grei's fist hovered as though it had just pulled free.

Every day at Highsun, different pilgrims came to the temple to give thanks to the Faia. When it had been built, Emperor Baezin decreed that there would be no central worship of the Faia, that each citizen should give their respects in their own way, but sects had sprung up, all claiming that their method of worship was what the Faia demanded. The most powerful of the sects in Fairmist were the Servants of the River Lady. Grei's father and step-mother belonged to that group, and they came to this temple at Highsun on the seventh day, Faiaday, and laid their offerings in homage. There were other sects, of course. The Supplicants of the Sun Goddess. The Dirt Bathers. The Wanderers. The Moon Crows, who worshipped on Seconday at Deepdark. The rare but chilling Teeth Gnashers, named for the sound their grinding teeth made as they proceeded to the temple.

The floating sphere of water in the center of the temple glowed blue, giving a ghostly radiance to the marble pillars and floor. It was called Baezin's Voice, and the legend said it translated speech so that the Faia and humans could understand one another.

Grei entered the temple, passing beneath the dome. He knelt among the strewn and wilting flowers of those who had come during the day. There was a multitude of offerings: prized keepsakes, precious stones, coins, jewelry. Some people even offered dead animals: a rabbit killed on the hunt, a rack of antlers with blood on the stumps. Dead animals. For the Faia.

He ignored them and stared at the blue sphere.

"Have you truly left us, then?" he asked. Rage and frustration jammed together inside him like logs.

The Faia could build hovering houses. They could make water float like dandelion fluff, could make stone burn. They could have stopped the slinks, but they hadn't. They could stop the Debt of the Blessed, but they didn't.

"I'll do it, then," he said. "I'll show them the truth. You can't just let people die so you can pretend you live a normal life. You can't,,," Grei choked on his words, bowed his head. "You can't just pretend they aren't dying," he whispered.

He turned away, and a flash of blue on the ground caught his attention. At first, he thought it was metal reflecting the glow of Baezin's Voice, or a huge sapphire dropped as an offering.

Grei gasped. Between the fitted stones of the temple floor grew a blue rose. The whispers became voices again, loudly repeating the gibberish singsong.

Grei had been from one end of Fairmist to the other, through the Wet Woods, to the northern plains of the Lowlands. He had climbed the cliffs of the Highward and seen the mist-shrouded valley in miniature. He knew the South Forest like his little brother's smile, and he had mapped out every bridge that ran through the city.

He had only seen a blue rose once before, just before the Forest Girl had kissed him:

Grei ran through the South Forest. The army of Highblades and refugees had just left Fairmist in the aftermath of the Slink War, and this was a dangerous place because there could still be slinks. But Grei had slipped his parents' leash and gone exploring. He wanted to see a slink.

He pushed a wet limb out of his way, ducking under the shower of water, and stumbled into the glade.

A green Faia floated by a drooping willow, her wings flicking. She was miniature, barely two feet tall. Her pale skin glowed green, and her hair looked like it was made of cascading leaves. Her eyes were shining emeralds. She turned at the noise, saw him, and vanished in a shimmer of sparkles.

Behind her in the fading green light lay an injured girl, crumpled against the tree's roots. Her heel had been ripped by something vicious, an animal's claw, and it leaked blood onto the grass. Her black hair looked like it had golden cords woven into it, and her eyes were deep blue. Beside her grew a rose of that same deep blue, glowing softly.

The Forest Girl's piercing blue gaze caught him, stirred something inside him he hadn't known was there.

He whipped off his cloak and laid it over her, told her it was going to be all right, that he was going to help her. He tried to gather her into his arms and take her away, but she was too heavy. He stumbled, sat down heavily with her across his lap.

"It's okay," he said. "I'll stay with you."

She leaned up and kissed him, lightly, on the lips. Blue light flashed through his mind, and he knew this girl, like they were twin souls in different bodies. Everything made sense: who he was and what he was doing here. He was here to protect her no matter what. She and he would walk hand-in-hand to the edge of the sunset. Together forever.

Then she broke the kiss, and her head fell back on his shoulder.

Father and Fern will look for me, *he thought, settling down with the Forest Girl, keeping his arms around her.* They will worry, and they'll come for me. I will take care of her and wait for them.

Hours passed. Afternoon turned to dusk and then to dark, and still his father and step-mother didn't come. Grei went to a nearby stream and rushed back with water in his cupped hands, but she barely drank any.

Night fell and the moon lit the forest. The blue rose glowed as though keeping watch. The Forest Girl slept, curled into him. He felt no fatigue, as though he had suddenly become a night creature, and he stared into the darkness, eyes wide.

Morning dawned, and still no one came. The day passed, and he talked to the sleeping girl in soft tones. As the sun fell

on that second day, she opened her eyes and looked up at him
again. He offered her the piece of bread and hard cheese
he'd thought to bring with him, but she turned her head
away.

"What is your name?" he asked her.

"I am no one," she whispered, closing her eyes.

"I won't leave you," he said. "I'm going to protect you."

She said nothing, but she leaned against him anyway.

The sun fell on the second day, and Grei's stomach hurt
from hunger. He tried to get her to eat some of the meager
store of food he had brought, but she wouldn't. He nibbled a
little himself, saving the rest for her. Where were his parents?
Why weren't they coming?

He stared into the night, imagining creating a litter. Two
long branches would do it. He would use his cloak to bind
them together, then he could drag her—

Hooves shuffled in the woods, and Grei spun around.

The slink emerged from between the trees, enormous. Its
bloated torso was mottled by bark-like skin, black and brown
in the darkness. Enormous arms hung low, twisted with
powerful muscles, and its knuckles almost touched the
ground. Its head was long and slender like that of deer, with
thick horns curling up to uneven points above. It saw him and
the girl, and a blast of froth shot from its nose. It raised its
enormous head, its dark gaze boring into Grei.

"No!" He leapt to his feet, standing between it and her.
"Back!"

"Run..." the Forest Girl said. "Run now!"

He grabbed a stick from the earthy floor and swung it at
the slink. "No!" He raised it over his head.

The slink snorted, watching him, but it did not charge.
Instead, its eyes glowed, changing colors. Brown first. Then
yellow. Lavender. A rainbow swirled through the glade. Grei
staggered back, dizzy.

"Please..." the Forest Girl said, her voice stretching long
and thin, wrapping over his head like a gossamer shroud.
Then he was falling.

That was all he saw. That was all he remembered.

Grei stared at the blue rose, dumbfounded. The Forest Girl had been gone when he had awoken, the rose too. He had found himself alone with whispers in his head, like his ears were ringing from some great noise he couldn't remember. He had shouted for the girl, searched for her. He had finally fallen to the earth, weeping uncontrollably because he had failed her. She had died and he had lived, just like with his mother. He had raged at the trees, throwing sticks and rocks and shouting until his throat was raw.

His father had found him like that, fingers twisted into the thick grass, rocking back and forth and crying. For his father, almost no time had passed. He claimed he'd been searching for hours. For Grei, it had been days. But in truth, something far stranger had happened. His breeches and tunic, dirty with stains not of his making, smaller on his body than they should have been, told a chilling story: He had grown, perhaps a year's worth of days, and he had no memory of it.

His father and Fern had hidden Grei for a month, claiming that he was ill. When he emerged from his "illness," his friends and neighbors commented on his sudden growth spurt, but none suspected it was magical. The whispers faded away after the first week.

Grei reached out a hand, then hesitated to touch the blue rose, afraid it might vanish. Instead, he leaned over it, his face only inches away. The whispered words grew louder, more distinct, as though something was coming. They sounded like—

"Not supposed to be in the temple after nightfall," came a deep voice.

Grei started. A hulking figure stepped into the blue glow of Baezin's Voice, and Grei's heart sank. It was Meek Furrows.

Grei was fourteen when he first decided to fight the Debt of the Blessed. Four years of watching it rip families apart was enough. That had been the first time he'd started asking questions. It had made him an outcast. Childhood friends were told by their parents to shun him. Adults who had been kind to him his entire life shut their shutters when he walked past. Then one day at the edge of the South Forest, three boys Grei's age had cornered him, pushed him about, told him he ought to shut his mouth. Meek had been their leader, and Grei's first and only punch had bloodied the larger boy's nose. Meek and his friends had beaten Grei senseless afterwards. And it wasn't the last time.

No adults would stop them, not even his father. It was everyone's way of showing Grei that they disapproved of his actions. Meek and his friends made the most of it. Grei took beating after beating. He had a scar on his head where Meek had thrown him onto a rock.

He'd endured more than a year of it, stubbornly refusing to give in, and that was when the delegate's men came for him. The torturers. They kept him for days in a dark room with the droning voices, the pain at unknown times. His birthday passed some time during his stay. When Grei emerged into the daylight at age sixteen, he played the normal boy, worked diligently in his father's shop. But the nervous tick at his eye had lasted for months.

The torturers had been more than a year ago now, longer since Meek had beaten on him. Neither would ever happen again. Grei stood up.

Meek came a step closer. He wore the battered blue tunic of a Young Blade with its stylized raindrop, which meant he had been admitted for training as a Highblade. Young Blades, as they were called, were given castoff uniforms and short swords, and often the less-coveted jobs, like policing the streets after dark.

"Meek," Grei said.

"Saw you," Meek said. "Knew it had to be you. Crazy Grei. Heard you're talking treason again." He smiled. One of his front teeth was brown.

"If only more people were listening," Grei said, wondering where Meek's partner was. Young Blade patrols always traveled in twos.

Meek nodded his head, smiling, as though Grei was singing his favorite song. "You're going to make me a full Highblade, is what you're going to do, when I turn you in. You're a conspitior."

"You mean 'conspirator'."

Meek's lip curled in a snarl, and he stepped forward, crushing the blue rose under his heel as he balled up his fist.

The rose's death burst inside Grei like splattered oil, and he staggered back. Bile rose in his throat, and he wanted to vomit.

Meek swung for his head, and Grei ducked, his fingers closing over the polished club he'd kept in his belt since the night he met Ree.

He yanked the stick free and smashed it on Meek's helmeted head with all his strength. Meek reeled and Grei got both hands on the stick and brought it down hard again. With a cry, the ox dropped to his knees. His helmet fell off and rolled to the side.

The whispers, so joyous before, had gone quiet. He could barely hear them. The crushed flower's stem had been severed. Destroyed. He knelt down and picked up the rose while Meek moaned. Rage boiled within Grei, and he glared at Meek, wanting to hit him again.

Meek tried to rise, lost his balance and fell over, slumping onto his butt. "No, don't..." he said, seeing Grei's fury. He waved one arm in a weak gesture of warding. "Don't kill me."

Grei gripped the club tightly. He could barely see Meek's face through the red haze over his vision. The flower's death coursed through him like poison.

"Kill you?" he growled. "I'm not a Highblade."

He pushed his anger down and forced himself to come to his senses. This wasn't just a scuffle between boys. Meek represented the delegate, the empire. He glanced around again for Meek's absent partner. Young Blades always traveled in twos.

He had to go.

He turned and ran. Meek shouted after him, but that was all the chase he gave.

Grei raced across the canal bridge onto Milkmist Street and south. He didn't bother with his cowl, and the floating water droplets splashed across his face, streamed down his cheeks and neck.

The innumerable waterways born of Fairmist Falls ran through the city like veins, and Grei knew all of them. Most of the streams had covered bridges, some open bridges, but many required boats or ferries to cross. He avoided the ferries. Depending which side of the river the ferry had been left, it could take five minutes to pull it over. If Meek decided to give chase, that would be a perfect place to catch up.

So Grei weaved his way through the city, leaping over the smaller streams and finding bridges to cross where he could not jump. He reached the edge of the city and plunged into the South Forest.

He charged through the trees, feeling the wet slap of the ferns against his legs, ducking leafy branches that showered water on him. Finally, he came to the place he had forsaken seven years ago and, breathing hard, fell to his knees.

He sat in the wet grass trying to control the shakes. His tongue tasted like blood. He tossed the club away and opened his other hand to reveal the beleaguered little rose.

He looked around the glade where he'd seen the Faia and the Forest Girl. He hadn't been here in years, but he could have found it with his eyes closed.

He dug a hole in the moist earth, put the rose's stem in it and pushed the dirt over, packing it delicately. The rose lay limp on the grass.

"I won't look away ever again," he said. "Not for anyone."

He let out a breath and stood up, watching the hopeless flower for a long time.

The whispers in his mind suddenly became deafening. He stumbled, tripped over himself and fell sideways into a thick, moss-covered tree.

> *A lost fair lady cried out in alarm*
> *The Whisper Prince offered his arm*
> *They both ran away*
> *And never did say*
> *Why a princess lay down for his charm*

It repeated. When it finished, it started again. He leaned against the tree, squinting as it barraged him.

Everyone knew *The Whisper Prince*. Fern had sung it to him and Julin when they were children. Every mother had sung it to every child since the beginning of time.

The poem repeated endlessly, and Grei felt a chill. Rat Mathens, one of those who had gone crazy after the Slink War, mumbled constantly that his dead wife was still alive. A dozen people had seen her ripped apart by slinks. But Rat endlessly repeating the story he wished was true: she's still alive; she just went to the north, that's all. Rat was a cautionary tale. Dwelling on the Slink War drove a person mad.

Grei shoved the thought down. He hadn't gone mad. He hadn't—

An image of the blue rose flickered across Grei's mind, and he spun around.

The rose had risen, its stalk firm and strong, its petals open to catch the floating droplets that touched it.

"By the Faia," he whispered, falling to his knees.

The rhyme quieted, repeating gently.

Chapter 5

ADORA

ADORA KNEW the rhyme *The Whisper Prince* like she knew her own heartbeat. She had heard it almost every day for seven years, since the Debt of the Blessed had begun stealing one Thiaran child a month, since the Slink War. She had studied the long version, had studied the short version. The old men of the Order had made her memorize it.

The Whisper Prince was in every household. Mothers and fathers sang it to their children. Lovers changed key words and repeated it to each other, giggling at their cleverness. It was as much a part of Fairmist—and the Thiaran Empire—as roads and houses, water-catchers and city symbols, Highblades and Ringblades.

To everyone else, *The Whisper Prince* was just a child's poem like *Milly and the Mouse* or *Seven White Towers*. It caught in the memory, a beloved rhyme everyone had heard since they were little.

But there was a deeper truth behind it. *The Whisper Prince* wasn't just a poem. The original version was much longer, a prophecy handed down to humankind by the Faia over a century ago. Only a handful of people knew of this prophecy which, if fulfilled, could save every man, woman and child of the Thiaran Empire.

Today, Adora was a traveling merchant's daughter. She had tucked her black and gold hair under a kerchief and dressed in working clothes: a dun apron and brown skirts, a white blouse that looked fancy to a lowland farmer, maybe. But a duke or delegate would not notice her anymore than he would notice a chair.

If someone thought long enough, they might consider her blue eyes or the gold streaks in her black hair. In the imperial city of Thiara where most were dark-haired, it would have made her more conspicuous. But not as much in eastern Fairmist, where the light-skinned northern savages sometimes came, sometimes raped women and gave their babies blue eyes and yellow hair. Adora had learned that the trick to hiding in the open was to show people what you wanted them to see, to fill their mind with what you offered and replace their own notions.

Today Adora would be introduced to Fairmist in her own right, under her adopted name. She had visited many times before, following Shemmel in his guise of a traveling merchant, as his daughter. Or more recently with Lyndion, escorting him as his young courtesan. The Bright Speaker had enjoyed that charade all too much.

But this was the next task. This was when she began her own life, separate from the Order. Today her new name would become her real name as others in Fairmist met her, defined her. Today she would begin the fulfillment of the prophecy. No more studying. No more learning. The Event that would herald the coming of the Whisper Prince was nearly here.

Today she would begin the journey that would end with the slinks' destruction.

She waited quietly by the tavern wall, darkened by years of pipe smoke. Shemmel talked with the owner of *The Floating Stone*, a man named Seydir, who was wiping out a

mug behind the bar. A large painting of the Sunset Sea hung
behind him, a long-necked monster rising over Seydir's head.

The tavern master could have been a blacksmith with his
wide, hairy forearms and thick-fingered hands. He was
balding, with prominent black eyebrows and bushy sideburns.
He glanced at Adora around Shemmel's head. She expected
him to look at her figure. Lyndion had warned her about the
way the outer world would appraise her. Men would want to
take her to bed. She had resisted rolling her eyes at him. As if
she did not know that already. Every man in the Order
besides Shemmel already looked at her that way. She wanted
to tell Lyndion that he looked at her most of all, but she
didn't. She'd nodded politely, knowing it was the only way to
make the "tutorial" end.

Adora was a woman now. She understood what it meant,
so when Seydir looked at her, she pretended not to notice.
Strangely, though, he didn't surreptitiously steal glances at
hip and thigh, breast and neck. He looked at her face, and she
was compelled to look back. He watched her eyes.

"I'm not needing another barmaid, Shemmel," Seydir
said.

"She will learn fast," Shemmel said.

"I don't need one."

"What about tending bar?"

"A girl?" Seydir raised an eyebrow.

"Why not?"

"I tend the bar."

"You need a break sometime."

"A girl cannot hold this job. The demand is—"

"I can do it better than you," Adora interrupted.

Seydir looked at her. He didn't smile.

"You've tended bar before, girl?"

"No," she said, which wasn't exactly true. The Order had
trained her for this. She had memorized drinks, worked taps
and glasses for months at the Order House. There was
pitifully little to know. The only challenge she imagined
would be the rush of people, demanding many things from

her at once. She looked forward to that challenge.

Seydir shook his head, turned his frown on Shemmel. "Look Shemmel, I appreciate what you have done for—"

"Give me one week," Adora interrupted. "One week for free and I'll run this bar better than you. Otherwise you don't pay me."

Seydir paused.

"Afterwards, when you see what I can do," she said. "I shall have two silvers a week and a room to live."

Seydir looked at her, again directly at her eyes. "It won't come to that," he said, rubbing gnarled knuckles against a sideburn. "If it did, you'd get five coppers a week and whatever the patrons see fit to tip you."

"And a room?"

Seydir ignored her, looked at Shemmel. "In a week's time, you come get her or she'll be on the street."

"In a week's time you'll want to marry me," Adora said. "But I won't let you."

Seydir laughed then, a deep rich sound, and Adora smiled.

Shemmel left her at *The Floating Stone* with a satchel of possessions. Some were actually hers, and some were carefully crafted keepsakes to prove her life as the daughter of a traveling merchant: an armband from a tribe of Benascan savages. A book of children's stories, containing a collection of pressed leaves from three corners of the empire. Four changes of clothing. A hair brush, half-a-dozen paper-wrapped cakes of soap, maps of the area—marked with Shemmel's supposed trade route—and a silver mirror, which was to be Adora's prized possession. And, of course, the cloak of a ten-year-old boy.

She lifted it from the satchel and pulled it softly across her fingers. Patches of the waterproof treatment had been rubbed away from years of handling. This was the only thing she really owned. When every person she loved had betrayed her, one boy had fought for her. A boy who would never betray anyone.

She put it to her face and took a deep breath. It smelled like him, like wet leaves and clean hair. It smelled like safety. She breathed into it for a long moment, then put it back into the satchel. This was her new life. It was time to get about it.

She laid her possessions out on the small table. Seydir said she could have the extra storage room above the tavern. It used to be a guest room, but he rarely used it. It was larger than she had hoped, and it had its own rickety wooden staircase and a door to the outside, which was good. Adora did not want Seydir knowing whenever she came or went.

There were a few boxes in the corner, a window that looked out on Clapwood Street, a window that looked out on the alley beside *The Floating Stone*, and a small side room that, she decided immediately, would serve as her washroom. Adora had given up almost all of her former habits, but she refused to give up bathing. She had learned to work in dirt, with animals at the Order house: pigs, horses, chickens, cows. She had learned to get on her knees and scrub floors, polish windows, change oil lamps, make meals and pour drinks. But she put her foot down about cleanliness. She would never learn how to be dirty for more than a couple of days. It was disgusting.

There was no bed, but that was no matter. She'd have Shemmel bring one from the Order house—a 'trade' he would have made for her in nearby Moondow—and then she'd either make a mattress or buy one with the tips she would receive.

After sweeping, mopping and scrubbing every corner of the room, she nodded her satisfaction. She emptied the large wash-basin into the alley, filled it again from the pump and brought it upstairs. She christened her new room by stripping down and washing the grime from her body. The floating droplets reflected the sunset that could not be seen in the city of Fairmist, and warm orange light filled the room when she stepped out, dripping and clean.

The first challenge was done. Seydir had accepted her, and she had a new home. The second challenge would come tonight, as she created herself for the rest of Fairmist.

And the most important challenge...

The Whisper Prince would be meeting her in that tavern below. Soon. Only a matter of days now.

He didn't know he was meeting her, of course, didn't know anything about Baezin's Order or how he had been written into the prophecy. He didn't know that Adora had watched him for the last seven years. She watched him help his father at his shoe-making shop, watched how he was gentle with his step-mother, how he looked after his little brother Julin, even as he acutely felt the bars of their prison.

They deserved better. They deserved a life free from the slinks, free from an emperor who demanded the Debt of the Blessed. Adora's own sister, so far away now, deserved it, too.

Adora's orders were simple. Seduce the Whisper Prince, become his confidante, and prepare him with the teachings of the Order. She must be bound to him when the Event occurred, which would be in the next few months. She had asked Lyndion incessantly when the Event would occur, and his frustrating reply was always, "When it happens, you will know."

Aside from that, Adora was free. She was free to explore Fairmist, free to make friends and to live for as long as she could. Cooped up for years with men who treated her like an exotic bird, she was excited to explore. Her body fluttered with sensations carefully held in check around the Order's ascetics. Before she left, she had asked Lyndion, "Can I take a lover?"

"Besides the Prince?" His face leaked a small smile. "Take ten," he said. "Become the strumpet of Clapwood Street if you like." He did a poor job of hiding how much the idea excited him. Lyndion could never have her, but she knew he imagined it often. "Use your body. With him. With another to make him jealous. Preferably both. Whatever keeps the Whisper Prince bound to you."

She knew the prophecy. They had drilled it into her from

the moment she had awoken scared, drenched and bloody. She knew her part. Shemmel had taken her to see the whores in Fairmist. She knew how it worked.

"And keep your emotions in check—"

"Lyndion, I know."

"You are there to guide him. Do not become confused."

"Is there anything else?"

"No," he had said. "Stay on the Path. Stay strong, my daughter."

She shivered. She hated that. She wasn't "his daughter" in this life or any other.

She dressed in an almost identical set of work clothes to what she had worn earlier, except black and brown instead of brown and dun. She remembered, wistfully, when she had worn reds and golds and bright yellows. Silks from Venisha and soft cotton from the Felesh plantations.

But not in this life. She was to play a poor bartender. She was to mix the confidence of her upbringing with the freedom of her low station. She was to become irresistible.

She left her little room, heard two water owls hooting above in the mist, and went downstairs to the tavern. *The Floating Stone* was already half-filled with customers, and Seydir was busy. Without a word, he motioned her over. She pretended to pay close attention, to go slowly at first and "pick it up" quickly.

After the first night, Seydir's frown disappeared. Adora served drinks like she was born to it and smiled at each patron as though she existed only for him. After the first week, Seydir watched her with guarded admiration as she owned the bar, flirting with patrons, drawing a crowd that was there for her as much as the liquor she served.

On the seventh day, an hour before Deepdark, the Whisper Prince walked through the door. He hung his cloak on the peg and ran his hands over the hot stone.

She knew him, would know him blindfolded. Barely a day had passed that she hadn't thought of him. He had found her, helpless and alone, and laid his cloak over her, stood fast as her guardian. She had kissed him, and he had made his promise:

I won't leave you. I'm going to protect you.

Then the slink had come. The last she remembered was a rainbow light, and the young boy standing bravely before it. She had awoken in the Order House; the boy and the slink were gone. The Order had healed her; then they showed her how she could make things right.

Barely a year later, when they first took her to Fairmist and pointed out the Whisper Prince, the one she must steward toward the prophecy's end, she knew him instantly. It was the boy from the forest. Of course it was.

Grei entered the tavern with a fire in his eyes that made him seem larger than the people around him.

He moved out of the way of two incoming middle-aged patrons, and politely held the door.

She looked down and watched him through her eyelashes, slowly filling a mug from the tap and passing it down the bar.

"He will burn with purpose," Lyndion had said. "Turn that purpose to the prophecy's need."

Grei hesitated by the door, then angled toward the bar, peering over the heads of the crowd as though looking for someone. She took an excited breath. She had to get on top of the situation from the outset; she had to move fast.

As he reached the bar, she flipped her hair back and looked up as though just noticing him.

"Can I wet your lips?" she asked, giving him an arch glance. His wavy hair tumbled carelessly to his shoulders, dripping from the mists, wildness framing an open face. Seven years ago, he'd been a boy. He was a young man now.

She'd crafted the perfect line for this moment, a few words to make herself unforgettable. What were they?

"I'm Grei," he spoke first. He seemed befuddled, as if he couldn't quite see her clearly. He was struggling with how he knew her. They had been children the last time they'd met.

"I'm Adora," she whispered. Seeing him, talking to him

face-to-face, hit her harder than she'd expected. She felt like she had come home.

They looked into each other's eyes. Then suddenly, it was awkward. They both realized they were staring.

"Where's, um, where's Seydir?" he asked.

"In the back," she said, then forced herself into her role. She owned this moment. She had trained too long to foul it up. She smiled. "Am I not man enough to find your drink?"

He opened his mouth to say something, but apparently had nothing to say. He shut it again.

She filled a mug with the nearest ale, regaining her balance as he lost his. She passed the drink to him. "Start with this. Come back and see me when you find your tongue." She winked. Grei shuffled back as though someone had thumped his chest.

Dazed, he turned with the ale and went to find a seat. He looked over his shoulder twice, as though he wasn't sure if he should really be walking away.

Did he see the injured girl he had held so long ago?

She banished the thought with a shake of her head. It wouldn't be the same for him as it was for her. She had studied him almost every day, paced this testing ground many times in her mind.

As soon as Grei sat down, Adora went to Seydir, who had just emerged from the kitchen.

"I need a breath of air," she said, holding her hands together to keep them from shaking. "May I?" She nodded at the side door.

"Take two. You're doing great, Adora."

She kept her steps slow, holding onto the persona, swinging her hips as she walked, and left the tavern. The moment the door closed, she rushed up the creaking stairs to her little landing, sank against her new door and hugged her shins. She looked out over the lantern lights of Fairmist with her chin on her knees. The water owls hooted. Floating droplets drifted in front of her.

Thrills fluttered through her, and she pushed them down.

She hadn't expected to lose her calm so easily.

Become the strumpet of Clapwood Street, Lyndion had said, and this was why. Sleep with others so she did not forget who was in charge. Grei was not hers to love. He was hers to snare, to guide, to manipulate. He belonged to the prophecy. That was why she had begun the rumors about herself. That was why she had drawn Highblade Ash to court her. He had visited her every day during the last week. He would probably show up at the tavern tonight.

She sat in the growing darkness, clutching her knees, fighting her optimistic heart and the dream of a life she could never have. Especially not with Grei. The Order had taken her in, nurtured her, because the empire needed her. She wouldn't let sentiment break a hundred years of destiny.

She wouldn't.

Chapter 6
GREI

GREI SAT at the little table, pressed between the wall and the stone fireplace, staring after the woman who called herself Adora. The haze of pipe smoke drifted in layers, and his fingers clutched the handle of the seven-sided mug so hard his knuckles were white. It was her. It had to be her. The puzzle pieces of his heart fit together again. Adora was the Forest Girl.

Except she had died. He had failed to protect her and the slink took her.

But...the black and gold hair. The same features he had stared at for days. The same everything except not as a girl. As a woman.

He turned his gaze to the side door through which she had left, got up from his seat and left his beer untouched. Seydir glanced at him, his bushy sideburns doing nothing to hide his smile, and he went back to polishing a mug with the rag he always carried on his shoulder.

Grei pushed through the door into the wet night—

—and almost ran into her.

She stepped back, graceful as a cat, and he stumbled past. She seemed startled, but then smiled and cocked her hips, resting her hands there. "The beer is inside, my lord. Are you lost?"

Grei cleared his throat. "No. I came for you."

"Not yet, I hope."

He opened his mouth, but couldn't think of a single thing to say to that.

He tried to rally his thoughts, but she took mercy on him and spoke first.

"I was taking a break," she said, nodding toward the door that had nearly swung shut, leaving only a line of yellow light across the shining cobblestones. "Come back inside where it's dry."

"I have to ask you something." The floating droplets caught on her hair and clothes, sparkling like diamonds.

"You can't ask me inside?"

He looked at her, and suddenly his gaze went inside her.

He fought to assimilate what came to him. The impressions weren't words. The only words he could hear were those of *The Whisper Prince*, growing louder. Purpose glowed like a bar of hot iron in her chest. And around it, fear. She was scared of him.

No. She was scared *for* him. About something to do with him. He could smell her tension, taste her apprehension. But it wasn't even that. It was some other sense, faint and ticklish. It went beyond sight or smell or sound or touch, some mixture of all of them. A new sense.

He stepped back. The colors of her desires flickered past him.

"Who are you?" he whispered, trying to understand what had just happened to him.

"A keeper of the bar," she said, watching him carefully. Then the colors, scents, and visions of her suddenly vanished as though she had closed a door. She paused. "I have worked here for a week."

"Have you ever played in the South Forest?"

The teasing smile returned. "You want to play in the forest?"

"W-when you were a child," he stammered.

"You want to know if I played in the forest as a child?"

"Your heels," he said, looking down at her half-boots, barely visible behind the hem of her skirt. "Show me your right heel—"

"Tell me this isn't how you court a woman."

Grei suddenly realized how strange he must sound, even threatening. "No, that's not..." he said. "I know this sounds strange."

She put a hand on his arm. "Not the strangest request I've ever had." She winked. "But I do not show my ankles to just anybody."

"Not ankles," he said. "Your—"

"There you are!" Meek roared.

Grei spun around. Meek's hulking form filled the mouth of the alley. He hunched, his huge arms and shoulders rounding his silhouette. He looked like a barrel with a head.

Meek staggered into the courtyard; he had obviously been drinking. His cloak had fallen back, and he was drenched from the water droplets. "I'll drive your face into the stones, Grei," he said. "You broke my nose." He pointed at the red bulb on his face.

Two of Meek's friends, Pad and Norcun, slipped into the alley behind him. Like Meek, they were close to Grei's age. Neither of them were Young Blades, but they had been there with Meek when Grei took his first beating.

"Gonna make sure you end up with worse than this," Meek said, pointing at his face.

"No one could end up with worse than that," Grei said. Adora laughed lightly, and Grei's heart lifted.

Meek's scowl switched to Adora, and his eyes narrowed. "You're Seydir's new whore, aren't you?"

Grei clenched his fists and stepped forward. Meek backed up.

"I told you to get him!" he shouted at Pad and Norcun,

who leapt forward. "Hold him still!"

Grei drove his shoulder into Norcun, but Pad got his left arm. Grei yanked, but before he could free it, Norcun had his right. They pulled tight, spun him around.

Meek drove his fist into Grei's face, and stars burst in his vision. A second fist slammed into his gut, and he doubled over.

Struggling to breathe, he raised his head and Meek nailed him in the jaw. Grei tasted blood. Through bleary eyes, he glanced over at Adora.

She stood with her hands on her hips. She seemed tense, but she didn't yell for help. Her blue eyes blazed.

Grei flinched for the next hit, but Meek paused, looking past him in surprise.

"Stay where you are," came a soft voice. Grei craned his neck upward. A two-foot length of painted black steel, the edges shining silver where they had been sharpened, rested lightly on Pad's shoulder. "And let the boy go."

Pad and Norcun dropped Grei. Coughing, he got to his feet and backed away, looking at his rescuer.

A tall, slender man with wide shoulders held the short sword alongside Pad's neck, pointed at Meek's face. The newcomer wore the telltale blue and silver tunic of a Fairmist Highblade, water beaded on its oil-treated surface, a silver raindrop embroidered on the left breast. Behind his head rose the pommel of his longsword. His curly black hair was pulled tight in a ponytail, and his eyes were dark and implacable. He watched Meek.

"Not a good moment to be a villain," Adora said smugly.

Grei recognized the Highblade, of course. Everyone in Fairmist who had ever seen a blades competition knew that crazy curly hair, those wide shoulders and those painted black blades. Galius Ash was Fairmist's standing champion in every category that involved swordplay. Last year at the Harvesthome Festival tournaments, he had swept the awards. Everyone thought it was a miracle that he hadn't been recruited to the Imperial Highblades right then.

"I am Highblade Ash," he introduced himself as though he needed to. "And it is my duty to ensure peace in Fairmist." His gaze never wavered. Pad and Norcun bowed their heads like dogs who had been smacked. Their open hands, so recently full of Grei's arms, quivered as they tried to hold still.

"This scene offends my eye," Highblade Ash said.

"But I'm a Young Blade," Meek whined.

Highblade Ash considered Meek. "Meek Furrows," he said after a moment. "I remember you. I disagreed with your admittance to training. Is this how you exercise your authority while you are off duty? Three to one?"

It suddenly made sense. Meek had been strutting around in his uniform when he wasn't on duty. That was why he had no partner at the temple. Grei suddenly dared to hope that he wouldn't be visiting the delegate's prison tonight.

Meek's eyes got wide. "But..." he said in a tiny voice. "He hit me."

"I see. Well, I wouldn't stand in the way of lads striving to improve themselves. Training is important," Ash said. He withdrew his short sword from between Pad and Norcun, held it pointed toward the ground. "You boys may go," he said to Meek's friends without looking at them. They glanced at each other, then scrambled to reach Clapwood Street. Pad gave one backwards glance to a very sallow-looking Meek before they disappeared.

"You," Galius said, flipping the short sword in his hand and deftly snatching the flat between thumb and fingers. He tossed it hilt-first to Meek, who jumped, then tried to catch it at the last minute. He hissed as it cut his hand, but managed to hang on.

Galius drew a dagger from his belt. "Now, if you would like to train, I will give you exercise. Come at me with that blade and we will see if we can improve your skills. We will trade hands."

Meek looked helplessly at the Highblade. "Trading hands" was a deadly Highblade contest in which two swordsmen agreed to fight until one chopped the fighting hand from the other.

"Or," Galius said in a dark tone. "You may place that sword at your feet, leave this alley and, for the offense you have given to me and the peace of sweet Fairmist, you may compose the apology that I expect to hear the next time we meet."

Meek swallowed, then knelt and put the short sword at his feet. "I-I'm sorry—"

Ash shook his head, and Meek stopped speaking. "A stammered, inadequate apology will surely turn my offense to anger. I expect something poetic from you, *Young Blade*, and I have given you the time you need. I recommend you use it."

Meek blinked. He looked at Grei, as though he might come to Meek's aid, then turned back to Highblade Ash. "I just leave?"

"Or pick up your weapon," the Highblade said.

Looking confused, Meek started toward Clapwood Street, looking at Highblade Ash as though expecting some kind of attack. As he reached the corner, he broke into a run and was gone.

Galius walked quietly to his short sword, picked it up and, with a double flick of his wrists, sheathed both blades at his waist. He glanced at Grei. "You pick your fights large, boy," he said. "Such a thing deserves assistance."

Grei said nothing. He didn't want assistance from this death-dealer, this protector of the Debt of the Blessed. Galius strutted as though he was somehow different than Meek.

Galius seemed not to notice Grei's sullen gaze. He turned to Adora.

"Thirsty work, gallant sir," she said, giving him a curtsey. He held out his hand, and she took it. "What can I get you?"

"Anything that includes your company. May I escort you inside?"

"You may."

They went into *The Floating Stone* like Grei wasn't there. He stood alone in the mist, staring at the closed door.

Chapter 7

SELICIA

SELICIA HEARD the almost-inaudible footsteps outside her curtain, glanced at the water clock across the dimly lit room, and knew three things at once. First, an outsider had come to the Ringblade Sanctum with ill news or ill purpose. Second, the messenger sent to alert Selicia was Liana. Third, and most interestingly, the message had upset her. Her footfalls were as quiet as always, but her usually confident swagger was absent.

That it was two hours past Deepdark meant the news was not a part of the normal Sanctum rhythm. The new initiates had just been culled, so there were no night activities. Yesterday, Ringblade Zela had sent seventeen of them back to their normal lives after giving them the drug that would erase their memory of this place. The remaining four, the newest Ringmaids, were resting, preparing their bodies for the sleep deprivation training of the first three dances. No one but the sentries and Selicia were awake.

Liana paused before the curtain, and Selicia spoke.

"Come in, sister."

Selicia could imagine the small bow Liana made before

parting the curtain. She was respectful, and Selicia loved her for that. She loved each of the sisters more than her own life, and the Ringsisters shared this same bond one to another. It was the reason the Ringblades were a powerful force for the empire.

Liana stood straight, her head inclined forward, shadowing her exotic lavender eyes. Her usual love of movement, of observing the Ringblade rituals, whether spinning or standing at attention to deliver a message, was absent. She was stiff. There was no joy in her body.

"A wave has reached the sanctum, Selicia," she spoke the ritual words. The outside world sent waves. Within the Sanctum, there were only ripples.

Selicia studied the tall Ringsister's manner, the little movements that betrayed her distress. No one except another Ringblade would notice, perhaps no one except Selicia. Liana was resilient and accepted the flow of life as it came; she was drawn to beauty and pleasure. There were only a few things that could make her this agitated. Selicia felt a weariness descend upon her.

"Ree has returned," Selicia murmured.

Liana glanced up, surprised. Her soft, lavender gaze was altogether too guileless for a Ringblade. Selicia could see the wonder on the young woman's face: *how could Selicia know?*

Ree and Liana had been the only two to graduate from their group of initiates four years ago. They had both blossomed into the finest Ringblades in the Sanctum. They were also, for each other, a shining example of the Ringblade bond.

"How many of our sisters have been exposed to her?" Selicia asked calmly.

"Jylla is on sentry at the Poison Door," Liana said. "She came to me first and returned to her post."

Selicia didn't like that Jylla had come first to Liana, who would be most likely to let emotion cloud her duty. But then, perhaps that was wise. It gave Liana an immediate test of loyalty. Subtle thinking. Selicia would have to commend

Jylla for that.

"Jylla did not let her in," Liana amended.

"That was well done." Selicia rose and walked to the doorway. "You may return to your room, Liana."

"Ringmother," Liana said. Selicia turned. There were tears in Liana's remarkable eyes. "Ree is our sister," she whispered, a quiet plea.

Selicia paused, and knew this was the moment. Liana would have to be dealt with right now.

"Emotion makes us larger," Selicia quoted the words from the twelfth dance. "But running wild, it pushes us out of step."

Liana pressed her lips together, as though she would take a defiant stance, as though she would challenge the wisdom of the Seventy-Seven Dances. The muscles in her beautiful jaw worked.

"They are not just words," Selicia said softly. "And there are no exceptions. We must follow them every moment, Liana. We let our passions fill us, not use us."

Liana bowed her head. "I love her," she whispered.

"As do I. As do we all."

"But—"

Selicia waited. She had already lost Ree the moment she broke faith and left the Sanctum on her own mission. Now, she might lose two Ringblades.

The Ringblade tests were the most rigorous in the empire. The dances were as deadly as they were powerful. But this was as difficult a test as Liana had ever faced. The betrayal of a lover. The betrayal of a Ringsister. Dancing the steps that were required to make it right.

"Say what you would say," Selicia said softly.

"You will kill her," Liana whispered. Her black-skinned, slender hand clenched her red silk nightdress over her thigh. Her emotions leaked, out of control.

"Tell me why I must," Selicia said.

Liana looked away, blinking tears. This was the moment. If Liana spoke now, while she was faced away, her words would be lies. Even if she said exactly what she must, her unwillingness to look at Selicia would show that she did not want to face the truth, and what *must* be done.

Liana looked back at Selicia, locking gazes with her. A single tear streaked down to her jaw, but there were no more. Liana found her bond with Selicia again.

"Because she left the circle," Liana whispered.

"And?"

"One who would break faith once would do it twice."

Selicia waited as Liana's own words hung in the air, waited for them to sink in and do their work within the young woman's heart. Finally, Selicia spoke. "Go to your room, sister. I will visit you after."

"Yes, Selicia." The young woman's hand no longer clenched her thigh. She was smooth again, her emotions channeled. Selicia stood aside as Liana passed and went up the hall.

Selicia went to the Poison Door. There were seven entrances to the Ringblade Sanctum. The Emperor's Door was known only to the emperor and Selicia. The Empress' Door only to the empress and Selicia. Of the other five, three were used by all the Ringblades: the Poison Door, the Water Door and the Main. The sixth was the Motherdoor, known only to Selicia and the previous Ringmothers. She had only used that door once after Ringmother Alynne had passed away in the manner of all aging Ringblades. The last was the Faded Door. The living did not touch that door.

Jylla stood at the Poison Door, regarding Selicia as though nothing was unusual, as though this wasn't unprecedented in her lifetime. No Ringblade had broken faith with the circle since Selicia was a Ringmaid.

"Rest, Jylla. I will finish your shift. Who relieves you?"

"Nyshen."

"Thank you," Selicia said. "I will visit you in the morning."

"Yes, Selicia." Jylla left.

Selicia drew a stiletto from the sheath on her waist and

opened the door. She waited the span of a blink to see if Ree would charge into the sanctum. When she didn't, Selicia slipped into the darkness.

Ree huddled against the wall like a stack of sticks in torn Ringblade clothing. Her bony legs, bent at the knees, had fallen sideways. By her atrophied state, Selicia guessed she had not eaten anything in the sixteen days she had been missing. Her left arm was hidden by her body, but her right had been severed at the elbow, horribly burnt. Her black clothing was torn, and dried blood covered her side. Her head looked large on her thin neck, but her gaze was piercing. There was purpose there. What little fire remained in Ree's shrunken body shone brightly in her eyes.

Selicia had seen horrible things. She had fought in the northern wars, slitting throats behind enemy lines, killing Benascan kraskas who were a bit too talented. She had seen men and women tortured in the emperor's dungeons. On the Sunset Sea, she had seen a Venishan sea monster devour a man as he screamed.

But this was personal. This was a sister who had left the circle, and yet still a woman whom Selicia loved deeply.

It was amazing that Ree had the strength to keep her eyes open, let alone to do the twenty-fifth and twenty-sixth dances to avoid the traps and reach this place.

Ree had always had tremendous will, imagination, and a gift for improvisation. She was a thinker. If, sixteen days ago, Selicia had been forced to choose her successor, she might have chosen Ree. The young woman had the courage to lead, to see what others might not see, and the willingness to act. Those prized qualities had also been her downfall.

"Welcome home, Ree," Selicia said softly, kneeling next to her.

"Home," Ree whispered in relief. "I longed for you. I longed to step back. I stepped too far, and it made me larger. In time to die. In time to die. I saw, and the ground slid sideways."

"Ree—"

"The soup is swirling. Burning and swirling. And the Slink Lord breathes on my back." She gasped as if in pain.

Ree reached out with her severed arm, as if she would touch Selicia, then she looked down, noticed that she had no hand, and a rasp bubbled out of her mouth.

"He ate it. He is the one." Ree held up her arm. "But do you see? It's still there!" She let out a croak of a laugh.

Selicia's heart hurt. She had sent four Ringblades to find Ree and kill her. But seeing this now, it felt like someone was branding Selicia's chest with a hot iron. Ree was ruined, taken by the slink sickness, talking like a madwoman. "You went to the slinks," she said softly.

"He'll have us in the end," Ree croaked, shaking as she lifted her head. "His mind is the web and he is the spider. He hangs over us. I understand now. I understand it all."

"How did you escape the slinks?"

"Do you see?" Ree croaked, waving her stump. "There is nothing to see!"

One look at her grisly wound told Selicia that Ree had reached the cave, but her brain might have turned to mush long before then.

"I saw the Whisper Prince," she mumbled, her head falling back against the wall again as she lost the strength to hold it up. She moaned in pain.

Selicia leaned forward, now very interested. "What about the Whisper Prince?"

"It was a lovely kiss." She closed her eyes, her jaw muscles rippling as though she was fighting to speak. "A young man's kiss, not a slink's."

"Ree," Selicia said, grabbing her upper arm. Ree's eyes shot open, and she reached again for Selicia, but the charred stump just waved in the air.

"Do you see?" Ree demanded. "You have to see. That was why I went too far!"

"Where is the Whisper Prince?" Selicia asked in a stern voice.

"There is nothing to see," Ree said. "Nothing..."

"Ree, where is he?"

"He sank his teeth into my mind. He chewed and chewed, and I brought this to you." She gestured with her stump. "Because I love you. Tell Liana and the rest. Tell her I love her."

"I will tell her, but you must tell me." Selicia picked up Ree's head. The woman's once-beautiful hair was lank and greasy, thick with dirt. Selicia made sure Ree's bulging eyes looked into her own. "Where. Is. The Whisper Prince?"

"I kissed him sideways." A ghost of a smile flickered across her cracked lips. "He came to me. I didn't know who he was, but I was right about him."

Selicia narrowed her eyes. "You kissed him sideways? At the Lateral House?" Ree had omitted her report when she had returned. Selicia cursed herself for a fool. Of course she had. Selicia had told her the news about her sister first, and then Ree had lied as smoothly as she had been trained to do.

"He chewed my mind. There are teeth in there still." Ree hissed as though it was happening right now. She twitched against Selicia's grip.

Selicia watched Ree in silence. The woman was incoherent. She babbled about the Whisper Prince. The emperor had commanded Selicia to look for the unusual in the seven main cities in the empire. A person doing something—anything—that a normal person could not do. Something only the Faia might do. It might be a little thing. It might be large. That was why Ree was in Fairmist, why Dya was in Moondow, Raria in Cliffgard, and all the rest. The emperor wanted this Whisper Prince found, wanted him subdued and brought to Thiara.

"It's so hot!" Ree hissed, her body convulsing. "It burns." Selicia gently set Ree's head back against the wall. "But I'm here. I'm really here. And I told you. Didn't I? Did you listen?"

"I'm listening now, Ree."

With a surge of effort, Ree shifted, bringing her left arm up from where it was pinned against the wall. This time she grabbed Selicia. "Please tell me that you see!"

"I see," Selicia said. "It's all right. I see."

Ree let out a long breath, and she closed her eyes. "Good. It is so hard to tell you. It's so hard, with the teeth. There is no dance for the teeth."

"Yes, Ree."

"I need sleep. I know I cannot sleep."

"You can sleep." Selicia brought out her dagger. Ree opened her eyes, saw it.

"I'm sorry," Ree said. "I came back."

"You came back."

Ree reached out with her good arm, the open hand trembling. "My blood. My fault. My hand. I know what I did. What I had to do. I will make the cut. I never knew. But now I know."

Selicia hesitated. There was a secret ceremony for the killing of Ringblades gone rogue. Seven steps. Only the Ringmothers knew them. Selicia had never had to use them before, but she remembered with absolute clarity.

Ree's hand shook violently with the effort to stay extended.

Selicia hesitated, then gave the dagger to Ree.

"There is nothing to see!" Ree murmured hoarsely. She put the point under her chin, but her shaking arm finally failed her, and the dagger fell from nerveless fingers, clattering on the flagstones. Ree looked at it hopelessly, her strength spent.

Selicia leaned forward and took the dagger from the ground.

"I'm sorry," Ree whispered.

Selicia watched her for a long time. Ree's bony ribs moved as she breathed, visible through a gaping hole in her tunic.

Selicia knew what her duty was. Loyalty to the empire first, the Seventy-Seven Dances next, and love after that. She felt all three in conflict.

Ree's head fell softly against the wall. "You see..."

But I don't, thought Selicia, and then her decision was clear.

She sheathed her dagger, gathered Ree's skinny body against her chest, and stood up. The woman weighed almost nothing.

"There is nothing to see," Ree murmured, finally closing her eyes. She laid her head against Selicia's shoulder.

That is what we will find out, Selicia thought, and took Ree into the Sanctum.

Chapter 8
GREI

GREI SAT down on the stone bench in the little courtyard in the alley. Blood trickled into his mouth, his eye ached, and the right side of his face felt too large.

Was he just seeing the Forest Girl in the face of an attractive bartender because he had failed to stop the Debt of Blessed? Because he had failed to discover anything of note about anything? Was he so desperate that he was conjuring hope in Adora's face? He stood up and clenched his fists.

"I am as crazy as Meek thinks I am," he growled to himself.

"Crazy boys are the best," Adora said. Grei snapped his gaze up. She closed the side door behind herself.

"What happened to your boyfriend?" he asked.

"Jealous?"

He said nothing.

"Wow," she said. "Crazy *and* jealous. I'm a lucky girl."

"Who are you?"

"I'm the one who has what you want," she said.

Grei stood up. "You do?"

She tapped her heels on the cobblestones in an impromptu dance. "Sexy ankles."

"Are you the Forest Girl?" he asked.

"I think you are fixated on the forest. But I *am* your friend," she interrupted. "Maybe more, if you—"

"If you're her, stop acting. Tell me."

She cocked her head to the side. "You're a difficult boy to interest."

"I'm interested. I want to know who you are."

She put her hands on her hips. "Seydir calls you a malcontent. 'Wants to stop the Debt,' he said." She watched his eyes.

"If your life depends on another's sacrifice, it's just a pile of stolen moments," Grei said. "Everyone knows it. No one tries to stop it. And you keep avoiding the question."

She smirked. "Ask me a different question." She stepped close to him and touched his arm. Why was she bent on seducing him?

He stepped back.

"*The Whisper Prince offered his arm,*" he said, speaking over the words that intoned in the back of his mind. He held out his hand.

She jerked, surprised.

"*They both ran away,*" he said. "*And never did say.*"

"*Why a princess lay down for his charm,*" she finished.

"Come on." He took her hand and tugged. With a gasp, she stumbled after him, and they ran out of the alley onto Clapwood Street. The floating droplets swirled at their passage.

Adora twisted her skirts into her fist, hiked them up to free her legs, and put on a burst of speed. She laughed.

They wound through the wet streets, and he led her to the Blacktale Bridge. The Blacktale was made of black granite, spanning the enormous Fairmist River in three arches. The thick pillars extended down, touched the top of the river...and stopped there, sitting solidly on the flowing water as though it was bedrock. Grei had swum the river before, exploring. You could pass beneath the pillars and never touch stone.

Fairmist's Great Bridges were famous, relics of Faia handiwork. People came from all over the empire to see them.

There were innumerable tiny bridges all over the city, but only seven Great Bridges, crossing the mighty Fairmist River and lacing the two halves of the city together. No two bridges were alike. Shieldbridge was made of iron, its rails as black and thin as a spider's legs, flowing from one arch to the next without any bolts or hammering. Skybridge was white marble with blue veins, one piece of seamless stone. The Lance was lacquered blonde wood, thin and graceful. Darkspan was mahogany, intricately carved with stories of Emperor Baezin building the fledgling empire with the Faia.

The lantern lights cast a yellow glow across the floating water droplets. The bridge was deserted except on the far side, where a pair of cloaked Highblades turned and walked away on their rounds.

"I'm drenched," Adora said, shaking her hair, flinging water off her hands. "I don't have my cloak."

He bowed low to her, like a noble at court, then straightened and extended his hand. "The Harvesthome Festival begins tomorrow," he said. "Fourteen days of drinking, dancing and masquerades."

"And?" She arched her eyebrow and put her hands on her hips.

"They'll dance to celebrate the life they've bought. Let's dance to something else. A life without slinks, without the Debt. Let's dance to a girl who kissed a boy seven years ago."

She raised her chin. He waited, his hand out for the taking. Then, she put her fingers in his. He pulled her close, wrapped his waterproof cloak around them both.

He danced slowly to the *Whisper Prince* in his head, and she moved with him. He felt the same grace he had when the Forest Girl had curled into him long ago. This was where he was supposed to be. This was his fate.

His racing heart calmed and *The Whisper Prince* sang happily. The puzzle pieces fit together again. Being with her. Moving with her.

"I'm sorry I got you drenched," he whispered.

"I don't care," she murmured.

She spun suddenly, uncurling from his arm and standing next to him, hands firmly entwined in his. She winked at him with that captivating smile, and they stepped lively across the stones of the Blacktale.

"Who are you?" he asked.

"Your friend," she repeated.

He twirled her, then brought her back, chest to chest. "A friend?" he asked.

"I'm whatever you need." She looked up, searching his eyes.

And then she opened to his magical sight, so quickly it took his breath away. That frustrating wall between them crumbled, and *The Whisper Prince* sang louder. He heard whispers underneath the song, and knew they were Adora's whispers. It was her own language, and it slowly transformed into images, smells, sensations.

Ten-year-old Grei leaned over her, worried, tucked his cloak around her. She was so scared. Everyone wanted to kill her. But not this boy. He didn't know who she was or what she had done. He didn't care. He was just good, and he wanted to protect her. She drank his kindness like honey water, and she kissed him. She was safe here. He would never hurt her...

The earthy scent of the forest and the little Forest Girl faded back inside her, and *The Whisper Prince* went silent.

They stopped dancing, holding each other in the wet night. He knelt in front of her and cupped the back of her right calf, felt the taut muscles there. He pulled softly, beseeching her foot to lift. She relented, and he slid the boot off. On the back of her heel was the vicious scar, curling and pink.

"You're alive. I didn't lose you," he said.

She knelt and kissed him. Her lips were soft and alive. She smelled of roses and desire, and he knew he wasn't ever going to let her go again. He grasped her tighter, stood up and lifted her onto the wide stone wall that bordered the Blacktale. The river rushed loudly below. She wrapped her legs around him, slid her fingers into his hair and kept kissing him, his lips, his ear, his neck. Desire forked through him. He had never wanted anything this much.

Then she stopped, hovering over him, looking down. Her wet hair created a curtain around their faces. "Stop," she breathed. She pulled back. Her legs released him. "Wait."

He could barely think straight. His arms tightened around her.

She pushed against his chest, her hands firm. "I..." Her voice was rough, and her breath came fast. She twisted her hips, hopped off the wall and ducked under his embrace. She stooped and snatched up her boot.

"Adora—"

"Let's..." She knelt, pushed her foot into her boot and stood up. The covered lantern behind her made her body a black silhouette. He couldn't see her face. "Let's go back to my room."

"Why run from me?" he said. "I want you. To know what you know. To know who you are."

Adora hesitated, then nodded.

"And the whispers? *The Whisper Prince.* Do you know what it means?" he asked.

"I know—" Her voice broke, and she cleared her throat. "Come with me. Come back to my room."

He wanted to see her face. Was she crying?

Her wet skirts flared as she turned and ran down the arc of the bridge.

Chapter 9
ADORA

DORA RAN, trying to keep ahead of Grei, trying to keep ahead of her pounding emotions. He hurried to catch her, but when he tried to talk, she shushed him, shaking her head as though she had some kind of plan, as though she had the slightest idea what she was doing.

Her blood rushed hot, and her face was flushed. She couldn't think straight. All she wanted was to keep kissing him. The overwhelming need was frightening. It pushed her off balance. She needed to clear her head.

She had a job to do. The most important job in the empire. She couldn't let her own selfish dreams interfere.

Lyndion's words pounded in her head as her feet pounded the cobblestone walkway.

"Tonight the Whisper Prince must set foot upon his path."

"Is this the Event?" she asked.

Lyndion shook his head. "No, it is the beginning of his transformation. Tonight, he must go into the forest to the east to pick a midnight lily for you."

"Into the Wet Woods? At night?"

"He must be in the woods three hours before Deepdark."

"It's half marsh out there. It's the most wretched place for miles."

"Entice him with your charms; he'll do what he must to sample them."

"Why a midnight lily?" she asked.

"Mind your part, my daughter. We will keep our eyes on all else."

"I am dedicated to the prophecy. Tell me."

"There are reasons for everything. Do your part and all will be well."

They had told her where to find him. The rest, she had trained for. When she'd enticed him, he had chased her. That was the plan.

She hadn't meant to open to his magic. They had trained her to resist, but she wanted him to see her, to know her. She wanted to kiss him, not for the prophecy's need, but for her own. When she wrapped her arms around him, she had seen him sweeping her away from Fairmist, away from the Order, away from the destiny that awaited her. She saw him as her husband, living in a small house among the floating droplets of Fairmist. She saw a little girl on Grei's shoulders, a girl with his brown hair and her blue eyes.

She had seen a life with him that she could not have.

Now she was fleeing, trying to regain her balance. But she wanted his hands on her. She wanted his goodness. His recklessness. His fire to make things right. He would never try to use her, would never betray her. He would stand against towering odds to protect her.

She shook her head. It was selfish. This wasn't about her, it was about everyone in the empire. Thousands of lives.

"Adora—" Grei began.

"Shhhh," she said, hurrying across Milkmist Street. She thanked the Faia there were no canals without bridges between the Blacktale and *The Floating Stone.* She didn't know what she would do if she had to sit on a ferry with him.

"I don't understand—"

She stopped, stood on her tiptoes, and kissed him softly on the lips. "Quiet, Grei," she murmured.

That mollified him, and she turned around, running now with his hand in hers. She would make this work. She could turn this to her advantage.

They turned on Stonewove Street and stopped at the mouth of the alley that went to her little room above *The Floating Stone.*

They both breathed hard from their exertions, but he didn't seem fatigued. His eyes were alive. He leaned closer.

"I need you..." She paused and breathed, talking a half-step back. "To do something for me."

He nodded.

"I need you to..." She paused again, then used the seductive tone she used on the patrons at *The Stone,* the tone that meant she was in control. "I need a flower."

His blinked. "You need a flower?"

She nodded. "From the cliffs. A midnight lily."

His face fell. "Adora, it's dark."

"It's the only time they bloom," she said.

He looked over his shoulder to the east. There was nothing but darkness brushed with silver fog. You couldn't see even two houses away, let alone the Wet Woods.

"I'll bring a bouquet tomorrow—"

"I'll wait in my room," she said. *And by the time you arrive,* she thought, *I will only be doing my job.*

That stopped him, and he considered. "If I've been too forward, tell me—"

She shook her head. "I want you. You want answers," she said. "We'll have both. But I must have the flower first."

His eyes narrowed. "Why?" he asked.

"You will see."

He looked at her hard, as though he would pierce her walls and get the truth. She held strong, whispering the mantra in her head that Lyndion had taught her, hoping it would be enough to turn aside his magic this time.

She kept her expression mysterious. He waited one more second, perhaps thinking she would change her mind. Finally, he turned and walked into the darkness.

When he was gone, she went into the alley and leaned against the wall, put a hand to her chest and felt her pounding heart. She was a liar. And he knew it. Her heart ached, and she hated herself for using him.

She could hear Lyndion in her head. "We do what we must. Always, what we must."

I have to calm myself, she thought. *Cleave to my purpose.*

It was almost four hours until Deepdark, and it would take Grei at least an hour, maybe as many as three, to find the lily and bring it back. They only grew against the cliffs on the eastern side of the Wet Woods. She would make herself ready in that time. The task was allowed to be enjoyable, as long as she did not make it personal. Grei did not belong to her, and she did not belong to him. They both belonged to the prophecy.

She went into *The Floating Stone* through the alley's side door. The smoky room already smelled like home.

"Adora!" Seydir said, giving a meaningful look to the water clock on the counter. He held his fists out, a mug of beer in each. "I'm to do this alone tonight?"

"Didn't you used to do this alone all the time?" she replied, slipping behind the bar and into her liar's persona. She gave him a winsome smile.

He slid the beers expertly, and they slowed to a stop in front of two waiting patrons, who watched Adora. Seydir tried to maintain his frown, but failed. He shook his head.

"You'll be the death of me," he said.

"But what a sweet little death it will be." She winked, stood on her tiptoes and kissed his bushy sideburn.

"How do I get one of those?" one of the rugged Lowlanders called from down the bar.

She turned her smile on him. "Keep drinking, my lord.

Soon your friend will look just like me, and you can kiss him."

Chuckles floated along the line of patrons at the bar, and the Lowlander grinned along with them. This was what she needed. Here, she danced like a spark over a fire. She was the vixen, captaining the bar. With Grei, she was a fumbling maiden who stepped on her own feet.

In the scant days she had worked at the *Stone*, she had become a part of it. The rumors about her flew, mostly about her promiscuity, a story that drunken men never tired of. Some said she was just a wanton, sleeping with whomever amused her. Some said she took money for sex. Some whispered that she was Seydir's mistress. She had started that one, because she knew Seydir would never try to make it come true. He looked upon her like a daughter.

Some said she was the long lost granddaughter of the man who originally built *The Stone*, that she actually owned the tavern and preferred to remain anonymous, slinging drinks behind the bar. The most popular rumor was that she was the bastard child of the city's Imperial Delegate, and this was where he had chosen to hide her. That one fit nicely ever since Highblade Galius Ash had begun courting her.

When asked to confirm or deny the stories, she would just smile enigmatically.

"Adora!" the Lowlander called back. She flipped her damp hair over one shoulder and fixed him with a gaze he would talk about later. She arched an eyebrow, loving this moment where she could forget everything and just be Adora.

He raised his empty mug. "The Thiaran Dark. One down. How many more before he looks like you?" He jerked a finger at his friend.

She took a mug from the shelf behind the bar and tucked it under the spout of a keg. She twisted the tap with her thumb while she smiled. When the mug was full, she thumped its thick bottom onto the bar and slid it down.

"At least one more." She winked at him.

"Got Stormy on an errand?" said a husky voice to her

left. The hair on the back of her neck prickled, and her newfound calm fled. She turned and narrowed her eyes, tried to keep the frown off her face. It was Blevins.

How did such a fat man move so silently? By all rights, he should stumble and bumble about.

She served up a drink and slid it down to another patron, wishing she could ignore Blevins. Everything about him annoyed her. He had a squinty-eyed gaze, seeking places where he could cause trouble. He was wealthy, which allowed him to be here, drinking all the time. And he never looked at her with desire, had no apparent interest in the saucy persona she flung about with abandon. He looked at her like he knew her game, knew she was false, and that this amused him.

Most of all, she hated that he was friends with Grei.

She let him sit without an answer while she filled a glass with Ox beer from a keg under the counter. It was expensive, made only in the southern reaches of Trimbledown, and it was as powerful as its namesake. Apparently, when Blevins had arrived in Fairmist three months ago, he had given Seydir a bag of gold large enough to buy the tavern twice over. The fat man quietly requested they serve him until the money ran out. Based on the size of the fortune, he would drink himself to death long before the bag was empty. She was surprised he hadn't died already.

She set the mug of molasses-dark beer on the bar and stared at him. "I'm sorry, did you say something?" she asked.

"Mad at me, Rose?" he asked evenly, using that stupid nickname. Heat climbed her cheeks. Blevins couldn't call anyone by their real name. Grei had to be "Stormy" and Adora was "Rose," which was also the name of the Imperial Delegate's parade horse. She wanted to slap him.

Blevins took a drink of the Ox beer and gave her a small, sweet smile, which disappeared as quickly as it had come. She glared at him.

He shrugged, took another pull. No smile this time. Adora filled a second mug and set it in front of him just as he finished. It never took him more than a few moments to drain the first. Quick as he drank, though, he never spilled a drop, as if each was precious.

Most gluttons had stains on their clothes, but not Blevins. He was well-dressed, usually in non-descript browns. His movements were economical, precise. He could obviously be something different than what he was, but he didn't care enough to bother.

"Did you send him on an errand? Offer him a dare?" Blevins asked. "Young Grei is reckless and able. The perfect combination for a good dare." He took another drink. "There's an adventurer in that cobbler's son."

She frowned, then turned to help another customer. She served up three Thiaran Darks, two shots of Thiaran whiskey and a Dead Woods liquor, forcing herself to smile and keep her gaze away from the fat man.

She turned away and knelt, rummaging through the cupboard on the pretense that she was searching for another bottle of whiskey. He was just another patron. Blevins didn't matter.

Grei did, and tonight she would begin. She would lay with him and use the skills she had learned watching the whores with Shemmel, and it would be business. The prophecy would begin—

A mewling sound came from outside, soft and distant.

The glass slipped from Adora's fingers, crashed on the floor. Everyone near stopped talking and looked at her. Adora never fumbled drinks.

No.

She thought of the Order as she stood up, looking about the room.

They can't have meant this. The Event couldn't be this.

The din of the tavern roared in her ears. It was so hard to see! Drifts of pipe smoke obscured her view of the room. She moved around the edge of the bar.

Return to your work. She could hear Lyndion as though he was in her head. *Do your duty.*

A man at the bar called to her for another drink, but she ignored him, moving through the patrons, drawing glances. She searched every face. Tears of frustration welled up.

Where was the—?

By the Faia, no!

With a gasp, she lunged forward, bumping a patron aside. This couldn't be happening. Not this.

Grei's parents, Resh and Fern, sat at a small table with his younger brother Julin. All of them were drinking. Grei's mother and father were toasting. Something had happened. Good news. It was a celebration.

They all turned their bemused smiles on her as she approached. Julin looked up and smiled shyly.

She wanted to explain, to soften the blow, but there wasn't time. Her stomach twisted.

"An Imperial Wand is here," she said, keeping her voice down. This went deliberately contrary to the Order's plans. She was opening herself to incredible risk, from the Order and the empire both. She could hear Lyndion yelling at her in the back of her mind.

Their smiles vanished.

"No," Resh said, barely audible. He looked, horror-stricken, at his son.

"You have only seconds," Adora said. "Use the back door. Go to Stonewove, not Clapwood. Run through the alley. Run east. Into the forest and keep going. Don't go home. If you go home, they'll find you." Her head felt light.

She saw the torture in Resh's eyes. He was an upstanding tradesman. He'd made a small fortune for himself and his family, possessed everything a middle-born shoemaker could hope for, but his life as he knew it was over tonight. One way or another. The hopes and dreams for his family were dashed, everything for which he had worked. Adora saw it all now, how this was part of the prophecy, how this would "temper" Grei, as Lyndion would say. The Imperial Wand could only be here for Julin.

A few people were looking their way. As soon as they

heard the mewl that Adora had heard, they would try to stop
Julin's escape. Everyone had heard the story of Moondow, of
what had happened there when they resisted the Debt of the
Blessed.

Resh bowed his head in resignation. "We cannot," he
said. "The Debt protects us," his voice was choked.

"Daddy?" Julin said, standing up.

"Resh—" Adora began.

"I'll do it." Fern stood up. Her thin mouth set in a line,
and she took Julin's arm.

Resh stood up, also, but as though he would stop them.
"The Blessed cannot hide." Tears leaked from his eyes; his
jaw clenched. "Don't make it worse."

"Worse?" Fern shouted, yanking Julin to her. She started
for the door.

Resh looked at Adora, then back at his retreating wife.

"Go with her," Adora said. She wanted to die.

"What about Grei?" Resh asked hoarsely.

"I'll—" She choked on the irony. "I'll take care of Grei."

"Where—?"

"Go!" she whispered, slamming her hand on the table.

Resh jumped up and followed his family. His limbs
moved jerkily as though his body wasn't working right.
Adora wanted to scream at them to hurry. The mewling cry
came again, and everyone heard it this time.

Boots stopped on the other side of the tavern door,
audible in the suddenly silent room, and the latch clicked.
The Imperial Wand would enter, and he would see Julin
fleeing. She had to distract him somehow. She spun around,
lunging for the door—

An enormous figure got in her way, his back to the door
as it opened, blocking the entrance. Adora drew up short.
Blevins!

He looked down at her with black, unreadable eyes. The
boots stopped on the other side of him, their wearer blotted
from sight.

"Stand aside, civilian," came a commanding voice.

Blevins turned, his belly bumping into the man hard enough to knock him down. Adora caught her breath. She was about to see Blevins die.

But somehow, Blevins had a hold of the Imperial Wand, steadying him.

"You oaf!" the Imperial Wand shouted, his snow-white hair disheveled. He brandished a steel rod in front of his body. Blevins bleared at it, then backpedaled as though it was a poisoned dagger.

Adora spared a glance. Julin, Fern and Resh were gone. They'd made it out.

"Apologies, master," Blevins slurred, swaying. He tripped on the edge of the door, stumbled, and crashed to the ground, smashing a chair to kindling. He did not rise.

The Imperial Wand kept his wand trained on Blevins, his mouth a resolute line. He held that deadly rod tight, but an unconscious man was a pathetic target.

Instead, he turned toward the crowd. Not a single murmur rose in the smoke-filled room, and most people wisely kept their eyes on their drinks.

Two Imperial Highblades entered, flanking the Wand. The telltale pommels of their great swords poked over their right shoulders at an angle. Their short swords were drawn.

The Imperial Wand scanned the room just as Adora had done, looking for that youthful face, that victim for which he'd been sent.

"Julin Forander?" The Imperial Wand inquired of the silent room. Crazy Rat Mathens stood up and glared at the Imperial Wand, who narrowed his eyes in return. The Wand crossed to the table and touched his five thin fingertips to the wood. "Did they run?"

Rat's gravely voice warbled out. "Cela went to the north. I saw her."

The Imperial Wand watched Rat.

"The slinks are everywhere," Rat growled. "Hanging from the ceilings and hanging from my hair. There are more of them when I stare. They took my wife. My wife, my wife.

My life. They killed her and she walked away. And I begged her to stay. She went to the north and she's waiting there. Hanging from my hair."

The Imperial Wand frowned, realizing what everyone else in the room already knew. Rat's mind was burned up by the slink sickness.

"My wife is alive!" Rat said, his eyes wild. "I saw her walk away! She's not going with you. I'm going to meet her in the north!"

Adora drew a long breath, hoping for every extra second. Let the Imperial Wand watch Rat while Resh, Fern and Julin made good their escape. Let them—

A cry of fear erupted just outside the door.

The Imperial Wand turned and strode out of the tavern, stepping high over the prone Blevins and his mountainous belly. The Highblades followed him. Adora wanted to run away. But she had run once, had run so far it had taken her here, and she had promised she would never run again.

Her feet were as heavy as river stones, but she shuffled to the doorway to witness the Debt of the Blessed.

Only a handful of people clung to the shadows of alleyways or shop archways on Stonewove Street, unable to tear themselves away from the blood-chilling spectacle.

Three more Imperial Highblades had been waiting outside *The Floating Stone*. One held Julin facedown on the cobblestones. Another held Resh upright, with his arms pinned behind his back, but the cobbler didn't struggle. He looked at his son. The third stood by Fern, whose shoulders slumped. She also stared at Julin.

Visions flashed through Adora's mind of another time, another girl taken weeping through the night. The shale slope leading downward into a nightmare filled with glowing eyes, the Slink Lord waiting with his wide shoulders and thin arms.

And then the green light. The Faia who saved her.

But for Julin there would be no green light, no salvation. No one had ever escaped the Debt of the Blessed. No one except that one lost girl.

With an animal cry, Fern suddenly grabbed for the Imperial Wand. She gouged his cheek, raking for his eyes, and he gasped, staggered back as he raised his wand.

"No, Fern!" Resh yelled.

A yellow stream shot from the wand and hit Fern in the chest. She flashed yellow, then was a stone statue with her hands reaching forward.

"Mother!" Julin cried raggedly from where he was pinned.

"No!" Resh screamed, then sagged in his captors' arms, hanging his head. "No Fern," he whispered. "Don't..."

"Give him to the cat," the Imperial Wand said, his shoulders slumped as though he'd just run a great distance. He pressed his hand against his ravaged cheek. Blood trickled through his fingers. After a moment, he straightened and threw back his head. Flecks of blood marked his snowy hair.

"The Debt of the Blessed protects us," he spoke loudly, glaring at the crowd as he turned in a slow circle. "Without it, *everyone* dies."

The Highblades dragged a struggling Julin to the Imperial Wand's mount. Two Highblades held Julin's arm under the giant cat's mouth. It obligingly sank the tips of its poisonous fangs into Julin's arm, and Grei's brother stopped struggling. His head lolled forward, and he went limp. The Imperial Wand swung into the two-seated leather saddle on the great cat's back as the Highblades lifted Julin up and strapped him to the second saddle.

Adora realized that she had not only screamed denial during the scuffle, but she was incautiously staring. The Imperial Wand turned his attention to her. He held a white cloth to his bloody cheek. "It must be done," he said. "We are safe for another month."

He turned the huge cat and loped off.

Chapter 10
GREI

REI'S SHOES left watery prints on the cobblestones, squishing as he approached *The Floating Stone*. His blood had been on fire when he'd set out for the Wet Woods. He had pushed past dripping ferns and marshy grass, weaving through the trees with Adora's face in front of him. The feel of her lips on his.

But it had taken hours to find the midnight lily, and now he was cold and wet. His thoughts were less on romance and more on dry clothes. But he had the flower.

He squished into Adora's alley and looked up at her balcony. Surprisingly, she was there, sitting at the edge with her knees pulled up to her chin, her blue cloak spread around her in a circle.

"Grei," she said, standing. The sight of her quickened his pulse. Her proud shoulders. Her lithe body. The swing of her hips as she walked to the top of the stairs. His annoyance vanished and he began climbing the steps.

"I got it," he said. "Sorry it took so long—"

"Grei—"

He stopped one step before the top. "You're crying," he said.

Her eyes were red, her cheeks flushed. Uncertainty washed over him. "Adora, what's wrong? What happened?" He put a hand on her arm, held the lily at his side.

She touched his chest. Her fingers were light, hesitant.

He took her into his arms, held her. She was trembling. "Adora—"

"It's your parents. Your...brother," she said.

"What about them?"

She held her breath, reluctant to say more, and Grei's pulse quickened.

"What happened?" he repeated, his voice more stern than he meant.

"They—" She swallowed, then spoke quickly. "Your brother was chosen tonight."

An invisible wind swept through his body, scooping out his organs and tossing them away. He couldn't breathe. The edge of his eye began to twitch. "No..." He looked away to the west.

"Grei—"

"Where did they go?" he rasped. He grabbed her arm, crushing the midnight lily against her.

She winced. He was hurting her. He let her go, and she stumbled back. The balcony creaked.

"Your mother tried to stop him," she said.

Cold fear twisted in his belly. No one stood in the way of an Imperial Wand. He threw the lily at her feet and raced down the rickety stairs.

"Stop," she said, and the quiet plea in her voice made him hesitate. He looked back at her. "They'll kill you," she said. "And you can't die. You, of all people."

She flung the mystery at him, knowing he had to pick it up. Knowing that he had to know.

Well, she was wrong. Dead wrong.

He turned away from her and sprinted into the night.

Chapter 11
GREI

GREI SLAMMED through the door of his house and skidded to a stop in the common room. His father sat at the table, a large, full bag in front of him. His hands rested on either side of it, palms upward, fingers half-curled. The painting he had bought last month hung behind him. Only wealthy merchants could afford paintings. It had been another step up the social stair. It was a pastoral scene, the Felesh plantations, far too calm for the guts that had just been ripped out of this house.

Grei vibrated with anger.

Father's brown hair, always so meticulously combed back from his face, had fallen down into his eyes. His long face stared at the bag, and his neck sagged as though the muscles had been cut.

"Father," Grei said, stepping to the table.

"They left this," his father said in a monotone. "They took my family and left me this."

Grei jerked open the top of the bag. It fell on its side, spilling gold coins across the table. The remains of the Forander family would never be chosen again, and they would never want for anything: their recompense for allowing an abomination.

"And Fern?" he managed to say, though he felt the truth of Adora's words like coals burning into his temples.

Father leaned over, so low that his forehead touched the table. A single sob shook his body.

And where was I when they came? Grei thought. *Splashing through the Wet Woods, looking for a flower.*

He stood over his father for a long moment, water from his cloak dripping onto the floor as he beat back the futility. The whole empire was bound in threads, each citizen tied tight, helpless to change their own destiny.

So we don't try, he thought. *We sob into our bags of gold.*

Adora's final words echoed in his head. *You can't follow them. They'll kill you.*

He went to the workshop and grabbed a hammer, a knife, and a leather puncher from the work table, and then he left, giving his broken father one last look as he slammed the door.

Adora stood in the street. She was without her cloak, drenched and bedraggled. Her blue eyes shone in the darkness, begging him like they had on that day seven years ago in the forest.

"Don't go," she said.

He clenched his teeth and ran the other direction, all the way to the stable where father kept the horse, the one he had newly bought to train Julin, to teach him to ride like the noble classes.

It was past Deepdark, and the stable was closed and locked.

He set the leather punch where the latch had been nailed to the gate, wedged it between wood and steel. He hammered three feverish strokes, pried the latch away and entered.

In the dark, it took several moments to find River, Father's horse, and bridle her. He didn't bother to look for the saddle. Every second brought Julin closer to the slinks.

Grei threw himself over River's back and burst out of the

stable. Adora was there, breathing hard from chasing him. She held up her hands in a pacifying gesture.

"You can't save him," she said. "But you can save the others. All the others. You can stop the Debt! Isn't that what you want?"

"And all I have to do is give them Julin, right?"

"The Imperial Wand will kill you!"

He wheeled River about and galloped away, hooves clacking on cobblestones. He rode out of the city, the covered lantern lights fading behind him as darkness consumed him. Giant elms lined the road, barely visible as they whipped by on both sides. Floating droplets smacked his face hard, blinding him, but he leaned his head forward and squinted, trying to keep the center of the road in view.

River whinnied in protest, but he shook the reins, kicked her flanks, and she pounded forward. He would catch them. He would make them—

He didn't see the brown-cloaked figure until River was almost upon it. The figure's arms went up, spooking the horse.

River reared, whinnying. Her hooves scraped on the slick cobblestones; she slid forward and sideways. Her rump smacked the ground, rebounded, and launched Grei headfirst over her neck.

He spun in the darkness, saw the tree a second before he struck it, and all went black.

Chapter 12
GREI

GREI AWOKE in his own bed. Adora leaned over him, her face pinched with worry. His head pounded and his body ached like he had jumped off Fairmist Falls. He vaguely remembered her arriving, and the brown-cloaked man helping lift him onto a horse under her terse orders.

He sat up, shook his head. He didn't want to talk to her. He had failed his brother. The slinks had him. They had Julin.

Grei threw the covers off and stood up.

"Grei, you should—"

"Don't tell me what to do," he snapped and limped out of the house, past his father who was still at the table, staring unseeing at the bag of gold.

Grei walked through the wet streets, ignoring the pain in his hip and his head, heedless of the water streaming off him, until he came to The Garden. He climbed to a good vantage point and sank into the wet leaves.

The Garden stood at the southeastern edge of the city, surrounded by a wrought-iron fence. It had once belonged to Lord Denshell, a minor noble whose entire family was slaughtered in the Slink War. The emperor had appropriated the spot after Denshell's death and had turned it into a graveyard for traitors.

The wide area outside the spiked fence had been cleared, and was kept that way by the Highblades. The lord's manor house stood empty, falling into disrepair over the years. There were no houses or shops nearby, and no one visited who didn't have to.

Twenty statues stood in the Garden. If there was some pattern to their positions, Grei didn't know it. They were from all seven regions of the empire, brought here after their betrayal as a warning to any who would defy the Debt of the Blessed.

Grei had only been here once before, when he was eleven. He had looked up at the statue of an angry woman for a long time, mesmerized. Her features had been twisted by rage; her fingers were like claws. Her long hair stuck behind her as she lunged forward.

He still had nightmares about that statue. In them, she grabbed him and screamed an inch from his face, filled with the hatred of every sacrifice to the Debt, of every life taken while Grei and the rest of the empire stood by.

With all the areas around Fairmist he had explored, he had never returned to the Garden after that first visit, not until today.

Leaves rustled behind him. He didn't have to turn to know it was Adora.

"Come for the service?" he asked tightly. He couldn't look at her. It hurt to look at her.

She sat down beside him, pushing her blue hood back and wrapping her arms around her knees. She stared at the Garden.

Grei could feel Fern's arms around him as a child, whispering comfort into his ear as she banished the nightmares about the screaming statue. He could see her warning him as a young man, quietly telling him he must stop talking about the Debt, even though he knew she hated it as much as he did. He could see Julin playing with a crude wooden figure that Grei had carved for him, unaware that Grei was watching him.

Grei would never see either of them again.

Adora shifted, as though she might say something.

"I should have been there," he murmured.

She was silent for a time, then said, "It wouldn't have changed anything."

He looked at her, and he let the anger drip into his voice. "You're just like everyone else."

Her gaze was sharp. "They would have killed you. Throwing away your life for no reason doesn't help anybody—"

"You don't know. I could have figured something."

"I *do* know. You would have died with them. And you can't. The empire needs you."

A darkness stirred in him. "Who are you?"

"You want to end the Debt? I'm telling you: you're the only one who can. And you can't do that if you're dead!"

"Secrets secrets secrets," he hissed. "If you're the keeper of secrets, tell me this: why did Fern and Julin have to die?"

She opened her mouth as though she would say something, then bowed her head. "That's not..."

"Not what? Not important to you?"

"I would never hurt your family."

He looked away from her. Down the street, the cluster of Mourners came, their faces lost inside the cowls of their cloaks. They carried his step-mother on their shoulders like a log.

There were seven of them. Mourners was the name the empire had given the local Highblades who had this duty, a name from the emperor. But they didn't mourn. Their flesh crept at their burden. He wanted them to take their bloody hands off her.

The Mourners passed through the gateway into the field of statues. They found a patch of earth that wasn't too crowded, then quickly and quietly lowered her. Her heavy feet thudded into the grass, and they stood her up. A base, two iron bars crossed in an "X", had been attached to her ankles, making sure that she didn't fall over. Grei couldn't see her face from here, but he didn't need to. Her hands reached out, just like Grei's nightmare statue, as if she was going to grab the men who carried her. But his step-mother would never reach her aggressor. Her hands would stay like that long after Grei was dead.

The Mourners turned without a word, walking quickly out of the Garden, weaving past the stone bodies.

He turned to look at Adora. Her black and gold hair plastered against her scalp. She was the Forest Girl again, wet and miserable, except this woman was different, dangerous. The Forest Girl had been his perfect fit. This woman was filled with hidden schemes.

"Did you know they were coming?" he asked quietly. "Did you send me into the Wet Woods on purpose?"

"No," she said. Within the core of his pain, he felt relief. "And yes," she whispered.

His heart blackened like burning paper. "You knew," he whispered.

"I didn't know the Imperial Wand was coming. I swear to you I didn't know that. But I knew something was going to happen that would endanger you, and that I had to send you away. More than anything, it is important that you live. Your safety is—"

"I don't want anyone to sacrifice themselves for me!" he shouted.

"Let me help you—"

"Help me? You want to help me? *Again*, you mean?"

"Don't—"

"Go back to your Highblade," he spat.

She put a hand on his arm. "Let's go to my room—" she said.

"You're poison." He yanked his arm away. The darkness curled inside him. "Spout your lies to someone else," he spat.

She stared, her mouth open and silent. She let her hand

drop. "Don't do this."

He let out a short, ugly bark of a laugh. "Don't do this? Yes, I'll do something else. Whatever you tell me to do, I'll do that. Maybe I'll take another trip to the Wet Woods so you can kill my father, too."

"I didn't kill them," she whispered.

"No, you just got me out of the way." His lips pulled back in a snarl. "I don't want your protection and I don't want you!" He plunged into the forest, the darkness coiling around him.

Chapter 13
KURUK

T HE NEXT Blessed is waiting," Malik said.

The Blessed was here, had been kept in a stupor for days. Still, Kuruk was not ready. He did not have the strength to make the spell and effect the soul transfer. Not yet. The fight with the Ringblade had taken more out of him than it should have.

"We can kill the boy and wait until next month, Kuruk," Malik said.

Kuruk rallied his despairing thoughts and looked for the opportunity instead. "No," he said. "We will use Turoh. We will test his claim." Kuruk's plans were finally coming to fruition, but his strength was failing. For seven years, he had filled the Blessed's human bodies with the souls Lord Velak sent to him from flaming Velakka. But Kuruk's brothers could not be transferred into human bodies as easily as the wispy Velakkan souls. Kuruk's brothers had to be born again of a human and a possessed Blessed, a flesh and blood birth, and that took time.

The first birth was a girl named Aylenna within whom he had planted the soul of his brother Turoh. Turoh's personality had finally surfaced within the girl seven years later, and now she had come to them. The plan was working. Kuruk just had to hold on.

And now there was a new development. Turoh had arrived with a strange claim, that he could make the Velakkan soul transfer without the draining spell that Kuruk used. It sounded unbelievable, but if it was true, then it would save Kuruk the almost unbearable strain of dominating the future Blessed.

"Wake the Blessed," Kuruk said, standing and leaving his study.

"He has awoken. He sits whimpering," Malik said.

Kuruk did not remind Malik that he had also whimpered when the Thiaran wizards had thrown them into Velakka. Malik was angry at all humans, not just the Thiarans. That anger kept them all going, but it also stripped away compassion. Kuruk suspected that compassion was something they needed if they were going to make the jump back to humanity. But he decided now was not the time to correct Malik.

"Where is Turoh?" Kuruk asked.

"He is with the Blessed, watching him. And he asks that we call him Aylenna now," Malik said, frowning.

Kuruk stopped, looked at Malik. "He wants us to call him by his new name?"

"Yes."

Kuruk thought about that. It distressed him that Turoh didn't want to claim his old name. But perhaps this was a rightness. This was a new life for Turoh, certainly not a return to their actual childhood. They could never go back. Perhaps Turoh had wisdom in this. How could he pretend to be who he was —how could any of them?— after what they had endured? They could only go forward.

"This is good," Kuruk said.

"It is *good*?"

"We will call him Aylenna. That is who he is now."

"Who she is."

Kuruk glanced at his frowning brother. "Yes, who *she* is."

Malik snorted. They walked the rough-hewn corridors and went to the little cave where they had left the Blessed. Malik's flaming head filled the cavern with light and revealed the boy, huddled and squinting. He had dirty, tangled brown hair and a skinny body. He was in that human stage between child and adult, the stage Kuruk and his brothers had not had the chance to attain. Yet.

Kuruk saw Turoh leaning against the wall in his girl's body, arms crossed, hungrily watching the Blessed. No. Not Turoh. Aylenna. The girl that was his brother glanced up at them, then went back to looking at the boy.

"Please!" the boy said. "I-I just want to go home."

"We all want to go home," Kuruk said. "But we can only go forward."

"What will you do with me?" the boy asked, his voice trembling.

"What do Thiarans do with children?" Malik hissed, grabbing the boy's arm. The boy gasped at the burning touch. "They betray. They make promises and they break them."

"Let him go, Malik," Kuruk said.

Malik let his rage run. His hair burned higher, and he leaned toward the Blessed. "What do you *think* happens to the Blessed?"

"Enough," Kuruk said.

Malik released the boy and stalked to the far side of the cave.

"Do it," Kuruk said. "Show us, Aylenna."

Aylenna walked toward the boy. She had long, dark hair, oiled back like they did in the capitol city, with a white streak along one side.

The boy recoiled from her, scrambling back until he hit the wall.

"Kiss me." Aylenna cornered him. She put a hand on his arm, another on the side of his neck. Her hand pulled, encouraging him to bend down.

"N-No."

"I will not hurt you," she whispered, her fingers caressing his hair. Kuruk narrowed his eyes.

Swallowing hard, the boy leaned down, and Aylenna kissed him. Her hands gripped the back of his head like talons. The boy lurched back and struggled like Aylenna was shooting fire into his mouth, but he couldn't escape her grip. They wrestled to the ground amidst his muffled screams.

Then Aylenna went limp, falling away from him. The boy rose to his knees, twitching and grappling with his mouth, as if he could snatch out what Aylenna had done.

"No!" he screamed, then fell forward onto his face.

Kuruk went to Aylenna's side and knelt next to her, watched her. Her chest moved. She breathed. She was not dead.

"She killed him," Malik said, toeing the body of the Blessed.

"Not killed, Malik." The boy said with his face against the floor, then he rose, shook his head, and looked around. His eyes flickered red, then returned to normal. He sucked in a long, thin breath. "Trans-formed!" he hissed. He flexed his fingers once, twice, three times. Kuruk recognized the gesture.

"Zyzzt?" Kuruk asked. Zyzzt had been one of the thousands of flickering flame spirits in Velakka. He used to do that with his flaming hands to entertain the boys.

Zyzzt began to laugh. "Yes!"

Kuruk felt hope swell in his chest. He would not have to perform the arduous spell. He could focus on keeping the yammering voices at bay. He need not worry about losing control every time. He willed his fingers to be cool and put a hand on Aylenna's forehead, a gesture he remembered from his mother.

"It works," Kuruk looked up at Zyzzt.

"And more," Zyzzt said. "You seek the Whisper Prince."

Malik raised his head at that. "Yes," he hissed.

"This human was his brother. I know where to find him."

Malik grinned, showing his Velakkan teeth. "Tell us."

Part II

The Whisper Prince

Chapter 14
GREI

A lost fair lady cried out in alarm
The Whisper Prince offered his arm
They both ran away
And never did say
Why a princess lay down for his charm

 REI LOOKED down at the slumbering form of the Duchess of the Highward. The fine silk bed sheet covered the curve of her hip and ended just below her shoulder. Her brown curls spilled across the pillow.

He gathered his clothes and walked to the far side of the room. The double doors of the veranda stood open to the Fairmist night, and a sea of floating droplets lay beyond.

The strong wine he had drunk earlier warmed his face and his chest, and made his danger seem small. But if they caught him here, they would kill him. Certainly the duke would.

Good.

He tugged on his pants, one arduous leg at a time, then

pulled his tunic over his head. The moon outside lit the droplets, casting a ghostly radiance into the room. Grei slowly pushed a heel into his boot and watched the sleeping face of the Duchess Venderré, who was said to have stood guard over her husband's injured body, keeping a horde of Benascan savages at bay until reinforcements from Fairmist arrived. That had been six years ago. Supposedly she had been pierced by two arrows and a spear while fighting the savages. Grei had felt the puckered scar on the right side of her hip, next to the bone. He had seen the fierce will behind those dark eyes. He did not doubt a word of the legend.

The night had gone according to plan. Blevins had dared him to add a noblewoman to his conquests. And not just any noblewoman; he had suggested the Duchess Venderré, a Fairmist icon.

Blevins had somehow secured an invitation to one of the royal masquerades, so Grei had walked into the palace unchallenged among the rich costumes, the high ceilings. The sights, sounds and smells were still fresh in his mind:

The ladies wore distracting fragrances, and amidst their colorful masks and heaving bosoms it was all he could do to find the duchess. But striking up a conversation, the most difficult part of it all, was easy for Grei now. He wasn't holding back anymore. He didn't care about these wealthy peacocks, riding their bejeweled boats down a river of blood. He didn't worry and he didn't hesitate.

So he swam in their waters, peering past their veneers. He used his newfound power against them, the ability he had discovered that night he had looked into Adora. At a glance, he saw that Lady Vargol wished a compliment for her meticulously coiled hair. Lord Gorenen was proud of his foolish dancing. Lady Suffayne had spent a fortune on her dress, and she preened. Lady Piretta was filled with randy thoughts and longed to be ravished by one of the young lords. Any of them would do. In fact, she would rather not know who it was. Such was the mystery of a masquerade.

He moved through them and found his quarry.

Duchess Venderré barely glanced at him when he approached her. She wanted an excuse to leave. She was angry at her husband, who was pawing every young woman he could.

Grei watched Duchess Venderré carefully, and he opened her locks.

"Their anonymity gives them an excuse to act badly," he said. "They have put on their true faces at last."

"And is that your true face?" she asked.

"I have a dozen faces. But this one is just for you."

She gave a frown. "How droll. And you think I have interest in your bad behavior?"

"It might teach your husband a lesson, if nothing else."

"You know who I am?"

"Some women radiate a strength that no mask can hide," he said.

Her hawk eyes narrowed, but he saw the interest kindle within her. Her gates opened on silent hinges, and the conversation really began.

He looked down at her now, memories of their passion like coals growing cold. She was every inch the lioness the stories claimed. She had hungered for him, devoured him.

She was his latest. She had done the most to mask his pain, but he didn't expect it would last. It hadn't with any of the others.

Grei had been with five different women in the last six nights of the Harvesthome masquerade balls. His first was Neviva, a childhood friend who had shunned him like all the rest when he first started questioning the Debt. He found her at Lord Nasbith's manor at one of the earliest masquerade balls. With a mask in place, he gave Neviva an elaborate lie, and she did not recognize him. And after half an hour, she took his hand and led him to Lord Nasbith's stables, and they lay down together in the hay. It was Grei's first time, that night.

The urgent sensations, the rise of his climax stole away his anger. It wiped away his helplessness for one precious second. When he was in Neviva's arms, breathing her breath, feeling her naked skin against his, he wasn't Grei anymore. He was someone new. He was a man who took what he wanted and ignored the suffering of others. He was a true Thiaran.

He awoke in the middle of the night, wrapped in a blanket that smelled of horses with Neviva's arm draped across his chest, and his reprieve had fled. In its place was a cold regret like congealed fat at the edge of a pan. The crushing helplessness returned, and suddenly he could barely be in his own skin without retching. Neviva's scent, which had enflamed him only hours before, was repellent. The hay was dirty, the barn suffocating. He left her underneath the horse blanket. It was only after he had begun walking back to his empty house that he realized he had never taken off his mask. She didn't even know to whom she had given herself. That wasn't uncommon at the masquerade balls, but he had never envisioned it happening to Neviva. She knew what she wanted, a man to be hers alone, with whom to raise a family. A man who would stay with her.

He ripped the mask away and threw it into the gutter.

He spent the next day and night alone, wrestling with the ruin of his life. His father moved through the house like a ghost, making outlandish shoes that would never sell, then sleeping, then making more bizarre shoes. They passed each other in silence.

Adora tried to reach him. She knocked on the door of his house, but he slipped out the window as his father answered. He didn't want to talk to her ever again.

The following night, he donned a new costume and went to another masquerade ball, this one on the arch of Skybridge. That night it was haughty Calinne, the daughter of a Venishan merchant come as a visitor to Fairmist during the famous Harvesthome Festival. She barely deigned to look at him at first, but that was before he started talking. Soon she was hanging on every word. After half an hour, she led him away from the bright covered lanterns, somewhere dark where she could kiss him.

The merchant's daughter rode him on the grassy bank under a little bridge by Bullbend Street, and Grei felt good again. As they lay sweaty on the wet grass, it reminded him of being on the Blacktale with Adora, of how that night might have ended. An implacably dark mood descended on him, then he recited *The Whisper Prince* to Calinne, just as he had to Adora. She breathed approval, whispered the poem back in Venishan.

But that cold satisfaction didn't last. By the time they had dressed, he wanted to vomit. He stayed with her long enough to bring her back to the center of the party at Skybridge. Calinne's father hadn't noticed her absence, and she was flush with the adventure.

"Tell me your name," she said in her light accent, gazing at him with excited eyes.

"Tell me your drink of choice," he said, plucking a red rose from a bush next to the bridge and handing it to her. "I shall bring it back with my name."

She did, and he left her standing on Skybridge holding a rose.

Three more, one every night. He wore a mask. He recited the poem. He left them a red rose. And the legend of the Whisper Prince began.

Word spread unbelievably fast for something that had happened in a matter of days, but that was how the Harvesthome Festival was. People sought out the juiciest stories and reveled in the telling.

Grei had overheard rumors of the Whisper Prince at *The Floating Stone* just the other night. Apparently there were already imitators, young men who looked up to the myth, young women who longed to be a part of it.

But there were some women who didn't, or perhaps hadn't heard the legend yet. Grei had listened last night to a story that gave him a brief smile. Apparently Meek had fulfilled his promise to Highblade Ash, delivered a flowery apology in the form of a poem, and saved himself from "trading hands." When Grei's exploits as the Whisper Prince began to spread, Meek took his poetic victory to heart and was overheard trying to woo a young lady from Thiara on the Darkspan Bridge. The story went that she had listened politely, nodding her appreciation. Meek then took it upon himself to fondle her backside, perhaps hoping she would succumb to his charms. Instead, she pushed him over the rail. The Darkspan Bridge was one of the highest in Fairmist, and somewhere in the fall or the inevitable tumble downstream, Meek hit his head. After his friends fished him out, he lay unconscious for a full day, then rose and put on his mother's clothes. Yesterday, he had been seen in an ill-fitting dress, his voice slurred as he spouted bad poetry at the gates of the palace.

That night, Grei had told Blevins the truth, that *he* was actually the Whisper Prince, and the fat man's eyes had sparkled with amusement.

"A fine game," Blevins had said, "Now for a real challenge. Turn your magic tongue to a fitting purpose," the fat man had said. "They took your brother. Take one of theirs. Take the delegate's daughter." Then he gave one of his dark chuckles and shook his head. "No. Not a girl. A woman. Take the Duchess of the Highward, if you dare."

And now he was here. He had talked his way into the bed of the most powerful woman in the city.

Maybe it was the danger, that the Duke would kill him if he was caught, but Grei didn't feel sick this time. Or maybe it was that Venderré was not young or innocent. She was a woman of consequence, ruler of the Highward east of Fairmist, and as much to blame for the Debt of the Blessed as anyone.

When he was finished dressing, he glanced at the open veranda and went quietly to the rail. They were on the fourth story, and the top of the stone rail was beaded with moisture. There was no way out except the front door.

He left the veranda and crept to the sleeping Venderré's side. He carefully arranged his gloves on the edge of the bed, then kissed the tips of his fingers and reached out to touch her bronze cheek. He stopped, hovering just above her skin.

He pulled the rose from the lining of his cloak, leaned close and mouthed the lines of the nursery rhyme he had spoken to every woman over the last week.

He lingered another moment, then laid the rose down and went to the thick, wooden door that led into the palace. As his hand reached for the handle, Venderré spoke.

"You're the Whisper Prince."

He stopped, and the imagined threat of his death became very real. He paused a half-second before turning. She pushed herself to a sitting position.

"Aren't you?" Her voice was abominably loud in the silence.

"The who?"

"Do you think me a fool?" she asked flatly. There was a serpent's coldness in her words. She lifted her arms, rested them along the top of the brass headboard, and shivered slightly. In the silver light, he saw goose bumps on her smooth, bronze skin.

She was the lioness again, ready to pounce and devour him.

"I told you. I'm from Moondow. I only heard of your Whisper Prince today," he said.

"Did you."

One scream from her and the hall would fill with Highblades. He made himself walk back to the bed and sit down, but his eye began to twitch beneath his mask. Venderré reminded him of Ringblade Ree. Both of them were women of power, except Venderré did not seem interested in ushering Grei to the door. "This Whisper Prince, he does what again?" Grei asked.

"He flies through the open windows of virgins in Fairmist, ravishes them and flies out again, but not before stealing their valuables, and not before speaking the nursery rhyme *The Whisper Prince*."

Grei forced a chuckle. Legends, he had noticed in the short time he had been a subject of one, had a life of their own. He'd never stolen valuables from anyone. Of course, "valuables" was a vague sort of word.

"I assure you I shall not fly out that window," he said. *Though they may well throw me out.*

"And I am no virgin," Venderré said.

"So you see?"

"And yet you spoke the rhyme to me."

"Downstairs at the ball? I was a little drunk, I admit—"

"Just now."

He did his best to look confused, then smiled again. "I have angered you. I only thought it would be prudent for me to stay the night elsewhere, lest your husband discover us. I would have woken you, but you seemed peaceful in your slumber." He slid his hand across the smooth sheets toward her hip. "But I shall stay if you wish."

"Touch me, and I will scream," she said, though she made no move to draw away from him or to cover herself. His hand stopped inches from her skin. Her lips widened in a cold smile.

"But—"

"What is your name?"

"I have already told you. I am Balish from Moondow—"

"Take off your mask."

"My lady—"

"Tell me who you really are," she said.

"I am—"

"Lie again, and I will scream." Again, that cold smile, so potentially sweet. So...not.

Grei paused. Blevins' words rose in his mind: *If you lie badly, you're a bad liar. If you insist on a bad lie, then you're a fool as well.*

He stood, shrugged. "It is a masked ball. The point is to remain unknown, is it not?" he admitted.

"The ball is over," she said.

"But the dance continues." He stepped to the door.

The left edge of her smile curved further upward, a lovely nuance. He would have been feverish with desire if only his palms would stop sweating.

"Tell me your name, and I will consider protecting your identity."

Grei stopped for a moment. He wanted to believe her. Perhaps he could. Her gaze did not waver. Those deep brown eyes pierced him.

The last time he trusted a woman, he'd lost a brother and a mother.

He smiled. "Alas, my lady, it is a risk I cannot take."

"It is the only chance you have of leaving alive."

Hearing the threat from her own lips set his resolve, and it reminded him who this woman was. Part of the empire. A champion of the Debt of the Blessed.

He took another step toward the door. "There are so many chances in life."

"Touch the door," she said laconically, "and I will scream."

His hand hovered over the brass handle. "And what will your husband think if he finds me here?"

"That you are a thief and a rapist."

"And if I tell him different?" he said, thinking of how her back had arched, how she had gasped his name. His fake name, but nevertheless...

"He will, of course, believe you. Especially with your mask in place."

With a sweeping bow, he said, "It was an unforgettable night, my lady. Your beauty is as eternal as the sunrise."

Her dark eyes twinkled, and she shook her head as she might at an errant-but-charming child. He opened the door.

She screamed.

Booted footsteps pounded up the hall. A Highblade turned the corner, spotted him and shouted.

"Hold there!"

Grei slammed the door, throwing the bolt. He left it and

raced across the room. She continued smiling, the lioness.

Let it be here, then, he thought. *Let it be now.*

He burst onto the veranda, slipped on the wet flagstones and slammed into the wide stone rail. He wrapped his arms around it to steady himself and looked at the very hard, very distant flagstones far below.

If he was to die tonight, he wouldn't make it easy for them.

Swinging a leg over the balcony, he blew a kiss to Venderré as the first blow landed on the door. Maintaining the role fed the darkness within him, and the darkness didn't care about anything.

He dropped off the rail and began scaling the stones of the slick wall. He took his time, found toeholds before moving, checked each handhold. He tried not to think about how his hands slipped a little each time.

He began shimmying across to a line of windows. The window ledges would give him better purchase. The door thundered, and then Grei heard the latch being undone. "Thank you for not breaking my door," Venderré said. "He's on the veranda."

Booted feet tramped to the balcony. Grei dared a look, clinging desperately to the side of the wall. He'd barely descended five feet. There were two Highblades now.

"Go get help," the first said. "Take some men to the street below. Make sure they have bows." The second guard disappeared back into the room. Venderré walked onto the balcony, the silk sheet wrapped around her. She watched with feline curiosity.

The first Highblade unsheathed a dagger that looked suspiciously shaped for throwing. The guard narrowed his eyes, raised the dagger, and threw.

The shining knife flipped end over end, straight and true.

"No!" Grei shifted to the side, and the blade clanged into the wall just to his left, slicing through his tunic and spinning away below him.

He slipped and fell.

"No!" he shouted. The cobblestones raced toward him. "No no no!"

He hit, and the fierce pain of snapping bones, the sickening crack of his head breaking—

Did not happen.

He splashed into the stones as if they were water. He spluttered, thrashing, grabbing for something solid. His arm slapped the street, and he hauled himself out. He jumped to his feet, backing away from the human-shaped hole in the stone. His heart hammered in his chest.

He looked up at the balcony. The Highblade and Venderré both looked down, open-mouthed.

"By the Faia!" the guard shouted, echoing the very sentiment that rattled in Grei's mind.

Grei looked at his hands. He brushed them. Solid, dusty stone flaked away, drifted to the ground. Not liquid. He was covered head-to-toe in white dust.

He walked over and touched the indentation with his toe. It was rock. Hard enough to break bones.

He heard the sound of pounding feet, coming his way, coming for him. He turned and ran into the shadows.

Chapter 15
ADORA

ADORA STOPPED near the side door of *The Floating Stone*, put one hand against the wall and one hand to her forehead. Her little alley was cold and wet, and there were no pleasant thoughts to warm it. Fairmist had been a wonder when she had first arrived, but now the floating water represented her broken heart and her absolute failure as a steward of the prophecy.

It had been a week since Grei's brother was taken, and everything was in ruins. Grei was slipping away. And yet the Order demanded she return to work and perpetuate the lie.

She'd gone to the Order House after the masquerades had begun. She had screamed at Lyndion.

"You knew! You sent him away while his family was torn apart!"

"I did not write the prophecy, Adora," Lyndion said. *"I follow it."*

"He's out there heartsick and alone, using his magic to seduce women. Is that what you wanted? Is that what the prophecy demands, you twisted old man?"

"His pain will shape him into what is needed. You will see."

"The man I knew is gone," she said.

"The man you knew was not the Whisper Prince."

"You're not human!"

"His hardship will drive him to save the empire," Lyndion said, then he paused as he looked at her. "Assuming he is properly guided."

It always came back to that, and the accusation was unmistakable. It was her job to set things right.

She took a step away as though the breath had been slammed from her body. Sometimes it seemed as if these old men cared for her. Sometimes she felt like she was just a tool.

"I am chained to your deceptions because of my blood," she whispered.

Lyndion showed his teeth then, like a feral dog. "Our world is on the brink of ruin. What are Grei's trials—what are yours—compared to that?"

"I know the prophecy!" she screamed.

"Then do your part! The suffering of the Whisper Prince is necessary. It will temper him."

"At what cost?"

"And what is his cost to you? He does his part. You do yours." His eyes narrowed, and she saw understanding in them. He knew she was smitten, that she loved the one person she was forbidden to love. He was calling her out, daring her admit she had failed.

"It's needlessly cruel," she whispered, turning away to deny him the satisfaction.

"And who would you be without the cruelties visited upon you?"

"Happy," she said softly.

"You would be blind to the deaths harvested for your comfort. And humankind would fall into the darkest reflection of itself before the slinks devoured us. Your hardships save us. So will his, with your guidance."

"I hate you," she said.

"What you think of me is irrelevant. You waste time here. The Event is almost upon us. Go to the Prince."

"The Event was not the Debt claiming his brother?"

"Of course not."

"Then tell me what it is."

"Go to him."

"He won't speak to me."

"If you have done your job, he will. You must—"

"Don't tell me what to do!" She picked up the nearest object—a little water clock—and hurled it at him. It missed, shattered at his feet, pieces skittering across the floor. Lyndion's lips tightened, but he didn't do anything. "I spent seven years listening to you and your teachings!" she shouted.

"Then remember them," he said.

She stormed out then, slammed the door so hard it shook the wall.

The memory fluttered away. Adora looked east, catching a view of the gently sloping city of Fairmist. The rivers snaked through the city like a hundred roots. There was water everywhere, even in the air. When the Faia had rescued her and brought her here, the mists had been a place to hide from the betrayal that had cut her to her soul, a place to forget that girl and become another, a girl who could fight, who would never allow herself to be betrayed again.

But there was no hope now. Not here or anywhere. Adora's path led to her death, and there would be no succor along the way. No love waiting for her. No happiness as reward. Grei could not be hers. Galius, who was a pleasant distraction from her real life, could not save her. There was only the satisfaction of fulfilling the prophecy. It would use her up, and no one would ever know except a small group of old men who probably despised her. They would sagely nod over her grave, checking one more thing off their list.

She let out a breath. She had thought she was doing good here, but what good could possibly come from the deaths of

Grei's brother and step-mother? He was no longer himself. Every day, he slipped further into the persona of the damned Whisper Prince. And the prophecy waited, silent and intentional, to use him as it used her.

After Fern was planted in the Garden, Grei had disappeared for two days. When he came back, he sat at her bar as though nothing had happened and he ignored her. He and Blevins talked in quiet tones like conspirators, and he turned aside every overture she made. This amused Blevins greatly, and her shame burned that he was now Grei's confidante while she was nothing.

Probably because of Blevins' prodding, Grei had begun his sexual exploits, creating the legend that everyone was talking about.

The masquerades happened every night in every part of Fairmist during the Harvesthome Festival, from the palace to the modest quarters known as Mudtown. Grei wore his mask and used his silver tongue. He spoke and others nodded. He seduced women, always leaving his conquests with a red rose and the rhyme *The Whisper Prince*.

After the first few nights, excited whispers ran through the city, rumors about a suave lord who appeared and disappeared, making love to his chosen lady of the night. Every Harvesthome Festival had its masquerade myths; this year belonged to the Whisper Prince.

Adora sighed, and the dreary view of the city was suddenly unbearable. She opened the door, strode into the tavern and set to work. Usually, there was a quiet satisfaction to her job, but tonight all she could see was the empty façade. Perhaps she had even fooled herself. But none of the lies meant anything now, except that she was a liar.

The Stone was full. The Lowland harvests continued to come in, and the masquerade balls were nearing their peak. Over the next week, the revelry would increase in intensity until the final Harvesthome celebration, which marked the end of summer.

Another masquerade was being held tonight in the palace

for the highborn and visiting dignitaries. And of course Blevins had dared Grei to work his magic on a noblewoman. And not just any noblewoman, but Duchess Venderré, a Fairmist legend who could have Grei killed with the snap of her fingers. Adora kept watching the door in the midst of her duties.

As she doled out ales and whiskeys, her mind wandered. Was Grei in the arms of his noblewoman right now, caressing her, making her gasp with pleasure? Was she running her hands through his long brown hair?

She closed her eyes and placed her hands flat on the bar, forcing the image away. She glanced sidelong at Blevins, who had taken up his customary spot one seat to the right of center. She watched him, his economical motions, lifting the mug to his lips and drinking, not looking at anyone. He stared at the wall as though some intricate play was unfolding that only he could see. It was always the same. Once he sat down, he didn't leave the bar until Seydir closed. Once, a brawl had broken out right behind him, and a chair had come near enough to his head to cause a normal man to leap aside. Blevins had ignored it all. Always the same.

Except the night Julin was taken.

That night Blevins had moved faster than anyone. Faster than Adora, who had known what was coming. Somehow he had been at the door when the Imperial Wand tried to enter. He had provided the distraction she needed, and he had almost saved Grei's family.

Blevins cared for nothing. Why that? Why then? Was it really the bumbling of a drunk, as it had seemed?

She moved along the bar and stopped in front of him.

"So you sent Grei to the palace tonight," she said.

He glanced up at her, his black eyes assessing. "Yes. I dragged him up to the gate and shoved him through."

"You know what I mean."

"Every man makes his own decisions," he said in his low voice. "And then he lives with them."

"And this is your decision? To sit and drink while

sending others to entertain you?"

"It's a comfortable stool." He took another sip of Ox beer. "And Grei is an entertaining young man."

"He could be imprisoned. He could be killed."

"Every man dies. Not every man dies in the arms of a duchess," he said.

She wanted to slap the smirk off his face. "You don't care about him, or anything else."

"I care about this beer." He sipped.

"Then why Julin?"

"Who?"

"Grei's brother."

"Ah," Blevins said.

"You stepped in front—"

"No," he said.

"You stopped the Imperial Wand. You delayed him."

He gave her a tight smile and raised his mug. "Drink, Rose, and clear your vision. I tried to get out of his way."

She bristled at the stupid nickname, but she wouldn't let his baiting throw her off balance. "What were you doing at the door?"

"I don't remember."

"Yes you do."

"Serve your beer, bar wench," he growled. His playfulness had vanished.

Anger flashed through her. She hated that she couldn't find this man's measure. He was a walking contradiction.

She turned away, furious, and looked down the length of the bar.

At the end stood Grei's ghost, just inside the door that led to the alley. His masquerade mask, his hair, his clothing was pale. She put a hand to her chest, wanting to scream denial. His wide eyes watched her.

"Adora," he said imperatively, motioning her to him.

She ran to him, grabbed his hands. They were warm and alive. He wasn't dead; he was covered with some kind of white paste. Chalk dust moistened by the water outside.

"You're okay," she breathed.

"I don't know. I don't know what I am," he said.

"What happened?"

He flicked a glance at the crowded tavern. People were starting to notice him. "Not here."

"Come on." She led him out the back door into the alley. She felt Grei's fear like a lump in her throat. It had happened at last. The Event was here, and he had come to her.

He had come to her.

Chapter 16

ADORA

DORA HUGGED him, reveled in the feel of him, the warmth of his strong arms around her, the smell of safety. The moment she let him go, he told her the story, tripping over his words to get it out, to confide in her. He told of his fall from the duchess' balcony, the stones turning to water. It was the act of a Faia. The proof of the Whisper Prince. The Event that Lyndion had dangled in front of her was here at last.

"You're going to be okay," she said softly, leaning back and looking into his eyes.

"You were with a Faia. Please, Adora," he said. "I need what you know. I'm sorry that I yelled at you—"

"You were right to be angry," she said.

"Tell me everything," he said. "Let's do this together."

"I will. We will. It's time. Almost time."

"Almost?"

She squeezed him once more, murmured in his ear. "Please trust me, Grei. Just a little longer, and I'll tell you everything." She drew a quick, businesslike breath. "But first things first. They're going to be looking for you, so we need

to get you cleaned up," she said, pointing at the white paste
all over him. "And I need to finish up my shift so I don't
draw suspicion. Draw some water. There is a tub in my
washroom. Fill it and bathe there. Stay out of sight. I won't
be long." She touched his cheek, took his hand. "I'll be back
as soon as I can."

She led him to the pump, got the bucket for him. She
hesitated, then kissed him quickly and left him standing in the
alley.

Adora could barely concentrate on her final duties at *The
Floating Stone*. She fumbled glasses, spilled three drinks. The
Event was here. It was time to fulfill the promise she had
made seven years ago.

She did everything quickly, as though it would speed up
time, and she nervously watched the door. She expected
Galius to show up. He had every night before, but now he
was the last person she wanted to see. If he just stayed away
tonight, it would save her from having to end it with him,
turn him away, make up some excuse. She had rehearsed that
meeting in her head several times, and none of them went
well.

Finally, the crowd thinned enough that Adora could
leave, and Galius had still not shown his face. She tossed her
apron under the bar and disappeared through the door.

She ran up the stairs and entered her little room, saw Grei
sleeping on her bed as she had asked him to do. He was
clean, a sheet across his naked body and his long brown hair
wet against her pillow. His light snoring filled the room, and
his wet clothes, washed clean of the dust, were draped over
her chair.

She smiled, and then looked around at what had become
home to her. This room was hers. It did not belong to the
Order. She had earned it from Seydir, and that meant more to
her than she would have thought. The old wooden walls, the
high ceilings, the warped wood along the western edge from
a long-since-repaired roof leak, all had become so familiar.
She had seen this room as a challenge when Shemmel had

brought her here two short weeks ago. A new adventure. A temporary camp on the road to her destiny.

She opened her chest of drawers and withdrew the child-sized cloak Grei had laid over her so long ago, rubbed it absently between her fingers. The Event was upon her, and things would move quickly now. She drew a long breath and put the cloak back in the drawer.

She didn't regret the decisions that had led her here, and she would not turn from her path, even at the end. But for the rest of her short life, she would regret at least one thing.

She turned to watch Grei sleep, memorizing his features. His face was as smooth as a child's. It was as though his anger and hurt went somewhere else when he slept, and all that was left was an innocent young man. *The boy who protected me when no one else would.*

She stretched her shoulders. Her body ached, and she stank of liquor and smoke. She wanted nothing more than to wash the grime away, curl up next to him, and fall into a deep sleep.

Enough, she thought, snapping her gaze away from him. *There are only a handful of hours before daylight, and I have much to do.*

Taking a deep breath, she crossed to her little wardrobe, took out her blue waterproof cloak and pulled it over her shoulders. She left Grei sleeping and went down the creaky steps. She started into the narrow alley—

—and stopped.

To her left, a large figure shifted between the buildings.

Her fist clenched the cloak where she had just been about to fasten the clasp. Her hand slid down her hip, gripped the reassuring bump of the dagger's hilt at her thigh and stared hard at the figure. A late-night reveler who had gotten lost, or—?

"Blevins!" she hissed.

The fat man stepped forward, emerging halfway from the shadows. The lantern light from Clapwood Street painted a line down the center of his face and vast belly, and he tipped a mug to his lips.

She moved closer, not wanting to wake anyone in the surrounding buildings, especially Grei. She needed to be gone and back before he roused.

"What are you doing outside my room?" she demanded.

"Someone's got to keep an eye on the prince." He swayed, then caught his balance. A chill scampered up her spine. She had seen Blevins drink enough to kill a normal man. She'd never seen him show it.

"You're drunk," she said.

"Not drunk enough," he said in a low tone.

On any other night, she would have spun on her heel and left him there, but not with Grei in the room above. It scared her that Blevins was waiting here.

"Go home," she commanded.

"Not tonight." He hiccupped. "Or any other night."

That was how he spoke when he baited Grei. She had to end this now. She had important things to do. Bantering with this lackwit wasn't one of them.

She stepped up to him. With a quick flick, she hiked her skirt and yanked the dagger from its hidden sheath, put the blade against his immense belly.

"I've handled drunks, Blevins. They do crazy things, which can be forgiven as long as they understand what's best for them."

"I'm sure," he said.

His hand closed softly over her wrist, so quickly she gasped. She jerked back, but his sweaty grip became steel.

Slowly, he pulled her forward. Her feet scraped on the ground and her body pressed against his huge belly. He lifted her up and her blue cloak fell onto the cobblestones. She stifled a scream.

"You'll want to kill me *here*, Rose." He set the tip of her dagger against the fat rolls of his throat and blinked lazily, breathing through his mouth. The fumes were pure alcohol. "Stab me in the chest and I guarantee you'll miss anything important."

"What do you want?" she whispered. She could kill him with a flick of her wrist. The dagger was as sharp as a razor.

He stared at her with a watery gaze. His lips peeled back to reveal straight, white teeth, and she knew that he was about to do something horrible.

But then the look vanished. His grip went slack, and she fell. She hit the ground and stumbled away from him. He took a deep breath, but didn't pursue her.

She stayed there, half-crouched, the dagger tight in her hand. Her wrist and forearm throbbed where he had hauled her up like a rabbit. Her heart beat so fast it hurt. Her cloak lay crumpled on the ground between them.

"Who are you?" she whispered.

"An oathbreaker," he replied, taking another drink from his flask.

"What do you want with me?"

"With you? Nothing before tonight. Nothing until you came out of that door looking like you had somewhere to go."

She paused, searching for a lie that would dissolve his suspicions. She couldn't think of one.

He smirked, as though he was inside her head, reading her thoughts. "I went to the palace," he said. "I saw where he fell. A hole in the street like he punched right through it. I have seen many things in my life, Rose. But who in the empire can do that?" He waited for her to respond. When she didn't, he said, "The Faia, that's who. They are the only ones. So either that boy is protected by the Faia, or he can do what they do."

Her mind raced. Blevins had gone to the palace. He'd seen what Grei had done. She had to say the perfect thing to dissuade him from his notion, but she couldn't seem to think.

"Either way," he continued. "They're going to come looking for him. Poking maidens is one thing. Poking holes through stone is something else. They won't stop. Not for that. Not for what he did." He took a deep breath, and his voice dropped to a rumble so low it vibrated her chest. "And you know it. So either you're going to alert the Highblades, or you're going somewhere else, to someone you think might help."

"You don't know anything," she said.

"I know you manipulate the boy."

"And what are you doing here?" she asked. "Are you going to turn him in to the Highblades?"

"No."

"Why should I believe you?"

"Because if I'd wanted to hurt him, I would have done it."

"You've tried to hurt him a dozen times! You and your stupid dares."

"A man wants to hurt another man, he does it. He doesn't play. I was curious about him. He has something..." He watched her with half-lidded eyes. "And now I need to know. Are you going to the Highblades?"

"I can't believe you would even suggest that," she said.

His black eyes glittered like coal. "Answer me."

She had backed far enough away that he couldn't catch her if she ran. He watched her, not moving, and doubt filled her. Her heart skipped a beat, and she knew with cold certainty that she was wrong. This man could catch her whenever he liked. She wasn't safe ten feet away from him any more than she was in his grip. Who was he?

"Grei is my friend," she said, hating the fear in her voice. "I would never hurt him."

"Of course not," he slurred, and the deadliness vanished. He looked down and away from her, suddenly tired. "Go ahead, then. Do your deed. I will watch over the prince."

She opened her mouth to refuse, but said nothing. She stood in indecision for a long time, facing down the drunk who seemed to have lost all interest in her. Then, without a word, she stooped, snatched her cloak, and hurried away.

Chapter 17
ADORA

THE MIST closed around her as she left the city, the droplets becoming larger as if the forest was their true home. She weaved her way through the forest, following a trail the Order had trained her to find, a trail no woodsman could see in this dark.

She continued past the little clearing where she had first met Grei as a boy and on to the two impressive elm trees that disappeared into the white overhead. She waited, calmly counting to seven in her mind.

"I seek an endless future," she said softly. The trees leaned outward, and she walked between them. As she passed the elms, the forest transformed. The floating droplets in the air disappeared almost entirely. Only a few could be seen, little rogue sparkles. The overcast sky was visible through the leafy canopy above, and the trees gave way to the home of Baezin's Order: seven tall houses of black stone. They looked like they had been pushed up by an earthquake, and they glistened like water at midnight. The largest was the Order House, Lyndion's home, and the place where the Order gathered to discuss matters of importance.

She took a deep breath and went to the double doors of the Order House.

They opened on silent hinges, and Shemmel stood there. His thinning, wispy hair drooped down on either side of his face. Shemmel was the purest of them, free of the Order's politics. He was one of the lucky people who never questioned his place in the world.

"Dear Shemmel," she said, taking the hand of Speaker of the Clerks. "It has been a long time since you've answered the door for guests."

"It has been a long time since someone important crossed the threshold," he said in his creaky voice.

"I've visited many times."

"But you were never as important as you are now," he said. It was something a father would say. A father who cared for you. "Child, your courage humbles us all," he continued.

"Not yet," she said softly.

He patted her hand, then turned and led her into the foyer where the white marble floor began. The contrast with the black walls was stark, and not unintentional. In this place, all decisions were black or white. Either you assisted the prophecy and sought an endless future, or you stood in its way.

They rounded the corner and Adora stopped just outside the council room. She put her hand on a polished area of the black wall. Under her fingers, she felt the chiseled letters of the prophecy, *The Whisper Prince*. Lyndion had told her the history. The Faia had delivered this map of a brighter future, and the Order had inscribed it here.

The version that had leaked into the world, the single stanza nursery rhyme that Grei murmured to his conquests, was so short it made no sense at all. Supposedly, that escaped verse had been a grave mistake. None were supposed to know the prophecy, even a small bit of it, except the Order. But the more Adora learned, the more she was certain nothing happened by accident when it came to the prophecy of the Faia. If *The Whisper Prince* was known all over the empire, it was because the Faia meant it to be known.

Flashes of memory ran through her, racing back across seven years to the moment she had first arrived here.

She swam through the air like it was water, swam for her life with the Faia right beside her. Harder, harder, breathing labored, arms aching, heel trailing blood, until she fell, exhausted, into the South Forest.

A young boy found her. A sweet boy, the only one beside the Faia who wanted to help her. He draped his cloak over her, and she kissed him. And then a slink found them. It came for both of them, and she begged the boy to run. The slink pointed at them, his rainbow eyes swirling, and she died.

Except she hadn't.

She woke up to seven old men standing over her, tending to her wounds.

"I am Lyndion," the tallest of them said, his voice deep and strong.

Lyndion the Conqueror had ruled Thiara a hundred years ago.

"Have I died?" she asked.

Lyndion smiled, one of the only smiles he would ever give her. "No, child. You are very much alive."

"Then how are you Emperor Lyndion?"

"I am merely named for him," Lyndion said.

"But the slink—"

"We saved you, but now we need you to save us. To save the empire..."

The memory faded and she was left with the words on the wall, the words that had shaped the rest of her life. They glistened in the lamplight.

The Whisper Prince
A lost fair lady looked into the mist
The Whisper Prince whispered of love
The lady saw slaughter, and terror, and rifts

The prince, he whispered of love

Love came swimming along the lost road
Her heel painted with blood
The shadows came charging with wrath born of old
Their claws dripping with blood

With blood and from fire the shadows unwound
Losing souls too many to measure
The flesh and the faces of others were bound
And the shadows all took of their measure

Their measure felled hordes; their fires untamed
But the prince, before them, he stood
One hand on the rose, one hand in the flames
The prince, before them all, stood

All stood when the horns of the realm gave alarm
Too late for all and for one
But he sent them away
And never did say
Why a princess lay down for his charm

She closed her eyes, looking away as though the poem had seared her. A tickle of premonition shivered up her spine, painful, and she knew in an instant that this was the last time she would come to the Order House. As they had told her, as the prophecy demanded, Adora would go to Thiara and Grei would take her life. With her blood and the training he would receive from the Faia, he could send the slinks howling back to their abyss. That was her destiny.

She shook her head and strode quickly to the double-doors of the meeting room and yanked them open.

Six men stood in the wide room, and they jerked to look at her as the doors banged against the wall. They were the Speakers for their Houses. The House of Academics, the House of Growth, the House of Consuls, the House of Clerks, the House of Seekers, and the House of the Lost. The seventh, Lyndion, the Bright Speaker, did not flinch. He merely watched Adora as though he had expected her entrance. Though old, Lyndion was tall and powerfully built. He looked more like a Highblade than an ascetic, and it was a rare thing that surprised him. He knew Adora better than any of them. He knew she would enter the chamber angry.

The long, oval table filled the big room, and each Speaker stood behind his seat, some with wide eyes, some with disapproving frowns, all with long, gray beards. They always waited to sit when she was a guest.

She paused there, fixing them with an imperious stare: one last rebellion before she did their work for them. What would they say if she left them here? If she walked away? If she went to Grei and told him there were spiders in the forest, spinning webs in between cracks of history. Told him to run away with her forever and leave this broken empire behind.

Lyndion's deep voice brought her gaze to him. "Seven years of courage will soon be bound into one moment," he said. "Are you ready?" He asked her that every time she visited. His gaze flicked to her bosom, then farther down the length of her before finding her eyes again, like he was appraising some chattel he owned.

"I will be," she said, the answer she always used, the answer that nettled him. He wanted an unequivocal 'yes', and that was one of the few things she could deny him. She had come to love many of these funny old men and their servants over the years, like Shemmel. But some she hated. And she hated Lyndion most of all.

"I hope you will be ready soon," he said darkly. "The Event is upon us."

She strode into the room. "I know what time it is. And I know who lies in my bed at this very moment while every Highblade in Fairmist seeks him."

The six Speakers murmured in approval, nodding their heads. Lyndion held up his hand, and they fell into silence. He turned a sour smile upon her.

"Then the time has come," Lyndion said.

"He goes to the falls," the Speaker for the Consuls said.

Adora nodded. "Tonight?"

"Yes," Lyndion said. "Now."

Chapter 18
ADORA

ADORA LEFT the Order House and returned to her room in Fairmist. As she closed the door, she looked at Grei. If either of them ever had a moment for innocence in their lives, it was over. Grei was going to have to work harder than he'd ever worked before. They were going to the Faia, and She was going to train him. Grei was going to become something more than human.

"Grei," she murmured, hating to break the silence. His face looked so peaceful in slumber, and she wanted him to stay that way. She sat down on the bed and touched his shoulder, shook him gently.

He blinked awake, his body tensing. He touched her forearm. "Adora."

"It's time for me to tell you. For me to show you everything," she said.

He smiled sleepily, sliding his other hand onto her thigh. "Show me everything?"

"Oh, so now you *want* me to seduce you?" she asked.

He sat up, stretching, then looked into her eyes. "Mmm, I

think I do."

She leaned over and kissed him. His hand slid across her hip to the small of her back, and she broke the kiss.

"Listen," she whispered, her forehead against his. "Do you want answers or not?"

"Maybe this answer first," he said. "And then we can move on to those other answers."

"Men." She rolled her eyes. "Look, I promise you that   "

A knock sounded loudly, and Adora jumped.

"Adora?" Galius' voice came through the door.

Grei stared at her, incredulous. "You called the Highblades?" he whispered.

She shot him an angry glance, mouthed the word, "No!"

"Who is it?" she said to the door, changing her voice. She tried to sound barely awake, her speech slurred with sleepiness.

"Galius, my lady," he said through the door. "Please open the door. It's been a long night."

She cursed softly, turned to Grei and grabbed him by the arm. She put a finger to her lips and shook her head.

"One moment, my lord." She yawned loudly. Grei grabbed his clothes, and she pushed him quietly to her washroom and closed the door.

Adora swallowed hard as the washroom door thumped shut. Her throat was suddenly dry. She couldn't deal with this right now. By the Faia, Galius was the last person she needed at her door. What was he doing here an hour before dawn? She looked down at herself, dressed for work, clothes wet from travel in the woods. With frantic speed, she undressed, unbuckled the dagger from her leg and kicked the entire bundle under the bed.

"Adora?" Galius called again.

She yanked the sheet away from the bed and wrapped it around herself, tried to calm her heart and look sleepy. She went to the door, tousled her hair, then opened it.

Galius' handsome face was tired, and her heart twisted at the sight of him. Beyond him, at the base of the stairs, two of his fellow Highblades waited.

"I apologize for the late hour of my visit," Galius said. "I meant to come by *The Stone* earlier, but you would not believe the goose chase I've been on tonight." He glanced at the sheet wrapped around her, and a smile came to his lips. "It is good to see you, though."

"And you, my lord," she said, hating herself. This was the tangle she had meant to avoid. He had been her lover these last three nights. Their relationship was supposed to be simple, a respite, a brief glimpse of what it might be like to be a normal woman.

But it had all been a horrible mistake, despite what Lyndion and the Order had encouraged. Three nights ago, while Grei was avidly creating his Whisper Prince legend with his different women, Galius Ash came into *The Floating Stone* for his regular visit, she made up her mind in an instant. She flirted with him shamelessly, hanging on his arm and whispering in his ear, and they drank together. They danced in the center of the tavern while the patrons clapped out a tune. And when the tavern closed down, she took him to her little room and made love to him. He was her first.

He was everything a lover should be. Gentle. Strong. Skilled. Attentive. Exciting. He wanted her, and he made it known with every touch. It was exhilarating, and for that night, she lost herself in him.

Galius was the type of man she might have married in another life. He was part of the delegate's court, a man of standing. An honest man. He loved her.

And she played the lucky, giddy girl who had snared the most dashing man in Fairmist. In those first glorious, sweaty moments, she could forget about the prophecy. She could even forget about Grei. The second night went much the same.

But last night, when Galius came to the tavern, the thin walls of her deception were weak and easily broken. One day she would just disappear and that would be the last that Galius ever knew of the mysterious Adora. He didn't deserve that. And their lovemaking left her cold. Apparently Adora could only play her part so far.

Now, standing in front of him with an even more elaborate lie on her lips, she was sick at heart, and frightened on top if it. The prophecy was now in motion. She might damage more than just his feelings. She wished she'd never even kissed him.

"My lord," she said, feigning sleepiness. "Is it dawn?" She peered at the dark mists.

"Nearly," he said. "I apologize for the late call. Truly, I do. But it is the delegate's business."

"What sort of business?"

"Can you believe we are to search every house in Fairmist before dawn? They were going to send Javack and his surly crew to this area. It was the luck of the Faia I overheard and took the task myself. That cur would have broken down your door and dragged you into the street, just to see you naked."

"What are you looking for?" she asked.

"You wouldn't believe it if I told you."

She desperately needed him to leave, but the unspoken expectation hung heavily over her. She had eagerly given herself to him these past three nights. To suddenly turn cold would arouse his suspicion, and Galius was the suspicious sort.

She pulled him into a kiss. "I might believe it," she murmured. "You can be very persuasive."

The two Highblades at the base of the stairway cleared their throats and turned away.

Galius blushed. "May I come in?"

She only hesitated a moment. "Of course, my lord." She closed the door behind him and led him to the bed. She must keep herself calm. She had to think her way through this.

She held his hand. "The delegate has you up all night, searching houses?"

"For the damned Whisper Prince," he said.

She narrowed her eyes, feigning confusion. "The

phantom of the masquerades?"

"The same," he said, his lips a flat line. "I would be the last to question the delegate's soundness of mind, but he's chasing mist. I don't know what he is thinking."

"But the Whisper Prince isn't real."

"The delegate thinks he is. Rumor is this man crept into his daughter's room, stole her virginity and her jewels. Now we're searching all of Fairmist for him."

"How will you know him? He wears a mask."

Galius gave a wry smile. "True. But we have a fair description of him. Not his face, perhaps, but apparently the girl got a look at the rest of him." He winked. "The boy has three moles across his chest." He touched each of his collarbones and between them. "That's what we're to look for."

"That could take forever," she said.

"It's a fool's errand. But I've already searched dozens of houses tonight. The Faia only know what they'll have us do tomorrow. But on my rounds," he smiled. "I saved yours for last." He touched the side of her cheek.

Adora's mind raced. How could she deny him?

He sensed her reluctance. With a sad smile, he took the decision smoothly out of her hands like the noble man he was. "I know this is horrible, coming here without notice," he said, shaking his head. "It was not my choice. If you will allow me, I will be about my business and leave you to your rest." He stood and turned toward the washroom. "I shall be quick."

She caught his hand.

"Don't be too quick," she murmured. "I'm awake now."

He turned, surprised, and a grin spread across his face.

Her mind raced. She had to get him out of here. A tryst out-of-doors. An adventure. He would agree to that. She could tell him to send his fellow Highblades home, then take him... Where? *The Floating Stone*? It would be dark and empty at this hour. Somewhere they could watch the sunrise? Time was running out for her. She needed to get Grei to

Fairmist Falls.

"If I am your last stop on an abysmal night," she said in a throaty voice. "We must make it a memorable stop."

He took her into his arms. She touched the leather tie on his ponytail and pulled it free, setting loose his mass of curly black hair. Her sheet slipped down her back, held up only by their chests pressed together. He kissed her, and Adora prayed that Grei would take the opportunity. There was a tiny window in the washroom, perhaps big enough for him to shimmy through. He could make it, if he thought quickly. If he was silent.

The scuff of a foot rose from the washroom.

Galius stopped kissing her, and his head swiveled toward the noise. The washroom door was slightly ajar. Adora thought her heart would stop.

She took a step back, let the sheet fall to the ground. "Galius—"

"What was that?" he said. He glanced at her, saw her nakedness, but it did not draw him. His lust had vanished.

"Galius." She took his hand.

"A moment, I heard—" But then he looked at her again, and realization dawned in his eyes. "By the Faia," he whispered. "Have you hidden someone?"

He batted her hand away, a look of betrayal on his face.

"Listen—" she said.

The door to the washroom banged open, and Grei emerged, his chest bare. The three moles that Galius had described were visible on his bronze skin, even in the darkened room.

"I'm the one you're looking for," he said. "So get away from her."

Galius stood with his mouth open, then his lips set in a grim smile. "The brave boy. The one who picks his fights large."

"I said get away from her," Grei repeated in a low voice, and his eyes narrowed. Adora recognized him focusing his newfound magic.

"Grei, no!" she said.

Galius staggered back, touching his head. "What slinkery?" He said, then threw back his shoulders and drew his longsword.

"No!" Adora said, lunging between them. The Order could spring Grei from the dungeons. They could not bring back his corpse.

But Galius caught her wrist, yanked her sideways. She gasped and fell to her knees.

Grei swung at Galius' face, and the Highblade ducked, head-butted Grei in the chin and sent him reeling backwards. Grei slammed into the bedpost, tripped, and fell to the floor.

The Highblade leveled his black blade at Grei's nose.

"Galius, listen to—" Adora began, then cried out as he twisted her wrist.

"Quiet," Galius said. "You've broken my heart, Adora." Without turning, he shouted to the door. "Gareth! Jhan!"

The door swung wide. Galius opened his mouth to give orders, but the words died on his lips. Blevins stepped into the room.

Galius shoved Adora over, and she fell hard. He leapt back, keeping both Grei and Blevins in view and pointing his blade at Blevins' chest. The fat man watched him, unfazed, then held up his hands in a pacifying gesture.

"Calm yourself, Highblade," Blevins said, his voice slurred.

"Where are Gareth and Jhan?"

"Resting."

Galius was flustered by Blevins' appearance. "Who are you?"

"A loyal patron of *The Floating Stone*. Adora is a very attentive bartender. I was worried she might get injured in this little scuffle."

Adora scrambled across the wood floor, grabbing the sheet and wrapping it around herself. Grei started to stand, but Galius flicked the blade in his direction. "Stay down, boy."

Grei froze, and Galius turned the sword back on Blevins. "Speak quickly, sir. Your life depends on it."

"Drop your sword," Blevins said.

Galius frowned. Perhaps Blevins thought he could bluster his way through, convince Galius to lay down arms. But Galius did not waste time, and he didn't banter with criminals. Adora knew what was coming next.

"No!" she shouted.

Galius lunged.

The stroke should have skewered Blevins through the chest, but somehow Galius missed. Or Blevins moved. It happened so fast that Adora wasn't sure, but the fat man suddenly had Galius' sword hand in his meaty fist.

He clubbed the Highblade on the top of the head with his other hand, then slammed an elbow into his face. Blood flecked the wall and Blevins wrenched the blade from Galius' numb grip. The enormous man held the sword like a dagger in his left hand.

Galius stumbled back, a thin crimson streak across his cheek.

Blevins had that deadly look again. His face was flushed, and he was sweating. He flipped back his voluminous cloak and drew a long sword from his side. The cross guard was smooth steel, but the hilt bore a ruby on one side and a scratched stone as black as night on the other. She knew that sword. Where had seen it before? Was it the delegate's?

"Unfortunately," Blevins said to Galius. "Your choices are few."

Galius looked at him incredulously.

Blevins continued. "You can submit, in which case things get interesting for everyone. Or you can fight." He tossed the black sword at the Highblade's feet.

"Blevins!" Adora said, aghast. "Are you mad?"

"Shut up," he said, then to Galius. "She's a good woman. A liar and a sneak, but a good woman. She doesn't understand a man's code, though. Some things must be settled the way they must be settled." The fat man nodded at the sword in front of Galius. "Which will it be, Highblade? Surrender or fight?"

Galius took the weapon and rose. Adora could see him trying to puzzle it out, but he was obviously as lost as she. "You are a man of honor," Galius said.

"I am a cursed man with a pretty sword," he said. "That is all."

Galius saluted, then slashed wickedly.

Blevins shifted his stance. Steel clanged. Galius' strike missed the big man's arm by half an inch. Galius scissor-stepped to the side, his blade thrusting forward again.

Blevins moved, and yet he didn't. His bulk shifted, but his feet stayed planted. Somehow Galius' sword missed him again, whispering through the air.

Galius stepped back, a deep frown on his face. He unleashed a flurry of attacks, coming at Blevins from the side, then straight on, then overhead. Each time, Blevins' sword was there, blocking, countering. Metal ground against metal, and Galius tried to push the big man off balance. Blevins sent the slender Highblade stumbling away with a violent shrug, then shuffled back a step, not making a sound. Adora could not believe her eyes.

"Who are you?" Galius asked, breathing hard.

"A loyal patron of *The Floating Stone*," he repeated. Sweat trickled down his ruddy cheeks.

Galius came at him again, and Blevins moved back a step, then two. Galius' blade flicked out, a blur. Adora thought Blevins must be cut a half dozen times, but his sword was always there, turning death aside.

Galius lunged, shifted, lunged again. Blevins' foot bumped against the wall. With a happy cry, Galius thrust at the fat man's enormous belly.

Again, Blevins deflected the strike. But the big man didn't simply block this time. He surged forward, grabbing Galius' sword hand again. He thrust the Highblade's arm up, sinking the blade into a ceiling beam and hammering the hilt of his own sword into Galius' face. Blood flew, and Galius sagged as if he'd been chopped off at the knees.

Blevins held the unconscious Highblade up by his fist, then tossed him to the floor. Galius' sword wobbled back and forth in the ceiling where it had been embedded.

Blevins glanced at the wide-eyed Grei, then at Adora. Without a word, he held up his blade and looked critically along the edge. Satisfied, he sheathed it, and the hilt disappeared beneath his huge brown cloak

He strode to Adora's only chair and sat down, managing the sword with grace. Pulling a flask from his tunic, he removed the cork and took a swig.

"Who are you?" she whispered. Grei opened his mouth to speak, but shut it again, as if Adora had asked his question.

"A loyal patron of *The Floating Stone*," Blevins said. "Haven't you been listening?"

"You just bested the finest swordsman in Fairmist. Only an Imperial Highblade can use a sword like that."

"And how would you know that, *barmaid*?" Blevins asked, regarding her through squinty eyes. He took another drink.

A cold wisp of fear curled around her heart. By the Faia, had he been sent to find her?

"Who are you?" she murmured again.

"A worthy question. I've tried hard to be somebody else. But I couldn't let go of the sword, could I? And if a swordsman cannot put down his sword, he will use it again. As sure as the sun will rise."

Adora's voice caught in her throat, and she couldn't speak. She knew that sword now. She took an involuntary step back.

He gave her a sour smile, then nodded. "Yes." He took another drink from his flask, wiping his lips with his hand. "A man looks different without a soul. And you were very young then." He leaned forward. The chair creaked as though it would snap, and he looked straight into her soul with his dead eyes. "Princess."

Chapter 19

ADORA

JORUN MAGNUS!" Adora stepped back, aghast. Memories erupted within her: Jorun lingering to play with her when her parents had no time, showing her how to wield a dagger when her father had told her no. He had spoken soft words of guidance as she drew a bow for the first time. She had loved him as only an eleven-year-old girl could, had envisioned their wedding someday. A girl's dreams. Because of Jorun Magnus, she had felt safe every time she closed her eyes.

Then the Debt of the Blessed came, and she had thrown her faith in him. When her father damned her to death, she had been unafraid because she knew Jorun would never allow it. Her parents might fail her, but Jorun never would. He would save her. He would fight the entire Thiaran Empire to save her. Instead, he had betrayed her. He had cast her aside as if she meant nothing.

"I am Jorun Magnus no longer," Blevins said.

"Jorun Magnus the emperor's champion?" Grei blurted.

"They said you died," she whispered, unable to catch her breath. Even in Fairmist they had heard the report of the emperor's champion slain after he had gone mad, cutting his way through the palace. The Ringblade Selicia had delivered the killing blow. "They killed you."

"They killed you too," he said.

She clenched her fist, dizzy. "You should have died. I wish you *had* died," she said, nearly shouting. She shouldn't be shouting.

Blevins had become part of the chair, unmoving.

"Let me get this straight," Grei said. "You, Blevins, the drunk of *The Floating Stone*, are the Emperor's champion?"

"Not anymore," Blevins said. He took another drink from his flask.

Grei turned to Adora. She stood absolutely still as his gaze swept over her.

"And you," he said. "You're..." But he didn't finish.

She turned away from Magnus. She didn't need his protection. He was nothing to her now, just a drunk from the bar. Only Grei mattered. "I am Mialene Doragon," she told him the truth. "Or I was."

"Your father sent you to die?"

"I was the first Blessed," she said.

Grei's gaze softened, and she saw him putting it together.

"The Faia brought you here, away from the slinks," he said. "That was why she was with you."

"Yes," she said. She glanced at Blevins, but the man was so still he might have been dead. His black eyes swallowed the light. "And I will tell you more, but not here."

"She doesn't trust me," Blevins drawled.

"And how should I?" She glared at him. "Murderer. Traitor. Oathbreaker. You dragged a little girl to the slinks. A little girl you made feel special. She loved you, believed in you. With all of her young heart. You want trust? You deserve death!"

"A little girl..." Blevins murmured. "You speak of her as though she isn't you," he said.

"She isn't. Not anymore," Adora snapped.

"Hmmm," he said.

She turned to Grei. "Come with me. The Highblades are searching every house. The delegate will have scoured Fairmist by the time the sun rises. We don't have much time."

"Less than you think," Blevins said. "Selicia was at the palace."

Cold prickled across Adora's scalp. "Selicia?"

"Her, the delegate and a horde of Highblades, all of them looking at the great hole Grei made. The Ringmother is here for him." Blevins watched Adora's face and smiled grimly at her expression. "Yes," He drew the word out as though he was following her train of thought. "Selicia is a whole different problem, isn't she? The delegate is an idiot. And Highblade Ash is a fine swordsman, but he isn't a hunter. He can be controlled, slowed by your charms. But Selicia doesn't care about your heaving bosom or your long lashes. She can outrace a grellik, teach a cliffcat to stalk. She will find you, if she hasn't already, and she'll strike in the quiet before you draw a breath. That's what Ringblades do."

Adora refused to respond, but she checked the impulse to look over her shoulder. Ringblades lived in the shadows. She turned to Grei. "It's time to know everything, just like I promised. I will take you to a Faia. You will learn about your newfound magic and what must be done with it. Come with me now."

"Could we save Julin?" he asked. "Like the Faia saved you?"

She opened her mouth to speak, caught by Grei's stern hope. The Order would tell her to lie to him, to tell him whatever it would take to make him go in the direction she needed him to go. Manipulation. Lies.

"No," she said softly. "The slinks have already slain him. Julin is gone."

"The Faia saved you," he persisted.

"She did so immediately. Magnus had barely ridden away when she arrived. And you..."

"I'm not a Faia."

"It is a lot to hope for," she said.

"I'll go with you," he said.

Relief flooded through her.

"I'll just stay here," Blevins drawled.

"Stick a knife in your eye. Drown yourself in the river," Adora said, kneeling to pull her clothes and her dagger from underneath the bed. "I don't care."

Grei politely turned his back. She let her sheet drop and pulled her tunic over her head, then belted on her skirt. Blevins stared at nothing, his dark eyes unreadable and unmoving.

"Come on, Grei." He went out the door first, and she spared one last look at Blevins, sitting in the shadows of her little room, with the unconscious Galius sprawled across the floor like a rug. She felt she should say something scathing, something that would scar him. The timbers of her life had buckled when her father betrayed her, and only Jorun Magnus had held them up. When he had dumped her on the slinks' slope and ridden away, he had crushed her spirit.

"Princess," Blevins said. His voice was rough.

"What?" she said.

He sat like a statue.

"Never mind. It doesn't matter," he said finally, then in a lower tone meant only for himself. "Nothing matters."

She slammed the door, and Grei stood waiting for her at the bottom of the landing. Grei, her salvation. Everyone's salvation. The clock was dripping. It was time to begin their journey, side-by-side until the end.

As she descended, she saw Galius' other two Highblades piled underneath the staircase. She looked at the sky. It seemed as black as Deepdark, but the sun was coming.

"Where are we going?" he asked.

"Fairmist Falls," she said. "Maybe we could stop at the Blacktale Bridge? Finish our dance?" She gave him a little smile.

"Don't expect flowers," he said.

Her heart felt lighter, hearing him joke. She walked

quickly into the darkness, heading east, staying close to the buildings and moving over the bridges swiftly. Grei knew the streets better than she did, but she had memorized this route, had committed it to memory months ago before she ever came to *The Floating Stone*. This was where she had been destined to lead him since the beginning. As they crossed one of the roped ferries, Grei spoke.

"Why the falls?" he asked as he pulled the rope in time with her. The river gurgled at the edge of the flat ferry. Long grass bent over the banks, trailing in the water.

"It is where the Faia lives," she said. The ferry bumped the dock on the other side, and she leapt onto land once more. He landed next to her. "I'm taking you to her."

"The one who saved you?"

"No. The Blue Faia." She started up the cobblestone path that bordered the northern edge of the Wet Woods. To her left, the ground sloped down to the river. To her right, a grassy field pocked with little pools of standing water stretched up to the beginning of the Wet Woods. It was a relief to be outside the city. The Highblades were feverishly searching every house, but they wouldn't search the outlying areas, especially the Wet Woods, until morning.

He picked up a rock from the side of the path and tossed it speculatively into the air, caught it. "The magic starts as whispers, Adora, and singing voices, sometimes," he said, pausing in the center of the path. "I thought the hushed voices had turned into the poem *The Whisper Prince*, but lately I've heard them underneath the poem, too. Did you know that?"

She paused.

"When I look into people," he said quietly, staring at the rock, "It's as though I'm listening to how their hearts speak. And everyone has their own language. Foreign to me. Indecipherable. Except as I stare at them, suddenly I can speak it."

"What do the whispers say?" she asked.

"When someone opens to me, I hear their desires. Or no, more than that. I hear their identity. Who they believe they

are. Who they want to be." He shook his head, frowning. "I
see them. Smell them. Taste them. All of my senses, but more
than that. A different sense. A whole new way of
understanding. If I concentrate hard, I know them the way
they know themselves."

He looked down at the rock in his hand. "This rock is
whispering right now." He looked around at the dark shapes
of the trees. "The trees too, further away, harder to hear. The
water in the air whispers. And the air itself."

"What does the rock say?" she asked.

He held it closer to his face, pressed his lips together.
"Strength. Hardness. Grit." His brow furrowed and he gave a
frustrated frown. "But it's not that. It's not really *saying* that.
I never realized how poorly words capture what I've been
hearing. The whispers aren't words at all. They're sensations.
The rock is talking about what it is, over and over." He held it
out in front of him, and his eyes narrowed. "And I," he said,
his voice lowering, "can ask it to be something else."

The rock suddenly went soft, so suddenly that Grei
cupped his hands around it. Trickles of granite water slipped
through his fingers. He whispered again and the stone went
back to its original shape, only a little smaller.

"By the Faia," she whispered. All her training, all the
knowledge, and still it didn't prepare her for seeing the
impossible made real.

"It wants to be spoken to," he said. He looked at her, then
dropped the rock and took her hand. The floating water
droplets glowed, casting ghostly spots on his face. "I tried to
hate you," he said softly.

"I know." She looked up into his eyes. "I tried not to love
you."

"That's what I don't understand. Why? We were meant
to dance. I saw it inside you. I've known it from when you
first kissed me in the South Forest."

Her heart ached. She wanted to nod, to agree with him.
He touched her chin, then he kissed her.

She hesitated, then slid her fingers into his long hair and

forgot about Lyndion's rules. The prophecy could have them both soon enough. But she would claim this one sliver of a happy life. For this moment, she would have Grei.

A snort of derision floated out of the mist.

Adora broke the kiss and spun. Her heart leapt into her throat, and she gripped Grei's hand hard.

Had Blevins followed them?

But Blevins would have said something stinging. Her skin went cold, and the fat man's words danced in her mind.

She will find you, if she hasn't already, and she'll strike in the quiet.

Grei went silent, peering with her. Little hissing sounds came out of the darkness, like water droplets on a hot stove.

Adora shifted quietly to the balls of her feet, ready to run. She cursed herself for a fool. Seven years of training and this is how she had let this night unfold. She hadn't expected Galius. She hadn't expected Blevins. She hadn't expected Selicia.

"Be ready," she whispered so softly it was only a breath on his cheek.

"Who is it?" Grei asked her.

"Whisper whisper whisper," a child's voice said from right behind them, clearer this time, and Adora's blood froze. That was no Ringblade.

She lurched into a sprint, yanking Grei with her.

"Run!" she shouted, shoving him off the path into the flat grass, pocked with little pools of water. If they could reach the stream, if they could only—

A figure rose up in front of Grei and struck him on the head. He collapsed in a heap.

The figure's hair became fire, sizzling the water in the air. The slink shook himself, and hissing droplets flew to all sides.

"So this is the Whisper Prince?" He looked down at Grei with burning eyes.

Chapter 20

ADORA

AND YOU are his takla?" the slink continued, using the Benascan word for "whore". The floating droplets continued to hiss as they touched the slink's burning skin. Despite his childlike voice, he was tall, with elongated arms and an overlong face. His sharp features were exaggerated as though sketched by a little boy's hand. Thin eyebrows slanted upward over burning eyes. His skin looked like layers of smoldering coal.

Grei lay unconscious on the ground, and Adora faced the slink who had stood at the opening of the cave where Jorun Magnus had left her seven years ago.

She would never forget that elongated face. It haunted her nightmares. And now he was here again.

She clenched her fists, fighting her fear. Lyndion had prepared her for every eventuality the Order could think of, and she recalled his words now.

"When the Event occurs," Lyndion said. "There will be those who seek the Whisper Prince. You must take him away

immediately. Take him to the First Place, beyond the falls."

"Who will seek him?" she asked.

"The empire, for one. We believe the emperor has a copy of the prophecy. He will be watching for the emergence of the Whisper Prince, even as we are. I don't need to tell you what a disaster it would be if your father gets his hands on the Whisper Prince."

"No," she said.

"And the slinks," Lyndion said. "If they find out about the Prince, they will seek to destroy him."

"What can I do against a slink?"

"One thing only. There is a reason the Order is in Fairmist, a reason the Whisper Prince will rise here. Listen carefully..."

Lyndion's words echoed in her mind as she faced the slink. She stepped two paces closer, and he watched her with amusement. She bowed her head and knelt in front of him.

He chuckled. "Where are you going so late at night? To mingle your foul human fluids?" His nose wrinkled in disgust.

"God of fire," she intoned reverently. Every hair on her neck prickled as she made herself vulnerable to him. One quick stomp, and he could snap her neck. "We have long awaited you."

The slink was silent, but she could hear the little hisses of water on his glowing skin. Hidden by her bowed body, she dipped her hands and forearms into the puddle over which she had placed herself.

To her left, she heard Grei groan. *Thank the Faia,* she thought. *Wake up, Grei. Wake up!*

She sprang to her feet, scooping as much of the water as she could directly into the slink's body. His chest hissed and his glowing eyes went out, as did his flaming hair. He howled in rage, staggered back.

She spun, her feet digging into the wet grass as she launched herself at Grei. She yanked his arm, dragging him upright.

"Run," she said. "Down the hill or we die!"

He squinted at her through his pain, but he stumbled forward. She supported him and strained to make them both faster. They had only seconds. They had to make the stream. If she could just reach it, they might have a chance.

"Tell me you have more than that little trick!" the slink said, his head bursting into flame in front of them. He lunged, seizing her arm. His claws burned as he dragged her forward.

"Water!" Grei shouted, grabbing the slink's wrist. The slink yelled and yanked away, dropping Adora onto the wet grass. His arm hissed where Grei had touched it. Grei pursued, stabbing a finger at him.

"Water!" he shouted again.

She saw a ripple in the dark air between them, causing the glowing droplets to shudder.

With a snarl, the slink pointed back and the ripple of water exploded into steam. A gout of fire burst from the slink's mouth. Grei screamed as his right arm was engulfed. His forearm burned like a torch, and he fell to his knees. He rolled onto it, trying to put it out.

Adora screamed like an animal. She pulled her dagger and leapt at the thing, slashing wildly. "No!" she shouted. "No no no!"

Her blade clanked like it had hit rock. The slink caught her by the hair and yanked in a circle. "Enough of you," he said, slamming her to the ground. He drew back his clawed hand, but stopped, his gaze jerking to the left.

Silver flashed between them, and the slink shrieked, stumbling away. Red fire blazed in the night, blinding her. She rolled desperately away from the heat.

Its flaming arm was still tangled in her hair, severed at the elbow, but it was no longer the burning-coal arm of the slink. Instead, it was the arm of a child, pale and slight, with pink skin and little fingers that ended in translucent claws. A gout of fire shot out of the wound. She yanked the limp fingers from her hair and tossed the arm away.

Rising to her knees, she blinked away the bright after-images.

Blevins' huge form blocked out the fire and the slink, shielding her. Baezin's Blade jutted from his fist like a shaft of moonlight.

The writhing monster on the grass had transformed. It was not a tall, imposing warrior with layered, burning skin. Instead, it was a little blonde boy. Its arm and part of its leg had been cut away. Grass hissed as fire blew out of the ghastly wounds.

"Let's see how fast you are now," Blevins growled.

The slink boy huffed as he scrambled backwards. His movements were a blur, but Blevins was faster, sword arcing downward, slashing the boy's other leg.

It curled toward him, claws grabbing for Blevins' arm as it keened.

Blevins blocked, stepped back and thrust, impaling the creature through the chest. Blevins withdrew again, his arm arcing high, and sliced the blonde head from the body.

The child's shriek ended abruptly.

Flame shot out of the neck and chest, sending a column of fire a hundred feet into the sky, and Blevins spun away from the heat. His silhouette was a hunched blot against the fire.

The boy's head rolled to a stop, hissing as the flames died.

Adora couldn't breathe. Blevins glanced at her then went to Grei, who cradled his smoking arm. Blevins picked him up, carried him to the stream, and dropped him in the water. Adora leapt over the slick reeds and slid down to him as he spluttered to the surface. She held his shoulders and steadied him.

"Keep him here. I'll be back," Blevins said.

Grei grunted, holding his arm under the water.

"Shhh," she said. "It will be okay."

Blevins returned. He had removed his voluminous cloak, filled it with the child's body, and slung it over his shoulder.

He dumped the severed parts into the water downstream, and they hissed before sinking beneath the surface. He whipped his smoking cloak back over his shoulders.

"It was a child," Adora said. "Why was it a child?"

"You are the one with the secrets. You tell me."

She couldn't think straight. There was something important about the fact that the slink had transformed into a child. The Order had never said anything about that. Why hadn't they mentioned that?

"I wasn't strong enough," Grei said through gritted teeth. "It burned through my magic like nothing." His whole body vibrated with pain. He kept his arm beneath the water.

"I should have let you both die." Blevins growled, looking at Adora. "So now you're going to tell me everything. No more secrets. Slinks don't come to Fairmist. Why was it here?"

"For Grei."

"Why?"

"He is the Whisper Prince."

"A slink came to Fairmist because Grei bedded the Duchess of the Highward?" Blevins asked with a frown.

She hesitated, but she was off course here. If not for Blevins, they would be dead, and the prophecy would be done. She had made a botch of everything, and the Order was not here to set it right. Blevins was. She took a deep breath, then said, "The rhyme is a prophecy, and the Whisper Prince is part of that prophecy."

"Whose prophecy?" Blevins asked.

She hesitated, then shook her head.

"Whose?" he growled.

"No." She shook her head. "You don't get that information."

His black eyes flickered, and he rose a little higher. "You said the Faia saved you," he said. "Who did they bring you to?"

"I owe you nothing, Magnus," she spat. "But they trained me. They told me about the prophecy, that the Slink War will come again unless we stop it. Grei is the key. He can send the slinks back where they came from."

Blevins stood as still as a statue, his squinty gaze fixed on her. "Because of what he did at the palace."

"Because of what he will do when we reach the falls. He needs instruction."

"From the Faia."

"Yes."

"When will the slinks go to war?" he asked.

"Soon."

"Don't be cryptic, girl." Blevins showed his teeth like a dog.

"Don't act like you care!" she shouted. She knew she should keep her voice down, but she couldn't. "You sat by my father for years, watching the things he did, the evil he created. You *made* the Debt of the Blessed! What do you care?"

"I don't answer to you," he said.

"Yes you do," she said. "Me more than anyone." Her voice dropped to a venomous whisper. "Why didn't they kill you?"

"Because I was lucky. Because I was better."

"And you came to Fairmist to drink? You came here to—"

"I came to Fairmist to die!" Blevins pointed his sword at Grei. "And I was managing it until him. Until you," he said to her.

"And you saved us instead," she said. "Well, it makes up for nothing."

His knuckles were white on the hilt of his sword.

"You're no longer my hope. Grei is," she whispered.

"I don't want hope," he growled.

"Then why not let the slink kill you?"

He shook his head, looking over her toward Fairmist. He was silent for a moment, then, "Where there is one slink, there are a hundred. A thousand. Not to mention every Highblade in the empire is looking for him." He nodded at

Grei. "And Selicia. That bonfire will bring them like hounds."

"Then let's go," Grei said, his teeth clenched.

She turned. "How bad is it?" She asked.

He pulled his arm out of the water, and a gasp lodged in her throat. It was a horrifying claw, only charred tendons and flesh remained on the bones.

Her heart thudded in her chest, and she looked up at his face.

He shook with the pain. His breathing came hard through his nose as he stared forward, eyes tight. He forced his gaze away from his arm.

"Grei—" Adora began.

"Forget it," he said through clenched teeth. He squinted at her, then at Blevins. "He's right. We can't stay here."

"We should wrap your arm—"

"No," he growled. His whole body shook as he cradled the burned arm against his chest.

"Grei—" She reached for his shoulder.

"Don't touch it!" He snapped. He lurched out of the water and started up the path.

Blevins and Adora fell in line behind him.

Chapter 21
GREI

GREI COULD barely think for the pain. If he stopped, even for a second, the searing would devour him. The floating droplets got larger as they headed uphill toward Fairmist Falls, changing slowly from moonlit silver to soft yellow. Dawn was coming.

Adora had promised a Faia at the end of this race, and he needed to believe her. A Faia could fix the Debt of the Blessed. A Faia could fix his arm. A Faia could fix anything, if She wanted to.

The squishy grass gave way to waist-high, broad-leafed bushes as they reached the cliff that shot straight up to the Highward. To their left, Fairmist Falls roared, tumbling into Thiara's Pool far below, creating the floating droplets that drifted into the city. They stopped at the edge of the slope that led down to the pool.

"Behind the falls," Adora said.

"There's nothing behind the falls," Grei said.

"There is nothing for anyone else. For you, it will open."

Blevins shifted impatiently, as though this was a waste of time. She shot him an angry look.

"I'm supposed to do something?" Grei asked. He gripped his upper arm with his good hand, squeezing.

"You have to concentrate—"

"I can't concentrate!" he hissed through his teeth.

Adora's cool hands touched his shoulders. "I'm so sorry," she said. "And I will apologize a thousand times once we are safe, but Blevins is right. It is sheer luck that no other slinks have found us. We must make this one last step. The Faia is in there. She can help you. You can do it, Grei. It was what you were born to do. Open the falls and take us home," she said.

Adora slipped down the grassy slope, nimble as a deer, finding niches and grassy shelves. Grei followed, leaning on his good hand. Blevins stepped lightly behind them. His gaze flicked all around, quick and efficient.

The floating droplets were thick now, some as large as apples. Water dribbled down Grei's face. The roar of the falls was deafening, and his teeth chattered.

"Here!" Adora shouted over the crashing noise. The top of the falls glowed with morning light, barely visible through the mist.

In the midst of Thiara's Pool, some thirty feet out from the crashing falls, was a flat rock. It barely stuck up above the waterline, creating an oblong platform that pointed to the very center of the falls. In the warmth of summer, young men and women swam out to it, playing games, splashing, sometimes hauling food in waterproof sacks to have lunch.

"Look!" Adora said, pointing.

Dodging the fat droplets of floating water were little blue figures, wings flicking like flippers. Each was two inches tall, distinctly humanoid. Their faces were flat with bulbous blue eyes, no nose and no mouth. Their heads sloped backwards to a point at the nape of their necks. Grei had seen them before, of course. Everyone in Fairmist who had visited the falls had seen a fyd. They were just one more curiosity in the city of Fairmist. They tended to gather around the falls or in the Wet Woods. Grei had seen them in both places, usually singly, sometimes in groups of two or three. But this was a swarm. It was as though they were waiting for something to happen.

"There must be hundreds of them," Adora said.

Blevins looked around, shaking his head. He didn't seem impressed by the fyds, and he didn't look happy. "The sun is rising. We're blind and deaf, cornered and on low ground. We cannot defend this spot." He looked at Grei. Blevins had never seemed so large as he did now. His girth had always made him seem comical before, but now it filled the sky, dark and dangerous. "I'm going to a better vantage." He headed back up the slope.

The fyds slowly came closer, hovering around Grei, their wings clicking.

"They sense you, what is in you," Adora said. She took his hand.

"I'm ready," he said, drawing his gaze away from the fyds. "What do I do?"

Water dripped down her face. Her hair was plastered against her head and shoulders, limp black and gold weeds. The creeping sunlight made the floating droplets glow like gold.

"Just listen," she said, and began to speak:

A lost fair lady looked into the mist
The Whisper Prince whispered of love
The lady saw slaughter, and terror, and rifts
The prince, he whispered of love

Love came swimming along the lost road
Her heel painted with blood
The shadows came charging with wrath born of old
Their claws dripping with blood

With blood and from fire the shadows unwound
Losing souls too many to measure
The flesh and the faces of others were bound
And the shadows all took of their measure

Their measure felled hordes; their fires untamed
But the prince, before them, he stood
One hand on the rose, one hand in the flames
The prince, before them all, stood

All stood when the horns of the realm gave alarm
Too late for all and for one
But he sent them away
And never did say
Why a princess lay down for his charm

She recited it as though she had read it a thousand times, as though it was as common to her as her name. Grei felt he should know this poem, that the single verse of *The Whisper Prince* that repeated endlessly in his mind was only a shadow. These words filled Grei with cool water, spreading to every part of him. It drove back the pain of his arm and the hollow fear that his body was ruined forever.

The whispers swirled through him. They became a light song, lifting him up.

Adora squeezed his good hand. "The slinks came for you because you frighten them, Grei. Because they know you can hurt them. You can send them away." She paused. "Make them regret not killing you tonight. Become the Whisper Prince."

He looked into her blue eyes. The reflected dawn light illuminated her lovely face. She leaned forward and kissed him, then slid her cheek against his and whispered into his ear. "Do it. Take us to safety."

He let her go and turned to the falls. He could feel it now, and the song tugged at him. He faced the platform in the center of the lake that pointed toward their destination.

He pictured a door opening in the falling water, a corridor that led into another land, to a place where the Faia lived.

He opened his eyes. Nothing had changed. The water fell

from the cliff and pounded into Thiara's Pool as ever before. The hovering fyds clicked their wings, creating a musical hum.

He closed his eyes, held forward his good hand. He imagined the gateway once more, imagined parting the water. This time, he listened for the waterfall's whispers beneath the song, listened for its language.

He felt something rushing and merry inside him, a desire to race downhill, to flow around the hard parts of the world. Music accompanied the feeling, changing to its cadence, blending perfectly with the words of the poem.

Grei suddenly realized that this was the voice of the falls, the voice of the water in Thiara's Pool, the voice of the river that flowed downhill, happily visiting everything along the way. The long grasses of the bank drank of her. The dark bridges hovered over her. The people put their little vessels upon her and floated.

"Open," he said to the waters, speaking to them within his mind. He felt them speak to him in return, and their happy language thrummed through him. He wanted to rush along with the water all the way to the Sunset Sea, to give life to a thousand creatures and plants and become something infinitely larger.

Grei opened his eyes. The falls had parted, like an invisible archway was pushing the water aside. The flat stone in the center of the lake had risen, extending like a bridge all the way to the shore. The way was open.

He was dizzy. This had been altogether different than when he'd turned the flagstones into water underneath Venderré's balcony, or when he had turned the slink's skin to water. He hadn't felt a thing then, only a frightening need. This time, he was floating on an ocean of power gathered in this place. There was no struggle. He had sent his request, and all things were possible. It was as though this had been prepared, and he had only triggered it.

He peered through the mists, trying to see beyond the archway as they stepped onto the bridge.

In the center, glowing blue, was the Faia. The fyds flocked to her, creating a cloud around her and making her little form seem large by comparison. The Faia floated forward over the pool. Behind her was a long, dark corridor as tall as the falls, a cascade of shadows overlapping each other. He could only imagine what was in there.

Baezin?

The Faia spoke the word in his head. She was too far away for him to see her eyes, but he felt something on his arm, like a feather lightly brushing his burn.

Pain.

The Faia breathed in. The opening in the falls rippled around Her, and the pain seeped from his arm, flowing into the pool and swirling away downstream. He gasped at the release. He looked down. His arm was still grisly charred bone and meat, unhealed, but there was no sensation of any kind. It was as though his arm ended just below his elbow.

He tore his gaze away from it and focused on the Faia. "We need your help," he said.

Union.

"Y-yes," he said, not sure what she meant. "We have come to—"

"Grei—!" Blevins shouted, and his voice was cut off. Grei spun in time to see a steel ring bounce off the big man's head, glimmering in the dawn light as it arced back the way it had come. Blevins went down.

A lithe figure leapt down the bank, suddenly visible as she caught the returning ring in a gauntleted hand. She hooked the ring at her hip, danced down the last bit of slope and pulled out another weapon, spinning it over her head. The weapon blurred in a silver circle, and she hurled it at them.

"Grei!" Adora screamed. Thin steel chains wound around Grei's ankles and steel balls slammed into his calves and shins. Adora shoved him, too late, and they fell into the shallow water.

Frantically, Grei turned. He looked desperately at the

Faia. The tiny blue woman drew back in dismay, like a little girl watching dogs tear at each other.

"Help us!" Grei said to her.

She bowed her head and withdrew, fading into the mists. The opening in the waterfall vanished under a deluge of water.

"No!" Grei shouted.

Adora pulled frantically at the chains around his legs. "We have to get these off!" she shouted.

"She left," Grei said, filled with a crushing despair. The Faia had seen, and she hadn't helped. She hadn't even tried.

Adora's mouth set in a line as she looked up at the falls, flowing over the ridge and crashing into the lake as though nothing had happened. The fluttering fyds had vanished.

"Do it again. Call her back," she said. She jumped to her feet and hiked her skirt, revealing a sheath strapped to her leg. "I'll take care of this bitch." She yanked the dagger out and ran at the Ringblade with a shout.

Grei struggled to his knees. "Adora, no!"

"Don't hurt her!" shouted a second voice, joining Grei's. He looked downstream to see Galius Ash leaping over rocks and sliding down the bank. Further downstream, three other Highblades sprinted toward them.

Adora slashed at Selicia, but the black-clad woman leaned into her, as though to embrace her, and Adora's strike missed. The two seemed to dance for a moment, then the Ringblade pirouetted neatly. Adora coughed and fell to her knees, clutching her stomach. The dagger thumped onto the mossy rocks.

"Don't!" Galius shouted, but the Ringblade hit Adora in the neck, and she crumpled in a heap. Galius roared as he charged her. "I said we weren't going to—"

The woman turned to him, and suddenly she had a dagger of her own, pointed at his face. Galius drew up short. "See to the fat man, Highblade," the woman said. "Disarm him. Do it now."

Galius Ash seethed, facing off against the Ringblade, his

teeth bared. He glanced at Adora, then he turned and scrambled up the slope to where Blevins had fallen.

Grei looked at the pool. There was no way he could concentrate enough to call the Faia back, despite what Adora wanted. And even if he did, the Faia wouldn't help. She wouldn't help!

He could dive into the water and let the river carry him away, live to fight another day, assuming he didn't drown with his legs tied together and only one arm to swim.

He looked back at Adora, unconscious on the ground.

"Don't try it," the Ringblade said over the noise of the falls, seeing his intention. "Or we'll kill the girl and fish you out downstream."

She sauntered toward him like a dancer relaxing after a performance. Her face was twisted by a red scar that ran from her eye to her chin. She frowned.

"You are the Whisper Prince," she said, her voice barely carrying over the noise of the falls. "These Highblades don't know what that means. But I do."

"Do you?" Grei asked, and he opened her with his magic. A scattered array of sensations washed over him: the rotting stench of ruthlessness overlaid with a fresh breeze of love for all women, especially her Ringblades. An imposing monolith stood in the middle of her. It was the purpose that gave her life meaning. It was the empire.

He saw Ree, huddled in a dark place, emaciated and dirty. Her right arm had been severed at the elbow. He saw Selicia gather up the young woman tenderly.

He saw the back of some man's head as Selicia silently reached around and cut his throat. This image repeated, many different men, many different times.

All to make the empire strong.

Grei gasped and pulled back. Selicia hovered over him now, and he used his connection to speak to her, to reach past her defenses. To bend her purposes to his own.

"The empire is on the brink," he said, just loud enough to carry to her.

Her eyes narrowed.

"You think you're doing right," he pressed. "But you're not. If you truly want to serve the empire, you'll help me."

Selicia paused as the magic influenced her.

Listen to me, he thought. *Do what I say.*

The three Highblades from downstream finally reached them, and they fanned out at a respectful distance, making sure Grei had nowhere to go.

"Ree knew," Grei pressed. "Did you listen to her?"

Selicia rose up, stunned.

"Help me, Selicia. Help us all."

Her nostrils flared, and she leaned forward. Something round and hard hit him just under his ribs. He coughed, doubling over. His connection to her vanished, and he tried to prop himself up with his good hand. Through blurry vision, he looked up at her.

"Your emperor wants to see you," she whispered, her mouth right next to his ear. "And no silver tongue will change that." Her scar was a furious red line down her face. Grei held up his burnt hand to ward off the next blow, but he never saw it coming.

Part III

Thiaran Masks

Chapter 22
KURUK

THE VICIOUS stab sliced into Kuruk's brain. It tore through the delicate balance, and the pounding surged. He staggered out of the cave, leaning on the wall. He couldn't see straight. He couldn't feel the ground beneath his feet.

The battle slipped from his control. For an excruciating moment, the Thiaran voices in his head broke free. Fire burst from his mouth, his eyes, his fingertips and his skin, lighting the pocked sides of the tunnel.

He ran up the shale slope, into the night, as though running would allow him to escape his own head, as though running would give him the strength he needed.

"No!" he shouted. He slammed his willpower down on the voices, stopped them, held them in, clenching his pointy teeth. He fell to his knees, and the rocks glowed beneath him.

His breath bathed the air in flames, and Kuruk struggled to his feet. He roared and charged up the slope, around the side until he stood atop the craggy tor, shouting his despair.

Malik.

The stab into his mind had been his brother's death.

Malik was gone.

Kuruk screamed his rage, fire roaring from his mouth into the sky. They were all betrayers! Vile murderers!

His rage took him back to the Thiarans' first betrayal, the slaying of seven innocents on this spot a century ago. He returned to the first time Malik had been murdered:

"Immortality," the old man whispered to Malik, running his fingers through the boy's blonde curls. "You will ensure the Thiaran Empire thrives forever. That is why you have been chosen. That is why you have been blessed."

"Where is my mother?" Malik asked in a small voice, his eyes wide.

"She sent you with me. She said she wanted you to be good, to listen to me, to help me with my problem."

Kuruk always knew when adults lied, and this man was lying. He had seen the violence. These men had killed Malik's mother, and the mothers of the other boys, too. There was supposed to be peace between Thiara and Benasca, but that was also a lie.

The six other old men lined Kuruk and the boys up like sheep. Their leader, a man they called Emperor Lyndion, took a glimmering sword from the sheath at his side and cut the air like it was an invisible blanket. Smoking red light poured out. Emperor Lyndion shouted strange words to the night. They were not Benascan words. They were not Thiaran words, either. They were words that sent spiders crawling up Kuruk's neck.

Malik cried for his mother, but Kuruk knew crying would do nothing against these men. Sometimes only fighting made a difference. Even if you were small and weak, sometimes you had to fight or you would die.

"You lie!" Kuruk shouted. He leapt at the emperor, clawing at the old man's face, trying to gouge an eye, but the emperor was too strong. He grabbed Kuruk's arm and brutally shoved him through the smoking red slit in the air.

"Liiiiiiiiie!" Kuruk's last word in this world stretched

like a scream, and then the fires consumed him.

Kuruk blinked the memory away. He brought himself under control, shutting the fire away within. The top of the hill plunged into darkness once more.

He had learned much in the last century, things he hadn't understood when Emperor Lyndion had killed him and his brothers. He knew that Lyndion had attempted to gain immortality by sacrificing them. Lyndion thought he was sending them to the realm of the dead. An exchange of souls. Young sacrificed for the old.

Except Lyndion had opened a rift to Velakka instead, a flaming realm with thousands of souls about which Lyndion knew nothing.

Kuruk had been the first to go, the first of his brothers to die. He had also been the first to be reborn at the hands of his master, Lord Velak. He and his followers had taken Kuruk in, remade him. Ironically, Kuruk's transformation had given him what Lyndion had so desperately sought: Immortality.

Velakka took Kuruk and his brothers, tormenting them, burning them, searing away their humanity. The seven children died a hundred deaths. But when the pain subsided, they remained, transformed into something new. For the next hundred years, Kuruk studied under Lord Velak, and when his master led him back to the rip, Kuruk and his brothers returned with power.

Power enough to wreak vengeance on Thiara.

The Tullawn Mountains hunched beneath the clouds, mimicking them in black. The wet air of this world bit at his skin, burned his lungs. When it rained, it stung him like needles. The oceans were vast tracts of death into which Kuruk could never go. The Thiarans had done this to him. They had torn his birthright away so completely that it hurt to even be here.

The human histories said Emperor Lyndion had died, but that was a lie, too. According to Lord Velak, Lyndion had found his way to the realm of the dead, had sacrificed more children to get there. No, Lyndion wasn't gone. The coward was hiding from Kuruk. And there would be enough time to go hunting once his brothers were safe.

Lord Velak wanted revenge upon all Thiarans; he wanted to engulf Thiara in Velakkan flames. He wanted more than the monthly sacrifice Kuruk made to him through the Blessed. He wanted Kuruk to battle the Faia and throw open the door, but Kuruk wanted his brothers back first. And that took time. Lord Velak raged at Kuruk's choice, but he was trapped behind the door slammed shut by the Faia. His only recourse was to accept what Kuruk sent to him.

For now, the Blessed grew in number, pacifying Lord Velak by putting more of his Velakkans in human bodies. When each one of Kuruk's brothers was safe in this world, Lord Velak would be paid. Not before.

And he was close. Soon, he could let go of all the pounding, clawing voices. Velakkan spirits now filled almost a hundred human forms, mating with them, producing progeny into which his brothers could be born. Kuruk would continue to open pathways into these bodies, until all of his brothers surfaced like Turoh had. It wouldn't be long now. It had happened once; it could happen for the rest.

He turned and made his way down the tor into the cave. He could not grieve for Malik now. Kuruk's grief could only come when his plan was complete, his brothers were safe, and the Thiarans bowed their heads to him.

It was time to end this Whisper Prince.

Chapter 23

GALIUS

THE FLYING hare sailed overhead. Its fur glinted white in the sunlight. Its giant ears cupped the wind and his long, feathered hind legs pointed straight back. It had been trailing them for an hour. Full-grown flying hares would eat flesh sometimes. Galius, watching it from below, wondered if it hoped for a meal.

The airborne rodents were unpredictable. They were generally mild, especially in large groups. A flock might scurry to hide from a child. But alone, flying hares were crazy. This one might do something as stupid as attack a fully armed caravan of Highblades.

Galius Ash trailed the procession, watching the hare finally choose the better part of valor and bank to the left, staying within the boundaries of the lush Lowlands as the Highblades' wagon prison entered the cracked ground of the Badlands.

It had been two days since Fairmist, and Selicia's pet Highblades had religiously kept Galius away from Adora's rolling cage. The bitch of a Ringblade hadn't wanted to take him at all, of course, but Galius had come up with a little luck there. The delegate ordered him to accompany them, and even Selicia could not deny him. It was a boon for which Galius was grateful, despite the delegate's reasons.

"You stay with them," the delegate had whispered before their departure. "Selicia will arrive in Thiara and claim she found the Whisper Prince. You make sure that the emperor knows that he wouldn't have his prize without you. Without me."

Galius had nodded stiffly, giving no indication that the delegate and his schemes made him ill. The delegate's only concern was receiving his due credit.

Galius' only concern was Adora.

He ached just thinking about her. She had woven a spell around him, and Galius had fallen hard. She was brazen, unashamed, and unrepentant in a land filled with women who stewed behind their petty desires and lacked the courage to show their true faces. Adora had lit a fire in his soul that he had never known before. If she was blameless in this strange business, he would see her freed. But if she had played him for a fool, he would see justice.

The last few days had been a whirlwind of action, secret agendas and half-truths, pieces of a puzzle Galius didn't fully understand. The Ringblade Selicia had arrived in Fairmist the night the delegate had sent them all searching for the Whisper Prince. The delegate seemed cowed by Selicia, and she immediately enlisted all of his local Highblades and put them under the command of her imperial Highblades.

Except who had ever heard of a Ringblade leading Highblades? Ringblades were a different order. They served stealth and deception. They fought as cowards, throwing their namesakes from a distance, attacking from the shadows. Ringblades kept secrets and withheld information, and Selicia was arrogant in her superiority, demanding obedience but giving no benefit to the loyal.

Still, the arrogant were prone to mistakes, and she had made one. Galius had his own secret now, a piece of the puzzle she wanted.

He felt the reassuring press of the sheath against his back, which held Blevins' magnificent sword. Galius had known its value from the moment he'd faced the fat man in Adora's room. When Selicia had ordered Galius to disarm Blevins, that is exactly what he'd done, but in her arrogance, she had overlooked the weapon. Only later did she call for it, but by then, Galius had made sure she would never have it.

It had taken Selicia most of the day to organize her rolling cage and finish her argument with the delegate, and Galius had used the time wisely. Instead of sleeping, he carefully painted Blevins' blade black, a nuance he'd used on all his swords over the last few years. With splints, a short cylinder of wood, and worn leather strips he had recently pulled from his favorite sword, Galius extended the grip another two inches and wrapped it tight. When the jeweled hilt disappeared beneath the sweat-stained leather, it looked like just another of Galius' swords.

And sure enough, the moment he returned to the palace to argue his way onto Adora's escort, Selicia demanded the sword.

Galius had made a good show for her, acting reluctant to obey the order. Resentful. The delegate had finally made him procure the weapon, and Galius handed her the richest sword he owned, his signature black paint cleaned away and the steel shining, all the while carrying Blevins' blade on his back.

She had barely glanced at the sword he offered, told him he could keep it, which meant she had been looking for Blevins' blade specifically. And that added more questions to the pile. What was so special about it? It was a wealthy man's weapon, no doubt, but also old, the style wider and shorter-handled than the standard Highblade longsword. It was the kind of heirloom you would expect to see on the wall at a lord's castle, some remembrance of a grandfather's exploits.

It begged to be in the hand, though. There was something about it that made Galius want to practice with it, to rush into battle with it. He itched to draw it even now.

Instead, he turned his gaze on the swaying rump of Vallyn's horse. Vallyn was his "partner" today, though they both knew he was actually Galius' guard. Yesterday it had been Highblade Bef.

Galius drew a patient breath and let it out. He could continue waiting. A swordsman parried, deflected, waited for his opening. He could see that Adora was unhurt, and that was enough for now. He had even seen Blevins' fat arm pointing an hour ago, so the big man was alive as well, which was a something of a miracle. Selicia had bounced her ringblade off his head. By all rights, he should be dead. He was a tough son of a bitch, that one.

As for the shoemaker's son, they were drugging him. Galius didn't know why. By his estimation, Blevins was the most dangerous of the three by far. What had Grei done at the palace? Surely a silver-tongued seducer wouldn't warrant such caution.

He let out a quiet sigh and looked over his shoulder, hoping that the flying hare had decided to follow after all, but the little beast was gone.

He blinked, focusing on remaining alert, waiting for the next bout of ill-treatment. He had been ordered to serve as rear guard every day. When they had camped last night, he had been ordered to search for firewood, and then take the long night watches until he was so exhausted he had had to sleep during the few hours they allowed him.

That, at least, was a battle Galius could understand. Let them try to grind him down. He was a Highblade. He was trained to overcome hardship and lived to serve the right. To protect the weak. To die for love.

He looked up from his thoughts to see Captain Delenne riding toward him. Galius straightened in his saddle.

Captain Delenne was a lesser legend among Highblades. The layman in Fairmist wouldn't know him, but he had made a name for himself in the northern wars against the pale-skinned Benascan savages. He was no Zed Hack or Jorun Magnus, but Nilus Delenne was a swordsman to be respected.

Under different circumstances, Galius felt he could have liked the captain.

"Come on, Fairmist," Delenne said, using the nickname the other Highblades had given him. He reached up and smoothed his long mustache on one side, then the other. "Time to make our first sweep for sand bandits."

Galius noted two other Highblades riding off in front of the procession. Vallyn moved closer to the rolling cages as the sixth Highblade dropped back to do the same. Selicia, who had ridden at the edge of the road to the north, closed in as well.

Galius wheeled his horse about and followed the captain. *Patience,* he thought. *Wait for your opening.*

Chapter 24
GREI

GREI BLINKED, groggy, and tried to remember where he was. He was in something moving, bouncing and jostling. A wagon with bars. He was bound at the elbows, just above the burned ruin of his right arm, which had been freshly bandaged, and his legs were bound at the ankles. Adora held his head in her lap, gently stroking his forehead.

The wagon had steel bars, and it trundled over cracked brown earth. A forest of burnt trunks stabbed upward like tusks all around them. Less than half a mile to the south, there was a living pine forest, dark and foreboding.

The front and rear of the wagon were solid wooden walls. There was the outline of a door in the back, and an iron clasp that was no doubt locked from the outside. Blevins sat with his back against the bars, half his face dark with dried blood.

The poem of the Whisper Prince had gone from Grei's mind, replaced by dark, indecipherable whispers. They sounded like murderers plotting a kill.

"You're okay," Adora murmured quietly. He could barely hear her over the creaking of the wagon. "Thank the

Faia. I was worried."

"Where are we?" he asked, trying to lick his lips, but his mouth was dry.

"Captured," she said.

"The Ringblade," he said, remembering the two fierce strikes with which Selicia had driven him into unconscious.

"Yes."

"It feels like a dozen hammers are tapping on my head," Grei said. "And my tongue feels huge."

"You've been drugged," Adora said.

He moved his tongue around, trying to get the metallic taste off, but it was no use.

His burnt arm was wrapped in bandages. He couldn't feel it. There was only the vague sense of weight at the end of his elbow. It made him sick to think about it.

"Where are they taking us?" he asked.

"Thiara," she said. "That's my guess. Selicia is the Ringblade champion. She'll bring you to the emperor."

The pain in his head was receding. Now it only felt like six hammers tapping. "We're in the Badlands," he said.

"Yes," she replied.

He started to sit up, but she kept a firm hand on his chest, kept him flat. "If you move, she'll see, and they'll drug you again," she said quietly. "Lie still."

He eased back onto her lap. It wasn't a bad place to be. "Okay."

"We've been on the road for three days. In the Badlands for half a day," she said.

"And now that the prince is awake, it is time to escape," Blevins said.

"If you're a crazy fat man," she said curtly.

Blevins grunted.

"There is nowhere to go," she continued, as though they'd been arguing about this for some time. "We wait until the Felesh plantations."

"Every second you wait is a second you don't have," Blevins said. "We killed a slink. The last time we did that, they chased us all the way to Fairmist. They are hunting us, and they will find us. Do you think these Highblades will stand for five seconds against them?" He shook his head. "It's the luck of the Faia that they haven't found us already."

"Charging into the Dead Woods is no escape," Adora said. "It's suicide."

"Then we take their horses," Blevins said. "Four of the complement are away. If we face them by twos, we have a chance. Now is the time."

Grei turned his gaze to the trees. Deadly whispers slithered through his mind. Instead of whispering of growth, sunlight and deep roots, those trees whispered violence.

He had heard of the Dead Woods, of course. The legends grew larger every year. When he was a boy, this entire area, Badlands and Dead Woods alike, was the Vheysin Forest. But after a terrible fire, all that remained were charred trunks and that stand of frightening pine trees, now called the Dead Woods.

The fire had been five years ago, and not a single blade of grass had grown back. Every year that passed without growth on that cracked earth was one more year of superstitious whispers. Farmers and travelers became ever more fearful. Traders were paid more and more to ferry goods across.

The Vheysin Forest had once been a popular place to hunt for game. It had been full of deer, flying hares and pheasant, but no one dared hunt in the Dead Woods now. They seethed fury. Travelers who passed through the Badlands tried to avert their eyes. The pines, with their cracked bark and hungry needles, looked ready to impale anyone who dared come close. No one who went into the Dead Woods ever came out again.

"We can't let the emperor have him," Blevins was saying. Grei blinked, trying to ignore the ugly whispers and focus on the argument again. "Making an escape in Felesh is a fool's gambit. Once you reach the plantations, two dozen Highblades will join this escort. Better to face the unknown than certain capture."

"It's not unknown," she said. "Those who enter the Dead Woods die. No one has ever emerged."

"You won't get a better chance," Blevins pressed.

"You don't care if he dies!" she hissed. "He's not going into the Dead Woods."

Blevins snorted and gave up, turned his head away. "It doesn't matter," he muttered, closing his eyes. "Nothing matters."

"What if he's right?" Grei asked. Despite their malice, the forbidding pines drew him. There was power there, and...sentience.

She frowned down at him. "He's not right. He's an idiot—" She looked suddenly to the side. "Close your eyes!" she hissed.

Grei closed his eyes. Selicia whistled loudly and rode her horse up alongside them. The other two Highblades closed in, dismounted and drew their short swords.

"You are awake," the Ringblade said quietly, as though she was talking to herself and not to them. She signaled something to the driver. The wagon creaked to a stop. Selicia kicked a leg over and dropped from her horse.

Grei opened his eyes and sat up, pushing past Adora's protective hands. The charade was over.

"You're an interesting one," Selicia said. "That should not have worn off until tonight."

One of the Highblades poked his sword through the bars and leveled it at Adora's neck. She glared at him, but kept still. The other put his sword at Blevins' neck. With a frown, Blevins closed his eyes as though taking a nap.

"Take this and no one gets cut," Selicia said, pulling a water skin from inside her cloak. She held it out to him.

"Why drug me?" he asked.

Her thin mouth turned up at the edges. Grei supposed it was a smile, but her scar twisted it into a grimace. "Because I felt you inside my head, 'Prince'. Play the proper prisoner, and your friends don't have to die. Drink it."

He took the water skin, twisted the cork, and closed his eyes. The whispers of the Dead Woods were loud and insistent, calling to him, but he tried to listen past them. He tried to hear the quieter voices.

Like the swords the Highblades held.

"Bend," Grei whispered.

There was a wrench inside him and a heaviness on his head as though a stone had been laid there. The Highblades shouted. Sharp steel twisted around the bars, safely pointing away from Blevins and Adora.

Grei blinked his eyes open. His mind was cloudy, and for a moment, his vision blurred. The whispers faded.

Selicia drew her short sword and lunged forward. He squeezed the water skin through the bars right into her face. The drug splashed into her eyes and nose. With a grunt, she spun. Her blade rang on the steel bars.

"The lock, my prince," Blevins said. "Quickly."

Grei could barely think. His head felt too heavy for his shoulders. What had happened to him?

"Lock," he murmured. It took him a second to realize what Blevins was saying. Steel rang on scabbards as the shocked Highblades drew their longswords.

"Grei!"

He fought to hear the whispers, but they were distant. "Water," he said, reaching out to the to the lock on the other side of the door. It dripped down the wood and Blevins rammed his shoulder against it. The door burst open.

"Run!" he roared, leaping to the ground. A sword sliced past him, somehow missing him and thudding into the wood. Blevins grabbed the man's fist and wrenched. Bones snapped. The Highblade gagged and released his weapon. Now Blevins had a sword.

"Blevins!" Grei shouted. The big man pulled the sword from the wood and swung. The arc was tight and powerful. It sliced completely through the Highblade's thigh. The man screamed and fell over. Blood sprayed the cage and the ground.

Grei gasped, feeling the man's agony like a hammer on his chest. The Highblade's screams filled the air as his life poured onto the ground.

"Don't kill them!" he shouted at Blevins.

"Go, Grei!" Adora said, shoving him.

Hobbled, he hopped awkwardly out of the wagon and fell to his knees. He forgot what he had been doing. His head was filled with mud. But then he remembered. They were escaping.

"I can't think," he said thickly.

Adora leapt down beside him and hauled on his arm, pulling him upright. Steel rang as Blevins deflected the second Highblade's strike. The third shouted, running toward the battle.

"He can't kill them!" Grei said to her. "Please—"

"Onto the horse," Adora said, grabbing the reins of the dying Highblade's mount. The horse raised its head and whinnied, snapping at her hand. She jumped back.

Grei moved to help her when she suddenly cried out and fell to her knees. Chains and steel balls wrapped tight around her legs. It was the same weapon Selicia had used on Grei at the falls. He spun around to see the Ringblade moving sluggishly toward them. Her shoulders slumped as though she could barely stand upright, but she held a short sword tightly in her fist. She put two fingers to her lips and let out a piercing whistle.

Grei dropped to his knees. His elbows were still bound, his bandaged arm tight together with his healthy one. Selicia rose over him.

"Water," he whispered, not even hearing the ground's whispers, but knowing the change he wanted. He forced his will upon it.

A ripple went out from his hand like the cracked earth was a lake. Selicia dropped straight down. She threw her sword as she fell, and it stuck point first an inch from his hands.

For a moment, he couldn't even remember his own name.

It was as though his intelligence had leaked away. He stared at the vibrating sword next to him. After what seemed like an eternity, he heard shouting.

"Grei! Get up! Ride!" the voice screamed. He turned and saw her, the lovely woman. Adora. Her name was Adora. Her knees were bound, and she pulled herself toward him.

"I can't think," he murmured. "I...I've lost..."

Grei felt another thudding strike inside his chest, and a man's scream split the air. He looked up, saw the last Highblade slide off the long, bloody sword held by a giant man whose name he couldn't remember.

"Stop," he murmured, bowing his head.

"Get to the horse!" Adora commanded, rolling toward him. "The others are coming. There are four more. We can't fight them all." She grabbed the blade Selicia had thrown and sliced through the ropes that bound his arms, then his ankles.

"Leave you?" he said.

She sawed at her own bindings, but they were chains, and the sword wouldn't cut them. Grei's ears felt like they were filled with cotton. There were no whispers. He tried to hear them, but he couldn't.

"I'm not leaving you," he said. Selicia spluttered to the surface of the dirt lake. Her face was covered with mud, and her hands slapped at the top, trying to find purchase. She went under again.

Adora grabbed Grei's tunic and twisted it in her fist. "You are going to leave me," she said in a quiet voice. "They won't hurt me. They'll keep us to bait you back. Run and you have choices. Stay and you have none. Trust me."

His mind was still so cloudy. He just shook his head. "Adora—"

The giant killer man appeared around the corner of the wagon, spattered with blood. Blevins. His name was Blevins. He grabbed the reins of the skittish horse and spoke a sharp command in Venishan. It quieted instantly.

"Listen to the girl," he said.

"I won't leave her, Blevins," he said. "I love her."

Blevins rolled his eyes and let his stolen sword fall to the ground. He grabbed Grei with bloody hands and flung him onto the back of the horse. Blevins slapped its flank and barked another order in Venishan. The horse leapt forward. Grei clung to its mane with his good hand to keep from falling.

"Not towards the Dead Woods!" Adora shouted.

Blackened trunks whipped past Grei as the horse ran. The reins dangled from its mouth, swinging back and forth. Grei fought to keep his seat. To his left, between the burnt trunks, two riders approached the wagon, clouds of dust rising behind them. He looked to the right and saw two more.

Blevins had his sword again, and he walked deliberately toward the two Highblades closing in on him. Grei could also see the wagon master running away from the wagon for all he was worth.

I've got to help, he thought. *There has to be an answer—*

Suddenly, Selicia surfaced from the earth lake, yanking herself onto the hard bank and rolling free. She sprang to her feet, clumps of dirt falling from her.

Grei yanked on the horse's mane, but the beast kept pounding between the burnt trunks, heading toward the pines. He swiveled back.

Selicia leapt toward Adora, who raised the sword. The Ringblade crouched, dodged, and kicked out viciously. Adora's head snapped back, and she crumpled.

"No!" Grei shouted.

Like a dancer, Selicia spun out of the kick into a dead run, unhooking her Ringblade from her belt. She went five paces, drew back her arm and threw. Sun glinted off steel as the ring shot between the trees. Grei was at least two hundred paces away, but it sank deep into his mount's back leg. The horse screamed and lurched, catapulting him into the air. He threw his hands up over his head and smashed into the ground, tumbling to a stop at the base of a charred trunk.

Dazed, he lay there. His ears were ringing, and he tried to shake his befuddlement. Dust rose all around. The horse was screaming, thrashing on the ground. Before him, the scabrous pines of the Dead Woods loomed.

Grei grunted and pushed himself to his knees. His whole body ached, warning him to move slowly. He looked back. The riders had almost reached Blevins. Selicia was closer, still sprinting, arms pumping at her sides. She was almost to the screaming horse. The woman was unstoppable. And Adora...

They'll keep us to bait you back. Run and you have choices. Stay and you have none.

Staggering to his feet, he plunged into the Dead Woods.

Chapter 25

GREI

ARKNESS DROPPED over him like the sun had set, thick limbs cutting off the daylight. He sprinted through the trees, dry branches striking his face, his arms. He ran until his lungs and legs burned.

Gasping for breath, he stopped and put his hands on his knees. Sinister whispers slithered through his mind, growing louder, then softer, then louder. Dry pine needles covered the forest floor, and he couldn't see the bright Badlands anymore.

He would double back, come up with a plan as soon as he could think clearly. His clouded head was slowly returning to normal. What had happened to him at the wagon? The moment he'd used his magic, it had made him stupid. It had never done that before. His mind had dulled until he could barely keep hold of his own name. What had changed?

Something moved ahead, and Grei sank to a crouch behind a tree.

Selicia flitted from one shadow to the next, barely visible. She breathed smoothly and evenly as though she hadn't just sprinted a mile. He tried to keep his own breathing silent, but her dark gaze fell on him.

"You're full of surprises, Master Forander," she said.

"I work hard at it."

He kept close to the tree in case she threw something.

She opened her hands in a peaceful gesture and stopped twenty feet away from him. She did not make any threatening movements, but he didn't believe her posturing for a second. He'd seen how fast she had crossed the distance from the caravan to the Dead Woods, and she was barely out of breath. "I don't want to hurt you," she said.

"That's what I want, too. Let's work together." Grei's eye began to twitch.

"Very well."

"Set my friends free."

A glimmer in one of her open hands drew him, and there was suddenly a dagger there. These Ringblades and their hidden daggers. Where had it come from?

"You're very convincing, Master Forander. I felt you in my head at the falls, persuading me. If I feel you again, I will do what I must."

Grei was overmatched. His only weapon against her was magic, but he wasn't going to use it until he figured out why his mind had gone numb. He tried to buy time.

"You said the emperor wants to see me. Why?" he asked. He squinched his twitching eye shut, then opened it again, forcing it to stop.

"I think you know why," she said.

So much for that. "I didn't know that Ringblades—"

The whispers of the trees suddenly became screams, stabbing his ears. He shouted and put his hands to his head.

"Wait!" He held up a hand to Selicia.

Behind her and all around, the forest suddenly filled with shadows shaped like people. They crept into sight, hundreds of them. Angry eyes glowed in blurred faces. Greens and browns flowed over their black bodies.

The screams vibrated into one, clear tone.

"Kill them."

Selicia leapt at Grei, taking advantage of his helplessness, oblivious to the horde around them.

The shadows expanded in silent puffs of smoke, their bodies elongating across the distance. Arms turned into claws. The nearest flew into Selicia and passed through her.

She cried out, the flat pommel of her dagger missing Grei by inches. She stumbled past him and crashed to the ground.

A shadow flowed through Grei's chest, and its claws raked inside his body, slashing his heart, his lungs, his bowels. He screamed and fell to his knees. Images washed through him. He saw trees burning, and they keened pitifully as they were consumed. All that was left were these angry spirits.

The sudden agony vanished. Grei fell forward onto his hands and knees. His entire body was covered with sweat. He heard Selicia's growl as she fought the pain.

"We haven't come to hurt the forest!" Grei gasped. Sweat dripped down his forehead, and the figure rose up before him. The closest shadow formed into the smoky shape of a woman, standing with hands spread wide, about to grab him. Her shifting skin matched the tree to her left.

"He hears us," she said.

"He sees us," another echoed.

"Humans do not hear us," a third hissed.

"Please, we're not here to hurt your trees!" he shouted again.

"We *are* the trees, manling," the woman said. Her form solidified. She cocked her hips, resting her hands there. The mannerism was hauntingly familiar, but he could distinguish no features on her shadowy face.

"We don't want to hurt you," he said again, trying to catch his breath.

"That is a lie," she said.

The other shadows began to take shape again, standing over Selicia, who trembled as she clambered upright. She held the dagger in front of her, but not in the right direction. She turned slowly, looking for her attackers.

"Kill them," one of the shadow women said.

But none of the others moved. They seemed to be waiting for the one who had attacked Grei, who stood closest to him.

"Wait," she said.

Wails of suffering went up from some of the shadows. The sound was so sharp that Grei bowed his forehead to the ground, pressing his hands against his ears.

"He hears us. He hears our pain," the leader said.

"Kill them!" the voice behind Grei insisted. Grei craned his neck about. This shadow woman was not as clearly defined. Her glowing yellow eyes were larger.

The leader moved toward him, hips swinging, and again he was struck with familiarity. He knew that walk. She stopped in front of him, her skirt swishing as she leaned over him.

Her smoky features solidified into Adora's face. Light fingers touched him, slithering down over his head like warm oil.

He felt no pain. Everything went dark.

Chapter 26

ADORA

ADORA AWOKE and the pain became real, swelling from a dull ache in the back of her head to a sharp throb in her forehead. She sucked in a breath through her teeth. Her cheek felt like it had been cracked open.

"Grei," she murmured. She opened her eyes, trying to see where she was. The Badlands were gone. She squinted into the dark, cool room. The floor and walls were rough-hewn planks of wood. It smelled like dirt and potatoes, and scant light trickled in from somewhere behind her.

Her wrists were bound with a length of rope, and she lay on a straw-stuffed pad. She started to sit up, and the pain jangled in her skull. She stopped. Lying down was fine. Lying down was good.

Gingerly, she reached up to touch her cheek. There was a thick bandage there, and her head felt cold. She ran her fingers into her hair—

Only to touch the scratch of stubble.

She gasped, frantically touching her shorn scalp. There was nothing but tufts of hair and patches of bare skin. She yanked her hands back, and they fluttered like butterflies over her belly.

Why? Why would they do that?

Trembling, she reached up and touched her head again. They had hacked it all off. There was nothing left.

She pressed her eyelids shut and took a long, shuddering breath. It was only hair, she told herself. Only hair. Grei was the important thing.

"Are you in pain?"

She choked on a sob and swallowed her emotions, looked toward the door.

"Galius," she said hoarsely, and levered herself onto an elbow. Her lanky paramour leaned against the doorway, watching her with an expression she could not decipher. Anger? Concern? He moved toward her and crouched down.

"I have something for the pain," he said, steadying her as she sat up. "Take this. It will help." He put a little leather pouch into her bound hands. Her knuckles were dirty, caked with dried blood.

"Poison to finish the job?" she asked, forcing the pouch open. It contained white powder.

He ignored the question, silent for a moment, then said, "Was it all a farce, Adora? You and me?"

She met his gaze. "No," she murmured, then looked away. *Not all of it. It wasn't supposed to be like this.*

He watched her, suspicious, then he nodded at the pouch. "Take some, please. For your sake."

"Did you do this for my sake, too?" Her fingers hovered over her scalp, but she didn't have the heart to touch it.

"It was that crazy swordsman of yours," he said angrily. "He's mad as a jackal. I bounced my sword off his head while he was bent over you."

"Blevins was fighting *you*," she said. She had almost said "Jorun". She had to be careful. There were so many secrets, and Galius was a perceptive man.

"And he killed three of us. When Nilus and I reached him, he was sawing at you with a knife. I thought he had killed you. Nilus and I put him down."

Adora could not imagine the reason for the farce. Was he telling the truth?

"Blevins cut off my hair?" she asked.

"Who is he, Adora? Who can best three imperial Highblades like that? I fought him. I've never met anyone so strong. And he's... He's grotesquely obese. How can he even use a blade the way he does?"

What reason could Blevins possibly have for cutting her hair? It didn't make sense.

Then it hit her. Blevins knew they would take her back to Thiara. So he had cut away the evidence of her heritage. Her telltale Doragon hair would have given her away in an instant at the capital. He had spent his last moments protecting her.

"Where is he?" she asked in a whisper.

"Upstairs. Dying. I cracked his skull when I hit him. He has three gut wounds. It won't be long."

"I see."

"He murdered Highblades, Adora. It's an execution for him either way. He deserves to die."

Adora would have agreed with Galius an hour ago. But her emotions about Blevins were mixed now. In Thiara, this shaved head might save her life.

"Will you tell me what is going on, Adora?" Galius asked softly.

"Where are you keeping Grei?" she turned the conversation.

Galius frowned. "He and Selicia ran into the Dead Woods."

"No!" She jerked upright, fighting against the sudden dizziness. The room swayed and she slapped the wall to keep her balance. She couldn't breathe. "He wouldn't do that," she said, hating that she was wrong. Of course he would. That was exactly what he would do.

"Please tell me what you know, Adora," Galius said. "I want to believe you aren't a part of all this—whatever this is—but..." he trailed off.

She tried to keep her face neutral, but the despair was ice water in her veins. Grei was dead. The hope for the empire. The Whisper Prince. He was gone. The prophecy was over.

Galius touched her arm. "I'm sorry about your friend—"

"He was my lover," she lied to him, lashing him with the pain she felt. *I have failed! Seven years, and this is how it ends.*

Galius stiffened. They sat near each other in silence.

"You should talk to me," he said. "There's no reason for you to keep silent."

"Go away, Galius." She didn't want his barrage of questions. She could barely hold the tears back, and she wouldn't cry in front of him. "Just go."

He shook his head. "What do you think they're going to do to you when they get you to the imperial city, Adora? How do you picture this will end? Thiara is not the safe haven we're used to in Fairmist. They're going to ask you these same questions, and when you don't answer them, they're going to peel the skin from your body until you scream the answers, until you—" He choked on the words and stopped, bowed his head.

"Some things are more important than my life," she whispered.

"I am trying to help you," Galius said.

"Then cut these bonds and let me go."

He looked at her, his jaw clenched. "I can't do that. The emperor commands your presence. But if you come clean..." He paused, and he looked at her hopefully. "If you tell them the truth, Adora, then there's a chance. Just tell them that you aren't a part of whatever is happening here. I will vouch for you."

She lay back down and turned her head to the wall.

"So that's it?" he asked.

"You've made your decision, Galius. What else is there?"

"They'll torture you!"

"I don't care," she said.

"You will," he snapped. He stomped to the door, but

paused. "I don't know what your game is. I thought you and I were..." He trailed off, his voice thick. "What could possibly be your reason for keeping silent?"

The door opened and thumped shut.

She licked her finger, dipped it in the white powder and put it on her tongue. It was bitter, but she swallowed it anyway.

She closed her eyes, letting the despair take her. It was over. It was all over.

She awoke later. Lemon light shone through the little window, high on the boarded wall. She didn't know if it was the same day or a new one. The pain in her head was improved. She sat up and took more of Galius' miracle cure.

She was testing the strength of the rope when the door opened.

Galius entered, a steaming plate in one hand, a cup in the other. The plate had a browned chicken leg and two biscuits. Adora's stomach rumbled at the sight, and she swallowed the saliva that filled her mouth. She looked up at him.

"Is this the beginning of the interrogation?" she asked, eyeing the food.

"You think I'm your enemy. I'm not." He approached, set the plate and cup down at her feet and backed up a pace. She looked at it but didn't touch it.

He shook his head. "It's not drugged or poisoned, Adora, any more than the medicine I gave you. I never lied to you, and I'm not lying now. I am everything I said I was. *You're* the one who isn't."

She pulled the plate toward her, took a ravenous bite of the chicken, and the meaty tang filled her mouth. Nothing had ever tasted so good. She devoured everything without a word, picking the bone clean. Galius waited, leaning patiently against the door.

Finally, she pushed the plate away. He watched her, like

he wanted to say something, but decided against it.

"How is Blevins?" she asked.

"The same."

"What happens now?"

"I take you to the emperor."

A thrill of fear raced through her, but she kept it from her face. "I've always wanted to see Thiara," she managed in a monotone.

He shook his head. "Why won't you just—"

A knock sounded on the short door. Galius looked annoyed, then opened it. A wiry old man shuffled in, bearing a small tub half full of water. He set it down, left, then returned with a large, steaming kettle, a scrub brush, soap and a towel. He also left a long tunic and belt for her, then departed without a word.

Adora looked at the tub with longing. She suddenly felt the dirt on her, the dried sweat of exertion and the stink of fear, the blood. She longed for the tub almost as much as she had the food. She looked at Galius.

"I know how much you love to bathe," he said. "I thought you might..." He shrugged, approached her and, drawing his dagger, sliced through the rope that bound her hands. "Go ahead."

She rubbed her wrists as she glanced at the tub, then frowned at him. "With you watching?"

"That's right."

She crossed her arms. "No."

He shook his head. "Don't mistake this for freedom. I'm doing what I can for you. But you're an imperial prisoner. I'm not leaving you alone, unfettered."

"And I'm not undressing in front of you."

"Again, you mean?"

She clenched her teeth. "I did what I had to do."

"Is that what it was?" he asked.

"Galius..." she started, trying to think of a way to explain without revealing anything. She came up blank. *It was supposed to be simple, you and me. A fleeting moment for a girl who cannot have anything of her own.*

She looked at the bath again.

"It's your choice," he said. "We can go as you are."

She paused, then went resolutely to the tub, poured the hot water in with the cold and began undressing. She tried to forget he was in the room and stepped into the basin. It was too small to sit down comfortably, but she could crouch. She washed herself quickly and efficiently. There were red, striped welts behind her knees where Selicia's flying chains had bound her, and they stung in the soapy water.

When she was done, she touched the bandage under her eye. With careful fingers, she unwrapped it. The pain wasn't nearly as bad as it had been before, and she gingerly probed the wound. It was feverish and swollen, and the skin had split about half an inch along her cheekbone.

"He hit you hard," Galius said. "Perhaps with the pommel of his dagger. The man is phenomenally strong."

"Blevins didn't do this," she said. "Selicia kicked me."

His eyebrows rose in surprise, but he didn't say anything. She methodically washed away the grime.

"I'm lost, Adora," he muttered suddenly, and she looked up. He gazed at the floor, and all of his Highblade certainty was gone. His voice was low. "Last week, I was First Sword of the City. I was in love with the most amazing woman in the empire. I thought she loved me back. And since that moment, I've been humbled by a fat man, commanded by a Ringblade, and I've discovered my lover is in love with a criminal." He looked away, as though he could see through the boarded wall of the cellar, then focused on her again. "I don't understand any of this. Does Grei truly have one of the emperor's artifacts? Is that how he did it?"

She shook her head gently, and for a moment he seemed hopeful that she was answering his question. Then he frowned.

"They'll force it out of you," he said. "Why not just tell me?"

"I can't."

He sighed. "Did you feel anything for me, Adora?" he asked softly. "Sometimes I think you did, but then..." he trailed off. "Can you answer that question, at least?"

It took her a long moment. Lyndion would demand she keep her lips closed. "Yes," she said quietly. "But I can't..." She shook her head. "I'm sorry, Galius."

She looked away, reached up to touch her hair. It was a hacked mess of stubble and tufts, like her life. *Oh Grei,* she thought. *I failed you. I failed everyone.*

"It can't be salvaged," Galius said, and the sadness in his voice made her turn back to him. He had loved her hair, had loved to bury his hands in it. "There simply isn't enough of it." He opened his hand, revealing a long razor. She wondered if he had been holding it the entire time.

"For shaving," he said. "It's mine."

She swallowed, slowly nodded. "Give it to me."

"I'm sorry, Adora. No."

"Galius—"

"I'm not giving you a weapon. But I'll do it for you."

They watched each other across the distance for a long moment.

"Okay," she said.

He came to her. Her naked skin prickled as he left her line of sight, crossed behind her.

"Kneel down," he said in a soft voice. "I'll be quick."

She did, and he took the soap, lathered his hand and spread it across her scalp.

"They say—" he began. He cleared his throat. "I've heard this is a fashion in Thiara. A shaved head. For some."

She pressed her lips together. It hurt her, just hearing him talk, knowing she must deny him something as simple as answers. He deserved them, if anyone did. She had been horrible to him. He was a good man, and she had used him.

But there were more important things happening than a Highblade's feelings. She couldn't let them take her to Thiara in chains.

She wondered if she could grab his dagger from his belt

while his hands were busy. He might gash her while she jumped away, but then she'd have a weapon.

And do what? Dripping wet with a dagger against Galius Ash? And even if she could somehow manage to overpower him, what would she do then? Would she—

"Adora," he said, interrupting her thoughts as though he could hear them. "Please don't try anything. I don't want to hurt you."

She cleared her throat. "Then don't."

"Okay."

He began shaving. It was the oddest sensation having cold steel scrape against her head. Steel on skin on skull. Again and again. Little clumps of hair fell into the water around her knees. She clenched her teeth and let it happen. He was proficient; it didn't take long.

He scooped water onto her head, and it washed over her. Her cheek stung.

"Stand up," he said. As he came around to her front, he stole glances at her breasts and hips, then grabbed a pitcher of water.

"I can do that," she said.

"Not as well as I can." He poured the water gently over her head, rinsing away the soap and hair. He walked around her, inspecting and pouring until she was completely rinsed, then he set the pitcher on the floor and went back to stand by the door.

She dried herself and pulled the tunic over her head, belted it at the waist. It was long enough to form a short skirt. Simple peasant clothing. She may as well have stayed naked, the way he looked at her. He still wanted her, beat-up and shaved and all. She could use that.

"I must be a sight," she said, gingerly dabbing at her wound with the towel.

"It's not that bad," he said.

"I'm bald and disfigured, Galius. I'm wearing a sack."

"And still the most beautiful woman in the empire," he said. "The hair will grow back."

She was silent; she hated how his words warmed her.

"Thank you," she said softly. "For the bath. For everything."

"You are welcome."

She stepped toward him, reached out and touched him on the arm. His gaze lingered on her, and she let the silence build. He raised his chin and swallowed.

"Let me go, Galius," she whispered. She glanced toward the small window. "I could fit. Help me, and I could get away."

The muscles in his jaw flexed, and she saw his conflict.

"Please," she said. "I will meet you later, back in Fairmist."

His hand closed over hers, and she felt his warmth, his strength. Slowly, intentionally, he took her hand from his arm and placed it at her side.

"I'm a Highblade, Adora. I serve the emperor."

"I see. Love only goes so far," she said.

"But betrayal lasts forever," he replied.

She glanced away, stung. She tried to look bored. "What now?"

"We ride."

"In this?" She pulled at the thin tunic. "I'll be raw meat by the time we arrive."

"You can wear your dirty clothes, if you like."

"Can we wash them?"

"There isn't time. You can bring them."

"Where are the other Highblades?"

"Pazzek and Captain Delenne are watching Blevins. They will stay here until he dies. I'll take you on alone."

"Can I see him?"

"Only for a moment," he said. "Then we ride."

He bound her again, tying her wrists together with rope, then made her walk in front of him. They were in the cellar of a small house, and he led her upstairs to the main room where Blevins lay on the floor. The big man's face was white with a splash of red across his cheeks and nose. A bandage, black with blood, wrapped his enormous belly, and he wasn't moving. For a moment, she thought he was already dead, then she heard his shallow breathing. She didn't know what to feel. There had been days she had burned him in her mind, that she had longed to see him suffer as she had suffered when he'd abandoned her. She turned away from him.

A Highblade leaned against the wall, a leg cocked behind him. He had a bandage around his head, too, a trickle of dried blood down his temple. He glared at her.

"We're leaving," Galius said.

"Go to hell, Fairmist," the man growled.

"Where is Captain Delenne?"

"Finishing the graves," the Highblade spat. He continued to stare at Adora as though he wanted to stab her.

Galius kept himself between Adora and the Highblade and led her into the yard. "You'll ride in front of me," he said, approaching his black horse.

"Won't that be fun," she muttered.

Chapter 27
GREI

A DORA!" GREI jerked awake, then blinked against the intense white light. The brightness receded, and she was there, hovering over him. Her tumbling black and gold hair hung low, framing her face—

Yellow light flickered in her eyes.

He scrambled back. This thing was not Adora. It was a seething Dead Woods spirit wearing her face.

Bright light emanated from white trees all around him. More of the spirits stood between the trunks, all of them dressed in long brown skirts, white tunics, half-boots. All with Adora's face.

"He sees a familiar face," one of them said.

"He sees what he wants to see," said another.

"He should not see us at all."

The closest Adora approached him. Her movements were Adora's, the swing of her hips, the way she crossed her arms. But her scent gave her away. This creature smelled of pine trees and grass.

"What are you going to do?" she asked.

"I don't know what you mean."

She tossed her hair, then bored into him with her yellow gaze. "We do not keep prisoners, manling," she said.

"My name is Grei."

"Humans poison their own grove. We name you pestilence."

"Do you serve the Faia?" Grei asked. The white trees called to him, their whispers more gentle yet more powerful than the angry pines. This was what had drawn him when he looked at the Dead Woods from Baezin's Road. These trees were charged, like the air before a storm.

"Not since your leader took Her from us," she said. She leaned over him. He tried to see through her, see the truth. It didn't work.

"How can you see us, manling? How do you hear us?"

"I don't know," he said.

The Adoras wailed, and he winced. The sound drove into his ears.

"Kill him."

"Kill him."

"Kill him."

The lead Adora was fierce. Her yellow eyes glowed brighter, casting shadows down her face that made her nose and chin seem longer. "Your leader took life from the earth and sky," she said. "He ripped a hole in the land and took the Faia, leaving an empty crust in Her place. Hundreds died, their lives uprooted to give power to one human. And you and your kind walk upon what is left. You ride back and forth on your enslaved beasts and pretend not to notice what you have done."

"I didn't—"

"The Faia tried to join with you, but you have chosen the Lord of Rifts."

"You said our leader. You're talking about the emperor," Grei said, trying to puzzle together her furious words.

"You alone can hear us. See us. You can speak and remake elements like a Faia. What will you do with it?"

Several of the Adoras came closer. Their hands gripped his arms. He pulled against them, but they were strong. They lifted him effortlessly and took him to an enormous white tree. It towered into the sky overhead. Its limbs looked like slender arms, and the fat white leaves were leeched of color; only the very edges were a pale yellow.

The Adoras slammed him against the smooth trunk, and the leader approached him, looked into his eyes. She whispered something, and the twisting words burned.

The tree became soft as mud, and the Adoras shoved him backwards.

"Hey!" he shouted, fighting them.

They let go, and the wood became solid, biting into his flesh like a thousand needles. He screamed. Hard fingers grasped his brow and cheeks and shoved his head in.

His bones splintered. His heart ruptured. His eyes melted to water.

He died, and then the pain receded. Somehow, Grei could think again.

He felt the slow creep of water inside the trunk, hundreds of tiny vessels carrying nutrients up from a thousand fingers in the earth. The leaves reached toward the great blue overhead, tasting the air, drawing life from the sun. He felt the connection to every tree in this forest, felt its pervasive force. It bound them all together, giving them strength.

He saw the memories of the trees.

Two men stood at the edge of the forest. One was powerfully large, muscles laid over muscles. His face was angular, the jaw chiseled as if from stone, and he had a thick mane of black hair. His chest was broad, his waist narrow. His arms were thick in the shoulders and biceps, slimming down at his bronze forearms. His leathery, scarred hands looked like they could crush a human head with one squeeze. He wore a breastplate and loose red pants, and his midnight eyes glittered. That man could lift a horse onto his shoulders and not wince. He could make an army of swordsmen drop their weapons and flee. He was the emperor's champion, Jorun Magnus.

The emperor was almost as tall as Magnus, but slender, and he had a three-pointed beard. The emperor was not the ultimate Highblade like his champion, but he had an air of command. He wore red-and-gold riding clothes and in his left hand he held a dirty brown net. He stared at the forest as though he would see through to the other side, and he whispered something. The whisper formed a brown bubble at the emperor's mouth, then detached, swirling and pulsing. It floated toward the trees, carrying the whispers around it and throwing brown light outward in streaks. The whispers transformed into a guttural song. The emperor held up the net in both hands. Brown light emanated from it, shooting between the trees.

Screams erupted, a thousand anguished voices. Yellow fire leapt from tree to tree, all coming to the net, but it was not a normal fire. This fire drew the life from the trees. They withered and burned as the heart of them was drawn out and pulled into the net.

The emperor was unmaking the world. A yellow Faia swirled at the center of the conflagration, buffeted by flames, disoriented, reaching out desperately to stop herself.

When the emperor was done, the forest had become the desolate, charred Badlands that Grei had seen from the wagon. At the emperor's feet knelt the tiny Faia, wrapped tightly in the net. The emperor pulled a steel rod from his belt, pointed it at her brow—

Grei staggered forward. The tree released him and he fell to his knees, gasping at the sudden absence of fire and fury. He touched the soft grass with his good hand, blinked with eyes that had not turned to water.

"He killed a Faia," Grei gasped, feeling the horror throughout his body. The bones over his eyes ached. His arms and back itched as though thick oil had been poured over them. "He unmade a piece of the world."

"The Lord of Rifts would rip out the roots of the world, and you humans rush to help him," she said.

"I'm sorry," he whispered. "I'm so sorry."

They watched him, seething, waiting. Finally, Grei asked, "Who is the Lord of Rifts?" He clasped his good hand, rubbing it against the grass. The slick, itchy feeling receded.

"If the slinks had a root, it is he. He tore his way into this world and sank his teeth into it. He will tear it apart if he can."

"What are the slinks going to do?"

"Destroy," she hissed, drawing the word out.

The spirit women swayed, and there was the sound of wind passing through leaves.

"You have power," she said. "You can cause great harm, even more than the emperor. You can unmake the elements."

"No!" he said. His heart hurt at the emperor's abominations. "I can stop the emperor," he said. "And the Lord of Rifts."

Adora's eyes narrowed, and she leaned over him. "That is why we spared you."

Chapter 28

GREI

GREI HAD taken off his boots, and his legs hung over the edge of the bank, his feet submerged in the cool brook. He couldn't walk after being joined with the Root Tree, so they had carried him here and put his feet in water. When he had been one with the tree, he had actually thought like a tree. Perhaps he had actually become the tree. He watched the water, imagining his toes were roots, and he felt nourished.

He looked at the tree spirit who sat next to him, wearing Adora's face.

"Can't you be someone else?" he asked.

The tree spirit curled her lip. "Humans see what they want to see. They are not interested in truth."

I left her, he thought. *To the mercy of those who may kill her, and here I am with my toes in a stream.*

He yanked his feet out of the water and began putting on his boots, fumbling awkwardly with the use of only one hand. The tree spirit watched him struggle. He frowned, flicked a glance at her. "What happens to those taken in the Debt of the Blessed?" he asked. "Do the slinks...eat them?" he asked, barely able to form the question.

"You see the Lord of Rifts as a ravening beast, when he is only ravening. The Blessed are used for a purpose. If the Lord of Rifts had achieved his desire, we would not be here. The world would be consumed in flames."

"He keeps them alive?" Grei slipped and almost kicked his boot into the water. He trapped it against the edge of the bank with his dead arm, which crackled under the bandage. He winced, but there was no feeling there at all.

"I do not know," the tree spirit said.

"Could my brother Julin still be alive?" He finally shoved his foot into the boot.

"If the Lord of Rifts has him, he is no longer your brother." She stood up, cocked her hips and put her hands there, exactly as Adora would. It made him dizzy, thinking that he was conjuring these images.

She rose and led him back into the pine forest. Behind him, he could see the light from the white trunks of the grove that the spirits called The Root. The sight drew him and frightened him at the same time. He didn't want to go back into that trunk again. Yet a part of him longed to return forever. He yanked his gaze away.

The forest was close with the scent of pine needles and bark. His guide came to the edge of a natural bowl in the earth. The trees were tightly packed around the rim like spears on a wall. In the center of the bowl was Selicia, spread-eagled on the grass. Thick roots grew up from the ground, binding her legs and arms.

She was awake and had obviously been there for some time. When Grei stepped to the edge of the slope, she spotted him. Her hawk eyes regarded him, but she remained silent.

"This human is filled with violent intent. She is a destroyer," the spirit said.

Grei stayed silent. Selicia had clubbed him unconscious and brutally kicked Adora. She'd flung her ringblade into Blevin's head, a strike that should have killed him. And the grisly deaths of countless others filled her memories.

"We have spared you because you might stop your emperor," the tree spirit said. "We spared her only because she came with you."

"She can't see you?" he asked softly.

Selicia's thin gaze flicked around the glade, searching for the person to whom Grei spoke.

"She can neither see nor hear us," the spirit said. "We leave it to you, what is to be done with her."

"And if I leave her with you?" Grei asked.

"We will kill her."

"I don't want her with me," he said. He could still see Adora's head snapping back, see her crumpling to the ground. Selicia had never broken stride. She might have killed Adora with that strike.

"Very well." The spirit gestured, and a dozen other Adoras slipped between the trees at the edge of the bowl and started down the slope. He saw their legs move, saw the impact of each footstep in their bodies, but they weren't really there. He blinked, trying to see their true form, but he couldn't.

Though Selicia could not see them, she sensed them and pulled against her restraints. One of the Adoras reached out her hand to touch Selicia's face—

"Wait," Grei said softly.

The spirit next to him turned, and the tree spirits below paused as one, their heads swiveling to look at him.

"You wish her to live?" she asked.

"I don't know."

Blevins had slain without compunction. At least two Highblades were dead because of him. Selicia was also a killer, no question, but she had been kinder to his companions than they had been to hers. Did she deserve to die?

"Let her twisted life end," the spirit said. "Let her be reborn as something better."

"Like what?"

"Grass. Perhaps a tree will grow there."

He should let her die. Anyone would call it justice, but he

couldn't shake the other image he had seen inside her: how tenderly she had collected a near-dead Ree in her arms, how Selicia loved her fellow Ringblades. He couldn't just let her die. By leaving her here, he was making that decision, and that was a power he didn't want.

"I will take her with me," he said reluctantly. His stomach tightened.

"This is what you wish?"

"For better or worse, she's part of my 'grove'," he said.

"Very well, manling," the spirit said with disgust.

The roots slithered off Selicia's body and disappeared into the earth. With a quick breath, she rolled to her feet, crouching as if ready to spring. Her gaze flicked about, still trying to find with whom Grei had spoken.

Wind whipped around him so fiercely that he caught his breath. Whispers he could almost understand rushed past him. Hands touched his hair, his arms and legs, and the trees were obscured by white air and ribbons of yellow light. He felt limbs and leaves pass him, thought he could almost see them, then the rushing sound was gone.

Grei and Selicia tumbled onto the baked earth of the Badlands.

The tree spirit stared at him from the edge of the Dead Woods. Her yellow eyes glowed with hatred.

"I'm sorry for what the emperor—"

"Do not come back to this place until the Lord of Rifts is destroyed," the spirit interrupted. "We will not spare you a second time." The spirit paused, put Adora's hands on Adora's hips and glared at him with yellow eyes. "Serve your grove. Serve us all."

She faded until only the pines of the Dead Woods remained, looking like a hostile fortress. He turned to find Selicia standing behind him, looking in the same direction. She seemed different without her weapons, smaller and thinner. Older. He questioned his own wisdom in sparing her.

"You were going to let them kill me," Selicia said. "I felt them drawing near. But you didn't." Her eyes were thin slits in her face.

He kept his hand free. He still hadn't figured out why using his magic had made him stupid at the wagon, but he'd risk it again to turn the earth soft beneath her. And this time he'd turn it back to rock afterwards. Let her get out of *that*.

"What happened in the trees?" she asked.

"They hate you," he said. *They hate me, too,* he thought, but he didn't say it.

Selicia looked at him as though she might see something more. "How did you get them to release me?"

"I have something they want."

"What do they want?"

"They hate the slinks more than they hate us," he said. "They want me to stop the slinks."

"Can you?" she asked.

"What were your orders from the emperor?" he asked, annoyed at the interrogation.

"You are an unusual man, Grei." She watched him with those unnerving black eyes. "You leave me with a difficult decision."

"Sorry to inconvenience you."

The red scar along her cheek tightened as she gave him a flat smile. "I am a Ringblade. I belong to the empress and to the emperor." She paused, seemingly reluctant to say more, but after a moment, she continued. "My life is bound to my honor, and honor says I fulfill my mission. Unto death," she said.

She didn't seem about to attack, but he'd seen how fast she was. She would lull him into a false sense of safety, and then strike.

"Do you know what a life debt is?" she asked.

"If you're implying that you have to save my life because I saved yours, then I like it."

Slowly, she descended to one knee and bowed her head.

He took a step back.

"My fealty is yours," she intoned softly.

Chapter 29

ADORA

ADORA WONDERED if the Order would rescue her on the road to the capitol city of Thiara. But as they rode away from the Badlands, across the open grasslands and then through the Felesh duchy over the next two days, she realized that they either couldn't come for her or they wouldn't. Since she had failed, would they leave her to her fate?

Galius watched her like a hawk. During the day, she rode behind him. During the night, he bound her wrists and tied her ankle to a stake he drove into the ground. She imagined escape, but he did not give her the opportunity. As with everything, Galius was thorough.

On the third day, they passed through the giant gates of the capitol city of Thiara, and Adora watched Galius marvel at the thirty-foot-thick red granite wall and the seven white towers that thrust up above the smaller buildings. Thiara was Fairmist's opposite. Fairmist was dark and cool; Thiara was hot and bright. In Fairmist, people hid beneath layers of waterproof clothing. In Thiara, people wore skimpy fashions that changed on a whim. Everything was put on display in the bright sunshine.

The royal Highblades received Adora and her escort in the courtyard of the palace. Their leader stood even taller than Galius. Instead of the silver and blue leather of a Fairmist Highblade, he wore a golden X harness over his muscular chest and billowing red pants slit up the sides: Doragon colors. The Highblade had shaved the sides of his head and dyed the remaining center stripe of hair red. Adora had been gone so long that the fashions of Thiara seemed bizarre to her, so loud compared to the muted colors of Fairmist.

"I will accompany her," Galius said.

"You'll do what you're told, peasant," the rooster-headed Highblade replied without looking at him.

Galius' face went red. "Your tone needs mending," he said. His grip on Adora's arm tightened.

The Highblade looked at Galius. "Shut your mouth, climb on your nag and ride to the imperial barracks, Highblade Ash. The Archon will deal with you later."

Galius' jaw clenched, but he managed to take a calming breath.

"The girl is in my charge. I will take her to—"

The Highblade struck quickly, brutally. The backhand snapped Galius' head to the side, drove him to one knee. Adora gasped.

Galius leapt to his feet, shook his head. His cheek was bright red and blood flecked his chin. His sword flashed out of its sheath.

Four red-clad Highblades stepped forward in unison. Steel rang as four blades cleared their scabbards and leveled at Galius.

The rooster-headed Highblade, who had not drawn, laughed. "Our poor eastern cousin has bravery, but no brains." His laughter died and his voice lowered. "Listen, 'cousin', you've drawn enough attention to yourself for a lifetime. Your entire, short lifetime, if you take my meaning. These prisoners were important to his majesty, and you lost all but this ragged girl. If you want to fall on your sword now, I will understand. Otherwise, the Archon will deal with you later."

Galius' swordarm vibrated with rage, and his implacable gaze never left the rooster-headed Highblade. Then, with a smooth motion, Galius sheathed his sword and inclined his head. "Thank you, sir," he ground out the words.

"Get out of my sight," the Highblade said.

The rest of the Highblades sheathed their swords. Two of them took Adora's arms and led her away. She glanced once at Galius over her shoulder.

His dirt-smeared blue and silver clothing looked pitiful and out of place in the shining palace. He stood stiffly as they pulled her away, like he wanted to do something, but didn't know what it was.

The Highblades led her through the halls she had grown up in as a child. There were many doors, and after several minutes of walking, they found the one they were looking for. The stairs went down.

"Where are we going?" she asked.

"Quiet."

"I want to know—"

"Quiet or I'll make you quiet."

Adora had never been to this part of the palace as a child. There was probably a reason for that.

They descended a long time before they came to the bottom, a six-foot circular landing with one wooden door. The Highblade produced a key, opened the door, and pushed her through.

The room beyond was large and square. There were no other doors except the one through which they'd come. A huge steel boot sat on the floor to her right, cracked open and ready to swallow a foot. Torchlight flickered off the spikes inside. A stool sat in front of a squat table just beyond that. To her immediate left was a large brazier filled with unlit coals.

In the center of the room, commanding immediate

attention, was a large wooden "X". It leaned back, and thick leather straps with shackles dangling from the edge of each square post. Behind the "X" were little wooden spools of rope attached to each restraint. The Highblades pulled her toward this.

"I'm not getting on that."

The Highblade hit her in the side of her face, right where Selicia had kicked her. She cried out. Stars burst in her vision, and her head felt like it would split.

They dragged her forward and wrenched her hands upward. The pain roared through her head, and they closed the first manacle, pulled her other wrist up and locked it in. She held her face away, flinching, waiting for another strike. She didn't fight them as they secured her ankles.

She needed to keep her wits about her. She was Adora, just a server of drinks. She had to pretend to be terrified, to be confused. She could have laughed at that. Pretending wouldn't be hard at all.

"Please, I didn't do anything," she said.

"Archon'll sort that out," one of the Highblades said, stepping back. They left, closing the door behind them.

The sudden silence was emphatic, and Adora watched the flickering torch on the far wall dance its crazy dance.

"This isn't how it was supposed to go," she whispered.

She pulled against the straps. Metal clinked. Leather creaked. She bit her lip, hard, to hold back the tears. There had to be something she could do. The Order said there always was. Obstacles could be overcome; she must have the vision to see her way through them. Lyndion had told her that when there was no answer, she must create the answer.

She stared at the flickering torch. *Create the answer.*

Chapter 30
ADORA

ADORA TWITCHED when the door opened. The torch left a black imprint on her vision, and she blinked. Duke Dayn Felesh, a man she had known from birth, entered. He had been like an uncle to her growing up. She and his son Biren had not only been best friends, they'd been betrothed before she had been sacrificed to the slinks. Dayn Felesh was the lord of the most powerful holding in the empire and also the imperial Archon.

A Highblade flanked him on the right. To his left was a tiny man, stooped and bald, whose hands clasped and unclasped anxiously.

The Archon stopped, looking Adora over from a distance. She held her breath, waiting for his spark of recognition, but he didn't know her. Blevins knew what he had been doing when he cut her black and gold Doragon hair. Without it, she was just a battered bald girl.

"She is secure?" the Archon asked.

The stooped man moved forward, checked each restraint. He nodded.

"Tighten them," the Archon said.

"My name is Adora," she said. "If you will, please tell me what I've done."

The stooped man leaned past her, out of sight. Wood clacked as the spools turned. Her wrists were pulled up, her ankles down.

"Please," she tried to put an edge of hysteria in her voice without succumbing to it. She had to keep her wits, stay calm. "Please, sir," she said. "I don't know my crimes."

"We all know our crimes," the Archon said. "Whether we want to admit them or not."

The stooped man came around to her left side, humming to himself. He touched her bandage, and she flinched.

"I spilled beer on a man once," she said quickly. "I meant to do it. On purpose. B-But I said it was an accident."

"Clever," the Archon said. "Who is the boy?"

"Which boy?"

The stooped man tapped his finger on her brow, just above her wounded cheek. The little tap seemed like a hammer. She gasped.

"Grei? Do you mean Grei?" she said.

"Very good," the Archon said. "Yes, let's talk about Grei. What is he to you?"

She swallowed. "My lover," she said. "I didn't know he was in trouble. I swear."

"Is not Galius Ash your lover?"

"We...were courting."

"And this Grei as well?"

"He was... Yes."

"Hmmm." The Archon paused. "Why do you think Grei was taken?"

"Magic, my lord," she said. They already knew that he could turn stone to water. She had to tell them what they already knew, but nothing that they didn't yet know.

"Indeed."

"He changed a waterfall. The water...he made it open like a curtain."

"What else?"

"He turned ground to water."

"And he escaped?"

"Into the Dead Woods."

"And do you think he is dead?" the Archon asked.

Adora flicked a glance at the stooped torturer. He had black eyes in a seemingly happy face. He was balding, with age spots on his head and thinning white hair that sprouted just above his ears, draping over them like ghostly curtains. He smiled. He was missing all four of his front teeth. She looked back at the Archon. "No one comes out of the Dead Woods, your majesty," she said timidly.

The Archon smiled a thin smile. "I am the Archon, my dear. Not the emperor."

Adora gave him a confused look.

"You may address me as 'my lord', not 'your majesty'."

"I'm sorry, my lord."

"And that is all you know?"

"Is Grei an enemy of the emperor?"

"Most certainly."

"I didn't know."

"Of course you didn't. Of course," the Archon said. "And you saw him part this waterfall? You saw him turn earth to water?"

"The waterfall. Yes, my lord. And earth to water."

"Hmm..."

"Can I go home now?"

He ran a light finger across her scalp. "Who cut your hair?"

"Blevins."

"The fat man?"

"Yes."

"Tell me, did the fat man have a sword with him? Red and black jewels on the hilt?"

Adora swallowed. The Archon knew about Jorun Magnus! Or was he fishing? Her heart began hammering.

"He had a sword, my lord. He fought with Galius."

"With jewels on the hilt?"

"It was just a sword. There may have been something on the pommel. A white stone. Opal, maybe?"

"Hmm..." He rubbed his chin. "And this Blevins cut your hair?"

"That is what Galius said. He said the man was wounded, and he went mad. Galius thought he was going to kill me."

"Why would he cut your hair?"

"I don't know, my lord." She let out a sob, and there was no need to fake that. "My hair was long and black," she whispered. Let him paint the picture that he expected.

The Archon tapped his chin, thinking, then he came out of his reverie and smiled. "Well, my dear," he said, leaning so close she could see the tiny dots of stubble on his chin. His breath smelled sour. "I think you're telling the truth."

"Thank you, my lord," she said.

He ran an absent hand over her shaved scalp. "But no one can know what you have seen. And you've been so forthcoming. I just know you're going to tell someone else."

"I won't, my lord. Please. I'll go to my grave with it."

"That much is true," he said. He touched her chin with a wistful expression. "I bet you were a beauty with your hair, weren't you? In truth, you look much like the empress—" He stopped in mid-sentence. His brow furrowed, and his smile vanished. The Archon stepped away from her, stunned.

"Are you all right, my lord?" The Highblade asked, moving to the Archon's side. The Highblade glanced at Adora suspiciously, as though she had cast a spell upon him.

"I'm fine," the Archon said, shaking his head. He stared at her.

"What is it, my lord?" the Highblade asked.

"I've had a change of heart," the Archon said at last.

"My lord?" the torturer said in a creaky voice, obviously disappointed.

"I want to kill her myself. Give me your dagger and leave us."

"But my lord—" the stooped man protested.

The Archon held out his hand. "Wait outside."

"Yes, my lord," the old man said, handing his curved dagger over reluctantly. The Highblade opened the door and the two of them left.

When the door thumped shut and latched, the Archon came close to Adora again. His glittering gaze devoured her, moving from her eyes to her throat, down her body and back up again.

"Please, my lord," she said. "I simply wish to go home."

"Stop begging," he whispered, his breath coming faster "Royalty never begs."

Chapter 31
ADORA

THE ARCHON didn't listen to her protestations that she was just a bartender from Fairmist; he said nothing further. Instead, he left the room and his Highblade unshackled her and took her through quiet hallways to the Archon's apartments. It had high marble walls, three open arches to the sea, and fluttering silk curtains. There was an immense, sumptuous bed to her left, lined with fat pillows. To her right was an archway that led to the baths. She had almost forgotten how spacious the palace was.

And the sunlight. As soon as the Highblade left, she went to the balcony and turned her face toward the sun's warmth. It was a forgotten, beloved memory. Sunlight on her face. Sunlight every day, except when the storms rolled past Thiara.

She bowed her head, suddenly feeling the weight of her exile more than she had ever felt it before. Here she was, back in the palace, a demeaned, abused bartender in borrowed clothes. No longer a princess. No longer belonging to this grand place. A hundred times she had imagined herself staring down at the palace from a high point, seeing through the stone walls to where her father lay crumpled in shame for what he had done to her.

The double doors opened, and she drew a swift breath, tried to master her feelings. Where was the strong Adora now? Where was the woman who had learned everything the Order had to teach her with speed and determination, the woman who had consigned herself to death without cringing, the woman who had fought a slink to save Grei? Was she, at the heart of things, just a scared little girl?

A young woman entered and closed the double doors behind her, turned and dipped in a curtsey. She wore a short red skirt and a white tunic, open at the sides and cut low to her navel. Thiaran fashions changed constantly. This must be the latest.

A shapeless bag hung from a cord around her bronze shoulder, and she wore wooden shoes. Her shoulder-length hair had been oiled back in a swoop, curling outward at the very tips.

"A bath for you, my lady?" she asked, maintaining the deferent posture.

Adora didn't say anything. The young woman remained at the doorway, her head bowed.

"Yes," said Adora. She had to calm her thoughts. There was always a way. Even the darkest night had a ray of light somewhere. She had to find it, had to follow it until she found daylight once more.

The woman nodded and preceded Adora through the archway. The bath was sunk into the floor, red tiles bordering it in the wide expanse of white marble. There was already steaming water there. It looked divine.

Adora peeled away the bandage on her face. The cut had scabbed on her cheek, and she touched it gently.

She stripped off her borrowed tunic and the riding breeches Galius had procured for her at the first Highblade station in Felesh and stepped into the hot water, sinking slowly up to her neck as she closed her eyes and leaned back.

The marble felt cool against her bare scalp. She had had baths almost every day while living at the Order House, but nothing like this. This was paradise. This was what she remembered.

It calmed her nerves, and when she opened her eyes she felt more like herself. All this—her capture, her near torture, her wound and disfigurement—they were just obstacles in her path. She could not abandon the teachings of the Order. If Grei was gone and the slinks could not be banished, then at least her father must be stopped. It was because of him that the Debt of the Blessed existed.

The Order said her father had killed a Faia, that the Dead Woods existed because her father had ripped that Faia away. Because of him, the empire was at the mercy of the slinks, and perhaps there was something that Adora could do about that.

She looked over at the young woman. The girl was Adora's age. Adora wondered what thoughts went through her mind. She was young in a way Adora had never been. Was the girl thinking about whom she would wed soon? Perhaps she already had a husband, even children. Did she look forward to raising them, thankful for her position in the palace, thankful for the emperor who protected them from the slinks?

She thought of Grei and their too-brief moment on the Blacktale Bridge. It brought tears to her eyes, and she couldn't have that right now.

The servant had pulled a washing cloth, a soft bristled brush, a cake of soap, a razor and a strop from her bag and laid them on the edge of the bath. Adora's gaze lingered on the razor.

"I am to shave you, my lady."

Adora touched the stubble on her head. "Of course."

The woman washed her. She was efficient, with gentle hands. She neatly shaved Adora's head without a nick, and then cleaned her wound, re-bandaged it.

"You are adept at your work," Adora complimented her.

The young woman nodded. "I have left new clothes for

you." She indicated the marble bench by the door, where there lay a thin dress of red silk.

Adora's gaze lingered on it, then she looked at the attendant. "Thank you. You may go."

"Yes, my lady." The girl rose to her feet with a graceful rocking motion and left through the archway, her wooden shoes clacking on the floor.

Adora rose from the bath, took the cotton towel from the edge and wrapped it around herself. She stood staring at the dress on the bench for a long moment, then picked it up and let it fall to full length.

It was a Venishan courtesan's dress.

Chapter 32
ADORA

THE ARCHON arrived not long after Adora had donned the thin dress. It was floor-length with a modest neckline, but the sheer silk hugged her body and was slit all the way up the sides to her waist. She felt more exposed than she had in the brief shift Galius had given her in the Badlands.

The Archon closed the doors quietly behind him, gave her an appraising glance, and nodded.

"Good. It fits," he said.

"It's a courtesan's dress," she said.

"Shall I fetch your royal robes, highness? Two servants and a Highblade know you have come to my room. It is easy to believe I have taken you as a chattel. If I order royal clothes for you, what will they say?"

Adora paused, then nodded. "Of course."

"Very well then. Now, what shall I call you? Mialene will not do. Neither will 'your highness'."

"Adora."

"Lovely. Did you choose it yourself?"

"Does it matter?"

He smiled. "There are such stories to tell," he said, crossing to the sumptuous bed and sitting down. He patted the spot next to him. "I don't have much time."

She hesitated. "Where is Biren?"

That made the Archon pause.

"He is the Lord of Felesh while I am in service at the palace. He is doing a fine job. Almost as though he was born to it." The Archon gave a hard smile, as though that meant something. He patted the bed again.

She sat down next to him, crossed her legs and put her hands on her knees. The dress wanted to slide away; she held it in place.

"Why haven't you told my father about me?"

"I don't think you want me to go to your father. Otherwise, why cut your hair? Why not tell your amorous Highblade who you really are? You want your anonymity. I can ensure you keep it."

She watched his face, but she couldn't read him.

"I am curious about your story," he said. "I can only imagine how you escaped your fate. Will you tell me?"

"No."

"Why would you come back to Thiara?"

"Perhaps you didn't notice. I was taken here against my will."

"And what do you want now?"

"To leave, Uncle. I appreciate your rescue. Let me go."

"And you would go search for your lover? This boy Grei who ran into the Dead Woods?"

Her heart ached. Was there a chance Grei had come out alive? He was the Whisper Prince, after all. But her heart felt that he was gone.

She wondered if love ever made any difference at all. She had loved her father, had loved Jorun Magnus. She had loved Grei. She had worked so hard to bring him to safety and the empire to freedom. Her love for him was forbidden by the Order, and now here she was again, broken and battered. For love? Grei would have made it to the Faia in time if she hadn't stopped to kiss him. If she hadn't loved him.

"He is a special lad," the Archon continued when she did not speak. "The Highblades say he has one of the emperor's artifacts. Perhaps he survived?"

"I don't know."

"Except he doesn't have an artifact, does he?" the Archon said.

"I won't betray him. If this is another attempt at interrogation, then take me back to your rack," she said.

"My dear, I'm not going to hurt you. I'm going to make you a bargain."

She waited, then said. "All right."

"I will keep you safe for one month. I will hide you from the emperor. At the end of which, I will let you go, and you can go look for your beloved dead boy, or go wherever you wish."

"You'll let me go."

The Archon nodded.

"And my part of the bargain?" She watched his eyes, feeling the weight of what was coming next.

"You will be mine. For one month."

Her heart hammered. "So the courtesan's dress was intentional, *Uncle*?" she said with emphasis. He merely watched her, unfazed by the stab.

"You can keep your secrets, Adora," he said. "I just want your body."

"Why?"

"I have my reasons."

"I grew up with your son," she stated. The plea sounded weaker than she meant it. She searched his eyes for a shred of humanity. "And if I refuse?" she asked.

He spread his hands.

She looked down at her knees. Become the Archon's lover, or back to the torturer's chamber. Or worse, be taken to her father.

And why not use sex to win her freedom? *Create the answer,* Lyndion would say. She had used sex with Galius to keep up her façade. For what else should she use her body except advantage? For love?

There is no love, she thought.

As with Galius, she could take the Archon in hand. One, maybe two nights. She could play the possession, even that she enjoyed it. He would relax, he would slip, then she could escape this place and return to the Order, find out what was to be done next.

She stood up and moved in front of him. Her throat was dry. She pressed her trembling hands against her legs and waited until she was sure her voice would come out steady.

"Now?" she asked.

"Do you know what to do?"

"I know what to do." Her shaking fingers began working at the first button on the side of her dress, but she was proud to see that they were steady by the time she undid the last. The silk fluttered to the ground.

Create the answer, she thought as she undressed him. He laid her down on the bed.

There is no love.

Chapter 33

LYNDION

LYNDION WATCHED Shemmel, the wrinkled lines on his face more pronounced than they had been last year. The price was coming due more often now. The first spell had lasted nearly a century. The latest had not even lasted two decades. They would need another, and soon.

Of course if the slink children caught them, they need not bother at all.

That was the entire point of the Whisper Prince. And now it was seven years wasted.

When Lyndion received news of the Whisper Prince's capture, he continued to have hope. Grei had not opened a connection to the Faia, but the Prince was still going in the direction he needed to go. Mialene was still with him. The Order had agents in the palace. Things could be taken back in hand.

But then the Prince escaped his captors and fled into the Dead Woods. He cursed his great granddaughter for her weakness.

Shemmel sat silently, his craggy face unreadable. He had

not said anything since Lyndion had related the foul news.

"So we have failed," Lyndion said, feeling the words like acid on his tongue. "The Whisper Prince is lost. Mialene did not have him in hand at the needed moment." He shook his head. "I told you we should have whored her out at sixteen, stripped her girlish notions away, and readied her for the job. She would have had Grei under her thumb the first night."

Shemmel shook his head. "Grei was an intelligent boy. We needed her innocence."

Lyndion snorted. "You needed it, maybe. You were soft on her. You liked that she loved you. I wonder what she would think of you if she knew what you have done with girls half her age."

"Could he have survived the Dead Woods?" Shemmel asked, seemingly unaffected by Lyndion's taunt.

Lyndion shook his head. "I know what lives there. The Dead Woods killed him the moment he entered. My great grandson saw to that when he slew the Vheysin Faia."

"Our allies were knowledge, secrecy and speed," Shemmel said. "We have lost all three."

"The slink boys have not found us. That is something."

"It is seven years now they have been searching. They will find us. Do we run?"

"Not yet," Lyndion said.

"Then how?" Shemmel snorted. "We wait for another Whisper Prince? How many protégés does the beast of the forest take?"

"That was luck, and we have wasted the opportunity." An idea dawned then. "But..." He thought through it quickly. "Mialene still lives. Her death will still open the rift."

"And who will speak to the Faia's temple when her blood joins the waters? Who will push the slinks through?"

"Perhaps it can be done without the Whisper Prince," Lyndion persisted. "Someone could stand in his place."

"Who else? Shall we dig up Baezin's corpse, place it at the temple and hope to fool the Faia?"

"No. We use the magic of the Faia themselves," Lyndion

said.

"The Faia will never help you. They have refused you every time." Shemmel bared his teeth, and Lyndion saw the blood-thirsty duke who had begun this journey with him, not the kindly-seeming old man he had become around the princess. "They'll never take a life."

Lyndion smiled. "But the emperor has made weapons of their deaths. No one knows what powers are locked in those artifacts. One of them might be able to duplicate what we need."

"And our agent within the palace can get these artifacts?" Shemmel asked.

"She is our only chance."

"She will never use it to kill Mialene."

"It need not be her. One of our brothers can wield it. Or you. Or me."

"Yes."

Chapter 34
GREI

GREI AND Selicia returned to the site of the battle, but there was no wagon and no Highblades. Selicia hadn't threatened him since they had left the Dead Woods, but he didn't believe the act. Nobody switched loyalties that quickly. He didn't care what oath she had sworn. People didn't just do that.

Selicia touched the edge of the ground Grei had turned to water before he'd fled into the Dead Woods. It rippled outward like a dirt-colored pond.

"Amazing," she murmured, her back to him.

He let his concentration relax and listened to the whispers that came from her, searching for her true purpose, seeking the betrayal she planned for him.

The images he received were confusing, not clear like they had been the first time he had looked into her: he saw himself through her eyes as she bowed to him, felt her solemn commitment. It was imperative she serve him. She was shamed at failing her emperor, but the code she followed demanded that she put herself under Grei's command.

Other images swirled in a fog that he couldn't penetrate.

When he started to force his way past it, a dull feeling oozed over his mind, just like when he had escaped the wagon.

He stopped.

She glanced over her shoulder at him, and her eyes narrowed.

He kept his face neutral. The tree spirits had taken away her short sword and dagger, her ringblade and the gauntlet she wore to handle it. They had even taken her belt with its little pouches on it. The woman had nothing but her black clothes, but she was still dangerous. Standing next to her felt like being near a wild dog that could bite at any moment.

The Badlands were ghostly quiet. Only the dark stains of blood from Blevins' victims remained, marking the ground.

"Time has passed," Selicia said as she stood up.

"I was wondering about that," he said. Perhaps it was just the dry nature of the Badlands, but it seemed like the battle had happened a long time ago.

She walked across Baezin's Road, through the dead trees, pausing over each ominous blood spot.

"These are days old. Like the horse," she said, her hand lightly touching one. They had passed the mount she had brought down with her Ringblade during his escape. It had been long dead, eyes sunken, skin tight, though not a single fly had come to feed on it. It had been damned eerie. "At least three days, probably more. It could be twice that," she said.

"We were only in the Dead Woods for half a day," Grei said.

She looked at him strangely. "Indeed? I lay in that meadow for much longer, or so it seemed. Did you ever see the sun?" she asked.

All he could remember from the Dead Woods was the shining white trees. The smell of the towering pines. The presence of the spirits.

"You're saying we lost time," he said, and he thought about the Forest Girl and the slink seven years ago. He had aged a year and had no memory of it. His stomach rumbled.

"Did you ever feel hungry in there?" he asked

She shook her head, then glanced at the hot sun overhead.

He cleared his throat. "Well, I'm going. If it was more than half a day, there is even less time to waste. I have to find Adora." He didn't want to spend any more time with Selicia than he had to. She could practice her oath to obey him by leaving him alone.

"We must hunt soon," she said.

He wanted to tell her no, but his stomach rumbled again at the suggestion.

"Okay," he said. As he thought of it, he realized that would work even better. Wherever they hunted, he'd make sure he escaped her, and that would be the last he would have to watch his back.

Selicia rose to her feet and moved toward him, and he stepped away. She acted as if she didn't notice, continued past him along Baezin's Road. "We will find no food here."

He fell in line behind her, and they walked for the rest of the day, emerging from the Badlands just as the sun slipped behind the horizon, plunging the world into a fading purple light. Selicia took them off the road and over the tall grass to the north. The stars came out, growing brighter as the sky darkened. The fields stretched forever under the scant silvery light.

"This is where it gets dangerous for us," she said. "But we are almost to a place we can rest."

"I'm fine," he said, though his stomach felt like a hollow log. He was dizzy with hunger.

A black shadow suddenly blocked out the starlight, and an enormous shape slid overhead. Grei flinched and stepped back, but there was nowhere to go. It was an enormous chunk of floating rock! The thing was larger than the delegate's palace, perhaps larger than the entire city of Fairmist. Selicia took hold of his arm to steady him.

"What is it?" he said, wondering how he hadn't seen this thing from miles off.

"Surely you have heard of the Night Mountains," she

murmured.

The Night Mountains! He wondered if this was how visitors felt when they saw the Lateral Houses for the first time. The Night Mountains were a legend that was only murmured about in Fairmist, because you could never see the sky through the haze of floating droplets, especially at night. Supposedly, the Night Mountains had always been there, even back when Emperor Baezin first came to Thiara and founded the empire. They were long chunks of earth that floated high in the sky. It was rumored that Emperor Baezin took his Faia-made floating ship up to them long ago, though there were no written histories of Baezin's adventures on the Night Mountains.

Some had pursued the legends, searching for the civilization that supposedly lived there. Some Thiarans had tried to shoot ballistae with ropes tied to them so they could climb up, but no ballista was powerful enough to shoot that far. There was a group who tried to harness flying hares into a flock and attach a wagon to it. But the hares could not be trained to work together, and they leapt frantically in every direction, never getting the wagon off the ground. Another woman made huge wings like a bird and jumped off a cliff. She flew quite fast. Into the ground. Some would call it falling.

But no one had ever been able to reach them.

"Why didn't we see them earlier?" he murmured as they slid silently overhead.

"The Night Mountains only float at night."

"I thought that part was myth," he whispered. How could mountains completely vanish?

"Hmmm," she said.

"How do they do it?"

"How do buildings float?"

"But those are mountains!"

"Floating houses are sensible but floating mountains are not?" she asked.

He watched the mountains slide overhead.

"Come, prince. We are not safe in the open."

She chose their camp, a distance away from Baezin's Road behind a small rise that hid them completely from any other travelers. The Fairmist River rushed loudly to the north just beyond a small copse of trees. She crouched, pulled together some rocks and gathered fallen sticks from the trees. Furthering the farce, Grei searched around and found some other pieces of wood. She started a small fire.

"Keep it alive," she said, producing a little steel hook from somewhere inside her tunic. A black thread that looked like she had pulled it from her clothing hung from her other hand. "I will bring dinner."

"You had that hook in your clothes all this time?" he asked.

She didn't answer him, but moved toward the river, a gray blur in the dying light.

Once she had disappeared through the small stand of trees, Grei rose and slunk off in the opposite direction. He walked softly until he was sure no one, not even a Ringblade, could hear him from the river, and then began to jog west toward Thiara. He ran until his legs hurt and his stomach was crying for food, and then he headed back toward the river. He found another spot like Selicia had done, with a stand of trees hanging over the riverbank, creating a sheltered hollow beneath.

He went down to the river, but he had no hook, and after an hour of splashing around in the dark, trying to catch a fish with his bare hands, he went back to the little hollow and hunkered down, hungry and miserable.

He needed rest. Forget food for now. The air was warm, and he was exhausted. Once he'd had some sleep, he'd make a plan. He would find a nearby farm, beg some food and continue on.

He closed his eyes and fell asleep.

He drifted through dreams. Images of Adora, of the Faia, of Selicia and Blevins flashed past him. He rose to the surface of consciousness, and he could hear the comforting rush of the river. The fire crackling. The smell of cooking fish.

His eyes snapped open, and he drew in a ragged breath.

Selicia sat on the other side of a small fire. Over it, four fish were cooking on a makeshift spit.

He swallowed. His heart thundered.

"How did you find me?" he asked.

She looked up at him, expressionless. Then she looked at the fish again, as though his question didn't deserve an answer. She turned one of them over, and he noticed they were all fixed on slender spears that looked suspiciously like they had been sharpened with a dagger.

He remembered how both Selicia and Ree had pulled daggers from nowhere, and a cool chill ran down his back.

"Do you have a weapon?" he asked, trying to come awake and absorb the fact that she'd been here, with him asleep, for however long it had taken to build that fire.

He barely saw her hand move, but suddenly there was a thin dagger there, glinting in the orange firelight. She made it disappear just as quickly.

He jumped to his feet and backed up. "The tree spirits took your weapons!"

She regarded him again, the firelight making her scar prominent, a crevice in the side of her face.

"You don't have to trust me," she said simply, "But the fact remains that I am yours, and I will serve you as best I can. If I wanted to hurt you, I would have done it long before now."

His heart thundered.

"Why didn't you?" he demanded.

She watched him for a moment, then went back to tending the fish. The small fire sizzled as juice dripped down. Slowly, Grei sat back down. His stomach growled, and he was dizzy with the smell.

It seemed only a few minutes before the fish were ready. She offered two of them to him, and he reluctantly accepted. They ate in silence. He pulled the hot meat off the bones and stuffed it greedily into his mouth. Selicia carefully ate one, then wrapped the other in a black cloth.

Afterwards, he sat with his back against one of the trees and gazed at the fire, making sure to keep her in view. He wondered if he could get her to leave the campsite again so he could run, but then what? He recalled Blevins' words.

She will find you. That's what Ringblades do.

"You should go back to sleep. You will need your rest," she said, her dark eyes watching him.

"Why don't you sleep?" he asked.

"I have trained many years to overcome my need for sleep. I will guard you."

"I bet you would. I'll just close my eyes and you can do whatever you want. Well, I'm not. I don't trust you any further than I can throw you."

"You should not waste the opportunity. Sleep."

"You sleep."

She nodded and went back to looking at the fire. With the orange light flickering across her face, lighting up the crease of her scar, it looked like she might be smiling. He couldn't tell.

Perhaps he could cross the river, escape that way. He stared at her, and his eyelids felt heavy. How could he get her to leave the camp again? Some kind of night patrol? Highblades did that sort of thing. Did Ringblades?

He blinked. His eyes burned, but his stomach felt good for first time all day, contented and full of fish. The warmth from the fire was soothing.

She sat there, stoic. The moon rose higher in the sky. The Night Mountains slid enigmatically by. Eventually, Selicia extinguished the fire, scooped dirt over it and scattered the rocks. She stood up and went to stand by a tree, looking toward the road.

He ought to walk around to keep himself awake, but he didn't feel like moving. He'd wait until she moved off a little further, then get into the river and float downstream.

His eyelids slipped closed, and he told himself to blink,

told himself he had to stay awake.

You are awake, his mind told him, but he was pretty sure it was lying.

Grei awoke with a start, his arms jerking and his legs kicking dead leaves. He blinked furiously, then he remembered where he was, and a different worry filled him. The last thing he remembered was deciding he must stay awake to keep an eye on Selicia. But night was gone. The thin light of daybreak crept across the plains.

He sat up, expecting to be bound, but his hands and legs were free. Selicia wasn't there.

He glanced at the scatter of ashes that had been their fire. He rubbed his eyes with his good fist, got to his feet and stumbled out of the grove. She'd gone for reinforcements. She had—

He pulled up short.

In the scant dawn light, Selicia danced through the tall grass. She wore only a black loincloth and a twist of black cloth across her breasts, knotted in the back. She shone with sweat, her body lean and hard. Her legs were smooth, and light ridges of muscle stood out on her flat stomach. Her arms were ropey, veins prominent on her forearms and hands.

She leapt and landed on one leg, holding perfectly still, arms level to the ground as her body leaned impossibly sideways. Then slowly, she pivoted, coming upright. The movement gained momentum after one revolution, then she snapped into a spin. She became a blur, her long black braid whipping around her. She jumped, right foot lancing out at an unseen foe. She landed, still spinning. Her fists struck. One. Two. Three. Four. Grei could picture the bodies falling in the wake of her furious attack.

The spin culminated in a drop that took her below the level of the tall grass. She emerged a second later, slowly rising, arms held toward the sun like a flower. She stayed there, facing away from him.

She breathed hard, her back expanding and contracting, and he saw two prominent scars there. One was a ragged circle the size of a fist underneath her right shoulder. The other was a long, pink scar that curved from the left side of her neck down to her right hip. A sword or dagger wound for sure, and not too old. Probably the same age as the scar on her face. He wondered if Blevins had delivered that one, too.

She turned toward him as though she'd known he was there, and nodded.

"That was amazing," he said.

"The fifty-fourth," she said quietly as she passed him, untying the strip of cloth over her breasts as she stepped into the river. She dropped her loincloth also, then crouched naked in the shallows to wash herself.

Her casual disrobing shocked him. He cleared his throat and turned around. "The fifty-fourth what?" he asked over his shoulder.

"Dance." Water splashed.

"I didn't realize you were a dancer."

She laughed, and it was all he could do not to look at her. Selicia? Laughing? Her laugh was husky, as though rusty from disuse.

"I didn't realize you had a sense of humor, either," he continued.

The laughter faded, and he regretted saying it. He half-turned, then thought better of it. He felt he should apologize, but before he could, she spoke.

"Dance is a Ringblade's path," she said quietly. "Silence is her art. A Ringblade moves, but is not seen." He heard her step out of the water. Clothes rustled.

"I thought it was about killing for the emperor."

She was quiet, and he listened to her dress.

"There are many purposes for the dancing," she finally said.

"The dance you just did?"

Again she paused, as though she didn't know whether to

answer him or not, but then she said, "There are seventy-seven. That was the fifty-fourth."

"I've never even heard of that," he said.

"No one knows except the emperor, the empress, the Ringblades," she said as she passed him, now fully dressed in her long-sleeved black tunic and tight breeches. "And now you."

He opened his mouth to reply, and realized he had nothing to say. Feeling like a child, he followed her. "No one?"

"No one alive," she said, unwrapping the fish she had cooked last night. She pulled it apart and offered half to him. He took it and put it in his mouth, chewed thoughtfully. She did the same.

When he had gulped down his bite, he said, "Did Ree do these dances?"

She stopped chewing and looked at him, then swallowed. "All Ringblades do. Or they die trying."

"Die?"

"Yes."

"Learning the dances?"

"Better to die among loved ones than to fail among enemies," she said.

"That's brutal."

"The world is brutal," she replied. "We prepare as best we can."

"Is that why you kill?"

"I kill because it is necessary."

"I don't think it's ever necessary," he said.

She paused, cocked her head. "You are a smart man, Grei. But that is naïve."

"It makes me ill, the thought of it. People doing that to other people. I don't understand how you can."

She mused a moment. "I would call you a fool, but it is this foolishness that saved my life."

"Ree could have killed me, but she didn't," Grei said.

"Ree broke more than one rule before the end," Selicia

said.

The end? Suddenly the taste of the fish was cloying, and he swallowed with difficulty. He remembered the image of Ree in Selicia's mind. Shrunken and bloody, missing her arm. "Is she dead?"

Selicia shook her head. "Not when I left her. But she is no longer a Ringblade. She betrayed the circle, the other Ringblades, her vows."

"What happened to her, if she didn't die?"

"She is at the Sanctum. She was halfway gone and incoherent when I found her. The slink sickness had taken her mind. I think she may have actually reached the slink cave and returned. She might be dead by now, but Ree has a powerful will. If it is possible to survive what she has endured, she will. But that would be two miracles. No one has ever returned from the slink caves. Likewise, no one has ever overcome the slink sickness."

"Are you betraying your vows by helping me?"

She nodded. "I won't return to the Sanctum. They would kill me, and I would expect them to. I have stepped outside the circle. I don't serve the empress or the emperor anymore. My life is yours, for as long as it lasts."

"As long as it lasts?"

"We are rogue, Grei. The emperor sent me to find you. If he sent me, he will stop at nothing to capture you, and you insist on heading directly to him. It is only a matter of time. He has Highblades, Ringblades, and other advantages at which you and I can only guess. He will find you. I'll help you avoid him as long as I can, but there is only one way this can end: with my death and your capture. Perhaps with both our deaths." She took another bite of the fish, chewed slowly, and swallowed. "The emperor is relentless, and you are far too valuable to let slip. We have only one advantage." She took a last bite and offered the rest of the fish to him.

He watched her, then took it. "We went into the Dead Woods," he said.

She nodded.

"He thinks we're dead."

"Possibly. But that will not stop him from looking. At best, it might reduce the number of Highblades he sends. I did not know what was inside the Dead Woods, but the emperor likely does. He might even know that they would let you go. I think he will at least consider your survival, which means our advantage is a small one indeed."

"What can we do to avoid him? To avoid the Highblades?"

"I am doing it. I am better than most, but you would still do better to run north to Benasca. Going to Thiara is a fool's gambit."

"I'm not leaving Adora."

She nodded as though she understood this. "Love is powerful."

He frowned, not sure if she was mocking him.

"Or is it the prophecy that drives you?" she asked quietly.

Grei snapped his gaze to her. "What prophecy?" He tried to make his voice convincing.

Her eyes were implacable black points. Ringblade. Mistress of secrets. "Do you know what the words mean?" she asked.

He hesitated. Adora's mantle of secrecy hovered over him, imperative, and he did not trust Selicia. But Selicia might know something he did not. "Adora was going to tell me," he said.

"Ah," she breathed suddenly, as though she had just realized something. Her quiet surprise was like a shout from anyone else. She leaned forward. "I should have seen that. Adora is Mialene. The princess escaped the Debt of the Blessed. How?"

"I don't know what you're talking about," he said too quickly, shocked by her sudden jump in logic. How could she have figured *that* out? He hadn't said anything about anything! His cheeks felt hot.

"Mmmm." Selicia nodded. "Then she didn't tell you. She was leading you."

"Leading me?"

Selicia was silent for a moment, then nodded to herself. "Of course. It is the meaning of the last line of the poem. You need her to send the slinks back. Her blood. Baezin's blood."

"What do you mean?"

"The last line, *Why a princess lay down for his charm.* What did you think it meant? That she makes love to you?" Selicia's dark gaze held his. "No. She must die so everyone else can live."

His scalp prickled hot. He thought of his mother. He thought of Julin and Fern. And now Adora. Sacrifices. Blood and more blood.

"I won't do it!" He jumped to his feet, clenched his fists. A light wind ruffled the tall grass behind Selicia.

"Some must sacrifice to give us the chance to live," Selicia said in the same quiet voice, unruffled by his sudden movement. "It has ever been so. That is civilization. The many cannot survive without the sacrifice of the few."

Grei chased the thoughts from his head, fought them with everything he had. He didn't believe that. Life couldn't be built on the deaths of others.

But Selicia's words harried him like birds. The prophecy said he could stop the Debt of the Blessed. He could achieve what he had always wanted. There would be no more Julins. No more Ferns, dying so everyone else could drink and hide behind masks. All it took was one last sacrifice.

He shook his head. "I'm not that man," he whispered.

"Then what will you do with her once you get her?" she asked.

He shook his head. "Stop the slinks. Some other way."

"Bold words. Others have tried. How will you be different?"

"Somehow."

She nodded, and he felt her absolute lack of faith. He had no plan, no idea what he was going to do.

Selicia looked down at the ground between her feet. "Why not go to the emperor?" she asked softly, then glanced up at him, and he couldn't decipher her expression. Curious? Beseeching? Was this why she had stopped trying to capture him? To try her hand at persuasion?

"Instead of dragging me to him in chains, you could just walk me up to his door. Is that it?" He tensed. The woman could strike unbelievably fast. Would she try to capture him again if he refused?

She shook her head as if she could read his thoughts. "I am yours. But if your goal is to stop the slinks, then you and the emperor are aligned," she said. "That is all he wants."

"The emperor and I are not aligned. We will never be aligned."

"You will defeat the slinks, you say. Somehow. You say this like a man who has never met a slink." She watched him.

"I've met two," he said. And he had been helpless against both. He'd been driven into unconsciousness by the first slink seven years ago, and the second had burned his forearm to a cinder. He would be dead if not for Blevins. He had no idea how to fight slinks.

Selicia nodded at his uncomfortable silence.

"The emperor is worse," Grei said. "Do you even know what he's done?"

"He sacrificed his own daughter and almost his sanity trying to stop them. It is all he thinks about," she said.

"He killed a Faia. Maybe more than one."

She went silent, looking at him with narrow-eyed skepticism. "What would make you say that?"

"Because that's how the Badlands came to be. It wasn't a fire. It was the emperor killing a yellow Faia. The trees showed me. I lived the memory. It's why nothing grows there. And I can't tell you which is worse: the slinks slaughtering hundreds of our people or the emperor killing one Faia. It's appalling. It's hard to even imagine."

She didn't speak again. Eventually she got up, erased all traces of their camp and dumped the fish carcasses into the river.

Before the sun had cleared the distant horizon, they were

on the move again. Selicia guided them through the fields, keeping Baezin's Road just out of view.

By day they traveled. At dusk, Selicia hunted or fished, and Grei built a small cooking fire, usually in some natural hiding place, either behind hills or trees or in a divot in the land that gave some cover.

Selicia was a superlative hunter. He'd never seen anyone so good. Mostly, they ate fish. The Ringblade could catch a half-dozen fish with just a hook and a piece of thread. Some days, she also brought game from the fields, a few groundhogs, a half-dozen squirrels, even one flying hare. She did all of this with just her mysterious knife, and she always hunted for less than an hour, between the time the sun began to set and full dark. Grei had known hunters in Fairmist who went into the South Forest, spent the entire day, and only emerged with a rabbit or two. And the South Forest teemed with game compared to this land.

He assisted when he could, trying to forage for roots and other leafy greens they could eat, but he soon realized how ill-equipped he was to survive in the wild, especially with only one arm.

Every morning, she would do her dances, and Grei would watch. He was drawn to them, and his admiration for her grew. He took to waking just so he could see her move. Sometimes the dances were fiercely contained; she spun and struck within a five foot square space. Sometimes they were grand and sweeping, covering great distances.

Her grace and precision made him hold his breath. He had never seen a person move like that. He didn't know a human body *could* move like that. Highblades trained for years to be the skilled fighters they were, but this was something different. This was a way of life, and the more he watched her, the more he realized that these movements were a part of everything else she did during the day.

One morning, after she had bathed and returned to the camp, he said, "You never stop."

She glanced at him, then sat down and unwrapped a piece

of cooked squirrel she had saved from the previous night. It was always the same. She hunted, divided what was caught between them, then ate half of her part and saved the other half for morning. She always offered him part of what she'd saved, but after the first few days, he realized his selfishness and started saving half of his own dinner for breakfast.

"It is what I have left," she said.

He felt a sudden pang of guilt. She had given up her "circle", her sisters, her life, for him. He forced the guilt down, forced himself to remember what she had done to Adora and Blevins. But it was difficult, looking at her, realizing day by day that everything she did, everything she was, had been only to serve the empire, to serve all of them. Including him.

She was ruthless, but in an odd way she was also selfless. He wondered if he was the unreasonable one, refusing to collaborate with the emperor. Insisting on going his own way when there were more people he could help than just himself, Adora and Blevins.

He cleared his throat.

"Don't you ever want to rest?" he asked.

She finished her bite of squirrel and swallowed. "I am resting."

He laughed. "I mean like other people rest. Let go. Take a moment to stop working. Stop the dances. Relax. Smile."

She nodded, looked at the ground, but she didn't say anything.

"Well?" he said.

She seemed to consider staying silent, but then she looked up at him, and her black eyes pinned him.

"Relax like other people?" she said. "Other people are selfish."

He felt himself flush. "You mean me," he said. "You mean I'm selfish."

"The few must sacrifice for the many. I must. Because I have the power. Because I was born stronger, faster. I use my gifts to serve others."

"I'm traveling across the empire on foot," he said. "I would give anything to find Adora!"

"You have the power of a Faia. You say you wish to stop the slinks." She shook her head, and he felt the weight of her judgment fall on him. "But you do not use this power. You do not train. Not once have I seen you do this."

Grei had been reluctant to use his magic since the battle in the Badlands. It had dulled his mind, taken away his sense of self, everything the delegate's torturers had tried to do to him.

"You don't know anything about it," he said.

"I know you are the Whisper Prince. And perhaps that means you are destined to succeed in your quest. Perhaps that is all you will need. But if I were you, I would explore all of my weaknesses." Her gaze moved slowly and intentionally to his burnt arm, still wrapped in the now-filthy cloth. "It is a horrible thing," she said softly. "To discover your weakness only at your moment of need. This is how the inexperienced die in battle."

Rage leapt inside him. "Is that how you got your scar, then?" he lashed back. "Did you lean on *your* weakness?"

She sat so still that she might have turned to stone. "No," she said. "I leaned on my strengths. Every strength I had. I fought better than I have ever fought in my life."

"But he beat you."

"He beat me." Her gaze was intense. "But he would have killed me. Instead, I kept my life and two scars to remind me."

"That you lost?"

"That there will always be someone better. That I must live at the edge of my ability, or next time I *will* die, and not just walk away with scars."

Grei's rage left him so suddenly that he felt hollow. For years he had fought against his father, hated the Debt of the Blessed, hated the emperor who would instate something so foul, even though Grei knew the reasons. He had always felt there had to be a better solution, but he had never found one.

This brutal woman did not hope for some answer; she found one, even if the answer was flawed. A prickle of shame heated his cheeks. He looked at her, scarred and ropey, unwilling to give in, and he suddenly felt so small he wanted to die.

She went back to eating, as though the conversation was over and Grei was a child who stubbornly refused to be dismissed. After a moment, he stalked away, winding his way down to the river.

I have been selfish, he thought.

Selicia had exiled herself from her own life, but every morning she rose and worked hard at her dances. Because it was what she had left, because it was what she could do. Every morning, Grei woke and worried over Adora. But what was he doing to ensure that when he found her he would be able to help her? Would he run into her arms and ask her what he should do next?

He looked at the rushing water of the Fairmist River for a long time, and the thoughts bubbled in him like boiling stew.

With a deep breath, he opened his heart and reached out to the water. He reached past the fear that he would become a blithering idiot, that he was doing something wrong. He searched for that feeling he'd felt at Fairmist Falls.

Sparkling, happy images flowed to him. The river reveled in its purpose. To rush along, to cut through the earth, to reach the ocean, to give life to all things along the way. To flow.

There was sentience there, but not like Grei's own mind. There was no worry. No effort. There was no "trying" to do something. There was only doing. There was only purpose. The river was itself, cool and wet and flowing, and that was all it longed to be. It reached out to everything it touched, giving giving giving.

Its language thrummed through him, and he was reminded of how he felt watching Selicia dance. The intrinsic grace. The resulting beauty. Selicia, the river, neither could be anything else but what they were.

And the river felt him, too, knew that Grei was a visitor. He closed his eyes, trying to feel its mind, and little images welcomed him, glimmers of sunlight on rippling water. They asked him what he needed. They were excited to help. To give. To flow.

He thought of the seven great bridges the Faia had made in Fairmist.

Can you do this? He thought, holding the image of the Blacktale Bridge. *Can you make this?*

He heard laughter from the rollicking water. He heard whispers from the wind as water and air talked to each other.

Grei opened his eyes.

Arcing gracefully over the Fairmist River was a shimmering water bridge, a translucent replica of the Blacktale. Each piece, from the carved flagstones to the thick hand rails on each side to the pillars, were perfectly wrought in shimmering water, direct from his memory.

It made him dizzy, just looking at it, and he reached out and braced himself on the trunk of a tree. He did not feel the ill effects he had in the Badlands. His mind was clear and light. He felt refreshed.

Hesitantly, he put a foot on the shimmering slope of the bridge. It was hard as stone. He took another step, still cautious, then walked to the middle. He could see the river rushing below his feet, distorted by the translucent bricks.

He laughed and stood in awe over what he and the river had made together. He saw movement to his left and turned. Selicia appeared at the river's edge.

He descended the arch until he stood next to her. He felt he should say something, but he couldn't seem to think in human words. All he could hear were the joyful murmurs of the river at Grei's happiness.

Thank you, he thought to the water. *Thank you.* He sent it an image of the bridge becoming the river again, flat and rippling and doing what it was born to do.

The water bridge collapsed, sending a wave of water downstream and overflowing the banks on either side. The spray soaked them, and the wave washed over their boots. He and Selicia leapt up the bank. The water receded.

He grinned and looked over at her. His vision automatically went deeper, went inside her. She was amazed. *This boy can do the impossible. What an asset he might be to all the citizens of the empire. With him, the emperor could defeat the slinks.*

But behind her excitement was staunch control. She still kept some of her emotions tightly under rein, and it made them harder to see. Still, a few things leaked through.

He needs discipline. Defeating slinks will not be this easy.

"I will work at it," he said. "I promise."

She looked at him, knew immediately he was reading her thoughts. He felt fear from her at this, and it dampened his joy. He closed his vision to her heart and promised himself he would stop doing that unless he was invited. Taking what was not freely given was a crime, the opposite of what he had just done with the river. He remembered the river's joy at their collaboration.

It hit him then. *That* was why his mind had been dulled in the Badlands! He had forced himself upon the elements he sought to change. He had stolen the identity of the swords, the lock, the ground. He had ripped them away in his need. It *was* a crime, and the punishment was losing his own identity just like he had taken theirs.

Flush with his new realization, he turned to Selicia. "I'm sorry," he said.

She nodded. They watched the river together for a time. Then she said, "I will make you a deal. We will both train in the mornings. You watch me dance, then I will watch you do this."

He nodded and extended his good hand. She took it and they shook.

"Deal," he said.

Chapter 35
GREI

THEY BROKE camp and continued on. Grei felt invigorated. He turned his gaze on everything, listened for the whispers of the grasses, listened for the whisper of the ground. He stumbled once, trying to understand and speak back to the disjointed song of the wind, and Selicia looked over her shoulder at him with a crease in her brow.

"Practicing," he said.

"Perhaps practice walking first?"

"Was that a joke?" he asked her, striding faster to catch up. "Did you just make a joke?"

She said nothing and kept walking.

Days passed and they slipped into a companionable rhythm. Selicia danced. Grei practiced his magic.

As they neared Thiara, the wild grasses became cultivated fields. Some grew food, but most were cotton.

"We have reached the edge of civilized Thiara," she said. "These are the Felesh Plantations, and we must be careful. The closer we come to the imperial city, the harder it will be to hide in open places."

"What about the city?"

"Once we are in Thiara, I can hide us. There are many secrets there," she said.

They made camp that night in the hollow of a tall, sandy embankment that was well hidden from the fields and the road. Grei cleared out a few crabs before settling against the curving back wall. It was damp and filled with the noise of the river, but warmer than Grei had ever experienced. He had taken to walking without his shirt during the day because of the heat. There was also a scent on the air: thick, salty, part decay and part fresh. Life and death at the same time.

Selicia joined him, opened a cloth filled with carrots and turnips and divided them in half.

"What is that smell?" he said.

She glanced at the vegetables, then looked at him.

"No. In the air," he said. "Salty. Cloying. Like fish left too long on the bank."

"It is the sea. Have you never traveled west before?" she asked.

"Never beyond Fairmist. Well, the Lowlands and the Highward, but that's all."

"Come." She scooted to the river's edge, and he followed.

The sun had slipped behind the hills to the west, which were dotted with white marble outcroppings. The dying purple light touched them, making them sparkle like diamonds.

"That is the Crown. Just beyond lies Thiara. Just beyond Thiara lies the Sunset Sea. It is the sea you smell."

"Then that is the Jhor Forest," Grei said, looking north at the tall, lush trees. His father had often talked about the richest forest in the empire, said he longed to hunt there as a young man. There were said to be immense predators moving through those thick trees, giant wolves and tree-traveling cats, but also more game than could ever be hunted. It was sport for the young nobles, and they had contests each year. To hunt alone in the Jhor and emerge alive was a test of manhood.

"That is the Jhor," she agreed.

"Have you been inside?"

"Yes."

"Is it as dangerous as the legends say?"

"No one would look for us if we approached Thiara through the Jhor, and it would put us within running distance of the wall." She glanced at him. "But we will follow the Fairmist River."

Grei heard what she did not say. Better to face the Highblades than the Jhor.

He looked back at the bumpy darkness of the forest's canopy, barely visible as the sun disappeared.

"Wow," he said, wondering what it would be like to slip through those lush trees, to see wondrous creatures he had never seen before.

"Many young men are seduced by the Jhor," she said, watching him.

He caught her gaze and grinned. "I have other forests to navigate," he said. "First things first."

Her scar bent a little, a nuance he had come to know as her smile.

"I'm wondering if there was ever a time in your youth that you laughed a lot—"

"Hsst!" She grabbed his shoulder and shoved him flat against the ground.

Fear spiked through him. Then he heard the voices approaching just above the bank.

Selicia's face was shadowed, but he saw her motions clearly. She tapped her chest, and nodded imperatively at him.

He understood and opened the doorway to her heart. It was easier this time, and vivid images came to him. He saw the two of them swimming across the river.

He nodded and took a deep breath. They rolled into the shallows, and the water seeped into his clothes. She draped one arm across his chest as the current pulled them toward the center of the river.

"Lie flat," she whispered in his ear. "Float, don't swim. Keep your head back, face up."

Splashes of river water jumped into his mouth, and he coughed. Instinctively, he tried to put his feet down, tried to swim.

Selicia's arm tightened across his chest, and she kicked his legs out from under him. She held his head still, and he found that he could breathe. She pointed them downriver and propped him up so that his head rested on her shoulder, just above the water.

"Relax. Lie on me. Float."

After a rigid moment of panic, he realized he wasn't sinking, and he relaxed against her. Her body was tense underneath him, her muscles working as her free arm paddled hard beneath the water.

The voices he had heard suddenly became louder. He couldn't understand them, but they certainly weren't farmers.

With Selicia's expert guidance, they drifted to the center of the river, and then to a large tangle of driftwood and debris on the north shore.

She dumped him into the water, caught his bad arm just above the elbow and snagged the tangle of branches. They swung into the shallows, and she rolled silently to her feet. He crawled after her as quietly as he could.

She sat down, pulled off her thin boots, then undid the laces at her breeches and removed them, slipping her boots back onto her feet.

"What are you—"

She put a finger on his lips and shook her head sternly. When she had the dripping bundle wrapped up tight in a ball, she crept to the edge of the river, keeping herself concealed by the tangle of driftwood.

She watched upstream for a long moment then, cocking her arm, flung the bundle over the river. It arced low, splashing just south of the middle.

She returned and grabbed his wrist, led him up the bank,

over the top and back down a little slope on the other side.

She grabbed his head and put it next to hers.

"Run low," she whispered, so quiet he could barely hear her. "Head down until I tell you. Quickly. They are on us."

They ran, and he tried to keep his fear controlled. They had been spotted. The Highblades knew there was someone here. They would pursue. He could only assume that tossing her pants into the river was supposed to serve as a decoy. He had a dozen questions, but if not for her quick thinking, they would already be caught.

He kept his head low and ran, though he thought the squish and thump of his wet boots and breeches must certainly bring every Highblade straight to them. Selicia moved silently next to him and did not comment.

When his lungs were burning and his back ached from bending over, she finally pulled him to a stop. They dropped to a crouch between the rows of cotton. He tried to control his breathing. Selicia seemed as calm as ever.

"We crouch to the end of this field," she said. "Then I want you to stand and run as fast as you can toward the Jhor."

"Are they still..." he huffed. "Behind us?"

"Go, Grei," she said, pushing him in front of her.

He did as she asked, crouching to the end of the row. He could see the dark edge of the Jhor Forest ahead, blotting the northern horizon. The crops ended a few hundred yards before the forest, as though the farmers refused to till too closely to it. The moonlit field sloped upward to meet the trees. A figure running up that would look like a black bug on a silver blanket.

"Run!" Selicia whispered harshly from behind him, and he sprinted, hoping his legs would hold out, hoping his lungs wouldn't burst.

He hadn't gone more than a hundred feet when he heard a thump and something tumble behind him, and he risked looking over his shoulder. Selicia was gone.

Fear gripped him. He stopped, gasping for breath and putting his hands on his knees. He searched desperately for her in the grassy slope. She rose, some twenty feet back, and he felt a wash of relief. She reached under her arm and snapped off the arrow that had sunk into her side.

Behind her, four Highblades ran through the rows of cotton. A high whistle went up from the group.

One of them nocked another arrow while running and let fly. Selicia watched it come, swayed to the side like a tree in the wind, and the arrow missed her by inches, sinking into the ground.

She opened her wet tunic, slipped it off her arms and whipped it to the side. It sprayed water droplets in the moonlight. Her dagger glowed silver in her fist, and she sauntered toward them in her small clothes, as though she was preparing for one of her morning dances.

Grei froze in indecision, wanting to shout at her to run, but it was obvious she wasn't going to.

"Baezin's blood," he cursed. He hesitated one more second, then ran down the slope toward her.

Selicia broke into a light jog as the running bowman nocked another arrow. He shot, but she spun in a neat pirouette and the arrow missed. She rolled out of the spin in perfect form, arms winging out to the side, never breaking stride. Something silver flew from her hand.

The bowman reached for another arrow, but he suddenly gurgled, her dagger in his throat, and fell to his knees.

Then Selicia was among them. She leapt high into the air, over the side-strike of the first, kicking him in the face. His head snapped back, and he crumpled.

She landed slightly off balance, stumbling as the next Highblade thrust at her heart. His sword sank deep into her side. He yanked the blade out, and she fell to one knee.

"Selicia!" Grei shouted, barreling into the Highblade, taking him bodily off his feet. They crashed to the ground.

The Highblade growled, head butting Grei with his helmet. Stars burst in Grei's vision, and suddenly his arms felt like limp reeds. The Highblade threw Grei off and rolled on top of him, letting his sword go as he drew a dagger.

Grei reached up weakly with his hand, touched the helmet. "Melt," he murmured, and the metal dripped over the man's head. "Steel!" he said, and it hardened.

Grei felt that thick feeling in his head that he'd felt at the Dead Woods. It disoriented him.

The Highblade shouted, muffled and blinded by solid steel. In panic, he reached up to grab his head, and Grei threw him off. But the Highblade recovered himself and slashed out with his dagger, just missing Grei's belly.

Grei kicked at the Highblade's encased head, but barely connected, and he stumbled past. The man rolled to his feet, swinging blind, and missed again.

Then Selicia was there. She swung a longsword into the Highblade's encased head. It rang like a bell, and the man dropped. He gave a muffled moan, struggling to rise. She clubbed him again, and he lay still.

Her shoulders stooped. The big sword fell into the grass.

A thin stream of very dark blood ran down her right side where the arrow protruded from her ribcage. An even larger swath painted her left hip and thigh red from the sword wound.

"You're hurt," he said stupidly. He fought the fog in his mind, and suddenly remembered there had been a fourth Highblade. He looked frantically across the field, then spotted the Highblade's crumpled body over a cotton plant behind her.

"You did it," he said.

"My thanks," she whispered, drawing a rattling breath. She sank to one knee.

"Selicia," he jumped forward and held her up.

"You must run," she grunted. "Brave the Jhor. Do not go back to the river. That whistle will bring more."

He glanced up the hill, then back at her. "And you?"

She let out another gurgling breath and leaned against him. "I told you how this would end, Grei. But you don't listen..." She leaned her head on his shoulder, her body slowly going limp.

He glanced back the way they had come. He didn't see any Highblades, but if Selicia said they were on the way, they were. The fog in his mind was slowly beginning to clear.

"You're saying I should leave you?"

"Only one way this can end."

"Everyone wants to tell me how it's going to end," he muttered to himself, leaning down. She gasped, and he lifted her onto his shoulders. She seemed so light, a wisp of a thing, not the unstoppable woman who had just felled four Highblades.

"You keep the blood in your body," he said grimly. "I'll do the rest."

He started up the hill.

Chapter 36
GREI

GREI HEARD another shrill whistle when he was halfway up the slope. He staggered toward the trees, so close now, but Selicia grew heavier with each step. Sweat ran down his forehead. He huffed, sucking each breath.

The grass rustled next to him and he looked down. A gold-and-red fletched arrow quivered where his foot had been.

He spun to look back at his attackers, and Selicia's weight threw him off balance. His ankle turned and they both went down. Another arrow whistled over his head. Selicia tumbled out of his grasp, hitting the ground in a limp tangle. She moaned.

A triumphant shout went up from down the hill. They thought they had hit him.

Get up, he thought. *Get up!*

He gathered Selicia into his arms, but she was slick with blood and hard to grip. He managed to cradle her, hooking her knees over his burnt and bandaged arm. Her head lolled to the side.

With a grunt, he staggered to his feet and managed a pathetic lumber up the hill.

A shout went up behind him, frustrated this time. He heard swords being drawn, and he pushed his legs forward, forcing them to give everything they had, waiting for the sharp bite of steel in his back.

An arrow whispered by his ear and sank into the trunk in front of him. He plunged into the trees, which blotted out the scant moonlight. The thick undergrowth immediately tripped him, and he stumbled sideways, slamming into a gnarled tree trunk and spinning around. He clutched Selicia to his chest, managed to stay on his feet, and staggered into the dark.

The Jhor spoke to him like the Dead Woods, except the voices were light singing instead of insidious whispers.

There were no pines here. The trees were fat and massive, the leaves wide. The burly limbs grew so low to the ground that he had to duck under them.

It was even warmer in the forest than the field, as though something breathed wet life into this place. Sweat rolled down his face.

Wet brown leaves covered the floor. Moss grew on exposed roots, and the forest swallowed all sound. The noise of the approaching Highblades, the ocean breeze, the night creatures of the field vanished. All he could hear was his own rasping breath, the squish-shuffle of his boots, and the vibrant voices of the forest, alive in his mind.

He tripped again, and this time he couldn't manage to stay upright. He and Selicia fell into the hollow between two roots as thick as his waist. She slipped from his grasp and slid to a stop, curled in on herself like a sleeping child.

He gasped, trying to regain his breath. Selicia's blood covered his arms and chest and had smeared on the roots below her. He had to stop the bleeding. He had to bind her wounds.

He pictured himself getting to his feet, tearing strips from his tunic to use as bandages, but his arms and legs were thick and useless. He remained crumpled between the two protruding roots and gasped for breath.

He strained to hear his pursuers, but there was nothing.

With a grunt, he scooted to Selicia and leaned over her.

He labored to pull his tunic over his head, and it seemed to take forever. But he had no knife, and he suddenly realized that ripping the oil-treated leather with only one hand was laughable. He tried to use his teeth, but then stopped, panting, teeth aching.

The magic. He had to try. Could he slow her bleeding? Turn the wound to flesh?

Breathing deep, he opened his mind to her, tried to hear the whispers of her body.

The song of the forest became a dozen voices singing in harmony, so loud he cried out. It was like the Faia at the waterfall. Bells rang and dozens of sweet voices rose together, intertwining.

The darkness peeled away, and suddenly he could see everything as though the sun was just setting. It was as though he had been given night vision.

"I need to help her," he said, trying to speak into the song, but his voice was an ugly intrusion.

He cleared his throat, tried to speak softer, tried to find the heart of the song. He felt its power flow through him, and he turned his attention to Selicia. She could only have a few moments left, if she wasn't dead already. She had lost so much blood—

Limbs cracked and snapped, and a Highblade emerged from the undergrowth, his short sword drawn. He had not seen Grei yet, but his gaze searched methodically through the darkness. This man was still almost blind, while Grei now saw with the eyes of the forest.

The Highblade approached, moving through a veil of thin vines that dangled from the branches of the tree under which Selicia and Grei hid. Grei didn't remember pushing through them when he entered the canopy of the tree. The Highblade reached up and batted them out of the way.

A new voice joined the song in Grei's mind, low and

loud, as though closer than the others.

The swordsman's gaze swept left to right, then focused. He gave a chuckle, and a grin spread across his face.

"End of the run, you little bastard," he said, spying Grei.

A long, inhuman arm descended behind the Highblade as the last strand of vines fell away from him. It was black as night and as thin as bones, the joints thick and glistening. At the end, instead of a hand, was a single, curved claw.

The Highblade pointed his sword at Grei even as he grabbed the whistle around his neck.

The black arm wrapped around the Highblade, burying the wicked claw in his belly. The Highblade gasped, dropping sword and whistle, and was hoisted straight upward. He disappeared into the leaves overhead and gave one ragged scream. Then, silence.

Blood fell like rain.

Grei wiped the gore from his face. The little veils of vines descended everywhere now, all around him, apparently seeking other warm bodies that might be resting under its branches.

Something whuffled in the blackness, and to Grei's left was an answering snort.

His heart beat in his throat, and he opened his mouth to breathe. A dozen enormous wolves slunk into view, their silhouettes barely visible through the dangling vines, which now almost brushed the forest floor. The nearest was inches from Grei's hand, and he forced himself to remain perfectly still.

The giant wolves circled, staying beyond the tree's reach. They were as tall as Grei, their paws as wide as serving platters. Their dark eyes glinted, and their muzzles pulled back to reveal long teeth as they sniffed the air in his direction.

He didn't know where the frightening black arm was, or if there were a dozen such arms in the darkness of the tree overhead.

He glanced at Selicia. Her skin was pale, and she wasn't

breathing.

Enough, he thought. *I can't just sit here and watch her die.*

He knelt down and picked Selicia up. She had been a true companion to him these past days. If they were going to die, they'd do it together.

He let his mind flow into the song and listened, searching for the words, but they still escaped him.

"I am here to help," he murmured to the forest. "I will stop the Lord of Rifts."

He walked into the vines. They slithered against him, light as paper, sticking to the blood on his body and clothes.

The long, black arm came down to his left, slowly like it had before. It dripped with the Highblade's blood. Grei tensed, but he kept walking, skirting it, waiting for it to snatch them up and turn them into red rain.

"I am the Whisper Prince," he said, louder this time. The vines tickled his neck, his ears. He kept walking. Another arm slid down to his left, and another in front of him.

He clenched his teeth and walked past it, leaving the last veil of vines behind as he stepped beyond the canopy of the tree. The wicked claw-arms didn't stab him.

The wolves spread out in a semi-circle, their heads low and their lips pulled back. Those enormous jaws could snap him in half with one bite. Their fur was tinged with a green light, and as he watched, the light grew, radiating from the leaves and the tree trunks all around. The wolves' heads sprang up, ears perked.

The song in his head changed again as one voice within the many grew prominent. The other voices faded back.

The wolves whined. One by one, they dropped to their haunches then lay down, putting their giant muzzles between their paws.

There was a light, feathery touch on his chin, as though beseeching. He lifted his head and saw her. Crouched on the lowest branch of the deadly tree was the green Faia he had seen seven years ago, the Faia who had protected Adora in the South Forest.

She was small; she might have come up to his waist if she stood beside him. Her hair was pleated green leaves, and diaphanous wings spread out behind her, flexing lightly as she watched him. A brief, sleeveless gossamer dress draped her slender body, and her green eyes glowed. She cocked her head.

"I'm, uh..." Grei tried to say. She turned her tall, pointed ear toward him as though he was whispering. For years, he had wanted to question the Faia. Why did they leave? Why didn't they help against the slinks? How could they let the Debt of the Blessed stand? Suddenly, all of his questions and demands seemed arrogant.

He descended to his knees and set Selicia in front of him. He bowed his head. "She needs help."

He heard the fluttering of her wings, and she landed in front of him.

He glanced up. Her skin was pale, tinged with green, glowing beneath the short dress.

"I am sorry," he whispered, and she cocked her ear toward him.

She opened her mouth as though to speak, but nothing came out. Instead, the air rippled. The song grew louder, weaving around him. The ripple and the song moved through him, and he drew a shuddering breath. In his mind, he heard a single word.

Grei?

Chapter 37
GREI

REI FELT the Faia in him, in his chest, like she was another heart beating. She walked forward, each foot so light it barely bent the grass. He drew a breath as she reached out, took his face in her tiny hands.

The song of the forest thrummed all around, owning him. It was in his chest, his belly, his arms and legs. Within his mind, he heard the Faia speak.

Grei... You are beautiful. To have you listen. To have you hear. Baezin was beloved, but his human children were deaf.

He felt her flutter in his mind, adding to his memories like the Root had done in the Dead Woods. But this time, there was no wrath, only the music of the forest, heightening, taking him elsewhere.

The forest vanished, and he was suddenly floating above Fairmist Falls.

The falls parted, and the blue Faia emerged, sapphire wings cupping the air. A man stood on the platform before her. He was powerfully built, with strong shoulders and a thick neck. His gold-trimmed red fur cape hung heavy in the mists. Upon his graying head was a golden crown, and at his side was the jeweled sword with which Blevins had slain the slink in Fairmist. The Faia floated in front of him at eye level, and her gaze was sad.

"The empire is at its height," the man said, his voice deep and strong. "The work you began with Emperor Baezin has finally come to fruition through me."

The Faia remained silent, watching the man and listening, but she did not speak.

The gray-haired man said, "I have brought the empire to this pinnacle, and I would continue to even greater heights."

The blue Faia cocked her head, as though trying better to hear him.

"I call upon you and your pact with Emperor Baezin. I call upon you to give the empire an endless future."

The Faia drew away, as though a wave of heat was coming off the man, but she did not leave.

"Make me immortal," he said, his strong voice dropping lower in its intensity. "And I will guide the empire forever. I will keep her strong."

The Faia backed away even more.

The man stepped toward her, reaching out his hand. "Your kind live forever," he said. "Give me your gift. I have made your dreams with Baezin come true. Make me immortal and I will complete your vision in Thiara and beyond."

The Faia lowered her head, but her gaze never left him.

"You may speak now," the man said.

She only watched him.

The man's outreached hand slowly curled into a fist. "I have never asked you for anything," he said. "Emperor Baezin asked you to build bridges. He asked you to build ridiculous floating houses, even a flying ship for his pleasure. I have asked for nothing, yet I have expanded the empire to three times what Baezin did. Now I ask for this one thing. One thing! Give me eternal life!"

The Faia's wings flicked three times, carrying her

backward toward the waterfall. With a sad bow to her body, she turned away.

"Don't turn your back on me," the man demanded, running up the platform of rock. "Speak to me, damn you. Speak to me!" He headed toward the falls. "I am the greatest emperor Thiara has ever known—!"

The opening in the falls closed on the man, cutting off his tirade and crashing over him. The rush of water swept him away, swirling him down the river.

The Faia's song brought Grei back to the Jhor Forest. The enormous wolves were sitting up now, ears pricked forward as they looked down at him.

He reeled with the information. The Faia had pulled away in sadness because of that man. He had been an emperor after Baezin, but which one?

"Who was he?" Grei asked.

The song rose, and it swept him away once more. The forest faded, and Grei floated over a bald hilltop that he didn't recognize.

Dark clouds hung low in the sky, and lightning forked between them. The same man from the waterfall stood atop the hill, but he was older. Behind him stood six other men, all dressed in rich clothes. Before them were seven Benascan children, all with the identifiable pale skin and blond hair. Their little wrists were tied together with rope.

"Immortality," the emperor said. "You will ensure the Thiaran Empire thrives forever. That is why you have been chosen."

The man drew his sword, pointed it at the tumultuous heavens, and began speaking a strange language. The words were a dark imitation of the Faia's song.

The emperor sliced a gash in the air. Red light and smoke poured out. He reached for the first boy, but the second leapt at his face, clawing like an animal.

"You lie!" the boy screamed.

The man held the struggling boy at arms length and threw him through the blazing rip. "Liiiiiiiie!"

The old men seemed deaf to the terror of their victims. The next richly dressed man stepped up, took the next little boy and hurled him through the rip...

The image swirled away, bringing Grei back to the forest, gasping.

"They were just children," he said to the Faia, who watched him with those huge, liquid green eyes.

He used new lives. Destroyed them so that he might live longer.

The song heightened again, and the forest faded a third time. Green leaves were replaced by a star-filled sky. Grei returned to the same hill, but now it was deserted. The trees surrounding the hilltop were different. Years had passed.

A shaft of light shot out of the air like a smoky red spear in the exact place where the emperor had tossed the children.

The hole turned into a gash, and clawed fingers poked out, wrenched it open. Smoke and fire burst forth, and a small figure tumbled onto the ground in a ball, its skin glowing red. It twitched painfully, then uncurled and stood up.

Grei gasped. It was the first little boy the emperor had thrown into the rip, the one who had fought and screamed. As he cooled, his red skin became pale. His flaming hair became blond curls. He turned, went back to the rip and shoved his hand inside. With a grimace he pulled, and another child tumbled through. He reached in again, and pulled through a third. He reached for another, but the rip suddenly snapped shut. The boy gasped, barely withdrawing his arm before the line vanished. He howled his rage at the sky...

The vision faded. The old, green trees of the Faia's forest returned. Grei gasped and fell back. He looked up at her.

"Those were the slinks," he gasped. "That's where they

came from."

He opened a rift. He has opened others.

"What can I do?" he said. "Is Adora's prophecy the way? Do I follow Adora?"

She smiled suddenly, like he had struck a spark with his last word.

Love, she said, and she came to him, knelt in front of him. *It is the human gift. She. You.*

She took hold of his bandaged arm and drew it out from where he cradled it against his chest. She unwrapped the dirty, blood-smeared bandages and let them fall, revealing the charred, numb forearm beneath.

She whispered, and the burning circle just below his elbow flared. Blackened skin grew over exposed bone, coating it like dripping candle wax, and he gasped as sensation returned.

He flexed skeletal fingers, and they moved! The bones of his forearm were covered with smooth skin the color of charcoal, and he could feel again. It felt warm, as though he was holding it close to a stove.

Love. The Faia said.

The Faia crouched next to Selicia. Green glowed within the Ringblade's chest. The broken shaft of the arrow in her side pushed up, out of her flesh and fell to the forest floor. The blood all over her body glistened and began to move, gathered together in little lines. Dirt and debris crawled out of the rivulets like insects, sliding away until her blood flowed cleanly up her legs, across her belly and chest, back toward the sword gash and arrow hole. The blood seeped back into her body, and the horrible wounds closed.

Selicia drew a long breath and opened her eyes. She gazed at the Faia, stunned.

The Faia looked at her for a long moment, then turned away. She gave Grei a sad glance, her little brow furrowed.

Voices flew around him, and the trees glowed brighter. The giant wolves turned their snouts upward and howled. With a flick of her wings, the Faia leapt into the air and alighted on a branch above him.

"Wait!" he said. "Don't go."

Behind him, trunks and limbs bent away from each other, creating a glowing green path straight through the forest.

"But I have so many questions," he said.

She gave one last smile, then turned and leapt high above the tree, disappearing from view.

"Please!"

The giant wolves rose and moved forward, creating a wall between him and the dark forest. This audience was over.

"Thank you," he said softly. He turned and started down the illuminated path with Selicia behind him.

Chapter 38
GREI

GREI AND Selicia followed the path all the way to the forest's end. The wolves paced them, staying close behind. The forest opened onto a breathtaking vista. Below was the imperial city of Thiara, a thousand lights in the night. Its seven towers rose toward the moon, white marble glowing. A latticework of bridges sparkled high among the towers, and a dusky red wall surrounded it all. To his right, mossy boulders tumbled down to the moonlit ocean, and the dark expanse stretched as far as his imagination could go. The breeze that blew up the slope was warm and salty with the scent of the sea.

He glanced back toward the Jhor. The path through the forest was closing, and the giant wolves slowly became shadows between the trees. In moments, only their glowing eyes could be seen, and then those vanished as well.

The trees now looked like the normal edge of a forest. All traces of the path had vanished.

He glanced down at skin-covered bone of his right arm, touched it with his good hand. He "felt" it move, how to make it do his bidding, but it was not like a real hand. It was though he had been given control of something not fully his own, a living artifact of the Faia like the Lateral Houses.

He turned to Selicia. She was smeared with dirt, but all of the blood on her arms, legs and torso was gone.

"You look better," he said.

"That is the second time you have saved my life," she said.

"The Faia brought you back."

She watched him silently for a moment, then walked forward and embraced him. He froze, stunned, then he slowly returned the hug, trying to keep his shock in check. Her muscled body molded to his, warm and vibrant. He would have thought a hug from Selicia would be bony, but it felt good. He suddenly realized how frightened he had been.

"We did well, didn't we?" he whispered, swallowing down his sudden emotion, not sure if she was giving him comfort or seeking it. He had never seen her evince more than a tight smile, but perhaps being brought back from the dead was enough to make her sentimental.

"I am sorry," she said.

He hissed as she scratched his neck. He drew back from her, reaching up to touch the tiny wound with his hand. A spot of blood came away. On her finger glinted a metal sheath, pointed at the end.

"What are you...?" His legs wobbled and his head felt light. He staggered back, holding up a hand to ward her off, but his eyes had gone funny. There were two of her. Then three.

The three Selicias watched him as he dropped to his knees and fell backward. His arms and legs went limp. He couldn't feel anything. He shouted, but only a gargle came out. She had poisoned him!

He looked up at the three images of her, slowly revolving around him.

"I hope you will understand someday, Grei," she said. "You are simply too powerful to be free. The emperor needs you. With you, we could win against the slinks."

"You..." he managed to say. "Swore..."

"It was what you needed to hear." She took a deep breath and watched him with that expressionless face, then murmured, "A Ringblade moves, but is not seen." As though that explained her betrayal. As though that could explain that she was a blackened husk with no soul!

He suddenly realized why the Faia had retreated. She had seen into Selicia's heart, had known this would happen. It was the same reason the Faia backed away from humans a hundred years ago. We backstab. We betray. We dominate and subjugate. The Faia wanted no part of this.

He screamed at her, but the noise came out as another gargle.

"I know you are frustrated," she said. "But you are serving your empire best this way. You don't see it now, but there are other things happening here, and only the emperor has all the pieces." She fingered the ring on her left hand. It had a large black stone, and she turned it. The stone came free and floated up.

"Above the Crown," she whispered to it. "Western edge of the Jhor. Immediately." The stone hovered for one more moment, then sped away, flying straight for the wall of the imperial city.

She let out a long breath and glanced down at him. "It is ironic," she said. "Using Faia magic to bring you in. I think you are a good man, Grei. But being good isn't enough. Too much is at stake."

He growled, trying desperately to move his body, but it was as though he only had a head. He tried to focus on her, tried to bring his magic to bear, but the whispers were gone, even the loud song of the Jhor.

"I urge you to accept your fate," she said. "You and the emperor could fly together, or he could cage you. The choice will be up to you."

She stooped, hooked her hands under his armpits, and dragged him to a nearby outcropping of white boulders. She set him down in the dark, blocked from view on two sides by the rock, on a third side by the forest. Only a thin view of the moonlit Crown was visible from her hiding place, and Selicia sat patiently, watching in that direction, waiting for someone.

He stewed in his thoughts, trying to focus his attention enough to use his magic, but whatever poison Selicia had used was effective in taking away his power.

Eventually, he just stared at her, waiting for the effects to wear off. After what seemed like an hour of frustrating torture, Selicia suddenly stood up.

"Well done, Liana," she said. "Your approach was silent, but you allowed moonlight to catch you there." She pointed.

Grei strained his eyes to see who Selicia was addressing.

Three images of the same woman, dressed in the tight black Ringblade clothing, appeared in Grei's field of vision. She was very tall, with strong shoulders. She had a straight, prominent nose, a wide mouth, and large eyes, the whites stark against her black skin. Her curly black hair was short, shaved above the ears.

"My apologies, Ringmother," the new woman said.

"You came quickly. That was needed most," Selicia replied. She turned to face Grei, then said, "You may come out, Jylla."

Another woman, her three images revolving slowly, hopped down from the tall boulder behind Grei. She was short and thickly muscled. Her braid was light brown, contrasting against her black clothing. She had a round face, and her black eyes glimmered in the dark.

"Ringmother," she intoned reverently, and all three of her bowed.

The Ringblades stepped back to flank Selicia and look at Grei.

"We will carry him back to the Sanctum," Selicia said. "The emperor—"

Selicia spun suddenly, hearing something Grei could not.

The Ringblade named Liana suddenly gasped and twisted as her tall body turned to stone. Selicia dropped and rolled away. In a blur, Jylla drew her Ringblade, looking for the attacker. She had it cocked back to fly when she was suddenly backlit by a yellow light. She also became stone.

Grei strained his eyes to the side. An image of three revolving figures came forward, cloaked and hooded like someone from Fairmist. The figures paused, bowing their heads as though powerfully tired, but they quickly straightened, keeping the steel rod trained on Selicia. The hooded figure was small and slight of build.

Selicia looked as calm as ever. She waited.

"You're not that fast," the figure said, and Grei drew a shocked breath. He knew that voice!

Selicia launched herself forward, then with a dazzling pirouette, spun to the side as the yellow stream of magic hit the ground where she had been, turning the grass and dirt to stone. She leapt straight at the figure, who threw himself backward with a cry.

She reached him, bowling him over. They both thudded heavily to the ground. For a moment Grei thought Selicia had overcome the attacker, until he realized she was not moving. She was frozen in her leaping position, hands out, almost grasping her foe.

The little man grunted and, with great effort, rolled the stone Selicia off him. He stood up, and his cowl fell back onto his shoulders, revealing the long face and brown hair of his brother.

Grei let out a gurgle. "Julin!"

"Happy to see me, *brother*?" Julin said, smiling thinly.

"Help...me," Grei gasped.

"Of course," Julin said, giving a sweeping bow. "You are the Whisper Prince. Your wish is my command."

Grei felt a chill. It was his brother's voice, but not his tone.

"Kuruk is very angry with you, *Whisper Prince*. And what Kuruk feels, we all feel. 'Find him,' he told me. 'Find him and make him know my pain.'"

Julin's eyes had red flames in them. "Die," he said, pointing the rod at Grei's face.

Grei saw the yellow stream approach, and his gurgle was cut off as he turned to stone.

Part IV

Slink War

Chapter 39

THE ARCHON

THE ARCHON closed the door to his study and smiled after this morning's rousing activities. He had intended to sire a son on the emperor's wife in payment for what the emperor had done to him, but the empress had spurned the Archon's advances. She knew her husband had lain with the Archon's wife, knew that the Archon's "son" Biren was actually the bastard son of the emperor, but she wasn't inclined to take her own revenge. The Archon, however, was not the forgiving type. If he couldn't have the empress, he had planned to plant his seed in Princess Vecenne.

Then Mialene had walked into the palace. Sweet Mialene, the instrument of the empire's salvation, would be the instrument of the emperor's humiliation and the Archon's revenge.

There were some times over the years the Archon despaired that he might never have his opportunity without sacrificing his own life, but apparently the Faia did grant wishes.

He laughed, then gave a playful knock on his desk. For

now, there was business to attend to, reports to read. He must play the role of the Archon. He looked through the scrolls on his desk. No news yet from the fourteen Highblades sent to find the boy, Grei. But that wasn't surprising. The search was a formality. Unlike the emperor, the Archon didn't believe anyone could emerge from the Dead Woods.

He opened the scroll on the very top. Prince Qorvin had almost beaten back the Benascan savages at Cantrup. Soon, the empire would be even larger.

He set the open scroll back down. He couldn't concentrate. These juicy bits of information always drew him, but this morning they seemed small concerns. Mialene was in his bed, and he would keep her there until he was sure she was with child. And once she had given birth, the Archon could kill the emperor, slowly, whispering that Mialene had returned, and that it would be the Archon's issue on the throne, not Qweryn's.

A knock sounded on the Archon's door.

"Enter," he said, turning and folding his hands into the long sleeves of his crimson robe.

To his surprise, his granddaughter Aylenna entered. She wore the green and white of the Felesh Duchy, and she bowed low to him. Her long, dark hair was oiled in the current fashion of Thiara, and the snow-white lock at her left temple was a striking accent to her white tunic.

He always enjoyed seeing his granddaughter. She was the issue of his true son, Bennor, who had been taken as the second Blessed. Unlike Biren, who currently ruled in Felesh, this girl was the Archon's own blood. For protection, he'd brought her and her mother to the palace when Biren became Duke. Supposedly Biren was unaware of his true parentage, but the Archon hadn't navigated the crooked politics of the palace by being trusting.

"Aylenna, I wasn't aware you and your mother were visiting this week. What a pleasure to see you," he said.

She bowed her head. "Thank you, grand-da."

Aylenna excelled in her studies, was always polite, and

had the same direct personality as his *real* son. The Archon planned to make her the Duchess of Felesh when he took the throne.

Aylenna had matured startlingly quickly. She had been born nine months after Bennor had been taken as the second Blessed. She was Bennor's last unknowing gift to his wife. The girl was only six years old, but with her uncommon height and piercing intellect, she could pass for ten.

She walked to him and took his hand.

"What brings you here, my little rose?"

She frowned. "Roses are weak, grand-da. They wilt in the winter. They break when you bend them, come apart when you pluck them. Is this how you see me?"

He chuckled. "Shall I call you my little iron maiden?"

"Do I torture you?" She cocked her head to one side.

"You are the joy of my life."

"I shouldn't like to be called 'your little joy'."

"I fall before your arguments. Tell me, what shall I call you?"

She smiled. "I have a perfect name."

"Shall I guess?"

She laughed, tugging his hands. "I love you, grand-da. Give me a kiss, and I will tell you."

He leaned forward. Every time she visited, she gave him a hug and a kiss on the cheek. This time, she kissed his lips. He began to draw away, but her hands gripped the back of his head with frightening strength.

She parted his lips and licked his teeth.

He jerked back. "What are you—"

His teeth burned, and he cried out, slamming into his desk as he tried to get away from her. She slumped to the ground.

He grappled with the desk, trying to shove himself upright as the fire spread to his head. Knowledge came with it. The slinks had not been pacified with the Debt of the Blessed, and the Blessed were not sacrifices at all. They did not die. They lived in the empire in quiet corners. They bred

with other humans, attempting to create more humans with
slinks inside them.

The Archon gaped down at his unconscious
granddaughter. All of his machinations were nothing. The
slinks were quietly overthrowing the empire from the inside,
and his own granddaughter was one of them. This was the
true Slink War, and Thiara was losing. He saw her history
now. Bennor had not sired a daughter on his wife *before* he
became a Blessed. He had sired one after. He had returned to
his wife, whispered assurances that he had escaped his death.
He told her that he could not stay, that he wanted one last
night with her before he ran from the Highblades who were
even now searching for him.

"It...was all...a lie!" The Archon gasped, reaching out to
her, but the girl had fallen as though in a faint.

The Archon collapsed on his face next to her, tearing at
his throat. He opened his mouth to scream, but by the time he
could expel the breath, his mind had been overthrown.

He lay there for a long moment, and when he pushed
himself to his feet, it was the mind of Gexxek who saw
through the Archon's eyes. He had left the fires of Velakka
behind, had been pulled into this world to live a new life. His
memories from Velakka and this human's memories mixed
together, swirled, joining as if they were one. He turned to
Aylenna and gently lifted her head in his hands.

"It works," Gexxek said softly. He looked down at the
girl who housed one of the brothers of Kuruk. The Benascan
boy was a marvel. Lord Velak was right to humor him.

Aylenna's eyelids fluttered and she looked up at him,
exhausted. She barely had the strength to raise her head.
"How do you like my kiss, grand-da?" she whispered,
smiling weakly.

"Kuruk is clever. We will come more quickly now. Lord
Velak will be pleased."

"And now we have you in the palace," she said. "Next to
the emperor's heart."

"We have more than that. You will not guess who this

man has imprisoned in his room," Gexxek said. "This Archon has the emperor's lost daughter."

Aylenna's eyes widened. She struggled to her knees. "I will return and tell him right away."

"A moment," Gexxek said, thinking. "Wait. Let us surprise him with a gift."

Aylenna smiled. "What shall we do?"

"If only you could see the schemes in this man's mind."

"Tell me."

"I will do better. I will unfold them. We will use them. What will your brother Kuruk say when we give him a Velakkan-born child of the royal line?"

Aylenna grinned.

"Come," he said. "I think it is time for the Archon to visit the princess again."

Chapter 40

ADORA

ADORA SANG *The Whisper Prince* to the wind on the Archon's balcony. She sang it for Grei, the boy who would rather die than betray her, for the loss of him and her pretty daydream of another life. She imagined Grei with their brown-haired, blue-eyed daughter riding his shoulders, a life without emperors and Archons, without slinks or Blessed. A daily routine of quiet happiness, where sacrifices were simple. Foregoing cream for the winter to buy a new plow horse. The exchange of time for the raising of children. Honest sacrifices.

A lost fair lady looked into the mist
The Whisper Prince whispered of love
The lady saw slaughter, and terror, and rifts
The prince, he whispered of love

Love came swimming along the lost road
Her heel painted with blood
The shadows came charging with wrath born of old
Their claws dripping with blood

With blood and from fire the shadows unwound
Losing souls too many to measure
The flesh and the faces of others were bound
And the shadows all took of their measure

Their measure felled hordes; their fires untamed
But the prince, before them, he stood
One hand on the rose, one hand in the flames
The prince, before them all, stood

All stood when the horns of the realm gave alarm
Too late for all and for one
But he sent them away
And never did say
Why a princess lay down for his charm

She drew the last note out, pouring herself into the song. *Take it, Grei. Wherever your spirit has gone, take mine with you. And we will live there, for this life has no place for us.*

Her song seemed to linger when she stopped. The wind captured it, lengthening it, carrying it like a feather into the world, and then it was gone.

She ran a hand over her bald head, her fingers lingering on the small red scar on her cheek. She breathed the sea air and watched the shadows grow long at the eastern edge of the Jhor. She faced west, watched the water turn orange in the setting sun. The ocean withdrew and surged, crashing unceasingly against the shore. Adora had spent seven years with men who predicted the future, but they had never seen this.

The Archon had just left, his need urgent today. He came to her often, and would likely visit again before long. His attendants arrived every day to bathe her, to dress her, to shave her head anew. They came to make sure she was well-hidden and well-prepared for the Archon's visits.

The doors to this opulent chamber were the doors of a prison, latched from the outside, and she was never sure when he would arrive. It could be an hour after he left in the morning. It could be after lunch or before. It could be two or three times in the afternoon or none. It was always at night, and after, he would lie with her while she stared wide-eyed at the ceiling.

She felt like she was watching everything from a distance. It should have been just another task, like the Order used to give her. She had been prepared to give her body in service to the prophecy. She had calculated the taking of lovers, like Galius Ash.

But the Archon was not a Highblade from quaint Fairmist, not a cobbler's son to be taken in hand and guided. He was a master of the palace, of politics, of people. He had planned all of this, perhaps from the moment he recognized her in that dungeon room.

She had tried to manipulate him, whispered words of love while he rode her. She had cried out in real pleasure, allowing herself to succumb to his experienced touch. She had taken down protective walls to snare him, but she had succeeded only in losing control of herself. Her shame burned.

The Archon remained completely unmoved by her attempts. Today, she understood why. She had spent two weeks staring into the Archon's dead eyes while he made love to her, and she finally realized the truth.

She was the Archon's revenge. This wasn't a forbidden adventure, bedding the emperor's daughter. This was a plan. She had never had a chance to sway him, had never had a chance to escape, and she would bet that he would not honor his part of the bargain when the time came. She was his prize. Herself, and what she could give him.

She knew enough to know that the emperor had betrayed the Archon some time in the past. That betrayal, whatever it was, went deep. The Archon hated her father. It was his sole passion. Adora's pathetic whispers of love, the orgasms that rocked them both, were thin arrows shattering on a decades-thick wall.

At first, she couldn't figure what the Archon sought in

his revenge. Was it a secret he could think of smugly whenever he faced his emperor?

This morning, she understood.

She felt she should care, that she should rage. But for the first time in her life, her passion was spent. She did not want to fight anymore. She just wanted it all to stop.

She wasn't a real person anyway, just one façade after another. There was nothing true inside her. Nothing that stood on its own; she was a thing to be used for another's purpose. Her father. The Order. The prophecy. The Archon.

There was no Adora. No Mialene. She was nothing.

She looked down at the city, the ocean in the distance, the hard flagstones four levels below. One jump is all it would take, one leap into the air. She would make sure her head hit first. It would happen quickly, the attendants wouldn't be able to stop it.

She could see her father standing over the corpse, wondering who she was, never knowing that he had actually killed this bloody woman seven years ago.

The dream resurfaced then, of her father whispering to her, the dream she'd had that last night in the palace before they took her as the first Blessed. "I'm sorry," he had said by her bedside. "I'm so sorry."

She had thought about it often in her beginning days at the Order House, as the burn of betrayal settled and the passion for her new purpose was born.

But the dream had only been a child's attempt to believe that her father wouldn't willingly give her up. When she had awoken from that dream, Jorun Magnus was there with five Highblades. He took her down the hall, and her father looked past her as though she wasn't there. So she looked to Jorun. He would never give her up.

But then he, too, had betrayed her, left her alone on that dark shale slope. She yelled for him to help her, and he rode away. And her innocence had blackened like paper in a fire. No one would save her. No one cared enough—

The door to her chambers clicked, and Adora started

from her reverie.

The Archon has come to claim his prize again. She did not turn to face him.

She considered jumping then. If he realized she was considering suicide, he would take steps to stop her. Who knew what protections the Archon would put in place after he caught her staring longingly at the cobblestones—

"Adora?"

Startled, she turned. Galius Ash stood in the center of the room, half-crouched as though he was storming the palace. He was dressed in an X harness and the loose red pants of the Archon's Highblades, and she crazily wondered if he had somehow joined the Archon's entourage. A naked dagger was clenched in his fist.

"Come on," he said urgently. "I'm getting you out of here."

Mirth bubbled up inside her, and she laughed. He was so pathetic, a lone soldier in borrowed clothes. In Fairmist, Galius Ash was a name to conjure with. In Thiara he was a joke, a failure who had been ignored, dismissed. His appearance here, now, said much about his own transformation in the last two weeks. He was disobeying direct orders in coming here. His career as a Highblade was over and likely his life, too.

"I thought you went back to Fairmist," she said. A light ocean breeze blew across her shaved scalp, raising goose bumps on the back of her neck.

"Did you hear me, Adora? I'm getting you out of here."

She saw herself as the spirited woman she'd been in Fairmist, before all of this. That woman would have leapt forward, taken Galius' hand and rushed with him through the halls. That woman believed there was a solution to injustice. But that woman wasn't any more real than any of her other faces. The prophecy was broken and useless. Grei was dead.

She turned away, looked at the orange-tinted waves. She could still hear her song on the wind.

"Are you drugged?" he demanded.

"Leave, Galius."

His hand clamped on her arm, and he spun her around. Her wooden shoes clacked and the flaps of her high-cut courtesan's dress flew to the sides.

She didn't want to look at him. "Does it matter?" she said. "Go, Galius. Save some other maiden. There are none left here."

He paused, stunned. He searched her face.

"You're not yourself," he said sternly, but there was fear in his voice.

"Not myself..." She laughed. "I'm not anybody."

"You're drugged. I'll carry you." He took her wrist.

She twisted out of his grip. "I'm not drugged. I am done."

He looked at her, unmanned by indecision.

"The Archon's attendants will be here soon," she said. "He visits...often."

"Adora, we can sort this out when—"

"I'm pregnant."

It was as though she had struck him across the face. His mouth was open to finish his sentence, and it hung that way. "What?"

She felt nothing. How could she escape when her prison grew inside her?

"Whose is it?" he finally managed.

"Yours, dear Galius," she said acidly.

"Adora—"

"What do you think I've been doing here for two weeks while you've been running around with your Highblade friends? Locked away in the Archon's bedroom. What could he possibly have me doing?"

"It's...his?" He seemed ill.

She closed her eyes, put a hand on the marble rail to steady herself. The Archon wanted his own issue on the throne. She was a fool that she hadn't seen it in the first moment when she'd made his bargain. And she was suddenly certain that was the nature of her father's betrayal of the Archon, that her father had lain with the Duchess of Felesh. It all fit. Of course. Biren was her half-brother.

"You don't know that," Galius said quickly. "It takes months to know—"

"Take your quaint illusions and go, Galius. I don't need you. I don't want you. I never did."

"You don't know that you're pregnant—"

"I know."

His tense form seemed to sag. He was silent for a long time. She watched the white, thin clouds stretch across the blue sky.

"So," he finally said in a husky voice. "You will just let him come again?"

"Go away." She looked longingly below. Her arms tensed. She could jump right now, right in front of him.

Galius waited. It was as though he was thinking of the perfect words to say. But there were no perfect words.

Go away, Galius. She thought. *I am a used thing. Nothing you can do will change that. I have no purpose. My passing will be like the discarding of old boots.*

"How could you let him, Adora?" Galius asked.

The accusation lashed her, a bright pain cutting through the numbness.

"Let him?" she whispered, turning, and her voice sounded distant in her own ears.

"How could you let that old man put his hands on you?"

There was a distant roar in her ears.

"Could you not resist him?" he pressed. "Is it simply in your nature to—"

"I had no choice!" she hissed. She shouldn't yell. The Archon would come. His servants would come.

"Did you enjoy it?" he asked.

Her own cries of pleasure echoed in her ears, her body betraying her heart. She couldn't breathe, and everything in the room was red.

"If you wanted to die, you should have done it then," Galius pressed. "Before he put his—"

"You bastard!" she screamed, leaping at him, clawing at

his face.

He caught her wrist, spinning her. His dagger clattered to the floor. Off balance, she fell into his embrace, and before she could twist, he caught her other wrist and pinned it against her chest.

"That's my Adora," he whispered. "That's who I came for."

She struggled, trying to get free. "Let me go!"

"You didn't kill yourself when you faced your trials. You went through them to the other side, and that is what you will do now."

"I hate you!" she shouted.

"Listen to me, Adora," he whispered. "You did what you had to do. That's all it is. And that's what you'll do now."

"Let me go!" she growled.

"You can't give up. I won't let you."

She slumped against him. "I can't have his baby inside me! I can't!"

"Shhhh. We'll find a way. I'm going to get you out of here, and we're going to find a way through."

She struggled against him, but he held her firm until she hung limply in his arms. "I'm not anyone at all," she whispered. "I'm just a thing."

"You're Adora. Strong and beautiful Adora."

"You don't know me. You think you do, but you don't."

"I know you," he said. "I would know you if all my senses were stripped from me."

"How rare," the Archon said from behind them. "A poetic Highblade."

Galius whirled, setting Adora free so quickly she stumbled, clacking to the side and losing one of her wooden shoes. The Archon stood where Galius had before, except he was not a tense man in a foreign place. This was his room, his palace.

"How did you get in here?" Galius looked at the double doors, the only entrance to the room. They had not been opened.

"Let's allow that I know more about my own rooms than you do," the Archon said, spreading his hands.

Four red-clad Highblades opened the double doors now and entered, flanking the Archon.

"No," Adora whispered.

"Now, *beautiful* Adora," the Archon mocked. "You and I made a bargain, and you have not fulfilled your end. I cannot let you leave."

Adora's hand unconsciously went to her belly.

The Archon raised an eyebrow, and a slow smile spread across his face.

"No!" she shouted, sprinting for the door awkwardly, one foot bare and the other in the high-heeled wooden shoe. The Highblades moved to block her, but Galius was there, his sword flashing out of its scabbard. A ribbon of blood trailed a spinning hand and a Highblade screamed, and Adora made it out the doors.

The royal wing was only a short distance from the Archon's apartments. She ran into the hallway and pounded up the stairs. Clack, thump, clack, thump. The sounds of pursuit were right behind her, and she looked back—

Out of the corner of her eye, Adora saw the woman on the landing a second before they collided. The woman gave a shout of surprise, and the two tumbled to the floor in a tangle of arms and legs.

"I'm so sorry," Adora said, breathless. "I need to—" She cut herself short as she stared into the startled brown eyes of her younger sister. "Vecenne," Adora murmured. Vecenne had been nine years old when Mialene was taken. She had cried as they took Mialene out of the room they shared. That was the last time Mialene had seen her sister, and that nine-year-old girl had grown into a woman in the last seven years.

"Who are you?" Vecenne said, shaking her blond braid over her shoulder, an angry furrow in her brow. She stood up, brushing off the front of her breeches and stepping away from Adora like she was covered in horse manure. Vecenne was dressed in riding clothes, boots, and a short leather vest.

On the ground between them was a small strip of leather with straps. Archery. She was going to practice archery.

"I'm sorry," Adora said again. She wanted to tell her sister who she was, but suddenly she couldn't find her tongue. Instead, she stood awkward and uneven with one foot in a tall wooden shoe and the other on tiptoes on the cool flagstone.

"This is the royal wing, girl," Vecenne said. Her gaze flicked to Adora's shaved head, the scar on her cheek, the concubine's dress, slit high up the sides. "You are not allowed here."

"Vecenne—"

"You will address me as 'your highness'." She frowned, and her gaze lingered on Adora's cheek where Selicia had kicked her.

The Archon's Highblades finally caught up. They slowed as they reached the top of the stairs. "Apologies, your highness," the first of them said, taking Adora's arm. "We're not sure what got into her. She won't bother you again."

The second Highblade took her other arm. Adora couldn't make her voice work. They began to pull her away.

"Wait," Vecenne said.

"Your highness?" The first Highblade turned while the other kept a tight grip on Adora.

"What did you do to her face?" Vecenne asked.

"The Archon—"

"She is the Archon's servant?" Vecenne pressed.

"Yes, your highness."

"I've never seen her before." Vecenne's gaze had changed. "Did he strike her?"

The Highblade hesitated. "I believe she was a prisoner."

"The Archon is selecting courtesans from the prison?" Vecenne said. Her lip curled. "What was her crime?"

"I was not told what she—"

"Release her," Vecenne commanded.

The Highblade who had a hold of Adora hesitated.

Both of Vecenne's eyebrows raised. "Did you not hear

me, Highblade? Release her immediately."

The Highblade squeezed Adora's arm in frustration, then reluctantly let her go.

"Go back to your master. Tell him I'd like to talk to him about what he's doing with prisoners in the palace," Vecenne said.

The Highblades bowed stiffly, but they lingered next to Adora. Vecenne's frown returned. "Apparently the Archon's Highblades are hard of hearing. Need I repeat myself?"

"No, your highness." They both retreated down the steps, leaving Adora standing awkwardly in front of her sister.

Vecenne's stern gaze turned compassionate. "Come with me, girl." She went back up the stairs and past the two royal Highblades standing at attention at the double doors of the imperial wing. Their pants and harnesses were predominantly gold, accented with red, a sign of the emperor's own. They had not moved a muscle during the altercation, but Adora knew that they would have slain both of the Archon's Highblades if Vecenne had commanded it.

Vecenne took Adora to the room they had shared as children, the room from which she had been plucked on that crushing morning. The memories rushed over her, and her throat tightened.

"Please sit," Vecenne said as she closed the door.

"Vecenne," Adora began, unable to call her sister "your highness". She felt that the moment she did, the lie would overpower her, and she'd never be able to speak the truth. Vecenne was a thin strand that connected her to her past; she was all that made Adora a real person.

The princess smiled a little. "You are unfamiliar with the court, aren't you? Where are you from?"

Adora hesitated.

"You may speak freely, girl. I will not hurt you."

"You want me to speak freely," she whispered.

"Tell me your name. Tell me what they did to you. If it was done out of cruelty, they will pay the price. Archon or no Archon."

"My name..." Adora began, and choked on it. She thought of the Order, of how they told her she could never reveal herself. It was the greatest danger to the prophecy. If the emperor knew about her, everything would be undone.

Vecenne waited, her head cocked to the side. Perhaps she wondered if Adora was scared of the Archon's reprisal, or if she was a simpleton.

"My name is Mialene," Adora said softly. "Mialene Doragon."

Chapter 41
ADORA

VECENNE'S EYES flashed in anger. She opened her mouth to say something as her gaze flicked over Adora's face. There, with her mouth hanging open, scalding words on her tongue, Vecenne saw something that stopped her. Perhaps it was Adora's blue eyes, perhaps it was something in the set of her mouth, something that reminded her of their too-brief childhood. Vecenne stepped back and sucked in a breath through a tight throat.

"No," she whispered.

"Vecenne..."

Vecenne put a hand to her mouth, a gesture so like Adora's. She began shaking her head. "You died. They took you." Her voice was so soft that Adora could barely hear her. She looked at Adora as though she would suddenly vanish. "How?"

"The story is long—"

Vecenne threw her arms around Adora and hugged her tight. "Mimi," she whispered the old name she had once used. "I thought about you every day. Every day since then."

"I worried about you," Adora said.

Vecenne hugged her and would not let her go. It felt so good, so warm that Adora cried into her sister's shoulder. She had made herself believe that her family was Baezin's Order, that her life was to be a pawn of their prophecy. But this was Vecenne, warm and real and loving, a woman who didn't care if she served a purpose, didn't care if she was able to seduce a boy or withstand torture without giving up secrets. This was her sister.

Finally, Vecenne let go of Adora's shoulders, but she kept tight hold of her hands.

"You must tell me how you came to be here," Vecenne said. "Why are you dressed like that? And why were the Archon's guards chasing you? We must tell Father right away. He will be overjoyed—"

"No," Adora said, so suddenly it surprised her.

"But Father has thought only of you for a decade. To know that you are alive. It would bring the life back into his eyes."

Adora swallowed hard. She remembered his face when he turned away from her, as though he was erasing her, as though she wasn't there anymore.

"He thinks of me?" she said, barely able to hear her own voice. *I'm sorry,* he had whispered in her dreams. *I'm so sorry.*

"Oh Mimi," Vecenne said, squeezing her hands. "You are all he thinks of. It destroyed him, making that evil pact. He has lost all joy for life. He runs the empire, but he lives for his time alone. He spends hours in his magical workshop, locked up, searching for a way to destroy them. He would do anything to bring you back."

"What does he do there?" Adora asked, but she knew. The Order said her father was killing Faia, turning their magical lives into weapons like the Imperial Wands.

"He is a beaten man, Mimi. But if he knew you were alive—"

There was a bang on the door, and Adora jumped. With a deep frown, Vecenne turned.

"Who would dare?" she said, letting go of Adora's hands.

"It's the Archon," Adora whispered. The helplessness washed over her, and she felt small.

She thought of Galius. She had left him there to fight a horde of Imperial Highblades alone. He would never have a chance against that many. She had as much as killed him.

Vecenne started toward the door, which banged again.

"Vecenne, get your bow," Adora said.

Vecenne turned an incredulous look on her sister. "This is the palace, Mimi." She opened the door.

The Archon stood on the other side. Four of his red-clad Highblades stood behind him, their short swords drawn. Vecenne's eyes went wide. "You have overstepped your bounds, Duke of Felesh!" Her gaze flicked to the bow that hung on her wall. Too late. Too far away.

The Archon completely ignored her, speaking over her head to Adora. "You have been a bad girl, Adora," the Archon said.

"Did you not hear me, Felesh?" Vecenne said. "My father will have your head! This is my sister, Mialene," she said. "Your trespass on the imperial wing will not go lightly on you. Take your lackeys and leave at once!"

"He knows," Adora said. "He knows who I am."

Beyond the Archon, Adora saw blood on the naked blade of one of the Highblades, and her heart turned cold. They had killed to get in. They would kill again if they needed to.

"Vecenne, run!" she shouted, moving forward too late. The Archon struck quickly and brutally, clubbing Vecenne alongside the head with the pommel of a dagger. Her sister crumpled to the floor. The Archon stepped over her. His smile was flat.

"You had to bring your sister into this. I would have been happy to let her live, if you had just given me what I wanted."

"You want a child." Her voice shook with rage.

"Wasn't it obvious?"

"You said one month!"

One of the Highblades sheathed his sword and lifted

Vecenne's unconscious body onto his shoulder.

"Leave her alone, you filth!" Adora screamed, lunging forward. The Archon caught her arm.

"Have a care, Adora," he said, nodding to the Highblade, who drew his dagger and placed it against the back of Vecenne's ribcage. "Shouting in the palace will bring unwanted attention, and we have so little time. You hold your sister's life in your hands."

"I will kill you if you hurt her," Adora said.

"Of course you will," he said, offering his hand to her.

Adora's cheeks burned. She loathed him so much her body shook. But what else could she do? Fling herself on him, scratch out his eyes and sacrifice both their lives for moment of revenge?

After an excruciating hesitation, she took his hand.

"Clean this up," the Archon said to his men. "The rogue Highblade Galius Ash has abducted Princess Vecenne. The emperor will tear apart Thiara looking for both of them, and we can uproot any other lurkers while we're at it."

"Where is Galius?" Adora asked.

"I don't leave loose ends, my dear."

He yanked her arm, causing her to stumble into him, then pulled her down the hallway past the bloody bodies of the emperor's Highblades.

Chapter 42

GALIUS

WHEN THE Archon and his lackeys burst in, Galius spun to face them. No legend would sing of this last stand, but he was ready. Let them come. There would be blood in the palace today, but not all of it would be his.

Never sever the line—

Then Adora bolted past him like a wobbly colt, one foot bare and one clacking in her tall wooden shoe. She surprised everyone, including him, but Galius leapt forward with her and his spirits soared. She wasn't done. There was life in her yet.

He charged in front of her, blocking blades, cutting hands. He made good her escape, killed the first who tried to follow her and gave the others a reason to pay attention to him.

Run, Adora, he thought. *Go with the Faia.*

Swords bristled in front of him, and he turned away from the door, unable to follow her. But the Highblades had amateurishly left a narrow hole in the other direction. Their captain would berate them later for that.

He spun and made for the gap, parrying three blades meant for his heart. The tip of the third scratched his bare chest and left a scar on the silly X harness.

This was a man's life. He wasn't skulking through the palace or traveling across the Badlands with a broken heart and divided loyalties. This was what a Highblade was meant to do. Give his life for love. Fight brilliantly.

The Highblades shouted as Galius darted across the room. He leapt the giant bed and skidded to a stop on the balcony, arresting his momentum before jumping onto the rail and balancing. With a salute, he spun, sheathed his black sword and dropped straight down. A blade whistled over his head, sparking on the stone rail.

He had planned this. Sort of. When he was young, he had been enamored of the stories of Zed Hack. Who wasn't? Highblade Hack was the hero of all boys who aspired to be Highblades.

The work of a Highblade, Galius had soon come to discover, was mostly mind numbing. It was protecting a duchess's heirloom masquerade mask deep inside her keep, a place no thief would dare go for a treasure no one would want to steal. It was standing guard duty at the palace through unending nights. It was following a fat noble as he visited a brothel.

Zed Hack, on the other hand, represented all of the excitement a ten-year-old boy wanted. Hack could best ten foes at once with his swordplay. He leapt onto horses. He swung from ropes. He jumped from balconies.

So this was something the legendary Hack would do, and while Galius had long since learned that the most effective route to success was usually the most practical, he had always longed to jump onto his horse, to swing from a rope, or to leap from one balcony to the next.

Every level on this side of the palace had one. In one Highblade Hack story, Zed had escaped six swordsmen this way.

Galius timed it as well as he could. He took that extra

precious second to drop from the balcony rather than jump and risk sending himself wide of the next landing. But the balcony that rushed up at him still seemed frightfully far away. He reached for it, stretching as hard as he could.

His forearms smacked into the rail. His hands slipped in that flashing second, and he careened past it.

"No!" he shouted, trying to spin as his body whirled headfirst toward the ground. He reached in vain to catch the next rail.

A huge hand shot out, grabbing his wrist. Galius shouted as he jerked to a stop. He slammed hard against the rail. His arm felt like it had been pulled out of its socket, and white-hot pain shot through him. For a second, Galius' vision went dark. He fought for consciousness and won.

The giant hand hauled him onto the balcony. Through watering eyes, Galius looked up. Blevins towered over him, his belly covered with blood.

"By the Faia!" Galius gasped.

Blevins grabbed the front of Galius' harness, lifted him, and shoved him against the wall with one hand. Galius gasped at the pain. Each wound on the man's belly should have killed him.

"Where is my sword?" Blevins growled, his blood-shot eyes flicking a glance at the leather-wrapped hilt at Galius' back, then at Galius. He didn't recognize it. He didn't know that the blade he sought was within his grasp. Galius clenched his teeth through the pain, trying to think of what to do next. This man should be dead!

"What happened to Pazzek? Captain Delenne?" Galius demanded. But one look into Blevins' black eyes, and he knew the truth.

"My sword," Blevins growled in a deadly tone that assured Galius that he was next.

"I will tell you where it is," Galius huffed. Blevin's meaty fist pushed so hard Galius could barely breathe. "But you will give me your story first."

Blevins pulled him close, putting their faces an inch

apart. "Give me my sword, and I will give you your life."

"In a pig's eye!" Galius growled.

Fury lit Blevins' face. He lifted Galius away from the wall and carried him toward the balcony as though he would hurl him over.

"Kill me," Galius said tightly. "I'm living on borrowed time anyway. Or tell me your story and I'll tell you where the sword is."

Galius waited for the huge man to fling him over. Instead, Blevins nodded. He dropped Galius to his feet. "Very well, Highblade," he rumbled.

Galius took a breath. He worked his arm in a slow, painful circle. It wasn't dislocated. Good.

"You tried to jump from one balcony to the next?" Blevins asked suddenly.

Galius nodded, watching his eyes.

A small smile flickered across Blevins' flushed face. "Like Zed Hack," he said.

"Like Zed Hack," Galius said.

A dark noise came from Blevins' throat, a bubbling sound, and Galius realized that it was laughter.

Chapter 43
ADORA

"VECENNE?" ADORA whispered, needing to hear her sister's voice. The room where the High-blades had shackled them was somewhere below the palace, cool and damp. She shivered in her thin clothing, praying to the Faia that Vecenne would answer her.

Her sister had not spoken, not since the Archon had...

Adora thrashed against her manacles. How could it be happening right here, right in the palace? She squeezed her eyes shut, trying to think of a way out, but there was no plan that could right the wrongs that had happened in this room.

"Vecenne?" Adora whispered again. "You have to talk to me. Let me know you're okay." Adora had brought that monster into Vecenne's room, had spilled this horror into her sister's life.

"I'm going to get you out of here," Adora said. Vecenne's screams still echoed in her head. When Vecenne had awoken, she had fought the Archon as he methodically cut her clothes away. Those screams of rage became two gasps of pain as the Archon stole her innocence, then silence as he had his way. Of course, the Archon hadn't touched

Adora this time.

"Please, Vecenne," she said to the dark. "You have to talk to me. Tell me you're okay."

Adora strained for the slightest sound, the smallest movement, but there was nothing.

Then a stifled cry, a body hitting the outside of the door. One of the Highblades raised his voice and was cut off mid-word. His cry became a gurgling sigh. Another thump hit the door, slid slowly down.

Keys jangled, fit the lock, then the door swung open. Torchlight leapt into the little room, and Galius Ash stepped through. Behind him, Blevins' huge silhouette filled the doorway, his body covered with blood and wounds.

"By the Faia!" Adora exclaimed.

Galius gave her a tight smile. "Yes. It's all madness, isn't it?" he said. "Your highness."

Adora couldn't speak. "You know?"

Galius flashed a look at Blevins. There was awe and fear in that gaze. "It's all madness," he murmured. He worked quickly at the spools behind the table. Adora's chains went slack.

"My sister," she said. "Vecenne first."

"Adora—"

"Please," she begged.

Galius nodded and moved to Vecenne. He took in what had been done to her and set grimly to his work. He had her unlocked in moments. Vecenne slid down the "X" and stood on wobbly knees. Her gaze was distant, unfocused.

"I didn't bring clothes," Galius said.

Blevins, who had remained facing the hallway, removed his huge cloak and handed it to Galius. He wrapped it around Vecenne, who stared unblinking at the bodies of the dead Highblades.

Galius turned to Adora and freed her. Her bleeding, raw wrists filled with pain when the manacles came away. She clenched her teeth against the stinging.

Impulsively, she threw her arms around Galius' neck.

"Thank you," she whispered. "Thank you. For coming for me. For being...for being Galius Ash. I didn't dare to hope."

"Men are crazy for love," he said.

"You're a true Highblade."

"A dead one if we don't hurry. Come on, your highness." He urged her to the door.

"Don't call me that," she said. "You don't need to—"

"Make your chatter later," Blevins growled.

Galius led Vecenne gently by the elbow. She stared at him, then listlessly followed him out the door. Galius shot a warning look at Adora. "Battle shock," he said, shaking his head. "Her mind is—"

"She's my sister," Adora interrupted.

Galius nodded.

"Now or never," Blevins growled.

The four of them started down the long, dark hallway. Torches flickered in sconces on the wall.

They turned sharply to the right, rounded the corner, and ascended the worn stairs quickly. Blevins led them through another twisting corridor that opened up into a wider, longer room with a stairway along the wall.

"We must go up," Blevins said suddenly. "It opens to the western edge of the palace proper. This will be the most dangerous, so stay close, and stay quiet." Then Blevins stopped, staring into the darkness beyond the stairway. He held up a hand for silence.

Adora heard it. The slightest scrape of metal against stone.

"We are found," Blevins growled. His black sword sprang from its sheath like a wand of darkness, and he roared, charging forward.

Adora didn't know what was happening at first. A flurry of whispers flew past her head, and she thought they had released bats or birds. Then Galius grunted, and Adora saw the feathered shaft sticking out of his thigh. He dropped Vecenne's hand and leapt in front of Adora.

"Get down! Get behind!" he shouted. Another flurry of

whispers. Galius fell to one knee. He leaned back into her, and she saw the arrow sticking out of his chest.

"Galius!" she screamed. His hand rose shakily in front of them, lifting his sword as though the thin blade could protect them from the next volley.

There was a steel crash as Blevins reached their assailants. Screams filled the corridor, and the arrows stopped. Blevins roared, and a body smashed into a wall somewhere in the darkness. Another man howled like his tongue had been cut out.

"I'm okay," Galius coughed, pushing to his feet. He touched the side of his ribs where the arrow was buried deep. "Come on. He is giving us time. We must...use it."

A Highblade's battle cry was cut off. More steel clashed.

"Get behind him!" another man yelled.

"I have—" Another death scream ripped the darkness.

Vecenne did not hesitate this time. Her eyes were haunted, tight with pain, but there was life once again. There was determination. Galius grunted, grabbing Vecenne's arm and hauling her forward. They ran up the narrow stairway.

"Got him!" a Highblade cried from below. "I—" His voice cut off in a sickly gurgle. Blevins roared again. It was no sound Adora had ever heard a human make.

"Galius!" Adora said as two of the Archon's Highblades raced out of the darkness to the base of the stairs behind them. One cocked a crossbow, peering up at them as he fitted a bolt.

Galius reached the top landing and threw the door open, pushing his way through. The light of morning was blinding, and Adora rushed behind him, suddenly unable to see. He stopped abruptly, and she bumped into him. Something sharp scraped her shoulder.

She drew away as Galius slumped forward with a sigh.

A tall man stood silhouetted against the light, his curved Venishan sword thrust through Galius' body. Galius sagged to his knees.

"No!" Adora screamed.

The man yanked the sword out, and Galius collapsed on the stones of the open hallway. Two gold-clad Highblades dragged him out of the way and through a doorway. The stranger with the bloody sword grabbed Adora and pulled her through too. He did the same with Vecenne, then slammed the door and twisted the key.

"No! He's my friend. That's my friend!" she said, throwing herself toward Galius, but the Highblades held her arms tightly. She looked up desperately at the man with the bloody sword.

"And who are you?" Her father stared down at her, his dark eyes flashing.

Chapter 44
ADORA

ADORA LUNGED for Galius, but she couldn't reach him. He locked gazes with her, eyes wide with shock. Then the pain in his face eased, and he smiled as if he was dreaming.

"Die for love..." he breathed, and it stretched into a long huff. The light in his eyes faded, and he stared at nothing.

"Galius!" she screamed. She twisted and the Highblades finally let her go. She crashed to her knees next to him. "No!"

He had only wanted to help her. She had seduced him with no intention of loving him, and he had clung to his honor when the honor of his profession had failed him.

"Galius," she whispered into his curly black hair. "Please, no."

She was supposed to sacrifice *herself* for the prophecy. Not Galius. Not her sister's body. When was the moment Adora paid for her own choices?

A rough hand grabbed her shoulder and hauled her upright, and she looked into her father's black eyes.

"A fine harvest," she spat. "Another innocent for your tally!"

He was just as she remembered. He still wore his beard tied into three points. The black and gold hair he shared with Adora was cut short just above his ears. His nose was long and pointed. The wrinkles at the edges of his mouth and eyes did not seem any deeper for the years that had passed. He was the father she had loved, the father who had betrayed her.

His gaze flicked over Adora's courtesan dress, her bald head.

"You're the bartender from Fairmist," he said. "You came with Highblade Ash." His lip curled and his grip on his sword tightened.

"No!" Vecenne lunged forward, grabbing her father's arm. The emperor hesitated. Blevins' cloak fell away from Vecenne, revealing her bare chest, the tatters of her pants at her belt. The emperor's eyes went wide with rage.

"What has been done?" he roared.

"The Archon," Vecenne said. "Not her. Not him."

"Let him kill me, Vecenne," Adora said, her voice low and trembling. "Let him do it twice." She lifted her chin, exposing her throat to him. "Death is his answer. Innocent children. Valiant Highblades. Even the Faia, isn't that right, Father?"

The emperor looked down at her, and his brow furrowed.

"Who are you?" he asked.

"Just kill me and be done with it," she said. "Let us come full circle." Her father released her arm and took a step back as though she had struck him.

"I don't know you," he whispered even as his eyes lighted with recognition.

"Father, not here," Vecenne said, pulling on his arm. "There is much to say, but not here. Please."

The emperor flicked a glance at Vecenne as though she was a buzzing fly, then stared at Adora.

"I don't know you," he insisted, but his words were frail.

"A killer should remember his victims," she said. "Or have there simply been too many?"

His curved sword drooped until the point clinked against

the stones.

"By the Faia..." he gasped. "Mia."

"You don't have the right to pray to them. You don't have the right to say my name!"

"Father, please!" Vecenne begged. The Highblades were watching everything.

"Take them—" the emperor stammered, his gaze never leaving Adora's face. "To my chambers. Both of them." His voice dropped, as though he barely had the wind to speak. "Do not hurt her." He looked at the leader of the gold-clad Highblades. "The man who hurts her dies."

He glanced at the closed door through which Adora, Vecenne and Galius had escaped. "Recover the rest of this group, alive if possible. And bring Lord Felesh to me. There is truth to be had here, and I will have it."

He stared down at Galius Ash, started to look up at Adora, then stopped himself.

"Take her. Now," he commanded.

The Highblades took Adora's arms and gently escorted her away.

Chapter 45

THE ARCHON

THE ARCHON slammed the door. He was Gexxek, his soul snatched from flaming Velakka. At the same time, he was Dayn Felesh, Imperial Archon, and the desires of this stolen body had colored his actions more than he would have thought possible.

For Dayn Felesh, the taking of the youngest daughter of the emperor was his ultimate revenge, the culmination of years of waiting and scheming. Gexxek felt Dayn Felesh's elation. The idea of planting his seed in both daughters of the royal line made his heart swell with victory.

Gexxek put his hand to his head, wanting to scratch hard with flaming claws he no longer possessed. Instead, fleshy fingers pressed against sweaty skin. He took his hand away in disgust. Sweat. Human water.

"I am not human," Gexxek whispered. He scratched at the desk with his pitifully thin nails. One bent backward, and he gritted his teeth. He was molded in weakness, and until today he had thought it was only physical. But Dayn Felesh had a hold on his mind. Gexxek was not riding in a foreign body. He had become one with it.

The realization rattled him. He must remember to think like a Velakkan. He would send Aylenna to Kuruk immediately, inform him of the tangle Gexxek had made of things. Gexxek would run and live for the hope that Kuruk could use him elsewhere in this water-soaked world. Gexxek looked around, thinking about what he must take with him: the beloved silk hangings, the many books and scrolls scattered on the table. He would have to pack a trunk—

With a low growl, he realized that Felesh was overtaking him again. There was nothing of importance here—!

The door slammed, and Gexxek spun around. He squinted at the dark slash of shadow that covered most of the eastern wall. A Velakkan's vision could pierce those shadows, but humans were half-blind in the dark. He couldn't see the intruder.

Imperial Highblades would have charged through, surrounded him with swords.

"Who are you?" Gexxek said, finally catching the silhouette of a human to the left of the door. Gexxek slipped his fingers over the hilt of a dagger lying on his desk.

"I like that question," the man said from the dark. "Let's try it again: who are *you*?"

"I am the Imperial Archon, Duke of Felesh," Gexxek said, using the authoritative voice so easily, as though it was his real voice. "And you will suffer in my dungeons for your trespass."

"You're a liar," the man said, stepping forward. "Your real name is Gexxek."

Gexxek felt hope catch in his throat. Only a Velakkan would know his real name. Was this man sent by Kuruk? Could he have anticipated Gexxek's need and sent someone to lead him out of Thiara?

"Did Kuruk send you?" Gexxek asked.

"That's twice I've heard that name. Is Kuruk the Lord of Rifts?"

A chill ran through Gexxek. Kuruk did not play jokes. He did not send ambiguous messengers. Gexxek snatched up the dagger, stepped quickly forward and thrust it into the man's—

The dagger clinked against solid air, unable to reach the intruder. The man whispered, and the blade melted. Gexxek yanked his hand back as steel dripped down his palm, cool as river water. He stumbled away, looking up in shock.

"Who are you?" Gexxek repeated.

The man grabbed Gexxek's robes with a blackened, skeletal hand and shoved him backward. He bared his teeth.

"I'm the Whisper Prince," he hissed.

Chapter 46
GREI

STONE SUFFOCATED Grei, eating his organs, his skin, his throat, taking away his life. He tried to scream, but nothing came out. The last thing he saw was Julin's victorious gaze, eyes glittering. Then the stone covered him, and Grei went blind.

He screamed without a voice. There was no escape because he wasn't anywhere. He wasn't anything. He was thought without a mind, and all around him droned the voice, that horrible voice that would not be silenced.

Stone. Stone. Stone. Stone.

Grei tried to get past the fear, but the repeating words suffocated him. He was already dead! The dark overwhelmed him, and he floated endlessly, surrounded by that thudding, never-ending mantra.

Stone. Stone. Stone. Stone.

When he had been battered beyond sanity, when he realized there was no escape, he accepted. He let the droning voice wash over him and gave in. There was only stone. There was no Grei anymore. No Whisper Prince.

No Whisper Prince...

Whisper Prince...

The Whisper Prince whispered of love...

A voice sang softly, slowly rising over the droning of "Stone. Stone. Stone. Stone." He knew that voice.

A lost fair lady looked into the mist
The Whisper Prince whispered of love
The lady saw slaughter, and terror, and rifts
The prince, he whispered of love

Adora!
The remains of his identity grasped at the song, at the poem, at the heart of Adora's purpose. He listening past the awful droning to the voice that called to him, called him to task.
I've been searching for you, *he said.* Where are you?
But the voice just continued, pulling at him, lifting him up from oblivion.

A lost fair lady looked into the mist
The Whisper Prince whispered of love
The lady saw slaughter, and terror, and rifts
The prince, he whispered of love

Love came swimming along the lost road
Her heel painted with blood
The shadows came charging with wrath born of old
Their claws dripping with blood

With blood and from fire the shadows unwound
Losing souls too many to measure
The flesh and the faces of others were bound
And the shadows all took of their measure

Their measure felled hordes; their fires untamed

But the prince, before them, he stood
One hand on the rose, one hand in the flames
The prince, before them all, stood

All stood when the horns of the realm gave alarm
Too late for all and for one
But he sent them away
And never did say
Why a princess lay down for his charm

I am coming, *he thought.* I will find a way. I will find you.

A green light appeared.

It was a tiny thing, the barest flicker of emerald, but he was transfixed. In a land of absolute blackness, that tiny smear of green was a world in itself. As he focused on the color, it grew and enveloped him.

Suddenly there was a sense of space. He felt inhuman skin pulled over smooth bones. There was Faia magic, music and growing things, and Grei realized he could think. The droning voice had retreated.

I am in my arm, *he thought.* The arm the Faia healed.

With that thought came memories.

Julin came for me, but it was not Julin. Julin had become a slave of the slinks; he turned me to stone.

Grei huddled desperately into that single, wretched part of himself, clinging to his identity. After a time, he mustered the courage to think again.

I can undo it, *he thought.* That is why I am the Whisper Prince. This is not oblivion. It is only stone. It owned me, but I am not dead. Not yet.

He spoke to the stone. He told it to change back, to become Grei Forander again. It ignored him. The voice yelling "Stone!" was far too loud for Grei to shout over.

He tried concentrating on a small part of his body, his elbow just above the bony, gray forearm, tried to convince it to listen to his voice instead of the powerful drone.

It didn't work.

He felt the pathways the droning voice had taken, turning muscles, skin, bone and blood to stone. There were minute distinctions in each, but try as he might, he could not turn even a fingernail back to its original state.

He retreated into the charred hand.

The wands were Faia magic, and Grei could feel its overwhelming power, but it was a power that had been twisted. The emperor had slain Faia, and this is what he had made with their deaths. The Faia would never create something like the rods of the Imperial Wands. They would never intend to torture humans in this way, turn them to stone and let their souls scream inside forever.

But Grei's bone arm had not turned to stone. So recently imbued with Faia magic, the arm had been powerful enough to resist the transformation. It had saved him.

And then Grei knew what to do. Instead of trying to shout over the ceaseless droning and give a command to his stone body, he spoke to the voice itself.

"Your task is finished. Stop," he said.

The voice ceased, so suddenly it was startling. A meek echo drifted into the back of his awareness, and then it was gone. The pressure and force of the Faia's magic had been released from doing what it did not wish to be doing in the first place.

"Revert," he whispered to his stone body, picturing it whole and complete. He saw blood becoming blood again, bones turning back to bone. He imagined his eyes and flesh and hair and clothes all becoming what they once were.

The transformation spread like wildfire. Without the droning command of the Faia magic, his voice was strong, and his body leapt immediately to do his bidding.

Grei fell onto his face in the dirt, gasping, then crying. The rich smell of earth and grass filled his nostrils. The silver moonlight lit his hands, his flesh-and-blood hands. His sobs turned to laughter. It seemed like he had spent lifetimes in the dark, but only minutes had passed. He stood on shaky legs and shuffled to the overlook, reveling in the strength of his muscles, the thud of each step through his body. He saw the Julin slink striding down the slope toward the imperial road. He listened for Adora's song, and for a moment he thought he heard it on the wind, but then it was gone.

Like a ghost, Grei followed the slink into the city of Thiara, straight to the palace and up to this room. Julin knocked on the door and spoke the name "Gexxek."

That was when Grei used what he had learned and turned Julin to stone.

Julin's statue was behind the door where Grei stood when "Gexxek" returned.

He regarded the two statues now, the slink Julin and the one he had just made of the Imperial Archon. Turning the Archon to stone had been impulsive, but not a complete loss. Grei knew his handiwork much more intimately now. His learning inside his stone self had been excruciating, but he thought he could change both statues back to flesh if he wished. Whether they would be dead flesh or living people when he did, Grei didn't know. Neither of them had a Faia-charmed arm or a song to pluck them from the darkness.

But if they were alive, he could question them, find the next link in the chain. Both interlopers had mentioned "Kuruk". Was this the Lord of Rifts?

Through our fear, he thought, *they enslave us. I stand frozen in indecision because of it. We enlist men as Imperial Wands because of it. We order Highblades to steal innocents, drag them to the slinks and throw them like shovels of dirt on the top of our graves.*

The Debt of the Blessed was part of a deeper plan. They were infiltrating human bodies.

Blevins' question from a thousand years ago at *The Floating Stone* rose in Grei's mind: *Why just take one each month? Why not kill us all?*

The answer was this. The slinks were taking bodies. Using them. But the slinks had the power to kill everyone in the empire. They had shown that. Why not use it?

He raised his head at the light clack of wooden footsteps. They came closer and stopped outside the Archon's door.

Another visitor. Another link in the chain. Grei faded back into the shadows.

Chapter 47

GREI

THE WOMAN who entered the room was tall in her elevated wooden shoes. Her gown was black, trimmed with deep red and gold with not a pleat out of place. Her long, raven black hair flowed down her back, shining in the morning sunlight from the far window. A circlet of twisted gold rested on her head.

She drew a breath as if to speak, then her gaze fell on the stone Archon by his desk, and she froze where she was. That brief hesitation was the only indication she was repulsed. She stepped toward the statue, her wooden shoes clacking lightly, and touched the Archon's face with light fingers.

Grei gazed at her back, into her. She had come here looking for the Archon, and anger simmered around his image. The Order had told her the prophecy had arrived at her doorstep, and she must look for weapons in the emperor's workshop. But they had also told her Mialene was in the palace in the Archon's hands.

The woman had decided to come here first. Her desire to see Mialene was tangled up with the foreboding of what she must do. These desires and thoughts halted in her shock at the

Archon's demise.

The woman straightened. The last image Grei received was fear, as she guessed that the Archon's attacker might still be in the room. Her emotions became shielded, just as Adora's had been in Fairmist.

She turned, her eyes searching the darkness, and spotted him.

He had received no indication that she was a slink, but she knew a great deal she hadn't told anyone.

"Come forward. I will not hurt you," she said.

"Your concern is heartwarming, Empress Via." Grei took a small step toward her, allowing the morning light to touch his boots.

The empress' façade was perfect. Her gaze asserted that it was his place to please her. If he had not just looked into her, he would never have thought she feared him.

The empress' blue eyes were Adora's. So was the delicate line of her jaw, her full lips, and that imperious stare. She was Adora, twenty years older. Only Via's hair was straight and black without a hint of gold.

"You're the Whisper Prince," she said.

"And you're part of Adora's Order," he said.

He caught a brief flash of her surprise through his magic. Nothing showed on her face.

There were so many lies. Were Adora and her mother collaborating? Had Adora fed him a false story about being sacrificed to the slinks as the first Blessed? About being saved by a Faia?

"I'm here to help you," the empress said. "I came here looking for you—"

"You came looking for your daughter," he said.

Her lips pressed together.

"How much do you know?" she asked.

He let out a short laugh. "Let's try this a different way," he said. "How much do you know?"

"The cusp is upon us," she said without missing a step. "Now is your time to shine."

Grei stepped into the light and brought his unnatural hand up to point at her. "I have only killed slinks so far," he said in a low voice. "But I will make an exception for you."

She lifted her chin, and he touched it with a blackened, skeletal finger.

"You threaten me?" she demanded, her blue eyes flashing.

"I'm sick of being manipulated. I'm sick of your Order."

"Take your hand away," she said in an even tone.

He lowered his arm. His body vibrated with the need to grab her, shake her. "Tell me everything," he said.

"The fate of the empire is at stake, perhaps today."

"And I think it's worse than you know. Did you know about him?" He gestured at the Archon.

She looked at the stone Archon, then back at Grei. "I knew about him."

"What did you know?"

She watched him, then said, "He held my daughter. He plotted against my husband."

He looked into her as hard as he could, but whatever skill was required to hide emotions from him, she had it. He couldn't tell if she was lying. Either she didn't know that the Archon had been a slink, or she was withholding the information, trying to manipulate him.

Grei clenched his fist. "Stone," he hissed through his teeth.

The empress gasped, snatching her hand back. He had turned a tiny square of her skin to stone. He knew the pain was excruciating. Her control slipped, and he saw her fear, but much greater than that was her purpose. She did not care so much for her own life as she did for her mission. Just like Selicia. Grei had had about enough of that.

"Tell me what I want to know," he growled, fighting through the fog that descended over his mind at having forced his will on her flesh. He felt ill.

"You mistake yourself," the empress said. "With a shout, I could have a hundred Highblades in this room."

"Do it," he challenged her. "And your precious prophecy can burn."

The empress held herself still, one hand over the injury he'd given her. She had begun to bleed at the corners where her flesh separated from stone.

"I'm not playing games with you," he said.

"What do you want to know?" she asked.

"I want to know everything. What is this damned Order that you and Adora serve?"

She nodded. "It is called Baezin's Order. They're Faia worshippers, keepers of knowledge. They're the only ones who knew the slinks were coming. They're the only ones who can send them away again."

"I'm the only one, you mean."

She was silent for a moment, then said, "They predicted you would come."

"And stood by while my family was killed."

"Destroying the slinks is more important than any one person's family."

He felt remorse slip through her guard. She regretted her part, but not enough to stop playing it.

"You gave her to the slinks, didn't you?" he hissed, feeling sorry for Adora that she had parents who would do this to her, but he also felt relief. Adora had not lied to him. "All this time, she has been angry with her father, but it was you—"

"No," the empress whispered. A muscle rippled in her jaw. "I didn't know about Mia."

"You know about her now, and you have for a while," he said. He was guessing, but how else could she have been so calm in coming here?

"Yes, but not then."

"Did they lie to you?"

"No. The Order predicted the Slink War. A man came to me before it happened. He warned me, and I thought he was mad. I ignored his warning and had him thrown out of the palace." She paused. "Things might have gone differently if I had only believed him."

"Go on."

"Later, after the unspeakable carnage, after we fled to Fairmist, the same man from the Order came to me again. He found me in the caves where we waited to die. He told me what we needed to do in order to survive, and I believed him. I would have been a fool to turn him away a second time. And the Order was right. The slinks agreed to a truce and relented."

"And you gave them your daughter as payment?"

"No!" she said vehemently.

"But you knew she hadn't died."

She shook her head. "Not at first. The Order contacted me later, told me they had saved her."

Grei narrowed his eyes. So the Order *had* lied. Adora said it was a Faia who had saved her.

"And you didn't go to her?" he asked.

The empress hesitated, then shook her head.

"Why?" Grei asked.

"Mia is at the heart of the prophecy. It isn't finished."

"She's your daughter. You'll sacrifice her twice?"

"And should I sacrifice my other daughter and my son as well?" The empress raised her voice. He felt her remorse more strongly now. The empress feared for Adora, but she feared more what would happen if she strayed from the Order's instructions again. "There is no easy choice since the slinks arrived," she said. "They will kill us all if we cannot stop them. The men of Baezin's Order are the only ones who have given me reason to hope. They say that Mia understands. That she has...accepted her fate."

"You're a nest of backstabbing snakes, all of you," he said. "Lies come easy as breathing. Who wrote this prophecy?"

"The Faia. And you have your part to play."

She hung her head, and her dignity slipped. She leaned on the desk, her hands splayed flat, as though she had lost the strength in her legs. "Don't make the same mistake I made," she murmured. "I could have stopped the Slink War. All those children. All those people. They would be alive if not for me." She paused. "The Order says the slinks came from somewhere else. A rift to a world of fire. Send them back, Grei. You're the only one who can."

"And Adora must die," he said.

"My daughter must die," the empress echoed.

Chapter 48

REE

REE SNAPPED awake. He was here. He was near. A kiss and a cut. Their blood bond called to her.

The swirling soup of her mind took her around and around, smacking words together, making them rhyme, but she felt him. A boat on the waves. Her thoughts surfaced and submerged like vegetables in broth, and she could not grasp any of them for longer than a few seconds. But there he was. Riding the top. A boat on her soup.

She raised her head, and the fire raged at her as it had since the Slink Lord had chewed into her mind. The bonfire flared to her left, burning her, driving her toward Benasca. No matter where she walked, how she turned, it always scorched her south side, pushing her north. The mere thought of Benasca was cool water. She felt she would be safe if only she gave in and went there. The pain could end. The soup would stop spinning, and she could be herself again.

But at the center of the soup was an iron pillar. It remained steady as everything else swirled. It had been thick when she had started out for the Sanctum, but now it was spindly, on the verge of breaking. The bar was her true self, the last spike of her identity. The bar knew that the Slink Lord's promises were lies, and she clung to it with what meager strength she had left.

In the first instant that He turned her mind into soup, she made her last coherent decision. Whatever He offered her, she must refuse, no matter the pain. She said it to herself over and over again, and soon the pain became her guiding star. As long as she suffered, she was winning.

It was the hardest thing she had ever done, returning to the Sanctum in the face of that horrible heat. One excruciating step at a time, into the flames. She had gotten turned around, had gone north several times only to turn around and fight her way south again. But she had eventually made it here, and they had imprisoned her. The Faia bless them, her sisters had locked her up, and she could rest for a time.

At first, she allowed herself to scream and rage against her prison, letting the compulsion take her. She beat her remaining hand bloody on the bars.

After a time, she took control, resisting the compulsion once more. The strain of picking up that burden almost killed her, but she managed it. She had no memory of whom she had talked to, only that she needed to give them the information she knew. The Slink Lord was in her mind, but she was in his, too. She had learned his secrets. He was weaker than they thought. And stronger. So much stronger. He was plotting to have them all. And he would do it if they didn't stop him.

She kept trying to tell the others, but they didn't understand her. Her words tumbled together, twisting and rhyming. Thoughts bobbed to the surface, and she tried to give them away. But she worried her words sounded like the swirling soup. Had they heard her? Could they make sense of it? Had they acted?

But the Whisper Prince rode the soup now. A little boat of hope. She knew him. She had kissed him sideways. A brave boy favored by the Faia. A protector of Fairmist.

He was the one, the only one, who could hear her. She would not need frustrating words to tell him. He could reach inside her and take the vegetables, take them all and make sense of them. He could make the soup stop spinning.

The Whisper Prince was near, and she had to find him.

"Grei," she whispered, his name bobbing to the surface of the soup. She felt his lips on hers. Young, surprised, excited. She felt her knife sinking into his ear, marking him, making him hers. She had made the blood bond, had taken his blood into herself so she could always find him. But he had found her instead.

She lifted herself to a sitting position. She was weak as a spindly cat. A scab broke on her hand and smeared blood across the floor.

She would have to move fast. She would have to be better than she'd ever been before.

Liana had left some time ago, and now her guard was Wehyan. Wehyan was slower. That was good. That would help.

Ree lay down, positioning herself carefully and slowing her breathing. The soup spun, information bobbing and disappearing. She calmed her breath, focusing on the hard core of herself, and gritted her teeth against the heat. She would look dead, expired at last after her ordeal. Wehyan would come in. She would come close.

And they would see who was faster.

I am coming, Grei. We must kiss once more.

Chapter 49
ADORA

THE HIGHBLADES took the sisters away, and Adora craned her neck, struggled to see Galius. She wanted to apologize, to set things right.

But he was gone.

The emperor's Highblades took her around the corner, onto the vast western lawn, and Galius' body disappeared from view. She blinked through her tears. It was all ruined. She didn't even know what she was doing anymore. Galius was dead. Grei was dead. Even Blevins was likely dead this time. The Order was so far away, and they had sent no one to help her.

She stared at her shuffling feet and thought about that aching moment outside her room when she had so badly wanted to kiss Grei, to take him to her room and make him hers, to have it be just the two of them against a world of cruelty. Instead, she had sent him after a midnight lily and spent their last chance of a life together.

She had no purpose here. Even if there could be another Whisper Prince, she was not the one to steward him. The Order had forsaken her. No doubt they were calmly checking her off as a failure and moving to the next plan. Her life may as well have ended in the slink cave when she was eleven years old.

She set her jaw. If there was no reason for her to exist anymore, if she couldn't challenge the slinks, then she could at least challenge the man who had bargained with them.

They took the sisters to the emperor's rooms in the royal wing. Vecenne seemed to have recovered her wits, and she glanced at the door and then at Adora. Adora felt she should say something, but she couldn't think of what that ought to be.

"What will happen now?" Vecenne asked.

"I don't know," Adora murmured.

"You survived what no one else survived. You have lived in secret. You have allies who would dare to break into the palace and kill imperial Highblades just to save you."

"That man was Galius Ash," Adora said. *Who now lies dead, and no one will remember his name except me.* "And Jorun Magnus."

"Jorun Magnus!" Vecenne said. "You return to the palace and you bring Jorun Magnus? Please tell me where you have been."

"The story is seven years long, Vecenne. And not a happy one. My life may as well have ended in the Badlands."

"Is that where you lived?"

Adora shook her head, but she didn't say more.

"You cannot tell even me your secrets?" Her sister asked. "I would never hurt you." Shrouded in Blevins' cloak, nothing was visible but her face and the curl of her fingers. "I love you, Mimi. I have lain awake each night, wondering what I might have done differently that morning, what I might have done to save you."

"Vecenne..." Adora began. "I was selfish for one instant. Just one. I ran from my duty without thinking, and I ran into you." She stopped, trying to manage the catch in her throat. "I did not think what the Archon might do to you. You paid for that selfishness. And now, I cannot predict what Father will do. You think you know him, but you don't. If I give you my secrets, he might do terrible things to you to get them."

"Father wouldn't hurt us—"

"And neither would the Archon," Adora interrupted, wishing she didn't have to be harsh. But Vecenne had to know. Their father was a man who would sacrifice one daughter. He would sacrifice the other if it came to that. "You have to tell him that you know nothing, and you have to mean it. If that is the truth, he will let you go."

Adora reached out a trembling hand and touched her sister's shoulder, so light that she could only feel the smooth cloth of Jorun's cloak. "Vecenne, I led the Archon to you, and he—"

Vecenne shook her head fiercely. "That doesn't matter."

"It matters," Adora whispered around a hard lump in her throat. "I'm so sorry."

"I would endure worse to help you, Mimi." Vecenne hugged her. "It is a wound, and I will bear it as you have borne yours." She squeezed her sister tightly. "I would have crossed the Badlands on bare feet to find you if I had known you were alive. Please let me help you now."

"No one can come with me where I must go. I don't even know if I can help myself," Adora said. "There was a man, and I was supposed to bring him here. He might have changed things..." Adora trailed off.

Vecenne pulled back enough to see Adora's face, but held on as though she didn't dare let her go. "Was he the man who led us up the stairs? The one Father killed?"

Adora shook her head. "No."

Vecenne searched Adora's eyes, looking for something to say. "I am sorry, Mimi."

"I do not know what I am supposed to do next," Adora said. "But I know that—"

The door opened then, and both sisters turned as their father entered. Vecenne secured her cloak with her fist.

The emperor looked haggard, his face ashen. He closed the door behind him.

No one wanted to be the first to break the silence. The emperor leaned against the door and stared at Adora.

"I had given up hope." His voice was hushed.

"You took away hope," Adora said.

"My precious Mialene—"

"I am not your Mialene anymore. You may call me Adora."

Vecenne looked surprised at the sudden steel in Adora's voice.

"Don't you understand—" he began again.

"I understand that you threw me to the slinks."

"If I hadn't, they would have come again—"

"I was eleven!" she screamed. She had meant to say the words dispassionately. She forced herself to speak in a lower tone. "I have wondered all my life how my father could hate me so much. Not a day has gone by that I have not thought on it."

The emperor slid to his knees, bowed his head. He looked like a crumpled bag of sticks. Adora approached him one step at a time, her fists clenched.

"How could you?" she whispered.

He looked up at her, his eyes red-rimmed. "I had no choice," he whispered.

"And what of the Faia you have slain? Did you have no choice as well?"

Vecenne drew a swift breath.

The emperor's eyes widened. "How—?"

"I know every sin you have committed," Adora hissed.

"Everything I did, I did to avenge you," he said raggedly.

She shook her head. "What you have done is serve the slinks. You destroy their enemies and feed them innocents."

"I have made weapons. I just need more time—"

"You have had seven years!"

"Mialene," the emperor said. "You cannot understand how I have dreamed about this day, the day that I could see you again, that I might have just one chance to beg your forgiveness—"

"Then beg, Father. Beg, and know what it is like to have your pleas ignored. Know what it is like to have the one you love turn her back on you."

"Please, Mia—"

"I was a child! I needed you..." Her voice broke. She swallowed hard, clenching her teeth until she could speak evenly. "But I don't need you anymore," she said calmly. "And you will answer for your crimes. Every one. You are the reason the Badlands exist. You killed the heart of the Vheysin Forest. You made the Dead Woods. And how many have died in those trees, Father? How many of your citizens have you killed in the name of protecting them?"

The emperor shook his head. "You saw the Slink War. They would have slaughtered every one of us! We had no weapons to fight them then, but I am changing that. I would throw off their yoke."

Adora shook her head. "How can you think killing Faia could ever save us? Such atrocity could only damn us," she said.

"Then what other way? Tell me and I will do it!"

"There is a group of wise men called Baezin's Order," Adora said. "And a prophecy—"

"Baezin's Order?" The emperor's eyes narrowed, and his voice changed. The crumpled majesty of the man rose again. "I know of them. I know of this so-called prophecy and the Whisper Prince. Had I known the Order held my daughter, I would have burned them down. Where is the Prince now? Did he save you from the slinks?" he asked. "Did the Whisper Prince save my little girl?"

She shook her head. "It was the Faia, Father. She came for me, lifted me up and took me to Fairmist."

The emperor's brow wrinkled. "But Magnus took you to the cave—"

"And he left me there. I saw the towering slink with the wide shoulders. The one named Kuruk."

The emperor's black eyebrows furrowed. "Are you lying to me?" he whispered.

"The Faia took me where I could be safe."

A knock sounded on the emperor's door. He paused, as though he would ignore it, but the knock came again, and he stood up. He held up a finger for her to pause. "Enter," he said.

The door opened and a Highblade, breathing hard, stepped through. He went to one knee and bowed his head. "The Archon is dead."

"I told you to take him alive," the emperor growled.

"He was dead when we arrived, your majesty. The empress found him. He was turned to stone."

"Stone?"

"As if by an Imperial Wand, your majesty," he said, never raising his head. "There was another man we didn't recognize. Also stone."

Adora's mind raced. What did that mean? Were there slinks in the palace?

"Who was he?" the emperor asked.

"From the east by the cut of his clothing. Young. I did not recognize him," the Highblade said.

"Find out," the emperor said. "And bring the bodies here."

"They are already being carried here, your majesty."

"Good. And the man who battled the Archon's Highblades?" the emperor said.

"Mortally wounded," the Highblade said, his breathing finally slowing.

"But alive?"

"For now."

"Bring him here as well."

The Highblade looked around the well-ordered room hesitantly. "He is a bloody mess, your majesty."

"Blood can be cleaned. Bring him. I want them all in my room. There is a story here and I mean to have it."

"Of course, your majesty." The Highblade nodded sharply and stepped back. He left, and they could hear his booted feet running up the hall. The emperor turned, stroking the center twist of his beard.

"Someone has stolen one of your weapons?" Adora asked.

The emperor looked up. "Apparently one of my Imperial Wands has lost the instrument of his office." He focused his attention on her, and his gaze was fierce. "I would do anything for you, Adora, but I must know. Did you bring an assassin into the palace?"

"I was brought here in borrowed clothes with my wrists bound. There was no assassin down my shirt."

"I need to know if this is your doing," he said.

"This is your doing, Father," she said. "Every bit of it."

The emperor's stern gaze softened, and he looked exasperated. "Mialene, I'm trying to help you."

"Those were the Archon's words to me as well, before he caged me and used me. Forgive me if I doubt you."

"What can I do to earn your trust?" he asked.

"Burn your workshop. Destroy everything you have made. Never harm another Faia. Start there."

"Then the Debt of the Blessed will be endless. Is that what you want?"

"Better for every Thiaran to die than a single Faia. Don't you realize what you've done?"

They all heard the approach of the Highblades again, and the conversation ceased. The knock came soon after, and the emperor opened the door.

"Put them here," the emperor said, pointing. The Highblades brought in three horrific bodies. First was the bloody mess of Blevins. It took six men to carry him, and they set him beside the door. His neck had been slashed halfway through, and there were countless punctures all over his fat belly. He was ashen-faced and unconscious like he had been at the farmer's house in the Badlands. Adora went to him immediately, touched his bloody forehead.

More Highblades carried the Archon and the other stone body, setting each down with a "clunk" next to Blevins. Adora's eyes widened as she looked at the second man. That was Julin! She stifled a gasp. How was that possible?

The leader of the Highblades passed a black, blood-smeared sword to the emperor, and he looked at the blade with tight lips. "You may go," he said. The Highblade captain put a fist over his heart in salute, then left the room, closing the door behind him. The emperor turned to Adora, saw her expression.

"What is it?" he asked her.

Adora tried to rally her thoughts. "It's...horrific," she said, covering her slip.

"Mia, if I'm to try to help you, I must know what you know."

Adora stood up. "Use your eyes, then. That is Jorun Magnus."

"I know," the emperor said. "I have been looking for him for six months." The emperor looked at the bloody sword, then set it against the wall. "And for this." His gaze returned to Adora. "Do you realize this is the only weapon to have killed a slink?"

"I was there," Adora said.

He nodded. "Why is Magnus back in Thiara?"

"I don't know why."

"If you are following the directives of Baezin's Order," he said. "Then your arrival heralds something worse, and I must know it if I am to protect against it."

"Is this where you sacrifice me again for the greater good?" Adora said.

"Mia—"

"You will get nothing just for the asking. Destroy your workshop. Promise me you will stop your heinous work. Then we will speak."

"Have you done what she says, Father?" Vecenne asked quietly, and the emperor looked at her as though he had forgotten she was there.

"You should go to your rooms, Vecenne. I will have you escorted—"

"No." Vecenne shook her head. "I let Mimi go once

because I was only nine and I didn't know what to do. I will not leave her again."

"Vecenne—" Both the emperor and Adora spoke at the same time.

"No," she said.

The emperor set his jaw, looking back and forth between them.

"Come with me, then," he said.

He went to the silk wall hanging of Venisha, pinched one of the crossed swords and moved it. The wall groaned behind the silk hanging, and he pushed it aside, revealing a passageway. The emperor led them up a winding staircase, and she felt an ominous feeling. Vecenne shivered, and Adora put a hand on her shoulder.

"I will not hide anything from you," the emperor said as they crested the edge of the floor. "But you must understand why I have done it. It was the only way."

Vecenne put a hand over her mouth as they stepped up onto the fitted-stone floor. The table in the center of the room had been wiped clean, but it reeked of murder. A chain hung slack over it.

Many things had changed. Two more chests of drawers had been added, and there were weapons hanging all over the walls, exactly spaced apart as though they could not be too close together. Each was oddly formed. There were three daggers that curved roughly like an 'S', each different, each asymmetrical. There was a bow made of long thorns that jutted out in every direction, a quiver of black arrows beside it. There was a sword that split at the end like a forked tongue. There was a weapon that looked like a 'T' after it emerged from the hilt. The blades were dull steel, the handles a myriad of sickly colors. Sallow moss and blood. Feces and urine. They tore at the eye and evoked despair.

"Oh, Father..." Vecenne whispered through her hand.

"An emperor must lead his people. He must find a way, even if it costs him what he holds most dear."

"Nothing is worth this cost," Adora whispered.

The emperor turned. "Would you condemn everyone in the empire to death then? The littlest baby? Your own sister? Your mother?"

"Some lines cannot be crossed," she said.

"Yes. But you Thiarans love to cross them," came a child's voice. Adora spun, drawing a swift breath.

A tall, grotesque shadow stood on the balcony, the bright morning sky at his back. His shoulders were inhumanly wide, and long thin arms hung past his knees. Within the shadowy silhouette, two red eyes burned.

"We have much to discuss, emperor," the slink said.

Chapter 50
ADORA

N O," VECENNE gasped, taking a step back. Adora felt small. Wild fear prickled through her. She wanted to flee down the steps, out of the palace. She wanted to run until her body could run no more.

Vecenne backed away, but Adora caught her elbow, gripped her arm hard, and gave a little shake of her head.

The slink was the same one Adora had met at the cave, the one who had nearly grabbed her, torn the flesh from her heel with his hot claws as the Faia lifted her into the air. He was their leader, Kuruk.

Uneven tusks jutted up from his long chin. He was stooped, his bulky shoulders three times the width of his torso. His arms were so long that his claws dangled past his knees. His legs angled backward then forward like a dog's, ending in cloven hooves sharp enough to crack stone. His black and red skin smoked, and Adora could feel his heat even at this distance. It filled the room.

The creature's eyes were dancing flames under his dark brow. It was difficult to know which way he was looking.

Adora felt like he was staring right at her, but he addressed her father.

"We had a pact," the slink said in his child's voice. Adora remembered the slink in Fairmist morphing into a child. She didn't know what that meant. And now this one also sounded like a child?

"You were never to come here again," Father said.

"You were to send me one of your subjects every month. You were to keep our peace."

"And I have!" the emperor said. "Blood for you and yours. Blood of innocents!"

The slink's thin lips curved in a snarl. "Thiarans lie. Betray. Murder." He nodded toward the wall of weapons. "Tell me, emperor. What did you intend to do with these? What could you possibly use them for? Is this how you honor our peace?"

The emperor's lips tightened, and he tensed, ready to leap.

Adora felt light-headed. This was how it would begin. She felt the strength of the prophecy building within her. They were caught, and there was no time to change anything. This was when the slinks would cover the empire with a second war. And there was no Whisper Prince to stop them.

Create the answer.

Her mind raced. She felt like she was in a room with no doors, looking for a way out. Then it came to her.

"Take me," she heard herself say. She stepped forward, let go of Vecenne.

"Mimi, no!" Vecenne said.

Adora held up her hand, walked toward the slink. She couldn't permit a second Slink War. The Order would have another plan. Perhaps there was another who could be the Whisper Prince, if Adora could keep the slinks from returning in force, if there was only a little more time.

"Ah, the lost daughter," the slink said, his flame eyes flickering. "I looked for you, but you eluded me."

"Then take me now," she said. "Forgive my father his

trespasses and take me as you did before."

"Mialene, I forbid it!" the emperor said.

She ignored him. "Take me."

"You are so willing this time," the slink said. "So reluctant before." He paused. "Why is that, I wonder?"

"I am a woman now, not a child. I know what is at stake. We cannot stand against you. We rely on your mercy."

The slink chuckled. "A woman, indeed. A woman who has studied and worked hard, I think. Your father is preparing for a war. What are you preparing for?"

"I only want the empire to be safe."

"You wish for what you humans call a 'second chance'?"

"Yes."

"Or do you just want more time to continue your plot against us?"

Adora's mouth dried up.

"Where is the Whisper Prince?" the slink asked.

She paused, unable to speak. It was so hard to think around the thudding fear emanating from the slink.

"Where is he?" the slink repeated.

"He is dead," she said breathlessly.

The slink narrowed his eyes, and smoke curled up from the edges. She felt his gaze like a hot hand across her cheeks, and he nodded. "Indeed." The slink looked at the emperor, then back at Adora. "If I give you your second chance, will you honor your part of the pact?"

"I will," Adora said.

The slink nodded, then pointed his taloned hand at her father. Fire shot from his finger, striking the emperor in the chest. Blood and flesh splattered the wall, and her father toppled over backwards.

"Father!" Vecenne screamed.

Crumpled against the wall, the emperor touched the hole that went clean through him. He gave a little sigh, then slumped over.

Vecenne lunged toward him, skidded on her knees. She yanked at him, trying to bring him upright. "Father! No!" Her voluminous cloak settled over the dead man as she pulled futilely, sobbing.

Adora stood completely still, shocked.

The slink turned his attention back to her. "I am dealing with you now," he said. "Do not disappoint me—"

"KURUK!" a thundering voice interrupted them. Blevins staggered up the stairs into view. His head was bent sideways. His body was dark with blood, and he dragged Baezin's Blade on the steps behind him. Clink. Clink. Clink.

"If you want to deal with someone, deal with me," he growled.

Chapter 51

ADORA

MAGNUS," KURUK hissed. His burning gaze went to the huge man's sword. Fresh blood dripped from Blevins, and his feet made red prints on the floor.

Blevins brought up Baezin's Blade, and despite his tattered appearance, the blade was steady. He shuffled toward Kuruk.

The slink bared his pointed teeth. "The girl has just bargained for Thiara. Is this how you would end her treaty?"

"I would end you," Blevins growled.

Kuruk's eyes narrowed.

"No!" Adora shouted. The Order told her that the slinks had come through a rip in the air, bringing through thousands of their kind in the first Slink War. The rip had closed when the pact was made, but the prophecy said they would do it again, and that only the Whisper Prince could stop them. Except there was no Whisper Prince. There was only her.

"Blevins, wait!" she said.

He ignored her. He was almost to the balcony. Vecenne continued to cry over Father, and each sob was like a knife in

Adora's ears. She wanted to shout at her sister to shut up.

Kuruk held up a hand and fear burst so strongly within Adora that the room vibrated. Cold sweat dribbled down her ribs and beaded on her forehead. She couldn't breathe.

Her sister fell quiet. Even Blevins faltered, but he struggled against his own balking muscles to take another step.

Adora grabbed his arm, stalling him for one moment. Then he roared. With the strength of a bear, he threw her aside. She skidded across the flat stones and went over the edge of the circular floor.

Her shoulder and neck slammed into the wall, and she dropped onto the steps, sharp edges hitting her like swords. She tried to protect her head as she tumbled. The stairs again. The wall again. She reached out, fingernails scraping futilely against stone. A stair crunched hard into her back, and she stopped, groaning, struggling to breathe.

Above, out of sight now, Blevins roared. Steel clanged on stone. Red fire lit the walls of the stairway, and he roared again.

"You have made your choice!" Kuruk shrieked.

Fire flared, and Blevins bellowed. Adora lifted her head. The pain in her side was like a knife, and she couldn't breathe. She had to get up to that room. Somehow, she had to stop him. The war couldn't start all over again. She couldn't let it. Adora rolled onto her hands and knees. She pressed her hand to her side and gritted her teeth. It felt like someone had taken a club to her arms and back.

"The pact is done!" Kuruk shrieked.

A strong wind whooshed down the stairway. A faint chittering echoed off the walls, and Adora's blood went cold. It was the same sound that had started it all, so long ago. It was the same sound she had heard as the slinks poured into Thiara.

Vecenne screamed.

"No!" Adora said. She fought herself, trying to get her frozen muscles to move. She had to reach her sister. "Please," she whispered. "Not again." Cold tears squeezed out the sides of her eyes. Her whole body shook, and she forced her foot up another step.

A terrible weight bore down on her, trying to shove her away from the room. Her fingers scraped on stone, and she pushed herself upright, moved her foot to the next step.

A slink's face appeared out of the darkness on a long, black neck. Not Kuruk. Another one. They were coming. Thousands of them.

Its bulging eyes were like white onions; its smile was lined with teeth as long as her fingers. It opened its mouth and gave a whispering laugh.

Her will broke, and she turned and ran down the stairs, slamming into one wall and then the other. She burst into her father's bedroom and spun around.

"Please," she whispered. "We'll be good. Please—"

She heard movement behind her, and a black claw closed over her shoulder.

Adora screamed.

Chapter 52
ADORA

DORA LAUNCHED herself away, but the claw kept hold of her, jerked her off her feet. She crumpled to the floor, squeezing her eyes shut. Images filled her mind: slinks rending, tearing, killing. "We'll be good!"

"Adora!" A hand slapped her. A human hand. Her eyes flew open.

Grei stood over her, his face stern. She sucked in a thin breath.

He pulled her to her feet.

"Grei!" she exclaimed. "What—?"

The long-necked monster slithered underneath the tapestry, hissing. Orange flame lit the stairway behind it.

Grei pulled her across the room and spun her around. The slink rose up, and Grei whispered, hugging Adora tightly.

The slink lunged, its long neck like a spear, jaws snapping. But Grei and Adora dropped through the floor. Then they were in the room below, falling from the ceiling. Grei whispered in her ear, words she didn't understand. They hit the next floor, and the stone became water. Then the next and the next, each splashing red and white marble on them, past them. Then the air grabbed at them, holding them, slowing their descent, and they landed in soft sand.

They were in the great room of the palace, four stories straight down, and she was knee deep in red and white sand the same color as the floor. She looked up and saw a hole in the stone ceiling slowly reforming, knitting itself together as drops of marble dripped down.

"By the Faia," she said, gazing at Grei.

He stepped onto the solid marble floor and helped her out of the sand. As she joined him, he whispered something, and the floor reformed into the red and white marble squares.

His once-open face was grim. He had light whiskers along his jaw, and his hair was pulled back in a ponytail. His left forearm had been transformed. It wasn't burnt flesh anymore but a skeletal hand wrapped in charcoal-colored skin.

"I thought you were dead," she whispered.

"You saved me," he said. "You pulled me back."

He touched her, and she flung herself on him, pressed her head against his chest. "I thought I'd lost you."

Images flashed through her mind. That little house in Fairmist, shutters closed against the wet. Grei opening the front door and pushing back his cloak, smiling. The little blue-eyed girl splashing through puddles. Then the three of them sitting by the hearth, together. Happy. Safe and loved. A normal life.

A scream rose in the courtyard, shocking her out of the daydream. The slinks were in the city.

She disengaged herself, and it was almost more than she could bear. She focused on his face, made herself into the woman she needed to be. The strong woman. The one who could face anything.

"It's time to save the children," she said softly. Every word was a tiny chisel, taking another curl out of her heart, and she let her dream die.

His haunted eyes told her that he had learned what the

prophecy meant, that he knew she had to die to send the slinks away.

More screams ripped through the quiet. More Thiarans dying.

With shaking hands, she touched his cheeks. "I knew this price from the beginning. I will pay it."

"What if we run?" he said. "Give ourselves time to think of something else."

"Listen to the screams, Grei. This is the moment we stop the slinks. This moment, and no other. For just one more death, everyone can live. Right now. Only now."

His jaw clenched. "I can't kill you."

"We'll do it together," she whispered, leading him forward.

They left the great room. A seven-legged slink loped down the hall after a screaming woman. One of the woman's wooden shoes turned, and she went down. The slink leapt upon her and ripped into her neck. Adora yanked Grei quickly in the other direction, through a doorway and into the open air.

Deep horns sounded, warning Thiara's citizens too late. Black slinks spilled into the courtyard, devouring, chasing anyone who ran. Already, bodies of the dead littered the ground.

Grei wrenched Adora out of the way of a flying slink. It hissed as it passed, and she felt the flecks of its spittle. It landed on a Highblade just beyond them, claws tearing into him. Its wings beat furiously as it lifted the Highblade off the ground. The Highblade struggled, and the slink tore his arm off. The arm fell on the ground next to them.

A woman at a third floor balcony leapt to her death. The slinks chased her, scuttling onto the wall outside the window as she smashed into the ground.

"By the Faia," Grei whispered.

"Come on!" she urged. She stooped and snatched a dagger from a dead man's belt. They ran toward the temple of the Faia.

The Thiaran Temple of the Faia was a circular structure with a dome overhead supported by nothing but air. A maze of water channels curved underneath the dome in concentric circles, folding back on themselves seven times as they worked their way toward the center. At the outermost ring, seven tongues of fire burned straight up from the water. In the center a fountain flowed upward, rising two stories tall before disappearing into the air. It represented all of the elements, a tribute to the Faia

She slowed to a stop before the rising pillar of water. *I was the first Blessed,* she thought. *I will be the last.*

Chapter 53
GREI

I'LL THINK *of something.* Grei recalled what he had said to Selicia days ago, but now he was here, he had no ideas, and he had run out of time.

His promise, so fervently given, was the empty promise of a boy. And now he was trapped. He hadn't been able to defeat even one slink in Fairmist. How could he defeat hundreds?

Maybe he could save Adora for a short time. He could run away with her while the rest of the empire went to slaughter. Or he could follow the prophecy and protect them all. All except one.

"Grei." She tugged his hand, leading him into the temple's shallow pool. He sloshed in next to her, and icy water seeped into his boots. He looked around like the answer might drop from the sky. All he saw were slinks, slashing and killing. All he heard were screams.

Adora drew her hand down his cheek, gently turned his face toward hers. "It's okay," she whispered.

She had the courage to do what must be done. To give up herself, her dreams, for the benefit of everyone else.

Grei wasn't a boy anymore. He couldn't blame his parents or the delegate or the emperor. He was the one, the only one, who could fix this.

She pressed the dagger into his palm. It was hot, as if the last of her life had seeped into the steel wire grip.

"Speak to my body like you spoke to the stones," she said. "Tell it to dissolve, to join these waters. The rift will open like the waterfall in Fairmist, and you will push the slinks through with the gathered forces. It will be like a great wind at your command. The magic of the temple knows what to do. The Faia will be with you. I will be with you."

"How do you know all this? How can you be sure?"

She pulled him down and kissed him, their last kiss. He tried to look into her, tried to see her true desires, but she had closed herself off to him.

"Make the empire safe for every other girl who loves a boy," she whispered. The dagger seemed to vibrate in his hand, and her fingers slid over his. "We'll do it together." She guided the tip of the blade to her chest, just under her ribs. Her breath came faster. "Upward," she said. "To my heart. Quick and strong." She gave him a nervous smile. "Don't miss."

He clenched the dagger hard. The chill in his legs seeped upward, through him. He would become like the rest of them at last. The delegate. The emperor. Selicia. He would do the horrific for a chance at a better life.

He put his skeletal hand behind her neck, bunched his shoulder. Her fingers tightened on his, ready to add her strength. One thrust. He would not miss.

He felt the tension of the sharp tip against her thin dress, her taut flesh.

"No," he whispered.

"Grei—"

"I can't," he said, forcing the dagger away from her, pulling it from her grasp. He dropped it into the water and hugged her, pressing her body against his, his cheek against her shaved scalp.

"You must," she said. She was suddenly sobbing. Her shaking hands lifted his head away so she could look into his eyes. "No, no, no." she said. "You have to. We have to."

"I can't," he repeated hoarsely. He had never felt so weak. "I'm not that man."

"It's not just us. It's—" She cut herself off, looking past him.

He turned.

On the far side of the courtyard, a tall slink emerged from the double-doors of the palace in a flurry of smaller flying slinks. He had wide shoulders, thin arms and a small head with jutting teeth, and his legs worked backwards like a dog as he strode into the courtyard. His gaze locked on them.

"The Lord of Rifts," Grei murmured.

"No!" Adora said frantically.

Grei watched the slink named Kuruk move toward him. Kuruk, the one who had slaughtered innocents. The one who needed to die.

"Do what must be done!" Adora begged. "Before it's too late!" She grabbed his shoulders, but he shrugged her off.

He leapt out of the fountain in a shower of water and screamed his rage at the Lord of Rifts. Kuruk pointed a finger and fire exploded toward them.

Chapter 54

ADORA

"GREI!" ADORA cried as the inferno engulfed them. She fell backward into the icy water, blistering heat all around. Then the flame was past, red turned blue again, and she surfaced, spluttering.

Cloaked within the roaring flame, Kuruk crossed the courtyard and slammed into Grei, pushing him out of the shelter of the temple. Somehow, Grei was still alive. He had kept the flames from burning him, had kept the slink's claws from rending him apart.

She snatched up the dagger lying at the bottom of the shallow pool and took a step toward the battle, but she stopped. That wouldn't help him. The dagger was no more than a twig to Kuruk. She—

"Princessss," a slurred voice said from behind her.

She spun, sucking in a shocked breath. "By the Faia!" She stepped back.

A hideously burned man stood at the edge of the fountain. Sizzling fat and muscle hung on bloody bones. His head was a grinning skull with patches of red, canted to one side. Tufts of black hair stuck out from the glistening scalp. White eyes looked unblinking at her.

"Thisss isss your prophesssssy?" the burned man said, his words barely coherent through the ruin of tattered lips and charred tongue. He gestured at the fountain.

"Who are you?"

"Noooo longerrr a ffffat man."

"Blevins!" she gasped.

Milky eyes slid inside the charred head, as though they could still see. "The daggerrr," he said. "Yourrr life?"

She turned to Blevins, the dagger tight in her hand.

"You," she said, feeling the cold clarity of it. Jorun Magnus was a killer. He could do what must be done. "It has to be you."

He paused, his grisly frame so perfectly still she thought perhaps he had died standing upright. Then his milky eyes rolled to the dagger.

"Grei can't begin the spell," she said. "But you can." She held the dagger out to him. "And then you make him finish it."

"Nnno," he slurred.

"Yes. You didn't save me at the cave, but you could save Grei now." She held out the dagger. "Activate the spell. Save him."

"I cannnot killl you. Nnnot twissse."

"I'm already dead. This has been my destiny since I escaped the Debt. But I understand this time. Please," she said. "For what you owe me."

"Miaaaa..."

"Kuruk is killing him!" She sobbed. She grabbed his sticky hand and slapped the dagger's hilt into it.

"Miaaaa, donnn't—"

"If you ever loved me. If you ever felt for me at all—"

His fist hit her ribs, rocking her body, and he roared like a wounded beast. She looked down, saw the dagger's crossguard flat against her chest, the icy blade inside her, a shaft through her heart. A perfect strike. She couldn't breathe. Red blossomed around his burned fist.

Her fingers and arms went limp. Blevins held her up, and his howl shook the temple.

"Thank you," she whispered. Cold slithered into her like a snake. "Thank—"

Chapter 55
GREI

GREI WHISPERED to the air, making it hard as stone. Kuruk slammed into it.

"We won't bow to you any longer!" Grei yelled at the slink.

Kuruk rebounded off the defense and stumbled to a stop. He calmly recovered his balance and stood as he had before, towering over Grei, blotting out the rising sun.

"You're done killing people!" Grei promised.

Kuruk laughed, high-pitched and mean. "What do you know about your 'people'? About the bloody price paid for your empire? What do you know about the mute monsters you worship as goddesses and call the Faia? You know nothing!"

"I know you pushed my brother's soul out of his body," Grei said in a low voice. He reached out to the slink like he had done with others and felt the monster's rage.

"And what of *my* brother?" Kuruk asked. "What of Malik?"

"Was that is name? He gave me this." Grei held up his bony forearm. "But he won't burn anyone again."

Kuruk's lips curled back from long teeth, and he launched himself at Grei, a blur. Grei whispered to the air again, making it stone just before the slink slammed into it. Kuruk's scaly claws broke through the half-made spell and raked across Grei's shoulder.

Grei cried out, scrambled backward.

Kuruk spat fire at him.

"Water!" Grei shouted to the air. The fire hit the barrier and became hissing steam. It scalded him, deadly hot, and Grei staggered away.

Claws raked his back again, and Grei crashed to his knees. "Hard!" he breathed. The air around him went solid, and he heard a second claw screech across it. The muddy feeling coated his mind. He didn't have time to move with the elements, to make a request. He had to end this quickly.

Grei rolled out of the steam, trying to ignore the excruciating burn from the scratches. He looked for Kuruk and caught a glimpse of the slink's silhouette at the edge of the steam cloud. He envisioned the air around the monster turning to water, then a box of solid rock around that, trapping the slink in a cage of death.

Grei mustered his focus. It took longer this time, and Kuruk charged through the steam.

"Water!" Grei shouted at the air. "Rock!"

The water splashed to the ground behind Kuruk. A cage of stone formed out of the light breeze, but the slink scrambled over it, so quick that the top crunched together as he leapt free. He landed on the ground next to Grei.

"No!" Grei shouted, his mind numb. He couldn't think of what to do next. Kuruk reached down with his claws, red eyes raging.

Then the slink jerked, screamed, and the claw barely scratched Grei's face. Kuruk spun around. A black arrow protruded from his back, feathers quivering. Beyond Kuruk, a young woman stood with a bow that looked like it was made of long thorns lashed together. She wore a burned cloak that dragged on the ground, shadowing her body. Her honey-colored hair glinted in the light. She nocked another arrow smoothly and quickly. To Grei's left, in the direction of the temple, an inhuman howl burst over the screams and growls all around them.

Kuruk hissed at the girl, leaping behind Grei. She kept the arrow trained on the slink, but did not release. Kuruk reached for Grei's neck, claws tickling his skin, but he spun away.

A black blade swept over Grei's head. It caught Kuruk in the side, adding to his momentum and spinning him in mid-air. The slink shrieked and crashed to the ground.

Grei looked up into the charred face of a horribly burnt man. The man lunged forward, moving with blinding speed, and swung the sword again. The blade crunched into stone, and Kuruk leapt away. Another black arrow whistled past Kuruk's shoulder. The woman with the honey hair ran forward, nocking another.

With a scream of rage, Kuruk backed up and circled. "It won't be that easy, Magnus."

Magnus?

Grei looked at the burnt man.

"Blevins?" he said.

"The battle isss not won, prinsssse," the shambling Blevins said. "Your ssspell isss ready. Your sssacrifissse made. Finisssh it."

Sacrifice?

Grei spun around. Adora was no longer standing in the pool. Instead, her body floated in the water.

"No!" he screamed.

Chapter 56
GREI

DORA!" GREI shouted, splashing into the pool. Blood flowed into the icy water, a long red cloud snaking into the twisted channels. The dagger lay on the bottom of the pool beside her.

"No!"

He wanted to scream at her, to rage and tell her that he would have found another way, but he knew it was a lie. If Blevins and the girl archer hadn't shown up, he would be dead.

He bowed his head over her body. *Make sure it's not in vain,* he thought. *Send the slinks back. Do what she gave her life for!*

The water glowed silver where her blood had spread, and he could feel the spell's prepared power. It had been created long ago. Different sensations and images came to him, smells and colors, emotions. An insidious sentience drove it, sucked Adora's blood out of her body and into the labyrinth of water. He saw images of the rift in his mind, bright flames beyond it, immense heat. The spell knew what it was doing. He could send them back. The rift longed to open.

But something stopped it.

He concentrated, following the source of the barrier, and he heard singing, the same song from the Jhor Forest. The Green Faia's song. It created an implacable shield, holding the blood-hungry water at bay. It kept the rift closed.

But if the Faia had created it, why would they create a barrier to stop it—?

A thin hand grabbed his face from behind, yanking him backward.

He cried out, struggling, but his attacker kicked his legs out from underneath him, pulling him over the small wall of the pool. They fell to the cobblestones. Grei swung blindly. He spun around, ready to fight—

And stared into Ree's face. She was gaunt, skin sunken beneath the bones of her cheeks. Her right arm was severed at the elbow, a wrapped stump, but her eyes burned with purpose.

"No time. No time," she mumbled, flicking a glance at Kuruk, who circled slowly around Blevins, looking for a way to get to the temple. "Words can't get past the rhyme. Listen, Grei. Listen, please. Listen close and set us free." Her scabbed hand fluttered around his face, smearing blood. She leaned into him, put her cheek to his like a dog desperate for affection.

"Get off!" He threw her to the side. He remembered Selicia's words. *Ree has been taken by the slink sickness.* "I need to finish—"

But she leapt on him again, wrapped her arm around his neck, entwined her legs with his. He fell to one knee.

"No!" she wailed. "Look, look. Open my book!"

"You're mad!" He lurched to his feet, tried to pry her off. She was skinny as a stick, but strong. With a grunt, he threw her to the ground. "Get off!"

She clawed at the front of her black tunic, ripping it open and bearing a swatch of bony skin between her breasts. "Prince, look inside! Deep inside the truth will hide. You must look! Open my book!"

A sudden chill ran through him, and he paused. Ree was crazy, her eyes wild, her speech like that of Rat Mathens.

Like Rat Mathens, who talked about secrets no one understood.

Something clicked in his mind. The true abomination of the Blessed was hidden: humans possessed by foul spirits from another world. But there were other secrets, questions that didn't have answers, like why a spell supposedly made by the Faia was being prohibited by the Faia, like why the slinks would trade the sure destruction of the empire for a monthly sacrifice.

Like why those who thought too much about the slinks went mad.

"You know something," he hissed.

Ree gasped in relief, reached for him again, and he didn't draw back this time. Her bloody hand touched his cheek, his neck. She leaned in, put her forehead against his chest. "Listen. Look. At all they took."

He reached into her with his magic, and she opened like doors to a sunrise.

He heard the voice of her heart, uninhibited by the stumbling rhymes. This was the Ree he had known in the Lateral House.

Look deep, Grei, she said. *See all that I have collected. The Slink Lord tried to scramble it, but I saved what I could.*

Grei staggered back under the onslaught of images and emotions. He bumped into the edge of the fountain and sat down heavily.

The Lord of Rifts was a boy named Kuruk, taken in sacrifice from Benasca a hundred years ago; he was the boy from the Faia's memories, the one who had screamed "Lie" at the emperor.

Kuruk's mind was inside Ree's, twisting, warping, making it so she could never speak of what she had learned. But she was in his, too, and Grei saw everything the Slink Lord knew. Velakkan spirits taking over the bodies of the Blessed, breeding with humans, making more monstrosities.

But the real secret, the one that Kuruk destroyed hundreds of minds to keep, staggered Grei's imagination. The slinks hadn't devoured the empire during the Slink War because they couldn't.

They were a *lie*.

"He's the only one," Grei gasped, looking at Kuruk. The image of the towering slink flickered, and Grei suddenly saw the truth. Kuruk was a little blond boy, and there were no other slinks. Not thousands. Not hundreds or even dozens. There had only been three little boys. And two of them were already dead, killed by Baezin's Blade. The slinks were illusions.

"He used our fear against us," Grei whispered, gazing at the carnage all around. It was impossible to encompass it, so strong was the fear that this slink boy pushed into his mind, into every Thiaran's mind. Those who had been "killed" by phantoms weren't killed at all. The grisly deaths were made real only in the minds of the observers. In the moment of the victims' "deaths", their minds were overthrown, and they were given a burning command to go north to Benasca and never return. Rat Mathens had babbled it over and over: his wife had gone to the north.

Grei forced himself to stagger upright, and Ree gasped as though someone had lifted a house from her shoulders. She smiled weakly, her eyes rolled back in her head, and she collapsed.

The rest of the slinks weren't real, but Kuruk was a being of staggering power. He had bent the minds of hundreds of Thiarans all at once.

And suddenly, as though Kuruk had sensed the exchange of knowledge, the slink boy was in Grei's mind, slamming heavy hands everywhere. The statue from his childhood screamed at him. The slink from the South Woods charged him, rainbow eyes swirling. The dark, smoky spirits from the Dead Woods came at him with their claws.

Grei cried out, staggering back. The fists kept pounding, pulling at the foundations of his sanity. The slinks would

devour him. They would destroy everyone he loved. He had
to—

Stop it, he told himself, clenching his fists against his
head.

"Out," he whispered, gesturing with his palm toward
Kuruk. Grei was master in his own mind, not this child
monster.

The fear fell away like rotting curtains.

He straightened and faced the fight between Blevins and
the slink, but Kuruk had backed out of range. He pressed a
hand against the wound that Blevins had given him, fire
glowing between his fingers. Blevins waited, still as a corpse,
sword ready. The girl archer moved sideways, arrow nocked,
waiting for the renewed attack, but Kuruk only glared at Grei.

Kuruk opened his mouth and flames spurted out,
engulfing Blevins. The girl spun, crouching away from the
inferno.

Blevins roared and charged forward, but Kuruk ran to the
courtyard's wall and climbed it like a squirrel, his clawed
hands cracking stone as he went up and over.

Grei watched, feeling Kuruk's rage echo in his mind,
then spun back to Adora. She floated just underneath the
surface, her mouth open and her skin ashen. Her eyes stared
sightlessly upward. Glimmers of silver light clung to her
body like seaweed, but the spell was fading. The useless
spell. There were no slinks.

He fell to his knees and keened, clutching her cold skin.
The blond archer let out a wail behind him as she saw Adora.

Grei pulled Adora onto the flagstones beside the pool and
cradled her cold body against his chest. "Don't," he cried into
her cheek. "Don't go..."

Chapter 57

VECENNE

VECENNE STOOD frozen in the Temple of the Faia. The young man Jorun Magnus had called "prince" sobbed at the edge of the fountain, curled over Mimi's body. The hot flow of battle in Vecenne's veins had allowed her to push back the horror of this day. The Archon. Her father's brutal slaying. The return of the slinks.

But the death of her sister had paralyzed her. Not Mimi. Not now. Not after all this. Mimi's shocking reappearance had been the dawn of new hope. In that first moment in Vecenne's room, when the lie of a bald courtesan became truth, Vecenne had seen the future, had seen the wounds of the past miraculously healed, the wrongs righted. She had pictured herself and Mimi sitting on the expansive balcony of the royal wing, looking at the blue sea and talking of things reserved only for sisters. A normal life. A happy life.

That flicker of hope died as she stared at the pale, still body. There was no justice in the world. She wanted to crumple next to this prince and weep with him. It was done. It was all done. What mattered now?

"Yooour Highnessss."

She started at the gravelly voice. The burnt figure towered next to her, smelling of sizzling fat. Jorun Magnus, the great betrayer. The one who had taken Mimi away in the first place.

Except that Jorun had saved Vecenne. She wouldn't have left her father's tower alive without him. Magnus had leapt in front of her, taking the slink's fire on his back. He had thrown the huge metal table onto its side, shoved it against the wall to shield her.

She had huddled behind the hot metal as flames roared overhead and Magnus battled the creature. Magnus had become something more than human. He could be burned alive and not die.

"We cannot ssstop," Magnus said.

"My sister—"

"Yourrr emmmpire," Magnus said, pointing at the screaming, running people, at the slinks who drove them like a herd of cattle.

"I can't stop the war—"

"There is no war," the prince said in a dead voice. He raised his head, and she could see his profile against the glimmering water of the fountain. His hair was half-wet, plastered against his head. The beads of water on his cheeks looked like tears.

"What?" she asked.

"It's not real."

She said nothing, glanced at Magnus' grisly face. Mimi's death had snapped the young man. He had been taken by the slink sickness.

"That ssslink wasss reeeal," Blevins slurred, glancing at the wall where Kuruk had fled.

"He is the only one. This," he waved a hand at the sky, at the bloody courtyard. "Is a spell. It is your own fears come to life. It has no substance."

Blevins was silent, staring with his eerie white eyeballs.

"That's impossible," Vecenne said.

With red-rimmed eyes, the prince looked at the battle near the palace. Two slinks were pulling apart a screaming child. Vecenne had to look away, but the prince's stony face didn't change expression.

The prince laid Mimi's body gently on the ground and stood up. Without a word, he shuffled out from under the domed ceiling of the Temple of the Faia.

"Kuruk is weak," he said dully. "Injured. Now is the time to rip the lie down."

Overhead, a slink with huge, bat-like wings spied the prince. He stared up at it and waved his hands half-heartedly. It stooped into a dive toward him, and Vecenne's heart leapt into her chest. She moved instinctively toward him, wanting to jerk him back under the shelter of the temple, but Magnus put a hand on her shoulder.

"Wwwait," the burnt man slurred.

"For him to be killed? His mind has snapped—"

"No," the prince said, holding up his black hand, bony fingers splayed. "Watch. See the truth."

The slink screeched, holding forward red claws, black arms covered to the elbow in gore.

It hit the prince, bones crunching as it slammed him against the ground. It tore at his chest, splintering ribs and yanking his entrails into the air. Its wings flapped furiously, hovering while it tore and bit. The prince gave a horrible death scream. Then the slink leapt into the air, taking half of the body with him.

"Grei!" Magnus roared. Vecenne drew and shot, but the arrow bounced off the slink, who flapped up into the sky.

She stood stunned. He had let himself be killed right in front of them!

Magnus swore.

"Blevins," Prince Grei said. Vecenne jumped. He stood next to them. A rushing sound filled her mind. She staggered back. The rushing became heat on her face and hands, on her chest and the front of her thighs, like she was standing before a bonfire. She gasped and spun, and now her back was scorched. The fire pushed at her. She needed to go north, as fast as she could, all the way to Benasca.

But suddenly there was a voice, speaking softly, laying a cool blanket over the heat. It was Prince Grei's voice, murmuring over and over.

"Fight it or it will make you mad." His hands were on hers. "It is the spell. It isn't you."

She looked into his brown eyes, this mysterious prince of whom she'd never heard before. He couldn't be dead and alive at the same time. He couldn't—

"Whaaat magic isss thisss?" Magnus hissed.

Vecenne bowed her head and put a fist to her temple, feeling the slink's compulsion trying to dominate her, but Prince Grei's voice was a shield, protecting her. Her mind felt thin, brittle, about to break.

"Kuruk's strength is not in numbers," the prince said. "But in lies. He has held us captive —we have held ourselves captive— for seven years."

The heat faded. She no longer wanted to flee to the north.

"He is weak," Prince Grei said. "Now is the time for you to defeat him." He gave one last glance to the chaos of the courtyard, then turned and went back to Mimi. He knelt next to her and lifted her bald head into his lap.

"Prince Grei..." Vecenne said, but he didn't look up. "We need—"

"Yourrr Highnesss. You mussst tell the empresss," Magnus said.

Vecenne swallowed, looking around. Chased by a slink, a woman jumped from a third story balcony. Her scream ended in a sickening crunch.

"By the Faia!" Vecenne turned away, then gave a desperate look at Prince Grei. He clenched Mimi's body and whispered, oblivious to them.

"Princessss—" Magnus began.

"Yes. Okay," she said.

"Gooood."

She gripped the thorny bow she had taken from her

father's workshop, clutched the cloak at her neck and strode onto the courtyard. People ran past her, screaming as slinks chased them. The spell tried to reassert itself, but she held onto the knowledge of what Prince Grei had shown her. The hideous slinks were everywhere, but they were like ghosts.

A slink lunged at her, and Magnus stepped in front, swinging his sword.

She saw the sword bounce off, saw the slink slip around Magnus and leap toward her.

She stood her ground. Every muscle in her body tensed. She needed to flee, to get as far away as she could. Claws raked her shoulder, her back, and she twisted under the pain. But she held the image of the prince standing before the diving slink. She held it and screamed.

She fell to her knees, and the pain of the scratches vanished.

"Princessss," Magnus said, towering over her. "Arrre you okaaay?"

She panted, throwing back her cloak to reveal her shoulder. No blood. No scratches. Not a single rip in her flesh.

"The empresss," Magnus rasped. He seemed more stooped than before. Wisps of smoke drifted from his smoldering back, and he smelled like roasted pig. She wanted to retch.

Vecenne got to her feet, secured her cloak and ran through the courtyard into the palace. They wended their way past slinks and people running from them. Ultimately, it was the fleeing Thiarans who were the true danger. Their wild eyes saw nothing but escape. They injured themselves and others in their terror. A screaming woman ran head first into a wall in her desperation, knocking herself unconscious. One man clawed at Vecenne in his effort to get past her, but Blevins threw him out of the way.

They found her mother in the great hall encircled by an army of Highblades and Ringblades. The empress fought to organize them for evacuation, and they moved slowly toward the doors. Grotesque slinks writhed like worms on the ceiling. They were everywhere, creeping down the walls, herding the empress and her entourage toward the doors. The room echoed with their chittering laughter and the terse commands of the Highblades.

Vecenne thought only of reaching her mother, of telling her the truth, but as Vecenne stood in the room, she couldn't think of any words that would sway the empress. The room was a nightmare come to life. Even with Grei's help, Vecenne was barely able to push back the fear of them.

"They won't even see me," she said to Magnus. "They'll drag me away before I can say a thing."

Magnus was silent as he stared with his lidless white eyes.

"Mmmake them sssee you," he hissed.

The Highblades and Ringblades saw shocking death all around them. What could possibly pull their gazes away? She looked down at her ravaged clothes underneath the cloak. Flashes of the Archon came to her. She grit her teeth.

Her gaze flicked around the room. "Hold this." She shoved her thorn bow and quiver of arrows into Magnus' sticky hands. She shrugged off her cloak, folding it and tying it into a makeshift skirt around her hips. She belted it in place and ran half-naked to the throne. Blevins shuffled behind her.

No one even glanced her way; she had to make them see.

She stood on her father's throne. Her hands shook, and she tried to calm them as she raised her voice in song.

The song was *The Sea Serpent's Wife*, a sad tale of a Venishan fisherman's daughter who liked to sing by the sea. The girl's beautiful voice attracted a Venishan sea monster who abducted her and transformed her into his serpent bride.

The song came out stilted at first, but Vecenne closed her eyes to shut out the slinks and focused her concentration. She had to create a sharp contrast, a sliver of beauty in this room of horrors.

She allowed the past day-and-a-half to flow out of her, to become the notes of the Venishan girl's heart-wrenching story. Finding Mimi again became the girl's joy at playing by the sea. Vecenne's brutal rape became the arrival of the Venishan sea monster and Mimi's death, so wrong, so unfair, became the girl being pulled into the sea, changed forever into a monster's bride.

Vecenne put the last of herself into the final note, holding it for as long as she could, then she stopped and opened her eyes. The Highblades and Ringblades stared at her like she was a deer sitting at a royal banquet, hooves on the table. Their gazes went from the grotesquely burned Blevins back to the half-naked princess and for one critical moment, they were not looking at the slinks.

Vecenne stood up on the throne, thrusting her fist into the air.

"Thiarans!" she shouted. "Listen to me!"

The slinks, swarming overhead as thick as locusts, stopped and swiveled toward her.

"You are being lied to! These slinks are phantoms. They are false, and you can overcome them without swinging a single blade."

Murmurs went through the assemblage. Many of them turned to her mother, who stood stunned.

"Get her down from there," the empress commanded. "Now."

"Mother," Vecenne shouted. "Listen to me!"

Four Highblades moved toward the throne in formation. From somewhere at the back of the larger circle, someone screamed as they were "attacked" by a slink. Vecenne saw the Highblade fall under transparent claws; but she also saw the illusion for what it was. The Highblade fought with nothing, then lay prone as if slain. Then the "dead" Highblade rose as though in a dream and ran through the doors. Another followed.

The small formation of Highblades hurried toward Vecenne, but Magnus leapt among them, throwing the first to the ground before his sword could descend. The second ran Magnus through, but he picked up the Highblade and threw him into the other two. The three swordsmen went down in a tangle of arms and legs.

"They've used your fear against you," Vecenne shouted. "But you must open your eyes. There are no slinks. Only citizens of Thiara stand in this room."

"Vecenne," the empress shouted. "Get down!" She wailed, reaching toward her daughter. Vecenne heard the slink chitter behind her, felt the claws curl over her throat, but she willed herself to feel the truth, and they did not cut her. They passed through her, and her head pounded as she fought the lie.

Shouts went up from the assembled Highblades and Ringblades as they "watched her die". She waited, wincing as the headache faded. Vecenne opened her eyes. The slinks in the room were even more transparent now. Only a vague heat at the back of her head told her she should run to the north.

"Noooo!" Her mother stood transfixed in agony, flanked by two Ringblades. The empire's protectors turned away, unable to witness the grisly carnage of their princess' death.

She could see the bloody illusion of herself sprawled beneath her on the throne. Did each of the empire's protectors see a different kind of mangled corpse, depending on their fears?

"My vision is nearly clear," she said to Magnus. He pulled the Highblade's sword from his burned chest and threw it away. His own blade lowered, point clinking on the ground.

He nodded, not speaking. His shoulders were so stooped he now leaned on his sword like a cane. He looked like he could barely stand.

"Are you okay?" she said.

That brought a bubbling chuckle from between his white teeth. "Go quiiickly, princesss," he said.

Vecenne jumped from the throne and ran to the pack of defenders surrounding the empress. Her mother still stood frozen to the spot, unable to move even as a Ringblade spoke urgently in her ear.

Vecenne moved past the tense Highblades, and they did not see her. In their minds, she was dead. She was invisible. They focused on the slinks, foreheads sweating, swords at the ready. Each was certain they would never make it out of Thiara alive, and each was bound to this spot only by his loyalty.

Vecenne slipped between them until she stood next to the empress.

"Mother," she said softly, but the empress didn't hear her.

"Mother," Vecenne repeated, touching the empress' arm. The empress turned and gasped, suddenly seeing her. Vecenne watched her confusion, saw the insanity Grei had warned of. Mother's eyes widened, and Vecenne gripped her arms.

"Look at me, mother," she said. "Trust in that. Trust in yourself."

"You died." Her voice shook.

"No. But he will take your mind if you let him. Do not let him. See what is real," Vecenne urged.

The war waged on her mother's face. Surprise. Fear. Hope for her daughter's escape. And the madness. It worked at her. Her mother's eyes squinted and her brow wrinkled. For a moment Vecenne thought that her mother's mind would break.

"By the Faia," Mother gasped, looking all around them.

Vecenne nodded. "See the truth, mother. The room is empty, except for your Ringblades and Highblades."

"Vecenne..." Mother said, struggling.

"He tried to make you believe I died. Yet here I stand. Use it. Use the truth."

"How could they—?"

"*He*. There is only one, mother. One powerful slink who has grabbed your mind with a spell. Don't let him have you."

Mother touched her forehead, closed her eyes. Vecenne waited in tense silence as the protectors around her fought against phantoms. They shouted. Weapons hit the floor, or hit each other. The dying—who were not actually dying—fell down then got up and ran from the palace with their own cloaks of invisibility, driven by the Slink Lord's will.

"Please, mother. You're stronger than what has been done to you," Vecenne murmured.

The empress reached out a hand to steady herself, and Vecenne took it, holding it firm. Suddenly, the trembling fingers calmed.

The empress opened her eyes.

She looked around as though counting every slink. Her eyes narrowed with the strain. "None of it?"

"None," Vecenne said, her heart leaping with joy. If her mother could pierce the illusion without Grei's help, there was hope.

"Not a single slink?"

"Only one, and we drove him away," Vecenne said.

Vecenne saw remorse twist her mother's face, the same shame Vecenne had felt. They had been duped. It was almost better to believe the illusion than to bear the reality: they had been enslaved by phantoms, by their own fears.

But the empress' self-recrimination came and went quickly. Her mother had always kept her eye on the necessities.

"Then this is a war we can win," she echoed Vecenne's thoughts, her blue eyes glinting. The empress looked down at Vecenne. "But dear..."

"Yes?"

"Let's get you some clothes first."

Chapter 58
GREI

KURUK'S ILLUSION had been exposed. The war was over, and the empress' Highblades had brought the body here. Grei stared at the covered corpse on the bier. No one else had visited except the empress, himself and Vecenne. No one else knew who lay beneath the sheet, and the empress had decided no one needed to know. The entire empire had accepted the original story, and the empress said there was no need to bring back the dead only to kill them again. Let the legend stay as it had been written.

Grei knelt before the bier, memories bubbling up in his mind.

After he had put every ounce of himself into attempting to revive Adora, he had lost consciousness. He had held her, clenching her ribs with his fingers, thinking of the dead blue rose in Fairmist, thinking of how the Faia had healed Selicia. He had begged Adora to live. That was the last he remembered until Vecenne woke him, telling him the war was over.

The attempt had nearly killed him.

"I am sorry, Grei," Vecenne said, neatly managing her short yellow skirt and kneeling next to him.

Grei admired Adora's sister for what she had done during the "Phantom War", as they were calling it now. She was fierce. She was beautiful and brave, a woman who could pick up a bow and fight the slinks, even when she believed they were invincible. The minstrels of Thiara would be writing about her for years to come, how she saved them, how she was strong, but it was her softness he liked the most.

"There was nothing you could have done," she said.

There was nothing anyone else could have done, Grei thought. He could have done something if he had been quick enough. If he had been stronger.

Though he could barely stand, Grei thought about trying again, gathering what life he could muster from himself and beseeching it to go into the dead body, beseeching it to live. But the thought alone made his muscles cramp and his Faia-touched hand throb.

Let the dead stay dead, the empress had said.

"Mother says she will arrange a burial tonight," Vecenne said.

"Above ground," he said.

"As you requested," she said. She was silent for a moment, then said, "I have so many questions for you. Did you know each other a long time?"

"Long enough," Grei said. He reached out his normal hand, touched the cold, white marble flagstones. Vecenne put her fingers over his.

He let her hand linger a moment. Vecenne's closeness was calming.

"I would like a moment alone, if I could," he finally said.

She hesitated, and her worry floated into him.

"Don't try to do what you did before," she said. "You're very weak. I didn't think we would be able to revive you the first time. I don't want—"

"I won't," he murmured.

She squeezed his hand and stood up. "You have a very

good reason to live," she said, smiling.

Her wooden shoes clacked on the floor as she crossed the empty room and closed the door behind herself.

With effort, Grei levered himself to his feet and approached the bier. He moved the sheet to reveal the burned, skeletal face of the man he had known as Blevins.

"I'm sorry, my friend," Grei said. "I'm sorry I wasn't quick enough."

Blevins' corpse was different than the other dead bodies Grei had seen. Even a corpse had a voice when Grei listened. But not Blevins. There were no whispers at all. Whatever Blevins had been, he wasn't human anymore.

"I asked them to bury you above ground. A stone tomb with a lid." He paused. "Sleep, my friend. Sleep and dream a hero's dream."

Chapter 59

ADORA

ADORA AWOKE to sunlight, blinked and drew an unexpected breath. It was her room in the palace, the room of her childhood. Whispers murmured in the back of her mind, forming words she couldn't understand. She turned toward the window. The sun was low in the afternoon sky, heading toward the Sunset Sea.

The green Faia crouched in the arch of the window, glowing. Adora's Faia. The goddess' emerald wings twitched. The leaves of her hair cascaded down her back and in front of her shoulders. Her little feet touched the sill so lightly she was almost floating. She smiled.

"Mimi," Vecenne said from behind her. Adora turned to see her sister standing in the doorway dressed in yellow, her long blonde hair loose and flowing.

Adora looked back to the window, but the Faia was gone.

Vecenne sat down on the bed, and her curious gaze followed Adora's. She had not seen the goddess.

"Am I dead?" Adora asked.

Her sister grinned, took Adora's hand. "No."

Adora blinked. "But the slinks—"

"Are gone. Grei broke their hold," she said. "He sent them away."

"But..." she faltered. "How?"

Vecenne gave a little laugh. "I won't lie. I'm still not sure."

"How am I alive?" she said. "Blevins stabbed me. And the prophecy—"

"I don't know about a prophecy. But the slinks are gone. And you are alive." Vecenne paused. "And you chose an exceptional man, Mimi." She winked. "Nicely done."

Adora put a hand to her forehead, dizzy. Was she dreaming? "I'm so confused. Where is he?" she asked.

"Probably right outside this door. He's barely taken a dozen steps away from you since he woke up. It's a new empire. I'll let him explain. He has a way about him. He knows how to say things so that they make sense. He knows when to be close, when to be away." The door opened, and Grei stood in the doorway.

Vecenne kissed Adora on the forehead. "See?" She rose to her feet.

Grei's wavy brown hair was washed and brushed. It tumbled to his shoulders in the way she loved. He was clean-shaven again, and his soft brown eyes glinted with the afternoon sun. He wore long sleeves and his right hand was covered in a dark green glove. Three thin, red scratches marred his left cheek.

"Grei..." she murmured.

Vecenne went to the door and took the handle. She nudged Grei inside with her hip and left. He crossed to Adora and sat down on the bed. The whispers in her mind grew louder as he neared.

"Now this is a pose I imagined you in many a time," he said, looking down at her.

His flirtatious tone brought her back to Fairmist, when she had first tried to snare his attention with promised secrets and the swing of her hips. But they weren't in Fairmist anymore. This was not the beginning of the adventure. It was supposed to be the end. Her end. But she was still here.

Fear forked through her, and she started to move a hand to her belly, then stopped herself. *The Archon's baby...*

She thrust the thought from her head and silently thought the phrase Lyndion had taught her to shield herself from Grei's magical sight. He couldn't know, could never know.

"Grei—" she began, then stopped. "Are the slinks really gone?" She couldn't bear to think about what the Archon had done, what he had left with her. Not right now.

"Yes." His smile grew smaller, but he kept it in place. "For a time."

"What do you mean?"

"For now, there are no slinks in Thiara, and I suspect that there won't be for a while."

"You didn't send them back," she said. A chill ran up her spine. "Through the rift. The spell."

He put gentle fingers against her cheek. "Forget about that. You did your part."

"I should be dead," she said.

"You were. You gave everything a person could give." The whispers in her mind reached out to Grei like fingers. She felt his strength. "You fulfilled your 'destiny', if it ever really was that."

She pushed her hand against her ribs, where the dagger had entered, had been shoved through her heart. "But I—"

"I brought you back," he said.

She stopped, stunned.

"And no." He shook his head. "I did not use the prophecy's spell, and I discovered some things about your Order that might interest you."

"Grei, if you thwarted the prophecy—"

His left hand took hers and squeezed. It felt perfect, like it was meant to be, like their dance on the Blacktale Bridge. "I can live without the prophecy," he whispered. "I can't live without you."

He leaned over and kissed her.

But the prophecy—

"Stop it," he murmured into her ear, as though he could hear her thoughts. "One life is enough. Save the next for yourself. For us."

"What haven't you told me?" she asked, fearful that he could read her so easily, wondering if he could see the secret of the baby.

He chuckled softly, his lips an inch from hers. "A lot. Shall I make a list this instant? Or could you just kiss me?"

She did, and pushed her concerns to the back of her mind.

"Grei?" she murmured finally.

"Yes."

"I hear whispers in my head."

He grinned. "What do they say?"

"That you love me."

"That's right." He took her into his arms. "That's right."

Behind them, where the Faia had been, a blue rose grew up between the dusky granite stones of the windowsill, its petals open to the sunlight.

Epilogue

GREI LOOKED down on the royal courtyard where the final battle had happened. The sun had not yet set on the third day after they had broken Kuruk's hold, and already streamers were being tacked up, lanterns hung from festive tripods. The empress had ordered a seven day celebration. She had commissioned a ballad from the famous Giallyn. Apparently, "Prince Grei" was to be a central character.

But it was Vecenne who was the real hero. Amidst the chaos, she had found the empress and convinced her. Without a prophecy, an army or any magic, she had saved countless lives. Grei was not present for any of it. After giving his life to Adora, he had lost consciousness. The next thing he remembered was waking in a bed in the palace.

Vecenne had told him that once the empress had been convinced, the spreading of the truth had become organized. The Ringblades had understood first and pierced the illusion, and the Highblades had joined shortly thereafter. The rest of the populace needed much more convincing. After seven years of living under the slinks' yoke, words were not enough. Each new person had to be shown, and during those precious moments, more citizens fled Thiara. More citizens died. Some ran heedlessly into the Jhor Forest to be devoured by beasts, others ran down Baezin's Road without thought to food or shelter. Ships sailed from the harbor. Some people even jumped straight into the ocean and started swimming, only to drown.

With every person who "woke" to the spell, Kuruk's hold had weakened, and it was easier for the next. But some simply refused to see the truth. Even now, citizens would fall prey to the illusion and flee, or worse, follow the compulsion northward after "dying" from a phantom slink. The empress now had Highblades and groups of volunteers searching the countryside and boats patrolling the shores for others who had disappeared.

Many had died in their panic, but only one body had been scratched open, ripped apart. Grei knew Kuruk had desecrated it for show, leaving an image no person could forget, and it was that body that stayed in the mind, as if there had been hundreds of them. If Grei let his mind wander, the slink fear took hold of him again, twisting how he saw the other deaths. Making it seem like all of them had died in that grisly way.

He contemplated going to the source of the this terror-evoking spell, trying to pry Kuruk's hold away permanently, but Grei feared he would be no match for the Lord of Rifts in that battle. Kuruk's kind of magic was unfamiliar to him. He didn't know how Kuruk could make him feel the spittle on his face from the flying slink that had almost "attacked" Adora or hear the cries of the dying who weren't actually dying.

His heart beat faster as the spell tried to take hold of him again. Even now, the compulsion was strong. Kuruk was still out there, fighting to keep his hold.

He wondered how many empty graves had been dug in the first Slink War, filled with "bodies" that were not there. He wondered how many citizens of the empire now wandered in Benasca, unable to return home because of the burning compulsion that prevented them. He would have to go looking for them—

Grei raised his head. He sensed her arrival before he heard her soft steps behind him. The hairs on the back of his neck prickled.

Selicia's guarded emotions gave her away, though her shield wasn't nearly as effective as it had been before. The more Grei used the magic, the clearer and quicker others' desires came to him. Everyone had their own "signature".

"It is still difficult to see the truth," Selicia said softly, coming up beside him. "Even though we know it now, thanks to you."

He forced his shoulders to relax and looked at her. One of Grei's first acts after waking had been to release her and her Ringblades from their stone prisons. There was no emperor and the empress had hailed Grei as a Thiaran hero, which meant Selicia had no reason to capture him anymore, no reason to hurt him. But he watched her eyes, let her whispers be loud. If she moved too quickly, she could be a statue again for all he cared.

"Kuruk is a master of lies," Grei finally answered. "Some people are like that."

Selicia took the sting without a wince. She kept her gaze on the moving people below. "Should one feel remorse for doing what she knows is right—what she knows will save countless lives—even if she later discovers she was wrong?" she asked softly.

"Is that your apology?"

"No apology will quell your anger."

"What do you want, Selicia?" he asked.

She paused. He wanted to rail at her. The Faia had all but warned Grei about Selicia's betrayal. The Dead Woods spirits had said it outright. Selicia had violence inside her.

But so did Grei. So did every human. There were other things within Selicia, too. Strong things. Good things. Loyalty to the empire, if not to Grei. Her love for her Ringblades was real. Selicia believed she worked above the rest of humanity, all to serve Thiara.

"It isn't over," Selicia said. "This Slink War."

"I know that better than you do," he said.

"Yes."

He let his magic flow into her. She smoldered with purpose. The empire was still at great risk.

"And you want to help," he said.

"I serve the empire." She paused, then said, "This Slink Lord is cunning. He knows most citizens still fear the slinks more than their own deaths. He will use that."

"You aren't my teacher anymore," Grei said.

"I am whatever the empire needs."

"The empire..." he said. He wasn't about to tell her his budding thoughts on the Thiaran Empire and the blood that had been shed to keep it standing.

"I am not your enemy," she said.

"Prove it."

She said nothing, and they remained silent for a long time.

"How is Ree?" Grei changed the subject.

Selicia nodded. "She is awake. No longer talking in rhymes. She asked to see you."

"I'll visit her today," he said. "Has anyone found the emperor's body?"

"No," she said. "Princess Vecenne thought he must have been incinerated."

Grei didn't believe that, and neither did Selicia. Vecenne was convinced her father was dead, and that was the official story. But something supernatural had happened to Blevins because of the horrific things he and the emperor had done to the Faia. It was likely the emperor was also affected. If there was no body, Grei didn't believe for a second the emperor was gone.

Selicia watched him. "You made the unexpected choice. You didn't kill the princess when you knew it would send the slinks away forever. I would have. The emperor would have."

"For seven years you've all done horrible things in the name of good," he said. "You, the emperor, Blevins, the empress. In the end, all those things only served the slinks. I wasn't going to commit an atrocity just because you told me to."

"You have wisdom, Grei," she said, and he hated the approval in her tone. He hated how good it felt.

She took his hand, and he flinched. She pretended not to notice, held his fingers firmly. The whispers grew strong in the back of his mind, and he prepared to lash out. But her black eyes, so intense, only watched him.

"Thank you, Grei Forander," she said softly. "You have saved our empire, despite me. That is a debt I can never repay. But know that I am your friend and I will do whatever I can."

He wanted to believe her, but he didn't know who she really served. The empress? The Order? Grei desperately needed an ally; he certainly had enough enemies. But was there anyone he could really trust?

Grei knew he had to start thinking about how he might use every single ally he could muster. To cast them aside through petulance was stupid. This crisis was larger than him, with so many pieces yet unseen. Like who was this Lord Velak he had seen in Kuruk's memories. Selicia, the empress, they had lived their whole lives thinking about the whole of the empire. He could learn from them. He *had* to learn from them.

"I will need your help," he conceded. *As long as I don't have to trust you,* he thought.

She seemed about to say something, but she was smart, so she didn't.

Kuruk was still out there, the most powerful being Grei had ever met, nursing his hatred of all Thiarans. Everyone in Thiara knew about him now, but there were other enemies that Grei wasn't sure he should talk about until he knew who to trust. The Blessed, Velakkans in human form, could be anywhere. Emperor Qweryn was also out there, licking his wounds, maybe waiting to unleash more horrors in the name of good. And there was the mysterious Lord Velak, a person even Kuruk feared.

But behind them all was one man, living between the pages of history, manipulating from his safe little web. This man had created Kuruk and his nightmarish brothers. This man had demanded Adora's death.

Like the Slink War, the Order's prophecy was a lie, a manipulation to save the Order from Kuruk's wrath.

"What will you do now?" Selicia asked, interrupting his thoughts.

"I will go home," he said.

And then we will see, Emperor Lyndion, if you have a prophecy for what comes next.

Other Novels by Todd Fahnestock
with Giles Carwyn

The Heartstone Trilogy:
Heir of Autumn
Mistress of Winter
Queen of Oblivion

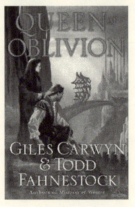

www.toddfahnestock.com

TODD FAHNESTOCK wrote his first novel in high
school because he "wanted a fantasy book with even more
action in it." Later in college, he published his first two short
stories in TSR Dragonlance anthologies. In 1997, he published more short stories with co-author Giles Carwyn,
winning the New York Books for the Teen Age award for
True Love (Or the Many Brides of Prince Charming). In
2006, Todd wrote *Heir of Autumn* with Giles under Harper-
Collins' Eos imprint and hit the Denver Post bestseller list.
Mistress of Winter and *Queen of Oblivion* followed, then
Todd went solo again. He currently lives in a 115-year-old
Victorian house in Englewood, CO with his wife, daughter,
son, one big blue dog and one big red dog. He splits his time
between Tae Kwon Do, playing with children, working at
Rose Community Foundation, and writing that next novel.

Visit Todd at:

WWW.TODDFAHNESTOCK.COM

@TODD_FAHNESTOCK on Twitter

Made in the USA
Charleston, SC
18 February 2015